THE
DARK
BONES

LORETH ANNE WHITE

THE
DARK
BONES

Montlake
Romance

Published by Montlake Romance, Seattle

www.apub.com

Amazon, the Amazon logo, and Montlake Romance are trademarks of Amazon.com, Inc., or its affiliates.

ISBN-13: 9781542091541
ISBN-10: 1542091543

Cover design by Caroline Teagle Johnson

Printed in the United States of America

For Jill and Ray,

who keep the Big Bar dream alive.

AFTER THE KILLING FROST

*Cariboo Country. Sunday, September 27,
just over twenty years ago.*

*Whitney's chest burns as she runs. Her throat is dry. Sagebrush, pine
needles, and flint cut into her bare feet. Blood pours down the insides of
her legs, leaving sticky traces on the dry grasses in her wake.*

*She drops into a crouch. Panting, she listens carefully to the ambi-
ent sounds of the autumn woods.*

*Grass pricks her naked buttocks. The ripped fabric of her shirt sticks
to her skin. Her left breast pokes through a ragged tear, and bite marks
puncture the flesh around the nipple. Her long hair—the same yellow-
gold as the wild grasses in which she seeks cover—is caked with sweat
and dirt.*

*A squirrel chirps angrily. She can hear the soft rumble of a distant
truck on a logging road at the far end of the lake. A hot, crackling
energy presses down over the forest—a thunderstorm is building. Wind
stirs, and the whole forest whispers and sways.*

But she can't hear them.

A kestrel keens up high. She glances up sharply. She doesn't know what to do. She's reached the forest fringe. Beyond the safety of the fringe lies an exposed meadow. It's full of fireweed gone to seed, tufts wafting like summer snow over the meadow as thunder grumbles and storm clouds shoulder together. Shadows creep over the forest.

She knows this area. Hidden among dense trees on the opposite side of the meadow are the decaying buildings of an abandoned summer camp. It's part of Haugen Ranch. She could hide there.

But terror traps her in a vise. They could be watching. Waiting for her to bolt out into the open like a wounded deer. Time stretches. Clouds boil thicker and muscle across the face of the sun. Shadow darkens the meadow.

Has she lost them? Is it possible?

Thunder claps. A wham of pressure slams against her eardrums. Fear spikes her into action. She lurches up and pitches forward into the meadow. Wildly, she smashes through the thick fireweed and grasses, her gaze fixed determinedly on a gap between trees on the other side of the clearing, her bare buttocks bouncing like the bull's-eye of a fleeing whitetail deer.

She hears a whoop behind her.

The growl of an ATV engine kicks into life from the opposite direction. She's being circled, cut off.

Tears stream down her face. But she doesn't stop. She keeps flailing through the tangled foliage, aiming for the sanctuary of those trees across the clearing.

A boom blasts through the air. Birds explode from the canopy. The hot whir of a bullet passes her cheek. She screams and veers sideways, changing direction. Thunder cracks again. The sky turns black. Fat marbles of rain begin to bomb to the earth.

Another crack.

She feels a blow on the back of her shoulder. It knocks the wind from her. The impact, the shock, spins her sideways, and she stumbles and falls into fireweed. For a moment she lies on her back, stunned, hidden by the vegetation. A hot wetness seeps beneath her shoulder. Pain. Incredible pain. All over. She can't breathe. Drops of rain begin to pelt her upturned face. The sky above her, she realizes absurdly, has turned an eerie orangey purple.

She thinks of her mother. Her mom likes thunderstorms. She thinks of all her mistakes. Of Trevor. Ash—everything that has gone so wrong . . . She begins to float softly away on a sea of indescribable pain. But a shrill whistle slices back into her consciousness. Her eyelids flare open. Her heart kicks into a wild stammer in her chest. She can't die—can't—will not die.

She struggles to roll onto her side. But she's unable to make her left arm work. With her good hand she clutches a fistful of fireweed, pulls herself up into a crouch. It's pouring now, rain pummeling down upon her back, slicking her hair to her face. Branches twist in a frenzy as wind whips and swirls across the meadow and through the forest. The lyrics of the song she'd been listening to in Ash's truck snake through her mind.

All I wanna do is live it up
In LA
Before I die, have some fun,
In LA. It's gonna be great.
Party all night, until the sun
Comes up over LA . . .

She was close.

So very close.

To living her dream. To seeing LA. She almost escaped this town. It was all going to be good. Fun. Now all she wants is to stay alive. To go home to her mom. Back to the familiarity of the trailer park.

Hunched over like a chimpanzee, she wobbles her way through the tall fireweed, her left arm dangling uselessly at her side and streaming

3

with blood and rainwater. She aims doggedly for that gap in the trees. But her vision is narrowing. She's getting dizzy. A clap of thunder explodes right above, and lightning forks in a jagged bolt to the ground. She barely flinches. She reaches the trees.

Then comes another rifle crack. Everything moves in slow motion as bark shrapnel explodes from a trunk near her face. Splinters pierce her cheek and blind her right eye. Mewling and blubbering now, she staggers into the dense woods on the other side of the meadow. Dark here. Very dark. Safe, maybe. The vision in her left eye adjusts to the shadows. Ferns and wild blueberry bushes carpet the forest floor. She locates the trail she knows is hidden beneath that growth and stumbles along it. Voices—she can hear voices. Yelling. Male. Coming closer. The roar of the ATV engine grows louder.

She sees the old cabin ruins covered in dead moss and lichen. Saplings push up between the rotted floorboards. In the shadows of the ruins stands a deer. She freezes. The deer watches her with big, liquid eyes, ears flicking.

But as the ATV comes closer, the deer bounds off with a loud crashing noise through the brush. Panic seizes her. She spins in a circle. Where can she hide? The old cabins will be the first place they look. Why did she even think she could be safe here?

Her gaze settles on a fallen log. It's a giant ancient cedar. Covered in moss and orange lichen and ferns. She staggers over to the log and drops to her knees. It's rotted hollow inside, offering the kind of place a bear chooses to hibernate safely through a winter, or where a cougar might den with her kits, safe from predators. She crawls inside, dragging her limp, slippery, bloody arm at her side. The wood encircling her smells like the old chest in which her grandmother used to store her fur coat. It smells familiar. Safe. Like family. Welcoming. Deeper and deeper she goes. Until the space narrows and chokes too tightly around her. There she curls herself into a tight ball deep inside her cave. The cedar

4

is scratchy soft against her bare buttocks and the skin of her arm. The ATV engine growls to a stop somewhere outside the log.

She hears another yell. Another gunshot. She squeezes her eyes shut, waiting to be hauled out by her feet. But the voices grow distant, as does the sound of boots crashing through the forest. The ATV engine fades into the woods.

And suddenly all is quiet apart from rain drumming steadily on her log.

They're chasing the deer, she thinks. The spirit deer sent to distract them and save her.

Great big palsied shudders take hold of her body. She clasps her hand hard over her mouth to stop her own whimpering. Just in case one of them is still out there, in case it's a trick to get her to come out.

But she hears them no more.

CHAPTER 1

Ottawa. Tuesday, January 8, twenty years and
just over three months later.

Sergeant Rebecca North strode down the marble corridor of the Supreme Court building alongside her legal counsel, heels echoing with the clipped cadence of confidence. Her suit was tailored, a dark blue in color, almost black. The cut of her silk blouse was classic. It projected professionalism yet gave a subtle nod toward femininity. Her thick, dark hair was drawn back into a soft bun at the nape of her neck. No jewelry. Minimal makeup. Her look, approved by the prosecution team, was calculated to appear effortless and to project the image of an accomplished, trustworthy detective with the commercial crime branch of the Canadian federal police force, someone with enough sophistication and smarts to help take down a high-profile white-collar criminal.

There was a lot riding on this trial. Media coverage on both sides of the US-Canadian border was intense. As was public scrutiny via social media. Outside the court building the wind was picking up, and temperatures plunged as cable news vans and tech support crews hunkered against a mounting January snowstorm. Inside, reporters with passes filed back into the courtroom. Recess was over. Rebecca was to testify next. But while telegraphing outward calm, inside she was edgy with adrenaline. The defense team was expected to ride her hard.

The lawyer striding beside her clutched a file of papers to her chest. She said coolly, her eyes fixed directly ahead, "Remember, Sergeant, a lot of excellent cops get snagged on the stand by issues that have nothing to do with their credibility, or with their level of professionalism. They get caught up with the little things that—"

"You told me," she said. "I got it."

Rebecca and her legal counsel rounded a marble column. She saw the crowd gathered outside the courtroom. As they neared the courtroom doors, Rebecca's phone buzzed in her jacket pocket. She hesitated. It could be her superior calling again.

"I better take this," she said quickly to the lawyer.

"You're up next," the lawyer said.

"I'll just be a sec."

She extracted the phone from her pocket and stepped into the relative seclusion of an alcove. When she saw the caller ID, her heart fell. Her father. Again. She'd allowed his last four calls to kick over into voice mail. She didn't have time for his paranoid conspiracy theory nonsense right now. She was about to kill his call but faltered. Her dad had not been well. He drank too much—always had, but it was getting problematic. And winters were lonely where he lived in the old family cabin. The closest town was Clinton. Forty-five minutes away on unpaved logging roads that were not routinely plowed.

The rural isolation, the booze, the creeping age . . . It was all addling his brain and causing confusion and depression. And to fill his long, lonely nights on the farm, he wallowed in old cases, obsessively going over and over the ones he'd been unable to solve, cooking up crazy theories he usually forgot by morning. Rebecca connected the call.

"Hey, Dad, listen, can I call you back? I'm about to head into court."

An odd, weighted silence followed her words.

"Dad? Are you okay?"

"I . . . need to talk to you, Bec. There . . . there's something you need to come clean with me about."

He was slurring his words. Rebecca glanced at her watch. It was barely noon in her father's time zone, and he was already three sheets to the wind. He'd be passed out cold by the time she was done this evening.

"Look, I'll speak to you when—"

"No, no, Becca, not over the phone," her dad whispered. "I'm in the lobby of the Cariboo Lodge, using the courtesy phone outside the Moose and Horn. People might hear." There was a pause. Rebecca could make out background noise from the pub. "I . . . I suspect he's been inside my cabin, took some papers from my case file."

"Who? *What* case file?"

The silence outside the courtroom was suddenly loud. Almost everyone had filed inside. Tension strapped across her chest. "Dad," she said firmly, crisply, "I can't do this conspiracy stuff right now. I need—"

"Last night. I think he was outside, among the aspens. Watching my cabin. The night before, I think someone followed me home in the dark. I think he knows what I know."

Rebecca hesitated. The tone underscoring her father's words was not something she'd heard before. She had little doubt her dad was imagining things, but his fear was real. She had to think about getting him professional help. It was time. She'd go home and deal with it all once this trial was over. But at the same time, returning to the ranch for any extended period was the last thing Rebecca wanted to do. There always remained the possibility she might run into Ash. But she'd put this off as long as she could.

"Dad," she said more gently. "Look, it'll be okay. I promise. As soon as this trial is wrapped up, I'll put in for time and—"

"I *know* he lied, Becca. You *both* lied. All those years ago. It wasn't a riding accident that gashed open his face, was it? What were you protecting him from that day?"

"*What* are you talking about?"

"Sergeant North—Rebecca!" It was one of the lawyers, eyes flashing with urgency. "Get your ass inside there, now! For Chrissake, Sergeant—do you want to lose this thing for us?"

Rebecca pinched the bridge of her nose. "Dad, I'm about to testify. I'll phone you tomorrow." He'd be too drunk if she called tonight. "I promise. Now get a room at the lodge, get some sleep. Whatever you do, just don't drive." She ended the call and pocketed her phone, but as she hurried after the lawyer, unease dogged her.

He lied. You both *lied . . . It wasn't a riding accident that gashed open his face.*

As she entered the courtroom, her mind catapulted back to a late September Sunday more than twenty years earlier. A massive thunderstorm had just erupted on what had started out as a typical Indian-summer afternoon, with the birch and alder trees shimmering yellow and gold over the hills.

Rebecca had been driving home from her weekend job at the vet's office when rain started coming down in sheets. Gripping the truck wheel, she'd bent forward, straining to peer at the muddy road through smeared wiper arcs across the windshield. Suddenly a man had appeared in front of her truck, walking slowly down the middle of the road, feet bare, arms hanging limp at his sides. His jeans were drenched and his T-shirt plastered to his body.

Rebecca had slowed her truck, coming right up behind him. He had seemed oblivious to her presence, had made no move at all to get out of the road, didn't even turn.

Thunder had clapped and rolled into the distance. The trees along the road had bent sharply in the wind.

She'd honked.

No reaction.

Rebecca had hit the brakes and stopped her truck. She'd sat there for a moment, rain thrumming on the metal roof.

What in the hell?

Then, suddenly, he'd turned. And her heart had faltered.

Ash.

His face—it had been gashed open down the left side. His eye was purple, swollen almost shut. Blood streamed with the rainwater down his cheeks and darkened the front of his T-shirt.

She'd flung open her door and run through the rain to him.

"Ash! What happened? What on earth are you doing out here?"

But he'd just stared, his eyes completely vacant . . .

Rebecca forced her focus back to the present. But as she took her place in the witness box, a chill trickled down her spine. She was barely able to register the court official in front of her, let alone recall how she'd gotten to the box.

"Do you, Sergeant Rebecca North, solemnly affirm that the evidence to be given by you shall be the truth, the whole truth, and nothing but the truth?"

He lied.

You both *lied.*

CHAPTER 2

Cariboo Country. Tuesday, January 8.

Tori Burton lay on her stomach, side by side with Ricky Simon on the snowy ridge among the bare aspen trees. They watched the old log cabin in the clearing below, waiting for the old man to visit his woodpile. Ricky had told Tori the old man always fetched a last haul of wood around this time of day. Then he wouldn't come out again for the rest of the night.

A few meters to the left of his cabin, next to the woodpile, was the shed—their target. The shed stood in front of another dense clump of trembling aspens that shielded the property from the snow-covered approach road. In the purple dusk of this January afternoon, the papery bark on the aspens glowed with a ghostly luminescence. The whiteness was punctuated by black marks that looked to Tori like kohl-lined eyes. She felt those Egyptian eyes were watching her and Ricky as they spied on the cabin below. It made her feel edgy. As twilight dimmed, further unease fingered into her, along with a biting cold that had started to blow in with wind that came all the way from the Arctic. It hurt her ears. She should have worn a toque, like Olivia, her bio mom, had told her. Olivia had also told her that all these trembling aspen trees were connected, one big organism joined by a root network underground.

If you cut a tree up on this ridge, the others down in that grove would know.

She wondered if they would all feel the pain of an ax strike at once.

She wondered if she could ever learn to love Olivia like she'd loved her adoptive mom. She doubted it. She missed Melody and Gage, her adoptive parents, like a big empty hole in her heart. Ricky was the only real friend she had now. He was the only kid at her new school who thought being the spawn of a serial killer was kind of cool. Ricky was *that* guy—the one who could make the bullies and the mean girls think *she* was cool, too, by mere association. Because Ricky was badass himself. He dared to do things none of the other kids would.

"There he is," whispered Ricky. He pointed to a window at the rear of the cabin.

Inside, silhouetted against a yellow square of quavering lantern light, the old man stood hunched, talking on a phone. He had a landline, but no electricity. He used propane from a big tank not far from the cabin's rear window. His warmth came from fire.

"You said he fetched logs every day at this time, and that he wouldn't come out again until morning," whispered Tori. "Why isn't he going?"

"He will, he will, he's just making a call or something. Look, I think he's hanging up now."

Sure enough, within two more minutes the cabin door that faced the shed opened, and out came the old man all bundled up in a jacket and toque and gloves. Bowed by time, swallowed by his overly large jacket, which had probably once fitted him, he trudged through deep, gelatinous slush toward his woodpile, which was covered with a tarp. He dragged a sled through the slush behind him. When he reached the pile, he threw back the tarp. Tori and Ricky watched in tense, excited silence as the man stacked a pile of split firewood onto the bed of his sled. He then re-covered the log pile and slopped back through the snow to his house, pulling the sled behind him with a rope.

"He's going inside now," Ricky said.

Panic flickered through Tori. What they were going to do suddenly felt wrong. Ricky's words ran through her mind.

It's not like he'll care, or even notice. Once he's inside, we duck into his hooch shed and nick a couple of bottles of moonshine. That's it. We run back up the ridge, hop on the snowmobile parked behind the aspen stand, and we're out.

"It's getting late," she said. "I . . . I promised Olivia and Cole I'd be home by dark."

Ricky turned his face to her and grinned, his eyes liquid black, skin dusky. His teeth glowed bright white and were dead straight. She felt that odd little sensation in her tummy when Ricky looked at her like that. He was almost thirteen but seemed so much older, so worldly. Ricky Simon had edge. He made Tori feel alive. He made her forget the mess that was her life, and quite simply, he made her want to get up and out of bed in the morning. Ricky was the sole thing in this world that made her new life on Broken Bar Ranch bearable. And suddenly it was all okay again.

"You're not chickening out now, are you, Tori Burton?"

"Of course not. We . . . we just gotta be quick."

"You got it."

They made it down to the old shed. The slush was already setting up with the rapidly plunging temperatures. When they reached the shed door, Ricky cursed.

"He's gone and fucking locked it. He never did that before."

Sure enough, a gleaming new brass-colored padlock had been hooked through a hinged metal plate across the door.

"Maybe he counted his bottles and saw some had been taken," Tori said, shivering now and glad the shed was suddenly off-limits.

Ricky dropped to his haunches. He examined the padlock at eye level, squinting against the fading light. He grinned suddenly. "I got this one." He reached into his pocket and removed a pocketknife. It was made of cream-colored bone polished to a translucent shine and inlaid with a small gold profile of a horse. He took off his gloves and opened out one of the little tool arms.

"Hoof pick," he said, showing her. He inserted the pick into the lock and closed his eyes, concentrating as he carefully maneuvered the pick around the inside of the lock. He cursed as his fingers got cold, and he continued to fiddle. "There!" It opened.

He stood up with a grin.

"Where'd you learn that?"

"One of the guys on the reserve. Hurry." He held open the shed door and shot a glance back at the cabin, which hulked like a sullen shadow in the lingering twilight, smoke snaking out of the stone chimney.

Once inside, Ricky panned the beam of a small Maglite over narrow shelves that lined one wall. The beam danced off glass bottles and mason jars filled with liquid. Some of the liquid was clear like water. Some was the color of pale fireweed honey, or burnt umber. Tori glanced around nervously. In a back corner of the shed, atop a rough wooden table, was the old man's copper still. Pipes connected it to a barrel-shaped container. Another shelf held two kerosene lanterns. Tools and various gardening implements hung on another wall. It was tidy. Tori hadn't expected it to look so neat and organized. She felt she really shouldn't be in here. She stared at the still. "Isn't making this stuff illegal?"

"Sure," Ricky said, taking a bottle off the shelf and stuffing it down the front of his jacket. He reached for another. "Which is why he can't go reporting any of it missing."

"I thought the old man used to be a cop."

"And when did being a cop mean that everything you did was legal? You of all people should know that, Burton, given what your father did."

"He wasn't my real father. He was my adoptive dad."

"Yeah, well, your real one was a sicko."

"Fuck you, Ricky Simon."

Ricky grinned and began to reach for a third bottle. But his hand stilled as they heard a sound. Both froze, listened. It came again—the distinct slurp and suck of boots moving quickly through the wet snow that was setting up fast.

"He's coming back," she hissed, terrified. "You said he wouldn't!"

"That's not him. Moving too fast. Quick, behind that table." They ducked down behind a workbench at the far end of the shed, just managing to squeeze between the bench and the wall. Ricky clicked off his flashlight. In the dark cold they waited. Wind began to moan through the trees outside, and branches creaked and groaned and scraped on the roof. Tori clenched her jaw and fixed her gaze on the door, waiting for it to creak open, waiting to see a wedge of yellow lantern light, or the muzzle of a shotgun.

No one came. Nothing moved. Then, just as Tori was about to get to her feet and hightail it out of there with or without Ricky Simon, they heard a boom. Her gaze shot to Ricky. In the dark his eyes had gone wide and round, the whites showing.

"Shotgun," he whispered.

Huddling side by side, they dared not move. Minutes seemed to tick by. Then they heard the boots in the slush again, moving even faster this time. Toward the shed.

"Oh fuck," he whispered as she grabbed his arm. Her movement bumped him against a shelf, and a tin clanged to the floor. The lid of the tin popped open, and some kind of paint spilled out across the planks. Neither said a thing. The yellow liquid spread silently out in a puddle and seeped under the bench.

The person outside turned away from the shed. The sound of the sucking boots went into the aspen grove behind the little building. They heard the cracking of twigs and underbrush, followed by the cough of an engine. A snowmobile roared to life. Ricky peeped up slightly to see outside the small window at the back of the shed. He ducked back down fast.

"I saw him," he whispered. "I saw his helmet."

They listened as the snow machine sped northward, toward a forest that lay along the opposite side of the valley. The sound whined into the distance.

"*Shit*," Ricky hissed. "We need to go see—check on the old man."

"No, we don't!" Tori lurched to her feet and lunged for the shed door. "We gotta get out of here!"

He grabbed her arm, halting her. "Tori, he could be hurt. He might need help. I'm going to check on him, with or without you."

Her eyes filled with tears. Her chest felt tight. She couldn't breathe. She shouldn't have listened to Ricky—shouldn't have come. But she sure as hell wasn't going to leave Ricky's side and venture off alone in the dark. Not now. Not with someone out there.

They left the shed and crept up the path to the cabin, painfully cognizant now of the noise their own boots made in the snow. They came around the rear, where the propane cylinder stood a short way from the house. Ricky peered carefully up into the living room window. Tori scanned the ridge behind them, worried that the person who'd fled on a snowmobile might return around the back.

"I can see his feet," Ricky whispered. "He's in his rocker by the fire, wearing slippers, but I can't see the rest of him." A pause. "He's not moving, Tori. There's a knocked-over glass by his foot . . . He's not moving at all."

He stepped back from the window. In the haunting twilight, his face looked like a ghost's, his eyes like dark holes. It scared her.

"I'm going inside," he said.

"No, Ricky, please." She grabbed onto his arm. "*Please.* Let's leave."

He shook free of her hold and made for the door, an anxious energy driving him. Tori hurried after him, terror growing deep in the pit of her stomach.

The door stood slightly ajar. Which was weird, given the plummeting temperatures and the mounting Arctic wind. Ricky knocked.

"Mr. North? Corporal North?" he called out.

Silence, apart from the brittle wind hushing through the leafless branches of the trees.

Ricky creaked the wooden door open wider. The kitchen interior was aglow with the flickering light of a kerosene lamp on the table. It was warm inside and smelled of woodsmoke and food in the oven. Two plates on the table. Ricky moved cautiously through the kitchen toward the living room. Tori started to follow. That's when it hit her— another kind of smell. Nothing she could identify, but it made every atavistic sense in her body scream to flee.

Ricky peered around the corner.

"Fuck!" He jumped back and shot out his arm to stop her. "Get outside, Tori." His voice was weird. She hadn't heard him sound like that before. His complexion was ashen.

She couldn't move.

"Now!" He grabbed her arm and spun her around, yanking her toward the kitchen door. The motion threw her off-balance. She flung out her free arm to steady herself, and her gloved hand whammed into the kerosene lantern on the table. The lantern toppled over and hit the floor with a crash. Glass shattered. Fuel spilled and whooshed into flame. She gasped.

Ricky dragged her to the doorway. They staggered outside. Ricky doubled over and retched into the snow. Fire was catching in the kitchen.

"R . . . Ricky?" Tori said.

He looked at her and said nothing, as if he were trying to organize his head, his words. His body. When he spoke, his voice was all quavery. "He . . . he's sitting there. In his recliner, but there . . . He's . . . got a shotgun wedged between his legs. The butt of the gun is on the floor, and the muzzle is pointed up to where his mouth . . . He's blown his brains out."

A bang and a whoosh sounded inside the cabin. Flames crackled and flickered up the kitchen drapes, making them billow as they burned in front of the window.

"We've gotta get help!" she screamed, panic beginning to suffocate her. "We need to get help!"

He took her arm. "No, Tori, *no*. We gotta get outta here."

"But old man Noah—"

"He's dead, Tori. Stone dead. Nothing in this world can help him now. Come!"

She resisted, tears burning into her eyes. "The fire, Ricky, the fire is—"

Another explosion in the kitchen blew out a window. Glass shattered and blasted outward and scattered about in the snow. Black smoke and tongues of flame billowed out of the window and the door, hungry for oxygen. Ricky tugged on her arm.

"Come on!"

They ran and stumbled up the bank, which was thick with snow starting to freeze solid. At the top of the esker ridge upon which the aspens grew, they ran through the trees. Tori fell in the deep snow, knocking her head against the slender trunk of an aspen. She scrambled back up to her feet and staggered after Ricky, to where he'd parked his snowmobile.

He was already mounted, engine running—a rough and loud old two-stroke, not smooth like the one they'd just heard. She clambered onto the back and wrapped her arms tightly around his waist. Ricky gunned the gas, and they took off at a clip in a cloud of blue smoke.

She didn't look back as another explosion boomed, and fire roared and crackled louder in the quiet landscape. The smell of smoke was thick and acrid, carrying on the icy wind. They bounded and slammed at high speed over the fields of snow, each jolt sending a shudder through Tori's body that made her feel as though she were being slammed in her lower back by a wooden mallet.

Above them the sky was a clear dome, stars starting to show in so many tiny pinpricks that they looked like a giant milky sweep of a paintbrush across the heavens. And far along the distant horizon, above the Marble Mountain range, a soft green haze of northern lights began to shimmer.

But all Tori could think about was old man Noah North burning in that cabin.

And that it was *her* fault. She'd started the fire.

CHAPTER 3

Olivia West watched Ace, her old German shepherd, dreaming in front of the hearth. His front paws twitched as he chased some imaginary hare through spring fields like the puppy he'd once been. Or so Olivia imagined.

But his hind legs lay motionless. It wouldn't be long before they were completely paralyzed. Degenerative myelopathy, the vet had said. Her heart constricted at the thought. Ace was everything to her. The day she'd stopped her truck to peel him off the road had been the U-turn in her existence. She'd saved Ace's life and he had saved hers. Before Ace, Olivia had been a sexual-assault-and-kidnap victim. With Ace she'd become bold. With Ace she had fought back against her victim label. With Ace she'd claimed her right to stop hiding, to be a mother. It was because of that old dog that she was here right now, sitting in this study-cum-library in the lodge on Broken Bar Ranch—a ranch that was now hers—with Cole McDonough, a man who respected and loved her and wanted to partner with her on this journey called life.

And she'd been reunited with her daughter, Tori, who'd been conceived while Olivia had been held in captivity and raped repeatedly before managing to escape while pregnant.

But therein lay the biggest challenge ahead of her now—mother-hood. She felt she was losing Tori before she'd even grasped what it meant to be a mother and to win a child's trust and love.

She inhaled deeply. It wasn't going to be easy, but she'd been through more than most humans could endure. She *could* do this, *would* do this.

"Ace will still be able to do some tracking when he gets his wheel-chair," Cole said from the corner of the library, where he sat at a desk going through his recently deceased father's papers.

Olivia glanced up. Cole regarded her with deep-set gray eyes. He was an astute observer, a student of human nature, a cataloger of facts, a reader of micro-signs. His skills had been honed through years of investigative reporting. Skills he'd turned to award-winning narrative nonfiction. Cole was a formidable mountain of a man who wrote with a rugged virility that matched his physique. He wrote about risk takers and what it meant to survive. But in spite of his apparent machismo, his muscular prose, his written words also bespoke a sensitive, empathetic view of the world and the people in it. It was with this side of himself that he had shown Olivia how to start trusting people again.

But she hadn't let him in fully—couldn't. Not yet. Not quite. She wanted to love him wholly but was still struggling toward that, prob-ably as much as Tori was struggling to accept her as a mother.

And Cole was also proceeding cautiously. One of Olivia's biggest challenges was sex. After months of sexual abuse in captivity, perhaps it would always be so. Cole had thus insisted that Olivia take the main bedroom in the lodge—a family home his father had chosen to leave to Olivia instead of to him—while he slept and wrote in one of the small cabins down by the lake. It kept the issue of a shared bed off the table. For now.

"Yeah, I think he'll still enjoy some tracking on wheels. Or on his skis, once he gets used to them. The wheel and ski carts should arrive at the vet's any day now." Olivia pushed up from her chair and went to the big picture window that looked out over the cabins and the snow-covered lake. It was almost fully dark outside. Aurora glowed in the sky. She crossed her arms tightly over her chest and turned her attention to the driveway. Not a soul in sight. She rubbed her arms. "Tori promised she'd be back before dark. I shouldn't have let her go with that kid."

"Ricky?"

"He's trouble. I wanted to say no, but I say no to everything. I . . . I just don't know where to draw the line with her, Cole. I don't know *how* to be a mom."

He got up and came over to her, put his arm around her shoulders. "Hey, you're doing great so far."

"No," she said flatly as she watched darkness descend. "There is no manual for how to raise your estranged daughter born of sexual assault. I killed her father—I killed my abductor and rapist with my bare hands, but he also fathered her. How does she cope with that? On top of the loss of both her adoptive parents?"

"By working with the therapist, that's how. You both take baby steps. We all just keep trying in life, Liv, one way or another, because what else is there?"

She bit her lip, nodded.

"And next time, insist she take a radio with her so she can stay in contact."

Olivia nodded again. Apart from a few pockets, including the area around the lodge, cell service was pretty much nonexistent out here. She tensed as a headlight suddenly appeared over the rise. A snowmobile. It bounced over the landscape, hit the approach road, and came at a hellish clip toward the lodge.

"I'm going to give that little Ricky Simon shit a piece of my mind for driving like that," Olivia snapped as she hurried for the library door. "He could kill them both."

Olivia rushed down the stairs to the front hall and yanked open the big wooden door just as the snowmobile skidded to a halt beyond the porch. She stepped onto the covered porch, the cold instantly biting. The solo driver yanked off his helmet, leaving his engine running. Her heart sank.

It was Dave Brannigan, their ranch hand, breathing hard, explosive white clouds crystallizing about his face.

"Fire!" he yelled over the chugging engine. "Noah North's cabin is totally engulfed! We need volunteers until the fire guys can get up here from Clinton with a pumper truck—gonna take them at least forty-five minutes on these roads."

Cole appeared at Olivia's side. "What about Noah?"

"I think he's still inside." Brannigan wiped his brow with the back of his gloved hand. "Can you set the volunteer phone tree in motion and get down there? I'm heading over to Haugen Ranch to see if Ash can round up help. I've got my radio." He pulled his helmet back on, dropped down the visor, and revved his machine. He took off with a roar, his headlight cutting a beam into the snowy darkness.

Cole caught Olivia's eyes. She could see he was thinking the same thought she was—that the old drunken ex-cop had probably knocked over a lantern, passed out, and finally set himself and his old log cabin aflame.

"I'll start the phone tree—get your gear," Cole said as he hastened back into the house. But just as Olivia was about to follow him, another snowmobile came down the driveway. Slower this time.

Ricky and Tori drew up in front of the house, his machine coughing and belching gas-laden fumes. Relief rushed hot into Olivia's chest. Neither wore a helmet. A battle for another day.

"Tori!" she called over the noise of Ricky's old engine. "Noah's place is on fire. Cole and I are heading over. Get inside and *stay* there. Roshan has made supper."

Tori dismounted. But Ricky stared straight ahead where his head-lights aimed into the darkness, gloved hands tight on the handlebars. A whisper of warning curled through Olivia. *Another time.*

Without even glancing at her, Tori clumped up the porch stairs and into the house. Head jutting forward, she started up the stairs without removing her snow boots.

Another time.

Olivia entered the hallway as Cole appeared carrying her gear—jacket, snow pants, heavy-duty mitts, and a helmet. He thrust the gear at Olivia as his gaze followed Tori up the stairs.

"Later, Liv," he whispered. "We gotta go."

——

From the library window upstairs, Tori watched Olivia and Cole speed off into the night. As the darkness swallowed them, Ricky's words rolled over and over and over in her head.

He's dead, Tori. Stone dead. Nothing in this world can help him now.

She sucked in a shaky breath as she replayed in her mind their flight from the blazing cabin. Ricky had stopped the snowmobile and turned to her.

"Tori?"

His voice is hoarse, his eyes wild. She looks away, her teeth clenched. She can't process what just happened. Everything inside her is twisted into a mangled ball. The wind has frozen tears down her face, and ice clumps her lashes. She can barely breathe.

"Look at me, Tori."

Slowly, very slowly, she meets his eyes. A whimper rises in her throat.

"We can never, ever tell anyone we were there, okay? Do you understand that? If the police find out we were stealing his liquor, or that we caused that fire, I strike out. Do you know what that means? They'll pull me out of the restorative justice program and I go into juvie. They'll take me away and lock me up. You can't tell anyone."

"Ricky—"

He grabs her frozen face between his gloved hands. The northern lights glow sickly green over his dusky features. "Listen. I've been busted for arson before. On the rez. I've been charged for breaking and entering in Clinton. I have no more strikes. And you—you're a sadistic sex murderer's kid, Tori. They're gonna ask just how much of your daddy's blood runs in your veins, how much of Eugene George's DNA drives your thinking. You got that? They're gonna ask why you started that fire. Do you understand me? You have got to promise on your life that you will never tell. Vow it, Tori. Now."

She's going to throw up. "We . . . we should call the firefighters. We—"

"Call them with what? There's no goddamn cell reception out here. And he's dead. Okay? There's nothing anyone can do now. And I can't go into the system. It'll kill me, Tori, kill me."

"I don't know why you insisted we nick that moonshine today." Her voice rises in pitch. "Why did you demand it had to be today, anyway?"

He falls silent, looks away. The aurora overhead turns from green to an eerie pukey yellow.

"Because it's my birthday," he says softly. "I'm thirteen today." His eyes begin to gleam. Tori realizes tough-ass Ricky Simon is sad. He hurts. He's crying.

She swallows. "Did . . . did you get presents? From your mom and dad?"

"Jesus, what kind of a stupid question is that right now? What family cares about birthdays anyway, once you reach thirteen?"

She wants to say, "Mine does." But the family Tori had a few months ago is not the "family" she has right now. She never even got a chance to reach thirteen with her old family. Her whole world was turned upside down when her adoptive mother died in a skiing accident, and then her adoptive dad set out to hunt the serial killer who had spawned Tori. Which led them all to Broken Bar, and to Olivia—her real mother. She's been living in a nightmare dimension since, a dark upside-down world that mirrors the right way 'round, and she doesn't know what to do about it.

"I care, Ricky," she says softly.

He rubs his mouth hard with his gloved hand. "Yeah. Well. That's cool. Because sometimes you just gotta make your own fun when no one else cares, you know?"

"I know."

He clears his throat and inhales deeply. "We weren't doing anything bad. Just taking a bottle or two of moonshine. Nothing bad."

He unzips the top of his jacket and pulls out one of the bottles he took. He removes the stopper and offers it to her.

"Have some. It'll make you feel better."

She takes a sip. It burns like fire down her throat. She coughs and her eyes water all over again. But he's right. The heat branching through her chest feels good. She takes another sip and hands the bottle back to him. He takes a few slugs himself, wipes his mouth, and recorks the bottle.

"Better?" he asks.

She nods, offering a half smile.

"Swear to me now, no telling?"

"I swear."

He leans forward and quickly kisses her right on the mouth. His lips are cold and rough from the weather, and he tastes like moonshine. Tori thinks it might be the most amazing taste ever.

It makes her brave enough to say, "What did you see when you looked out the shed window—you said you saw the man's helmet. What did it look like?"

"I'm not going to tell you. That way you can't tell anyone else, and we will be safe."

Inside her belly she begins to shake.

"Tori!"

She gasped and swung toward the source of the voice that had called her name. Roshan, the lodge's new housekeeper and cook, studied her oddly from the library doorway, her hand on the doorknob. Tori's heart banged against her ribs. She felt as though Roshan had heard her thoughts, as if she'd spoken it all out loud.

"I've got some nice hot soup ready for you in the kitchen," Roshan said.

"Not hungry." Tori pushed past Roshan and headed for the stairs.

"Where did you go with Ricky tonight?" Roshan called after her.

She hesitated a fraction of a second at the bottom of the staircase. "Out. Nowhere special." Then she took the stairs at a run. She rounded the corner at the landing, breathing so hard she thought she might die.

CHAPTER 4

Cariboo Country. Monday, January 14.

Rebecca sat on a plastic chair in the Devil's Butte hospital waiting area, still wearing her suit from court beneath her parka.

Across from her, a giant of a man in his sixties fiddled nervously with the ends of his gray beard. He was dressed in what was basically the Devil's Butte uniform—lined flannel shirt, lined Carhartt pants, fur-lined boots. Beside him a woman wearing the dull-brown uniform of a local fast-food outlet scrolled through her cell phone while chewing gum. At the far end of the waiting area, a young mother struggled to comfort a snotty toddler in a snowsuit. The smell was all hospital. Rebecca felt ill.

Once again the message she'd discovered on her phone late Wednesday afternoon looped through her brain.

Rebecca North? Sergeant Rebecca North? This is Corporal Buck Johnstone of the Clinton RCMP. Please call me at the following number, it's urgent.

She knew Buck. She'd been at school with him. When she'd heard his voice, she'd known instantly that something terrible had happened to her father. She'd called at once.

I'm so sorry, Becca. Bad news . . . Shotgun. Twelve-gauge. Self-inflicted. Fire . . . They've taken him to the morgue up at Devil's Butte. Autopsy to be performed . . .

She inhaled deeply and fought back the raw emotion that hovered so close to the surface. Fatigue, jet lag, and shock just made it all harder to control.

We took a good look at the scene, Becca, and there's nothing to warrant a criminal investigation. All the evidence pointed to suicide. The coroner's office is now the lead on the case.

Because of the record-breaking snow and ice storms that had locked down airports and caused untold havoc from the East Coast through to Calgary, it had taken Rebecca five days to get here, her nights spent sleeping on airport seats along with hundreds of other stranded passengers.

At least she'd managed to book into a motel in Kamloops last night, where she'd found a hot shower and donned clean underwear and a fresh blouse before driving up to Devil's Butte in a rental.

Her hometown of Clinton was too small for a morgue of its own, so her father's remains had been taken to the larger and more northerly town of Devil's Butte, which had a proper hospital and ancillary facilities.

And now they'd already conducted the postmortem.

It was protocol, she knew, in a sudden and apparently self-inflicted death like this, for the coroner's office to order an autopsy and confirm identification as soon as possible. Family consent was not required. Rebecca also knew that by law the fire investigator would have had to investigate the blaze within three working days.

Her eyes burned.

She should have taken her father's phone call more seriously, seen it as a cry for help.

Now this. Now he was dead and burned and autopsied. And she was too late to do anything.

"Rebecca North?"

She jumped as a perky woman in her mid- to late forties approached, sporting white-blonde hair in a spiky cut. Bright-blue eyes danced behind her tortoiseshell frames, and an electric energy seemed to crackle from her.

"It's been a long time, Becca." The woman proffered a delicate, pale-skinned hand. "I do wish it was under more favorable circumstances."

Confused, Rebecca came slowly to her feet. She stood much taller than the slight woman. She shook her hand.

"Have we met?"

"Dixie," the woman said. "Dixie Scott McCracken. I'm the local on-call coroner now." She smiled gently. "I know, it's been a really long time."

"I . . . *Dix*? From Dr. McCracken's office?"

"One and the same. His wife. We married before you left town. But I'm sure you had your own things on your mind back then."

"I didn't recognize you."

"Age." She smiled. "It's a magician. I'd know you anywhere, though. Saw you on the news with that big trial."

Rebecca swallowed. No one called her Becca back east. In that reality, in her world as a white-collar-crimes detective for the Royal Canadian Mounted Police, she was Rebecca. Or Sergeant North. This tiny wife of her old family physician calling her Becca made her feel small. Young. Like the gawky teen she'd been when she'd walked out of town and never looked back.

"Are you certain you want to view your father like this? The burn trauma is intense, and we have made a positive ID. So there's no need for—"

"I need to see him."

Dixie paused. As if giving Rebecca time to reconsider, to bow out. But Rebecca stood her ground in silence.

"Come this way." Dixie led Rebecca toward the elevator.

"I gather Constable Johnstone told you that the coroner's service is now the lead agency on this death investigation?" she said as she pushed the down button.

"He did." Rebecca met the little coroner's gaze. "You're all certain it was self-inflicted? That there's no criminal investigation warranted?"

Dixie's brow crooked up. "The official report will take a while to finalize yet, but yes, we've made the preliminary determination that Noah died from a self-inflicted shotgun wound around the time the fire started." The elevator doors opened. Dixie fell silent as they stepped inside. She pressed the button for the hospital basement. The doors slid closed.

"The initial investigation was handled by the local RCMP," she said. "And by the provincial fire investigators, but they found nothing suspicious. Everything about the case points to your father taking his own life. I really am so sorry, Becca."

Rebecca's blood pressure climbed as they descended. She wasn't sure she could handle this—seeing her own father's charred body on a morgue slab. Her face grew hot. The elevator space pressed in on her. She cleared her throat. "How did the blaze start?"

"The point of origin appears to have been a kerosene lamp in the kitchen, which was knocked over before he shot himself in the living room."

"He was definitely deceased prior to the fire?"

"No evidence of smoke inhalation in the trachea."

The elevator doors opened into a basement corridor. Fluorescent lighting flickered.

As they approached the opaque glass morgue doors at the end of the corridor, Rebecca asked, "How did you make the ID?"

"The contact gunshot wound was intraoral, the trajectory going up through the back of the roof of the mouth. So most of his jaw was left intact. We were able to use antemortem dental records for comparison, plus X-rays. Both his dentist and his family physician—my husband, Bob—provided us with Noah's health records."

Such was the nature of small towns. First names. Everyone knew each other. A Gordian knot of connections. Here Dix was—a nurse who'd worked as Dr. Bob McCracken's assistant before marrying him, now the on-call coroner presiding over the death of one of her husband's patients.

And here Rebecca was. Also one of Doc McCracken's old patients, waiting for Dix to show her her dad on a slab.

If only she had managed to come home when he'd called, seen him alive one last time. Perhaps she could have stopped this.

"I've asked pathologist Dr. Bert Spiker to be present. He can walk you through any specific questions you might have about the postmortem." Dixie hit a button on the wall, and the opaque morgue doors slid open.

CHAPTER 5

It was recess, and Ricky and Tori hunkered out of the wind behind the wall of the gymnasium, where Ricky was sneaking a smoke.

"I'm scared, Ricky." She kicked at a lump of dirty ice as she spoke. She'd been feeling sick since the event and *needed* to speak about it. Except she couldn't tell Olivia, Cole, or her therapist—nobody. Telling could get Ricky sent away.

"Quit worrying. It's been almost a week, and everyone says it was suicide and an accidental fire—the cops, the firefighters, everyone. *No one* knows we were there."

"But *we* know someone was there when Noah North died."

Ricky took a drag on his cigarette. She didn't like the smell but tolerated it on the grounds that it looked rebellious. He blew out a stream of smoke. It crystallized with his breath in a giant cloud around his face. He had a fresh black eye. She wanted to ask him how he'd gotten it, but the last time she'd inquired about one of his injuries, he had gotten mad and hadn't spoken to her for a week.

The wind gusted across the soccer field and swirled around the corner. She dug her hands deeper into her down jacket. Her toes were going numb, and her ears burned. All she could see in her mind, over and over, was the fire. Those trembling aspen trees had eyes. The trees *knew* the truth of what they'd done. She felt the record of their actions was somehow trapped there in that aspen grove. Her adoptive dad had been a homicide investigator. He'd told her that every action a man took left a trace. Even if not immediately apparent, the trace lingered there for those who knew how to look. She felt convinced that someone would go out to Noah North's place and discern it. Learn that she had burned a man.

"Look." He took a last drag, dropped the butt, ground it out in the ice with his runners. "You did nothing wrong, kid."

"Don't call me 'kid,'" she snapped. "You're not even a year older than I am."

He angled his head, that wicked little Ricky twinkle entering his black eyes. His lips quirked into a teasing smile. She felt a flutter in her stomach as she remembered his lips against her mouth. It eased the knot in her. A little.

"Don't mess with me, Ricky," she groused. "It's not funny."

"I mean it," he said. "*You* didn't nick the liquor, I did. You only bumped over that lantern because *I* jerked you around and made your arm swing out." Silence. He was giving her a mental escape route.

Take it, Tori. Take it . . . Safety net.

"So if you tell, maybe they'll forgive *you*, Tori. But me? I get sent away." Ricky paused. "You're still good, right?"

The school buzzer sounded. Tori hesitated. "I . . . I just can't help wondering if Noah North was murdered by that man on a snowmobile. If he finds out you saw him, he's not going to know that I didn't see him, too. It's not like I'm safe not knowing what he looked like."

Ricky's face turned dead serious. "That's the other thing. Right now he *doesn't* know we were in that shed. But if you talk, that man could find out, and yeah, then he might come after us both to shut us up." He watched her face. "Have you thought about that?"

She swallowed. Because of course she had.

"We *need* to keep this quiet, Tori," he whispered.

———

Olivia bent into a cloud of fine snow crystals blowing off the lake as she made her way down to the tiny log cabin where Cole spent the bulk of his days writing his new book. She'd left Ace in the main house. The ground was too icy for his failing legs.

As she reached the cabin door, she heard the sound of a snow-mobile approaching the lodge. Through the trees she saw someone pulling up in front of the porch. Roshan could take care of whoever it was.

Olivia hesitated before knocking on the cabin door. She was leery of interrupting Cole's writing time. But the door swung open before she could change her mind. He stood tall in the doorway, a smile upon his rugged face. The cabin exuded warmth from the cast-iron stove. It smelled comfortingly of coffee and woodsmoke.

"I saw you coming." He stepped aside for Olivia to enter, and he shut the door behind her.

"You could work in the lodge library, you know," she said.

"I like it here." His grin deepened. But the undercurrents—the reasons he was giving her space—simmered. He was waiting until she was ready for more intimacy.

"Coffee?"

"No, no thanks." Olivia hesitated. "I . . . I'm not staying. I just need your advice, Cole, before I head into Clinton to pick Tori up from the therapist."

His smile faded. "What is it?"

Olivia breathed out a heavy sigh. "Tori's been having nightmares. Since the fire. I've heard her crying at night. And this morning when I went into her room, I found this."

She opened her jacket, took out an empty bottle, and handed it to Cole. He upended the bottle and examined the markings on the bottom. He glanced up sharply and met her eyes.

"I think she's been drinking in her room," Olivia said.

"Liv, this is Noah North's moonshine. These markings are how he dates and records his batches."

"I know." She paused. "I think she was there the night of the fire. With Ricky."

CHAPTER 6

The autopsy suite was like so many others Rebecca had visited over her years of being a cop—exposed pipes, drains in the tiled floor, formalin-filled jars holding excised body parts lining shelves, utensils that looked big and urgent. A temperature-regulated stainless steel cooler for corpses. But the smell—that was something she'd never grow accustomed to.

At the center of the room was an autopsy table with a large metal grocery-type scale hanging over its foot. On the table lay a shape covered by a white sheet.

Rebecca's stomach fisted. A buzz began inside her head.

"Rebecca," Dixie said, "this is Dr. Bert Spiker."

Dr. Spiker, a formidable hulk of a man, stood at the sink washing his hands. He turned around, and drying his hands, he came forward. He was round in face as well as fleshy in body.

"I'm sorry for your loss, Sergeant North," he said, reaching for and snapping on gloves. His voice was nasal and strangely high for such a bass-looking tuba of a body.

Dixie offered Rebecca a stiff white mask. Rebecca shook her head. She wanted—needed—to be fully cognizant of all sensory input, almost as a form of self-flagellation. For not having been there for her dad. Dixie donned a mask herself.

Dr. Spiker partially drew back the sheet to expose her father's head and the top part of his shoulders.

Rebecca flinched and fought the urge to take a step backward.

The head was a blackened, lipless lump with white teeth clenched in a wild rictus.

Despite the coolness in the room, despite the fact that her father's remains had been kept at controlled temperatures, the scent of cooked human flesh was instant. Porky, livery, almost a musky sweetness. The kind of thick smell molecules that got right into one's mouth and nested into the hairs of one's nostrils.

She'd once been told by firefighters that when a whole human body burned, the iron-rich blood that cooked inside could smell coppery, metallic. The internal organs—which rarely burned completely because of their high fluid content—smelled more like burned liver. And the cerebrospinal fluid burned up into a musky, sweet perfume. Bile shot instantly up the back of her throat, and her stomach heaved.

What was on the table didn't look human to her, let alone anything like her dad.

Crispy critter was a term homicide cops sometimes used for burn fatalities. Gallows humor. It helped defuse normal human reactions. But nothing—*nothing*—could have prepared Rebecca for this burned, blackened skin, split in places to expose white-and-cherry-pink flesh and yellowish fat beneath. The buzzing in her head grew louder. It blurred time. Logic. Reality.

"Move the sheet down farther," she demanded.

Dr. Spiker glanced at her, then at Dixie. Dixie gave a small nod. The pathologist peeled the white sheet down farther over the twisted remains. Her dad's hands were curled into twisted black claws.

Dr. Spiker had done his Y-incision in the cooked flesh. Skin had been sloughed off in places on the abdomen to expose pinky-white flesh beneath. This once-human shape twisted and charred beyond recognition had been her father. The single dad who'd raised her.

The dad who'd held her hand, who'd patched her knees, who'd taught her to shoot.

Who had sat with her nights reading to her after her mother had died so suddenly of cancer on a spring day when Rebecca was twelve.

Rebecca's heart beat so fast she feared she might faint.

She was going to throw up, couldn't fight it. The smell, the sight, was so overpoweringly nauseating. And as she battled for composure, for control, to just breathe without sucking in the smell, she was besieged by a sudden hot spike of rage. *Bastard.* How could he do this to her?

How could *she* have let this happen?

"You're certain it's him?" she demanded, voice crisp. She'd asked it before, she knew that. Yet she couldn't help saying it again. She wanted to not believe it. For it to be a terrible mistake.

"From comparison with antemortem health records, yes," Spiker said in his nasal voice. And as if he saw she needed convincing, he explained, "There are around two hundred and six bones in the human body. Each is unique to a given individual. They provide a solid basis for positive identification if X-rays taken during life are available. The decedent in this instance had fractured a left radius sometime in his life, and he has a surgical plate in his right hand—"

"From an old police K9 bite." Rebecca cleared her throat and stepped closer, forcing her concentration onto the body. The jaw was oddly intact, but Rebecca had never personally seen the effects of an intraoral gunshot wound before. She felt both Dixie and Dr. Spiker watching her, weighing her. And something began to whisper inside her soul. It rose in crescendo and raised the fine hairs of instinct up the back of her neck. She could *not* believe her dad had done this. Especially not in the context of that phone call. Or the tone of fear she'd heard in her father's voice.

Last night. I think he was outside, among the aspens. Watching my cabin. The night before I think someone followed me home in the dark. I think he knows what I know.

"And his weapon was found with him?" she said.

"Mossberg twelve-gauge pump-action shotgun," Dixie replied. "The scene was consistent with him having been seated in his living room chair with the Mossberg positioned between his legs. Latent prints that match your father's were recovered from the weapon. Latents are capable of withstanding temperatures of about one hundred degrees Celsius for several hours," she explained. "Almost one in five items recovered from fire scenes yield fingerprint ridge detail following normal development treatments."

"Why is he in that pose—his arms and hands curled up like that—if he shot himself in his chair? Why is his skin on the backs of his forearms split as they might be in defensive-type wounds?"

"Intense burning causes bodies to demonstrate characteristically pugilistic postures," Spiker said. A pause. "He was definitely deceased before he burned, Sergeant North, if that's any consolation."

Small goddamn fucking mercies.

"And you're certain it was the gunshot wound that killed him—that was the cause of death?" She needed to ask it, to hear the pathologist confirm it. Again.

Spiker nodded. "If you take a look at the radiographs on the screen here"—he pointed to a monitor on the wall at his side—"the shotgun barrel made contact with the roof of the mouth, the pellets moving with an upward-and-backward directionality. Some of the shotgun pellets are still inside the skull, as you can see here. Here you can see the brain tissue is massively lacerated. No intact brain stem can be identified here"—he pointed—"including medulla, cerebellar tissue, midbrain, pons, cerebral peduncles."

Spiker turned to his notes, lying on the counter beneath the monitor. "The decedent had a large amount of aspirated blood in the right lung. Left lung weighs 440 grams, the right weighs 970 grams. A normal adult male is 400 to 450 grams. Section of the lung tissue shows congested, atelectatic, edematous, hemorrhagic lung with extrusion of hemorrhagic frothy fluid . . ."

His words began to blur as the noise in Rebecca's brain grew louder, trying to crowd Spiker out.

"Blood alcohol content was .242—more than three times the legal limit for those driving."

Dixie said, "The positive toxicology, combined with Noah's history of alcoholism, plus his medical records for treatment of depression, are all consistent with the conclusion of suicide as the manner of death."

Her gaze shot to Dixie. "My father was being treated for depression?"

"Bob had referred him to a therapist, yes—Dr. Rio Miller in Clinton. Additionally, Noah had publicly expressed dissatisfaction with his life."

"Where? When?" Rebecca demanded.

"At the Moose and Horn pub. Over the last few months. This was revealed by police interviews. Patrons and friends reported him saying that he felt he'd been a failure as both a cop and a father."

Rebecca's eyes began to fill with emotion. *Focus.* She wiped her nose with the base of her thumb. "No note was found?"

"If there was one," Dixie said gently, "it would have been destroyed in that fire—the blaze was intense and additionally fueled by the explosion of the propane tank." The coroner exchanged a glance with Spiker.

Rebecca felt denial rising like a stone wall around her, and clearly both the coroner and the pathologist sensed it.

Dixie added, "As I'm sure you know, Rebecca, the approach of agencies involved in assessing a fire fatality is always to treat it as suspicious until no sign is shown otherwise, and to assume at the outset that it will not be a straightforward case. There is nothing in your father's case to indicate the fire or death was suspicious."

Nothing to warrant additional funds, or calling in a major crimes team, or getting expensive forensic expertise and lab tests for a dead old paranoid drunk who'd considered his life and himself a failure.

Her father's voice snaked through her brain.

I suspect he's been inside my cabin, took some papers from my case file.

What "case" had her father been working on? Why had it made him feel threatened? Had the threat been real, or imagined, or some combination of the two? Rebecca was going to find out. One way or another. Come hell or high water. She was going to peel back the layers of her dad's last days, because this was not right. She did not—would not—believe it.

"I'd like a copy of your full report when you're done," she said.

"Of course," Dixie said. "I'll send it your way as soon as it's official. And once I've signed off on everything, we can release the body, and you can make arrangements. Will you be using Dunwoody and Smithe undertakers? I can call them if you like."

"I'll handle it." Rebecca gave a nod to Spiker. He re-covered the body.

After thanking him, she exited the morgue and rode back up in the elevator with Dixie, who then walked with her to the hospital exit doors.

"Thank you," Rebecca said as they reached the exit.

But as she was about to step out into the cold, Dixie placed her slender hand on Rebecca's arm. She regarded Rebecca intently for a moment, assessing something.

"You don't feel that he did it," she said.

"I know you've done your best, Dixie. Thank you for that."

Dixie's hand remained on Rebecca's arm. "But you still—"

"I can't." Emotion threatened suddenly, and Rebecca glanced away for a second to compose herself. "I . . . I just cannot believe he'd do that."

"It's a normal reaction, Becca. Denial."

"Thanks."

As Rebecca stepped through the hospital doors, the north wind sliced across her face as it howled and twisted around the ice-encased cars skulking in the lot. She welcomed the bracing blades of cold. She wanted the clean Arctic wind to wash the thick smell of her father's burned corpse out of her hair, out of her nostrils and mouth and pores.

She unlocked her little silver Prius rental and climbed into the driver's seat, shivering. As she started the engine and cranked up the heat to defog the windows, she caught sight of Dixie watching her from the hospital windows, a clipboard of papers clutched to her chest.

And Rebecca knew that as much as she'd tried to escape this place she'd once called home, it had found a way to claw her back. It was not done with her. Not yet. Not by a long shot. Nor she with it.

She was going to find out what had triggered her father's death.

But in order to do that, she'd have to go back more than twenty years into the past, to Ash Haugen. The man who'd cloven her heart in two and shown her the raw meaning of betrayal. The man she'd done her damnedest to avoid seeing whenever she'd returned home for her brief and obligatory visits to her dad.

I know he lied, Becca.

You both lied.

All those years ago. It wasn't a riding accident that gashed open his face, was it? What were you protecting him from that day?

She consulted her watch. Daylight hours were few at this time of year. She had to move it if she wanted to check in to the Cariboo Lodge Motel, see Corporal Buck Johnstone, and still manage a pre-liminary visit to her dad's burned-out cabin before darkness fell.

I GOTTA FEELING

Cariboo Country. Sunday, September 27,
just over twenty years ago.

All I wanna do is live it up
In LA
Before I die, have some fun,
In LA . . .

It's the hit song of this summer, and Whitney considers it her tune. It's
playing on the truck radio as she settles into the passenger seat of the
rusty red pickup while he tosses her old suitcase into the back.

It's a sign, she thinks. The fact that her tune is on the radio when he
picks her up. A sign that she is finally going to escape this shithole town,
and it's going to be great. She bobs her head to the beat.

It's gonna be great.
Party all night, until the sun
Comes up . . .

Her bag is packed. She's left her mom a note. She's got her money.
Hollywood, LA, here she comes.
He climbs into the driver's seat. She smiles at him.

But his face remains grim. The look in his ice-blue eyes is acid. Jaw tight, he shifts his old work truck into gear and releases the brakes. As he pulls into the road, her mood shifts. She watches him drive. His profile is rugged. It reminds her of the hard crags of the Marble Mountain range that she likes to sit and watch when the sun sets.

Maybe she'll miss the mountains.

His hands clench the wheel. His sleeves are rolled back on tanned arms. The hair on his forearms is starting to bleach gold after a whole summer of working on the ranch. Even his thick, dark hair has lighter streaks.

The truck smells like him, *she thinks. And of hay. And dust. It's coated with a fine layer of the stuff, inside and out. The dry dirt roads have made it so. Although it's the end of September, it's warm again, even early in the mornings, and the scent coming in through the open windows as they reach the highway is of sagebrush and manure. Indian summer. A last kick at the can before winter rolls in and squeezes the beating heart of this town in its icy grip.*

Winters will be warm in Cali, *she wants to say.* This town can die under snow and ice for all I care now.

"You've got the cash with you?" he asks without looking at her.

She feels a deepening frisson of unease. "Yeah." And then some. But that's not for him to know.

The song on the radio segues to another. Something more mournful. A tractor trailer rumbles past.

"Got everything else—everything you . . . need?"

"What's it to you anyway?" she snaps, irritable because the blush is gone off her mood. "What do you care what I've got, or don't?"

He shoots her a hot look. The anger in his eyes pierces right through her soul. The intensity of it screws with her breathing. She reaches for her smokes. Lights one, breathes out the window.

"You shouldn't do that."

"Fuck you. It's over. It's not like it's going to matter to me what you say."

He drives in silence, and after a while he casts her another look. And this time she sees pain. The guy's a fucking mess, and it frightens her.

"You gonna drive any faster, or what? I don't wanna miss the bus."

As they round the bend, she catches sight of Trevor waiting under the Renegade Bus Lines stop sign. He's dressed in black jeans, black leather jacket. His backpack rests in the dirt by his boots.

"What the fuck!?" He slows the truck and fires a look at her. "What in the hell is that asshole doing here?"

"What's it to you?"

He pulls instantly off the road and drives along the dirt shoulder almost right into Trevor, who stands defiant and does not move an inch. At the last minute he slams on the brakes so hard that she jerks forward against the seat belt; then her head rams back on the rebound, slamming up against the hunting rifle mounted in the gun rack behind her.

"Jesus!"

"Tell me what he's doing here!" He reaches over and yanks the cigarette out of her lips.

"Hey, asshole!" She grabs for it.

He chucks it out his window.

"I'm talking to you. Fuck you, Whitney. You owe me that much."

"Fuck you, Haugen. I owe you jack."

He stares at her as if stunned. Energy pulses off him in hot waves.

Suddenly he unbuckles his seat belt and flings open the driver's-side door.

"Stay in the truck," he demands.

CHAPTER 7

Cariboo Country. Monday, January 14.

Rebecca sat opposite Constable Buck Johnstone at his metal desk in the Clinton police station. The tiny RCMP detachment was manned by two members and ancillary staff, with backup drawn from other jurisdictions for serious crimes. It looked exactly as it had when her father had worked here. It was probably even the same desk.

Buck had a file folder positioned squarely in front of him and a box of doughnuts at his side. Heat blasted from the old vents, but Rebecca kept her parka on. She suspected the cold deep inside her bones had more to do with what she'd seen in the morgue than with the Arctic outflow.

She'd managed to check in to the Cariboo Lodge Motel a few blocks down from the station. It was the only accommodation in town. She'd left her Prius in the motel lot and walked up the main road, thinking physical exercise might help warm her.

It hadn't.

"Coffee?" said Buck. "I've got some pastries from Dot's Donuts and Diner up the street." He pushed the box toward her.

"No, thanks."

"Dot's is still there, can you believe it?" Buck pulled his chair closer to his desk, clearly uncomfortable and making small talk to defuse the tension that rolled off Rebecca. She'd never imagined Buck would become a cop. He'd been awkward at school, and tubby, and the kids had bullied him about his weight. But he had shot up to well over six feet and grown into his fat. His eyes were big and blue-green, and his brown hair was buzz-cut short and thinning. He had the ruddy skin and lined eyes of a rancher, and the chapped fingers of a cold-weather hunter, and Rebecca wondered if he'd inherited his parents' place and whether he'd married. No ring on his finger.

"Except it's no longer Dot who runs it but Marcy Fossum," he said. "Remember Marcy? Her daughter's in college in Vancouver now. Marcy bought the diner probably not long after you left town—"

"Buck, if it's okay with you, I'd really like to cut to it. I just need to know what happened."

His face changed, eyes narrowing slightly.

He opened the file folder, cleared his throat. "The fire was fully engaged when the firefighters got out there. There was nothing they could do apart from control any spread." He glanced up from the folder and met her eyes briefly before returning his attention to his notes. "It was only safe to enter and search for Noah at dawn. And it was a challenge because damage from the propane tank explosion pretty much flattened the place, plus water from the pumper truck had frozen over the scene, encasing the whole thing in thick layers of ice. But we—Constable Amy Beckett and me—photographically documented the scene at first light. I had print copies made for you." He selected several glossy photos from his file and spread them across his desk as if dealing Rebecca a hand of cards. He paused suddenly and met her gaze again.

"I liked him, Becca," he said quietly. "We all did. Noah was larger than life. And we owed him for his years of service. He inspired me to become an officer . . . This shouldn't have happened. We should have seen it coming, done something. Intervened."

Rebecca watched his face. In Buck's eyes she read sorrow, empathy. He had guilt, too, she was startled to realize. She'd never known that her father had been Buck's inspiration. And in his features she also read accusation, blame. *She* should have seen it coming. She who was not loyal to her dad or this place, she who'd deserted her home to become a bigger, better, fancier cop in some more populous part of the country than this rural backwater overseen by Corporal Buck Johnstone.

And it struck her that Buck Johnstone was doing this favor—giving her prints of his scene photos—for her dad, not her.

She felt naked suddenly. Vulnerable. It was not a feeling she was comfortable with.

"Thank you, Buck," she said softly.

He inhaled deeply and tapped his index finger on the first image. "The point of origin is believed to have been a kerosene lamp in Noah's kitchen, here. This is the fire guys' interpretation of the evidence."

Shock sliced through her body as she stared at what had once been the kitchen in her family home. The place was unrecognizable. Razed. Black and scarred and twisted with mangled appliances, all of it sealed in thick ice and ghoulishly draped with jagged, teeth-like icicles. An image of her father's body came to mind. Her heart began to race.

Focus.

She forced herself to narrow her attention to the tip of Buck's finger.

"The evidence is consistent with the lantern having been knocked off the kitchen table, breaking, spilling fuel, and igniting under the wooden table."

His finger moved to the next photo. "Shotgun shells. They went off in the blaze. It's the same as the ammunition Noah used in his

Mossberg. The gun safe by the door over here was empty, unlocked." He looked up. "The theory is he took his shotgun from the safe, and he put a box of shells on the table. He then proceeded to load his weapon at the kitchen table, after which he went through to the living room, where he seated himself in his recliner and positioned the shotgun. The timing—the spread of the fire—suggests he could have knocked the lantern over during the loading process, and either he didn't notice because of his high blood alcohol level, or he didn't care because he was going to eat his gun before the fire got to him."

Rebecca rubbed her brow.

Compartmentalize. Intellectualize. You can do this.

"Where's his rifle? My father had a rifle as well as his Mossberg."

"It's in his Silverado. Locked in the gun box on the truck bed. The vehicle is parked out back here in the public safety lot." Buck opened a drawer and reached inside for a set of truck keys. He slid the fob across the desk. "His rifle and ammunition are securely stored, so we left it there. We've been through the rest of the vehicle. Nothing amiss. Just an open bottle of moonshine, which we removed—we also confiscated the moonshine from his shed, along with the illegal still. The shed was the only structure untouched by the fire because the wind that night was blowing fierce in the opposite direction." He rubbed his chin, clearly uncomfortable with all of this. "And there's also some clothing and other gear on the back seat of the truck cab. Snowshoes. Some other bits of junk. Tools." He glanced out the window and appeared to study the flag snapping sharply in the wind outside. Frost filigreed the sides of the windows.

"The Silverado has good studded snow tires," he said quietly. "You might want to use it if you plan on heading up there—"

"I do. This afternoon. Thanks." She reached for the keys. "So is that where he was found? In his recliner in the living room?"

Buck nodded. "Melted right into the synthetic fabric. And then froze under the pumper truck ice. Had to chip him out together with

51

the recliner as one unit after we'd photographed and sketched the place, or he'd have frozen solid through to the core within hours, and then the pathologist would have had to defrost him slowly over an extended period or the outer layers would decay while the insides remained froz—"

"I got it."

He moistened his lips and showed her another photograph. Her dad's body in the burned and melted recliner, entombed in ice.

"We marked where he was before chipping him and the recliner out." Buck glanced up. "From everything at the scene, from us tracing back his movements that day, and even farther back in the weeks preceding the event, from his expressions of discontent to patrons at the Moose and Horn, from his medical records, his blood alcohol content, his state of mind . . . At some point during those days or weeks, Becca, your father formed an intention to take his life. He drank through his final day to a point he was clumsy and stumbling. He loaded his weapon, bumped things about, went to his living room, and shot himself."

She shifted rapidly through the other images, her mouth tight.

"Did you know he was working cold cases?" she said.

"Noah? He was always working some so-called case."

She met Buck's blue-green eyes. "Anything that was worrying him in particular?"

"Becca, your dad would come up with crazy conspiracy theories and get paranoid all the time." He paused. "We *all* knew this."

"What time was the blaze reported?"

"Five forty-five p.m. Called in by Cole McDonough on neighboring Broken Bar Ranch. He was organizing other neighbors to go help."

"And where was my father earlier that day?"

"Moose and Horn, from opening."

Nausea churned in Rebecca's stomach. He'd phoned her from outside the Moose and Horn. She herself could vouch for the fact that he'd been drunk by noon that day.

"Fire investigation started the following morning. No evidence of accelerant. No evidence of fuel having been loaded. Or windows opened for air, or the environment otherwise modified. No indication the structure was prepped to burn. No neutral indicators, either, which would be the absence of things like valuable furniture or jewelry, photos, taxidermy—"

"He didn't have anything valuable." *Apart from his precious case file papers, which will be gone now.*

"Nor did he appear to have any debt or foreclosure problems, or insurance motivation," Buck said.

She smoothed back her hair as if it might help her control her thoughts.

"Sometimes things are exactly what they seem, Becca. I'm sure you know that."

"Right. Sometimes the questions are complicated, and the answers are simple. I think Dr. Seuss said that." She reached for the images and gathered them up. "Thank you for the copies. I'm going to head out there now."

"Not much to see under all that ice. Been growing hoarfrost for a few days now, too."

"I just need to see it, you know? Touch base with the place."

He nodded.

As she positioned the photographs in a neat pile, it struck Rebecca. "If his truck is here in the public safety lot, how did he get home from the Moose and Horn to his cabin that day?"

"He got a ride from Ash Haugen."

Something inside her froze. She stared at him.

"Ash?"

"Yeah. He found Noah in the PetroGas convenience store right around noon. Noah had left his Silverado parked at the Cariboo Lodge because Solly, the barkeep, wouldn't let him drive. Noah told Solly he was walking up to visit Clive Dodd, who lives behind the PetroGas. Sometimes he'd crash on the sofa at Clive's place. Ash offered Noah a ride back to his ranch since he was headed up that way. Said he dropped Noah off around four p.m. They had a drink. Ash left the cabin shortly afterward and went home."

Rebecca's skin went hot.

"It takes forty-five minutes to get to my father's ranch from the PetroGas. What happened between noon and when they arrived at four p.m.?"

"Ash had some errands to run along the way."

"*Ash* was reportedly the last person to see my father alive?"

"He was the last person to see your father alive."

The moment stretched. Wind gusted outside, making the old building creak and the halyard clank loudly against the flagpole outside. A dark, inky chill trickled slowly through Rebecca. It sank cold and deep in her bowels. And with it came the sense of a looming, monstrous cloud.

He lied.

You both *lied.*

What were you protecting him from that day?

CHAPTER 8

Rebecca exited the station. Unwanted memories of Ash reeled through her mind as she made for her father's truck: How Ash had cheated on her. How he'd screwed Whitney Gagnon in the horse barn during the annual Clinton Rodeo Fair on that sweltering July night more than twenty years ago. The night that everything changed.

How the smell of cotton candy had hung heavy in the summer air, braided with scents of hay, manure, bonfire smoke, burgers, fries, distant forest fires. The band had been belting out a song she liked, and she had wanted to dance with him and had gone looking for him. She'd caught him and Whitney coming out of the barn, hurriedly pulling their clothes back into place, faces flushed and hair mussed. Her heart and dreams had snapped in two in that one moment her eyes met Ash's.

Ash had vowed to her that it was a onetime thing. A terrible mistake. Rebecca had, over the rest of the summer, begun to slowly believe him, believe she might be able to trust him again.

But then she heard from town gossip Marcy Fossum that Ash had been seen huddling in a bar with Whitney up in Devil's Butte. Not once, but many times through August and September of that year, after he'd promised it was over. And Rebecca's sense of betrayal had been complete.

She'd been in her last year of school, and she'd vowed that the moment she graduated, she was getting the hell out of Dodge, like Whitney and Trevor had at the end of that September. Ash was expected to take over Haugen Ranch from his father, and she could not bear the idea of continually bumping into him and her own pain. She'd never loved anyone like she'd once loved Ash. And she never wanted to see him again. Not then. Not ever. Certainly not now.

Because in spite of herself, a dark little part of Rebecca buried down deep had been unable to stop loving Ash. And every man she'd been with since had in some way been measured against him. And had come up short.

I know he lied . . .

Yeah, he'd lied. Plenty.

What were you protecting him from that day?

Rebecca almost faltered in her step as it struck her.

That day had been the last Sunday in September.

The day she'd seen Ash wandering down the road, wounded and confused, in the storm.

The same day Whitney and Trevor had been seen getting into a white van with Oregon plates as they'd left town for LA.

The cold, black sensation she'd felt in Buck's office darkened and thickened like bitumen inside her. She wasn't comfortable with the way things were suddenly adding up in the context of her father's death.

She found her dad's dented gray Silverado in the lot beside a shiny, late-model, black Ford F-350.

Rebecca crouched and checked her dad's tires as wind tore at her hair. They were indeed studded, and the treads looked good. At least he'd kept on top of that. But the rest of the vehicle was a rusting and clunky farm workhorse that should probably be put out to pasture. It stood in stark contrast to the large and blinged-up Ford beside it.

Rebecca glanced at the shiny Ford F-350 again as she beeped her dad's lock. The black vehicle boasted big-ass wheel simulators, a fancy chrome grille, bull bars, and other cosmetic accessories, including a decal on the back window that depicted a snarling wolf. It screamed testosterone. She wondered if it was Buck's truck.

The door lock on the Silverado failed to open. Rebecca cursed. It took her three more tries before the frozen locking mechanism released. Shaking with cold, she climbed in. With numb fingers she inserted the key into the old truck's ignition and turned it halfway to prime the globe. She waited for the light on the dash. When it came on, she turned the key fully. The engine churned over once, twice, coughed, stuttered, choked, then died.

She swore.

Shivering harder, she attempted the process four more times. Finally the old engine turned over, coughed once more, then chugged to uneven life as the truck belched out a cloud of black exhaust smoke.

She cranked the heater up to full blast and rubbed her hands, waiting for the vehicle to defrost. While the truck took an age to warm, she rummaged through the clothes on the back seat. In the pile she found an old trapper's hat lined with sheepskin, a fleece neck gaiter, big gloves, a padded rancher's coat, ski pants, and her dad's old Sorels. Shivering uncontrollably now, Rebecca pulled the neck gaiter over her head, followed by the hat. She lowered the fleece earflaps. She then shrugged into her dad's oversize coat. It smelled of him.

She stilled.

The smell had triggered memories that hit so hard and so suddenly and were so powerful they felt physical, and all she could do was sit for a moment and feel her father's presence, as if part of him still lingered here in his truck, as if his arms were wrapping around her with his coat. As if he knew, somehow, she'd come home. Emotion filled her eyes.

I love you, Dad.

She swiped tears away. How had she not said those words to him in so many years?

How had it been so very long that she'd not come home and stayed, really stayed? Rebecca wiped her nose and pulled on the gloves.

I'm going to do this for you, okay? I'm going to figure this out. I'm going to stay awhile. I promise.

She found an ice scraper in the glove box, got out, and scraped the rest of the ice off the windshield. When she climbed back into the cab, the interior was warmer. But as she reached for the seat belt, she registered the fuel gauge. Her heart sank. The diesel tank was almost empty.

She decided she would fill up at PetroGas on her way out. It was nearby, at the north end of town. Besides, she wanted to know if anyone at the gas station had spoken to her father when Ash had found him there during the last hours of his life. Maybe they'd even captured her dad on the security camera. She *needed* to see him one last time, see how he'd looked that final day of his life. Perhaps she might discern some tiny clue in his demeanor.

Or maybe she just needed to plug the maw of loss gnawing into her stomach with one last glimpse of him.

Enveloped in the scent of her father's clothes, wrapped in the arms of memory warmth, Rebecca navigated the belching old Silverado out of the public safety lot and headed for the gas station. And as she refamiliarized herself with the workings of her dad's old vehicle and the winter road conditions, she felt as though she were being sucked down a wormhole of time—her job back east, her sterile apartment, her designer clothes, her on-off boyfriend, Lance—all growing distant and unreal with each step she took back into the past.

Rebecca filled the tank, then headed for the convenience store to pay.

A bell pinged as she pushed through the door. The woman behind the counter glanced up, and a guy on a ladder stocking shelves turned and looked down to see who'd entered. Both were East Indian in appearance.

"Cold out," the woman said, studying the gear Rebecca had decked herself out in. She caught sight of herself in a store mirror and did a double take. Her face was ghost pale under the old trapper's hat. She looked windblown and red eyed and red nosed. Like some homeless person. She offered a smile as the woman rang up her diesel purchase and took her credit card, but Rebecca's face felt stiff from cold.

Before she could voice her questions, the guy descended from the ladder and jerked his chin toward the window. "Isn't that Noah North's truck out there?"

"It is. I'm his daughter, Rebecca North. I . . . I came as soon as I heard, but the weather . . ." She cleared her throat. She was trying to explain, to justify. Because she felt guilt, and she was projecting her guilt as judgment on their part.

"Terrible news," the guy said, wiping his hands on a cloth. "I'm so sorry." He held out his hand. "I'm Abdul Malik. This is my wife, Kamala. Noah mentioned he had a daughter. A police officer, also."

Kamala handed Rebecca the fuel purchase receipt.

Rebecca took it. "I believe my father was in here on the day he died. Were either of you perhaps working that day? Did you see him? Talk to him, maybe?"

Abdul pulled a wry mouth. "When are we *not* working twenty-four-seven, eh, Kamala?"

"True," Kamala said. "Noah came in to buy cigarettes. He was often in here. Like most folk in town. Only one gas station at the north end, and one on the south."

Rebecca frowned. "*Cigarettes?*"

"Denali Plain, I remember," Kamala said.

"Did he . . . Had he done that before—buy smokes here?" Rebecca pocketed the receipt. Her father didn't smoke. Then again, how much did she know about her dad, in truth?

The couple exchanged a look. Abdul shrugged. Kamala said, "He might have. Can't be sure. Mostly he came for gas. Sometimes a newspaper, and some of those hunting magazines." Her eyes ticked toward a rack filled with magazines and a few paperbacks. "Sometimes a carton of milk."

"Did he seem okay to you, normal?"

The couple exchanged another glance.

"I do know he'd been drinking all morning," Rebecca offered.

Abdul nodded. "He sometimes came in like that, yeah." He gave a small apologetic shrug as though he were sorry they couldn't keep this from her.

A motorbike growled into the station and pulled up alongside a pump outside. The rider was dressed in black. He was followed by a dark-gray truck with two snowmobiles on the back. Clots of ice and snow still lodged in the sleds' tracks.

The couple tensed as the biker dismounted and pulled off his helmet. He wore a face gaiter with the design of a skeleton drawn up over his nose and mouth. He yanked the gaiter down under his chin as he strode toward the convenience store.

Abdul climbed back up his ladder and resumed stocking the shelf. Rebecca sensed that her window to get information from this couple was closing fast.

"Did my father say anything?" she asked quickly.

Kamala shook her head, the diamond in the side of her nose winking. Quietly she said, "He didn't say a word. He just went to stand by that window over there." She indicated the window with a nod of her head. "He stared out for some time. Long enough to make me wonder what he was looking at, or who he was waiting for. I asked him, and he just shrugged. That's when Mr. Ash Haugen came in. Ash had been around back filling up his propane tanks. He came in to pay, saw Noah was drunk, and offered him a ride home."

The door opened. The bell chimed. The biker entered. Big man. Shaved head. Weathered face. "What time was that? Do you recall?" Rebecca asked as the man walked to the back of the store, where he began to pour himself a coffee.

"About noon, eh, Kamala?" Abdul said from his ladder.

Kamala nodded. "I know because the guy with the tanker truck was pulling in to fill the tanks. I went out to cordon off part of the station."

The biker approached the counter with his coffee. He stood behind Rebecca, waiting. Urgency mounted in her.

"And those security cameras," she said quietly, nodding to the screen behind the counter. "You wouldn't happen to have the footage from that day? Outside and inside?"

Kamala grew edgy. She said to the guy behind Rebecca, "I'll be right with you." And then to Rebecca, she said, "Our system overwrites every seventy-two hours unless we specifically save the digital footage."

Rebecca nodded. "Thank you both very much for your help."

She turned to leave and almost bumped into the biker. He stepped aside slightly.

Rebecca exited the store, and the icy wind slapped her face. She glanced back. They were all looking at her. And she got the sense that the biker had asked the Maliks who she was and what she wanted. She had little doubt the Maliks had told him. They appeared nervous about him, and Rebecca figured she knew why. Immigrants, minorities like the Maliks, were not always welcome in redneck rural backwaters, despite liberal sentiment in the bigger metropolises of the country.

Either way, she was sure that the news of her return—and of the questions she was asking about her dad—would now spread like wildfire.

Drawing her dad's coat more tightly around herself, she returned to the Silverado via the other side of the gas bar. As she passed the bike, she noticed it was a Harley. A thumping bass beat issued from the slate-gray Chevy truck parked behind it. The truck windows were tinted, and on the bumper was a sticker with a skull that said SLED-NEX. Rebecca could not see the occupants, but she had the sense she was being watched. Again she was seized by a sense that her arrival in town would be common knowledge by dusk.

She climbed into the Silverado and started the engine, thinking about the Denali Plain cigarettes her father had bought. It seemed odd. If her dad had been going to visit old Clive Dodd, maybe he'd bought the cigarettes for him. A visit to Dodd was on her list. After a talk with Ash—the ex-lover she'd done her best to avoid for twenty years. It had come down to this.

At the gas station exit, while she waited for a delivery truck to pass, a pink neon sign diagonally across the street caught her eye. DOT'S DONUTS AND DINER. And she realized she was famished.

Craving a sugar fix and the warmth of coffee, Rebecca decided to pull into Dot's quickly and pick up something for the forty-five-minute drive to her old home.

CHAPTER 9

Olivia sat opposite Tori in a tiny booth in front of the street-facing windows of Dot's Donuts and Diner.

The air inside was warm and heavy with the sweet scents of maple, vanilla, and chocolate, overlaid with the vague muskiness of jackets and hats and mitts thawing over the backs of chairs and hanging on the hooks near the door.

Ace lay under the table at their boots. Olivia had brought him into town for a checkup at the vet, and she'd promised Tori a visit to Dot's as a treat for going to the therapist after school.

Tori poked at her doughnut for a few moments before taking a bite. Colored sprinkles flecked her lips as she chewed.

Olivia had an urge to reach for her napkin and dust them off her daughter's face. But Tori had erected an angry wall of defensive energy around herself today, so Olivia restrained her impulse. Even so, watching her kid chew with happy-looking sprinkles on her grumpy face filled her with a feeling she could only describe as love—bitter and sweet and all-encompassing. She desperately wanted to touch her daughter the way she'd seen other mothers touch theirs, the way her own mom had once touched her, before Eugene George abducted her and turned her into a tainted thing not even her husband wanted to touch. Olivia needed that human connection, as much as she'd resisted it in the years after her ordeal. She ached to gather her twelve-year-old up into her arms and just hold and comfort her and stroke her soft, dark hair. She ached for it with every molecule of her maternal being, and she ached to hear Tori say—maybe just one time—*Mom*.

Olivia inhaled as memories surfaced. Of Tori as a tiny newborn. How painful breastfeeding had been due to the trauma she'd incurred to her breasts during her captivity and abuse at the hands of Eugene George. How at first she'd fought against even looking at the offspring of rape, against acknowledging the little dark-haired infant crying in the crib as her own. How a journalist named Melody Vanderbilt had come to interview her in the hospital. How Melody had ultimately given Olivia a way out when she'd finally asked if she and her policeman husband, Gage Burton, could adopt the baby Olivia had hated to touch at the time, yet also needed to love.

How Melody had died in a skiing accident, and how Gage had then come hunting for Eugene in order to make the world safer for Tori, because he himself was sick and his days numbered. How Gage had wanted to bring Tori into Olivia's orbit so she'd know her biological mother and have family after he passed.

Olivia looked out the misted window, trying to breathe under the weight of the memories. The emotions. The pain. The poignancy of love and what people did to each other in the name of it. Melody had never written her news feature. Instead, she had written a manuscript based on Olivia and Tori's story. And in that manuscript she'd written words that came to Olivia's mind now.

Can you pinpoint the exact instant your life starts on a collision course with someone else's? Can you trace back to the moment those lives did finally intersect, and from where they spiraled outward again, yet from that point they remained forever entwined, two lives locked one with another?

She returned her attention to Tori, who was sipping hot chocolate and studiously avoiding all eye contact.

"How did it go today with Dr. Miller?" Olivia asked gently.

"Not going back."

Olivia reached for her cappuccino and sipped as she counted to twenty slowly. She cleared her throat, then asked, "Why not?"

"Don't need a shrink."

"Is that what Ricky said?"

Heat flared into Tori's cheeks, and her eyes flashed angrily to Olivia's.

"Dr. Miller keeps asking *why* I think I'm not sleeping, *why* I think I'm having nightmares, *why* I think I get angry with the kids at my new school, *why* I beat up that girl at my old school, how I *feel* about losing Gage and Melody—" Her voice choked. Tears glittered into her dark eyes. She rubbed her hands over her face, hard, her skin flushing deeper red. "If I'm supposed to come up with my *own* answers, why do I need Dr. Miller anyway? It's stupid!" Tori shoved her half-eaten sprinkle doughnut aside. "How did Dr. Miller know I was having nightmares, anyway?"

Easy, Liv, she could hear Cole's voice telling her. *Baby steps.*

"Tori." She inhaled, leaned forward, and lowered her voice in the ambient buzz of the restaurant. "I called Dr. Miller and told her."

Tori's jaw dropped. Her eyes gleamed with the heat of betrayal and a dark hostility.

"I was worried. I do need to talk about it, too. We both do."

Tori's mouth flattened and her eyes narrowed. Olivia could almost hear the clatter of her child's emotional drawbridge cranking up.

"I heard you crying in your sleep. I've heard you every night since that evening you came home late with Ricky. And then I found one of Noah's moonshine bottles in your room."

"You went through *my stuff*?"

"I went into your room to get Ace. He was sleeping next to your bed after you went to school. Your top drawer was open. I saw the bottle in there, Tori. I couldn't help it."

Tori began to get up.

Olivia placed a firm hand over her daughter's. "I *need* you to talk to me, Tori. I'd like a relationship where we can talk openly. Not judge."

"Adults always judge."

"I think Ricky said that, didn't he?" Olivia held her gaze. "I can help you, and I *want* to help you, but you need to trust me. You need to believe I love you, Tori. Unreservedly."

"Why? Why do you even *care*?"

"You know why. You're my baby girl. You're my daughter."

Tori stilled. Her eyes pooled with tears.

"My blood is in your veins. We share that bond. We need each other. I need *you*."

Tori looked away, focusing hard on something outside on the cold street.

"Were you at Noah's cabin on the night of the fire, Tori?"

"No."

"When did you take the moonshine from Noah's shed?"

"Didn't take it."

"How did you get it?"

Silence.

"Look at me, Tori. This is serious, and you know it. How did you acquire that bottle? From Ricky?"

"Some guy at school gave it to him."

"Sold it to him?"

"I don't know."

"You sure you weren't there, at Noah's cabin, on the evening of the fire?"

She faced Olivia and glowered at her. "No. I was not. I never went there. Ever."

The door opened behind Tori. A woman entered Dot's Donuts and Diner with a blast of icy air. Olivia glanced up. Someone she didn't recognize. The newcomer was attractive but oddly dressed in a tattered old jacket that was too big and a trapper's hat that looked like it had seen its fair share of traplines. Yet her pants and boots were dressy and belonged on city streets. The woman's gaze met Olivia's briefly as the door swung shut. Her eyes were the color of pale honey. She made her way to the counter.

Olivia watched her, a curiosity rustling through her.

Other customers also noticed the stranger's entrance and looked up. And for a moment, Olivia was seized by an unsettling sense that this woman had just brought in a chill wind of change.

CHAPTER 10

"Becca North?" The woman behind the counter wiped her hands on her apron. "Is that *you* under all that gear?"

It took a second for Rebecca to realize the woman was Marcy Fossum—town gossip—herself. But she'd lost the huge boobs, and some serious work had been done to her face. Her naturally mousy-blonde hair had been colored a rich auburn that set off her blue eyes in a startling fashion. "Marcy." Rebecca forced a smile. "Wow, you look fabulous. I'd never guess you had a daughter in college already. Buck told me. He also told me you own this place."

Marcy offered a smile of perfectly straight and clearly whitened teeth as she came around the counter and gave Rebecca a warm hug. "Oh my heavens, it's so good to see you. I'm so, so sorry for your loss, Becca. Are you okay? Is this Noah's gear?"

"Not my best look, eh? It's taken me five days through snowmageddon to get here, and now this Arctic outflow weather pattern, which is going to last who knows how long. I needed something warm."

The three men in a booth nearby glanced Rebecca's way. They were all within earshot and appeared to be listening with keen interest.

"Will . . . you be organizing some kind of memorial service for Noah?" Marcy asked. "Because Solly Meacham at the Moose and Horn started a collection. We . . . we weren't sure if you'd come back.

I mean, we've been seeing you on the news and knew you were tied up with that big case back east and all. Noah told us all about it, too. He said your career was going so well. He was so proud of you, Becs."

Guilt, remorse, humiliation, grief all pinged through Rebecca. The whole town must see her as the prodigal daughter returned, but too late. It steeled her desire to stay, sort this all out. For her dad. Not leave until it was done. Only then would she properly be able to lay her father to rest and say farewell.

"I will be organizing something, yes," she said quietly. "But I need to sort out a few things first." She didn't want his body to leave the morgue yet, either. Just in case.

Marcy frowned. She drew Rebecca aside so her employee behind the counter could serve others. And she lowered her voice. "Was there a problem with the postmortem?" Conspiratorial tone. *That* part about Marcy clearly hadn't changed.

"Just looking into a few questions I have."

Marcy's frown deepened. She angled her head. "Do you think Noah didn't do it?"

"I want to believe he didn't."

Marcy stared at her. Rebecca could see her mind racing.

"What are you going to do?"

"I'd like to order a coffee and two apple fritters to start. And then I'm going up to the cabin, what's left of it."

Marcy's blue eyes widened. She turned and asked her employee for the coffee and fritters to go. Then she told Rebecca they were on the house.

While her employee poured the coffee and warmed the apple fritters, Marcy nodded toward a booth under the street window. "See that woman and kid there?"

Rebecca followed her gaze. An attractive woman sat across the table from a dark-haired girl of around eleven or twelve. They seemed to be having a heated, but quiet, argument.

"That's Olivia West and Tori Burton," Marcy almost whispered. "Olivia inherited Broken Bar Ranch, which should have gone to Cole and his sister, Jane. But oh no, old Grinch Myron McDonough left it to that woman and her dog, of all things. It was Cole, you know, who called your father's cabin fire in."

A bolt of recognition shot through Rebecca as she watched the woman and girl. "Olivia, who used to be Sarah Baker? The woman who was kidnapped by serial killer Eugene George?" she said.

"Yep. One and the same. Held captive by chains in a remote shack, like an animal, and sexually abused for months. Tori is the offspring. The rape child."

It had been all over the news. Olivia West and Tori Burton were victims, or rather, survivors both. And Rebecca was filled with a sharp and sudden distaste for Marcy. The same feeling of repugnancy she'd experienced twenty years ago when Marcy had told her that she'd seen Whitney and Ash together in the Devil's Butte bar where she worked.

Marcy handed Rebecca the hot coffee and bag of fritters.

"Cops and doughnuts, eh? Try to deny it, but there it is." She grinned.

Rebecca did not return the smile. "Thanks. I need to be on my way. Must get up there before dark."

Marcy's smile faded. "Sure. Don't be a stranger, 'kay?"

But as Rebecca took her leave, Marcy called after her, "Noah was here that day. With Ash."

Rebecca stilled. Drew in a breath and faced Marcy. "What time was that?"

"Just after noon, I think. Ash ordered two chicken sandwiches to go, but then he and Noah got into an argument right here in front of the counter. Ash said to forget the order, and he marched Noah out to his truck, which was parked outside the window there." She pointed.

"What did they argue about?"

Now Marcy looked smug. She'd cast out the lure and hooked Rebecca. She was reeling her in. Marcy Fossum really had not changed a bit.

"No idea. But they were still going at it when Ash forced your father into his truck."

"Forced?"

"Well"—she moved a fall of auburn hair off her face—"I can't be sure, but it did look rather aggressive."

CHAPTER 11

"She's back in town." The voice came through the vehicle's hands-free system.

"I know," the driver replied, gloved hands firmly on the wheel. "It'll be fine."

"She's asking questions. A lot of questions. She doesn't believe he did it. She's gone out there now, looking."

A pause as the driver pulled sharply off the highway and came to a stop on the shoulder next to a snowbank—a sign of mental distraction. Of a need to focus exclusively on the gravitas of this conversation. "There's nothing to find. Even less so since the fire."

"And if there is? She knows *how* to look. She's a smart-ass detective who's put away some seriously major criminals. Stubborn like her father, only more dangerous because she's not an old drunk."

Silence as the driver considered the changing play of things.

"Maybe her old man told her something," the caller insisted. "Maybe she *knows*."

"No. No way." The driver spoke quietly. "She'd have returned sooner if that was the case." A pause. "I'll go out there, check into it."

"Yeah, you do that, because if she starts talking and raising the suspicions of other law enforcement agencies, this thing gets a life of its own. She needs to be contained before that can happen."

"I've got it. I've *got* it, okay." The driver killed the call and uttered a soft curse, anger and fresh worry curling at the edges of what had looked to be a perfect murder.

Clearly this wasn't over.

Not by a long shot.

The driver sat in silence for a few moments, thinking, then placed another call.

CHAPTER 12

Rebecca hit the highway north, aiming for the Broken Bar Lake turn-off at the top of the plateau. From there she would head onto unpaved roads through a derelict cross-country ski area, then deeper into forests and remote ranchlands.

Heater blasting and hot coffee in the holder, Rebecca munched her fritters, icing sugar falling onto her lap. Music played on the old truck radio. The station was cycling through top hits from years gone by, which served only to slide her even further back into her own past.

On either side of the undulating ribbon of highway lay bleak, wintry farmland covered in snow and pocked with an occasional listing barn or squat ranch house with smoke snaking from a chimney. In places where corralled cattle clustered to feed in steaming groups, the snow had been churned up into dark-brown earth.

There was not much in the way of wealth out here. And not much had changed in twenty years.

The highway climbed. In her rearview mirror the small town shrank. Behind her, keeping a steady pace, was a dark-colored truck. But it stayed far back enough that she couldn't make out the model. For a brief moment she wondered if it was following her. She shook the notion and wiped sugar from her mouth before reaching for her phone.

She'd lose cell reception once she hit the top of the rise and turned off the highway. She called Dr. Bert Spiker while she still could.

"Sergeant North." Dr. Spiker's nasal voice came through her phone on speaker. "How can I help you?"

"You mentioned the condition of my father's lungs. Are you able to tell me—despite the aspirated blood—if my father had recently started smoking again?"

"Hang on. Let me get to my notes."

Rebecca waited as a country song on the radio ended and the host took a request from a listener who'd phoned in. Spiker came back on the line.

"Let me see . . . There was some old scarring, but no, not a smoker for some many years." A pause. "Why do you ask?"

"Just checking on something that came up. Thanks, Dr. Spiker."

"Bert, call me Bert, or I shall have to go on calling you Sergeant."

She smiled, thanked the pathologist again, and hung up. Rebecca thought of quickly phoning Lance before she exited cell range. She hadn't spoken to her on-off lawyer boyfriend since informing him that her father had died and she was going home. If she could even call this place home—she hadn't for so long now. But she wasn't certain she could refer to her sterile rental apartment back east as "home," either. Her career was her life back there, and she was always ready to move at a moment's notice, depending on where the force might send her. Not even Lance was a constant, although he'd recently asked for a more serious commitment from her.

Rebecca reached for her phone again, but as she did, the requested tune started playing on the radio. A late-nineties hit by the Hazmat Suits.

All I wanna do is live it up
In LA
Before I die—

She slapped the radio off, anger riding suddenly through her. It had been *the* big hit song of that horrible summer—the song that had sent her searching for Ash and a dance on the night of the rodeo fair.

The Broken Bar sign at the top of the hill came into view. Rebecca indicated and turned off the paved road. The old Silverado juddered across corrugated ice and potholes frozen in snow. She engaged the four-wheel drive and slowed as she felt even the studded tires begin to slide on thick ridges of ice.

She passed the entrance to the dilapidated cross-country ski area. The road narrowed as it entered dense forest. Trees pressed in around her.

The noise of the erratic diesel engine grew loud inside the truck cab as she navigated deeper and deeper into endless white forests that muffled outside sound. Suddenly vehicle lights appeared far behind her.

Was it the same truck that had been behind her on the highway? Had it followed her onto the turnoff?

The lights disappeared from sight as the road curved. But unease filled Rebecca, and she kept glancing into the rearview mirror. It distracted her. Because when she looked back at the white road ahead, a deer was suddenly right in front of her hood.

She slammed on the brakes. The truck skidded sideways. Coffee shot out of the cup in the holder. She came to a shuddering halt at a diagonal angle across the road.

Shit.

She stared at the road where the deer had been before it had bounded off into the forest, and Rebecca realized with a sickening sensation that this was almost the exact spot where she'd seen Ash appear, dazed, in the middle of a thunderstorm more than twenty years ago. Her chest clamped tight. Her skin went hot. Memories sparked down disused neural pathways and crackled to life.

She runs through the rain and grabs his shoulders as water pummels down over them. "Ash?" she yells over the noise of the thunder. "Talk to me! Are you okay?"

Silence. He's shivering. She takes his arm and leads him to her pickup. She turns her back against another blast of rain as she opens the passenger-side door.

"Get in."

He obeys. He's a zombie. Showing no emotion.

Rebecca slams the passenger door shut and hurries around to the driver's side. She climbs into the cab, wipes water off her face, turns up the heat. She digs in her bag on the back seat for a clean shirt that he can hold to the bleeding wound on his face. She balls up the shirt. "Here, press this to your cut. Hold it tight." She helps him, guiding his hand to hold it there.

Finally he looks into her eyes, and she sees a hint of the familiar Ash inside.

"What happened?" she asks.

"Horse," he whispers. "New gelding. Bucked. Threw me. Got my foot caught. Got dragged over rocks."

"Jesus, I'm getting you to the ER." She leans forward and engages the gears.

"No!"

She shoots him a look.

"Not the health-care center. I . . . I can't. Not there."

"Why not?"

"Just help me, okay?" He grabs hold of her arm. His grip is like a vise. "You do it. Fix me. You know first aid. Just patch me up. I know you can."

"Animal first aid, Ash. I work part-time for a large-animal vet, not a doctor. You need proper stitches."

"Flesh is flesh, Becca. Looks worse than it is. Just stitch it up, or use butterfly sutures . . ." He slumps back into the seat as his voice drifts off.

She fights down panic at the sight of all that blood on his shirt. His bruised and cut knuckles. That swollen eye. His dazed appearance. He could have a concussion. And she fights how much she still loves and still cares even as she hates him for everything he's done to her. Fights herself. Part of her wants to say, Just fuck off. Now that you need me . . . *But the other part can't.*

———

A flock of blackbirds exploded into the sky, shocking Rebecca out of her memory. She swore, the aftereffects of the adrenaline rush making her tremble. Angrily she swiped spilled coffee off her pants and off the seat. She cursed again. What little control she might have had of her emotions going into the fire scene had just been rattled clean away.

It was this place, this cold, the memories—it was all sucking her back into the dark forests of her past and closing an icy fist around her throat. For a mad moment she feared this wilderness was sentient, that it had sent the deer to stop her right here, that once this place got its claws into her, it might never let her go. She glanced at the road behind her. The truck seemed to be gone.

Engaging gears, she maneuvered the Silverado around and straightened herself out on the road. She drove deeper into the forests and the landscape of her youth, gloved hands overly tight on the wheel. In the sky above her, the blackbirds swarmed in undulating, ominous patterns.

Another twenty minutes of driving brought her to clear-cut land and a fork in the road. She took the north road, crested a rise, and suddenly it was there.

She stopped the truck.

A black bomb appeared to have been dropped into the pristine white landscape where her family home had once stood. She stared numbly, trying to process the scar of devastation as the faltering diesel engine grumbled, white exhaust fumes crystallizing in clouds around the truck.

All that remained among the blackened and charred debris that had once been their cabin was the stone hearth and chimney. The chimney rose above the ashes and pointed straight to the sky, like a finger of rock flipped to the heavens.

Up high above the chimney a raptor circled lazily on outstretched wings.

But on the ground, nothing moved apart from yellow police tape fluttering in the wind.

And there, behind the razed cabin, squatting in front of the grove of trembling aspens, was the moonshine shed. The irony was not lost on Rebecca. Her dad's vice, his dark passion, had outlived him.

And now the shed was hers.

CHAPTER 13

By the time Rebecca parked behind a row of trees that had once screened their home from the farm road, the sun had slipped below the horizon, and purple shadows were creeping slowly, insidiously, over the land. Wind howled down from the ridge and rocked the Silverado as she pulled her neck gaiter up over her mouth and nose, leaving just a slit for her eyes. The ear flaps of the trapper's hat protected her ears. She tugged on her dad's snow pants followed by his Sorels.

Once she was kitted out against the biting cold, she exited the truck and unlocked the gun box on the back. She found her father's ammunition and loaded his rifle with fast-numbing fingers. She slung the rifle across her back. She couldn't say why, but after her near miss with the deer and the weird sense of being followed, she felt naked without her regulation sidearm.

Tugging the big gloves back on, she left the truck and attempted to navigate over the slick ice and ruts left by the fire crew and the pumper truck. She slipped almost at once, going down hard. Cursing, she came carefully back up to her feet. Moving even more gingerly now, she picked and slid her way to where the kitchen door had once stood.

She stared at the devastation come to life out of Buck's photographs. He was right. Hoarfrost grew inches thick in delicate filigrees atop the ice. It obscured anything trapped below the ice. Yellow tape that had blown loose snapped at her.

Rebecca stilled. Listened. The wilderness all around hissed with the sibilant sound of wind skimming over ice and frost and through the bare, stiff branches of aspens and alders and frozen conifers. Papery bark rustled. Things sounded different in this brittle cold. Sharper edged. She glanced up at the esker ridge behind the razed cabin. Another grove of aspens grew up there. A sense of being watched from those trees suddenly prickled the hair on the back of her neck. She thought again of the truck behind her on the road. Fear beaded small and deep in her chest.

She shook it off. It was just the sense of death and destruction trapped below this ice.

But it was also the fact that if she couldn't accept that her dad had killed himself, she *had* to entertain ideas far more sinister.

Murder.

Arson.

And if this was a homicide scene, it could be tied to something that her dad had learned about a very old crime. Something that someone was prepared to kill to hide.

It meant a predator could still be out there. One who might kill again.

Or not.

Maybe it really was all just as it seemed. As Dr. Seuss had said. And she was being infected by her father's paranoia. As if it were a germ that still clung to this place and his clothing and his truck.

The raptor shrieked. Rebecca jumped and looked up. The bird circled lazily with fluttering wing tips over the carnage.

She turned her back to the destruction and faced the shed. Shadows had lengthened as she'd stood there, the sky darkening already. She didn't have long. But the shift in the angle of the light caused something to glimmer in an ice hollow near the shed door.

She made her way over, hoarfrost crunching beneath her oversize boots. It was a new golden-bronze padlock. Open.

Rebecca crouched down and examined it. It had fresh scrapes in the metal, made by some kind of sharp tool. As if it had been picked. She glanced up at the door and saw the metal plate where the lock must have hung. Removing a glove, she retrieved her cell phone from her pocket and photographed the padlock where it lay.

She remained crouched there a moment, thinking. The wind grew colder as the sun slipped farther away. Someone had broken into her dad's moonshine shed? When? Before the fire? Or after? Buck had said he'd removed the liquor and the copper still, but maybe some opportunist, upon hearing of her father's demise, had come looking to take his booze.

She picked up the lock with her gloved hand and examined it more closely. It had definitely been picked. She slid it into her dad's coat pocket.

Rebecca creaked open the door and entered the shed. It was dim inside. She activated the flashlight function on her smartphone, but using it in this fashion came with the price of urgency—the battery could shut down at any moment in these kinds of temperatures. It had happened to her more than once before.

She shone her light over the shelves. The bottles had all been removed. Only shapes remained in the layers of dust on the shelves.

The dust patterns on the wooden table showed where her father's distilling equipment had recently stood. And near the back wall, beneath a tiny window, was the old workbench her mother had once used as a sewing table. The beam of Rebecca's phone light revealed a fine coating of dust on that surface, too.

She ran her gloved hand over the top of the workbench. Memories breathed in and exhaled as the dust lifted in a cold cloud. Her mom.

How they'd all been a family unit. How Rebecca had always believed she'd live out here on a ranch. Marry Ash. Emotion squeezed her chest. But as she was about to turn away, she saw fresh scrapes through the dust along the back edge of the workbench. Her pulse quickened.

She brought her light closer. Fingerprints. Not glove prints but bare hands had grasped the edge and been dragged along it. As if the person had been ducking behind the bench and facing the door. Small hands. Small person. Like a child. Or a small female. Her heart beat faster.

She took photos, tension hastening her movements in case the battery froze.

Carefully, she then panned her light down behind the bench. Trapped in the splintering wood of the table leg were two long strands of hair. Dark brown. With a slight wave. About twelve inches long and wafting in the air currents caused by Rebecca's motion. And on the floor a spill of yellow paint had set up and dried. But in the dried puddle was a full handprint and a partial boot print. Her instincts began to buzz. Quickly she snapped more photos. Her gaze went to the shed door.

Had a small female—presuming the long hair strands did not come from a male—ducked behind here in hiding? That's when she noticed two more partial yellow boot prints on the shed floor, heading toward the door.

Taking care not to step on the prints, Rebecca moved to the wall where her dad's tools hung neatly. She found the square ruler he'd used for woodwork. She also found the paper envelopes her father had kept to store tiny nuts and bolts and fishing hooks. She returned to the bench and removed the hairs. She secured the strands in an envelope and pocketed it. She then got down on her knees and, using the square ruler for reference, photographed the patent prints in the paint. The fingerprint ridges showed up well. As did the partial pattern of the boot sole.

Rebecca bent sideways to angle her light better for a last shot. Her beam caught the shine of something white farther under the bench. She got down lower and peered underneath. It was a translucent bone pocketknife that nestled in a wide crack between the floorboards. She documented the pocketknife in situ, then used a gloved hand to fish it out. The polished bone was inlaid with a tiny gold horse's head. She slipped it into one of the paper envelopes.

Her phone light went dark. Shadows leaped at her from the corners of the shed.

Damn.

Rebecca tried to restart her phone. No luck. The interior of the shed was now almost fully dark. She'd have to return tomorrow with better equipment to see if she'd missed anything. Moving along the edge so as not to stand on the yellow paint prints leading to the door, she exited the shed.

A purple twilight glowed over the snow. The wind had increased and the temperature was dropping fast.

Rebecca checked the markings and boot prints outside the shed with renewed interest now. Her pulse kicked up as she detected a yellow mark in the ice, then another. The small yellow-paint boot prints led straight toward her father's kitchen door, but there they disappeared in the morass of prints and markings made by fire crews, police, and whoever else had responded to the fire. Her gaze moved back to the esker ridge.

Although it was getting dark, she thought she could detect two sets of deep tracks heading up that ridge. Whoever had made those had to have made them in soft snow before or around the time of the fire and not after, because everything had frozen up solid that night, from what she'd been told of the weather patterns that day.

It would be fully dark any minute. She should drive back to town and return to the scene tomorrow. But curiosity fired her to take a quick look at those tracks before she left. She wouldn't ruin them, as everything was solidly frozen into place and would remain so until a front big enough blew in to dislodge the cold dome of air pressing over the region.

But as Rebecca neared the back of her father's razed cabin and looked up at the esker ridge, a disquiet whispered through her again. She stilled and studied the shadows between the ghostly white trees, trying to discern movement in the gloaming.

A click sounded. Then a crunch on frost. Every nerve in her body snapped tight. With her gaze fixed on the trees, she slowly reached for her gun.

CHAPTER 14

He tucked the cold Mossberg stock snug against his cheek and curled his gloved finger around the trigger, training his eye on the armed trespasser at the bottom of the esker slope. His breath was steady and crystallized in clouds around his face.

Time stretched. Bits of loose, papery bark rustled in the wind. His dog, Kibu, a Karelian, lay flattened on the snowpack near his boots, gaze fixed on the "prey" below. Kibu had been bred and trained to hunt large predators. One movement or sharp whistle from him and Kibu would charge. Fearless. But Kibu was young. Still a work in progress. And sometimes the dog got away from him.

"Shh," he whispered. "Stay."

In this faint light he couldn't identify the man. Average height. Maybe five feet ten, he guessed. Coat was old school. Shabby and faded black. Looked too big. It obscured body shape. The intruder's gait was also clumsy and awkward on the ice. A ski mask hid his face, and a trapper's hat was pulled down low over his ears. Armed and uneasy. Didn't look good whatever way he considered it.

Sound carried in this cold. He'd heard the approach of an unserviced diesel engine. It had alerted him, and he'd come over the ridge to find the trespasser exiting Noah North's shed. From this vantage point he couldn't see the vehicle that had snared his attention earlier.

But right now his gaze was riveted on the intruder, who'd shrugged the rifle off his back and was aiming up at his hide in the trees.

Kibu sensed the tension and whimpered, inching forward through frost, hungry for a charge.

"Shh," he whispered.

The wind gusted. A branch strained and cracked with breaking ice.

Kibu exploded in a flurry of bone, fur, teeth, and saliva froth. His dog barreled down the ice slope. Aiming straight for the intruder's throat.

The man caught sight of the blur, spun. Aimed at his dog.

Fuck!

"Kibu! Stop!" he yelled, breaking cover out of the trees. *"Stop!"*

A boom split the air. A scream.

The sounds ricocheted over the frozen land, echoing over and over and over toward the distant Marble Mountains.

THE LAST SUPPER

Cariboo Country. Tuesday, January 8,
almost one week ago.

Ash carries in a pile of split wood while Noah lights kerosene lanterns in his cabin. There's an Arctic outflow forecast. It's going to be brittle cold tonight. Everything outside will freeze solid within minutes once the system hits. Ash stacks the logs next to the hearth and then builds and lights a fire. While he's busy he can hear Noah knocking and stumbling about in the kitchen.

Once the fire starts crackling, Ash dusts off his hands and pants and goes into the kitchen. His dog, meanwhile, lies down on the once-colorful rag rug in front of the hearth. The rug is something Ash considers fondly. Paige North, Noah's wife, brought it back from Mexico the year before she died. Ash was very fond of Becca's mother. She was kind. Warm.

In the kitchen, Noah is pouring two glasses of moonshine. The gas oven is on. A casserole dish of food waits atop the stove as if to be warmed when the oven reaches temperature. Two white plates have been placed upon the table next to a packet of Denali Plain cigarettes.

The wooden surface of the table is well worn. As Ash gazes upon the old knots and dents and scratches in the wood, his mind goes back. To a day when he was twelve.

His father, Olav, had brought Ash with him to this cabin because he'd wanted to discuss some business with Noah in the barn. Something about fertilizer or cattle feed. Whatever it was, it took the men out of earshot while Ash was left to watch Mrs. North rolling dough out on that table. Becca was helping, her hands full of flour, her cheeks flushed pink. A spot of flour smudged her chin. She'd been eleven. And she was the most beautiful thing he'd ever seen. And so was this vignette—Becs and her mom working together in the warm kitchen that smelled of yeasty dough. Ash could almost feel the love in the house, like a tangible yellow thing, and it made his young heart swell.

For a few moments he just stood and watched Becca. Her dark hair pulled back. Wisps escaping around her face. A smatter of dark freckles over her nose, a gap between her front teeth. Her eyes the color of wild honey. She looked up and smiled. Right at him.

Ash feels that smile now. How it hit him. Hard in the pit of his stomach, like a physical missile fired across that table of dough and flour and pastry and sense of family. He knew in that very minute, while his father was away in the barn, that while Becca might be only eleven years old, he was going to marry Rebecca Jayne North, the rancher-cop's daughter. It all made perfect sense in his mind. He'd take over his dad's ranch one day, when his dad was gone. Becca would come and live with him, and she would make his kitchen full and warm, just like this one. It was like an ache in his heart.

"Want to stay for some, Ash?" Mrs. North asked. "First batch is going to come out in two minutes."

Ash figured if Becca grew into even half of a Mrs. North, he'd be doing more than okay marrying her. Mrs. North had a smile and a magic in her eyes that could light up a whole room.

"Here you go," says Noah, and the memory shatters like a broken mirror as Ash is rammed back into the winter present.

He shakes himself and accepts the shot glass from Noah. He knocks it back, thinking how the smell of baking bread can still send him back to that day when he was twelve.

"Come on into the living room," Noah says, pouring another drink.

"Thanks, but I'm not staying to eat," Ash says with a tilt of his chin toward the plates.

"Not asking you to. Come. Come to the fire. I need to talk to you about something." He was slurring his words. He'd been slurring when Ash found him in the PetroGas convenience store.

"I can't stay, I—"

Noah's gaze locks onto his. Suddenly he seems half-sober. And intense. Disquiet fingers into Ash's chest.

"It's important," Noah says.

It's warmer inside now that the fire is going, so Ash hangs his ranch coat on a hook behind the kitchen door, next to Noah's olive-green long-gun safe. The safe key, he notices, is in the lock.

He follows Noah into the living room.

Noah has set a file folder on the coffee table in front of the fire. He plops heavily back into his recliner, splashing his drink onto his hand as he goes down. Lanterns flicker orange light into the room. Noah licks the spilled moonshine off the back of his thumb, all filters of civility gone out the window at this stage of his inebriation. However, even after the amount of alcohol this old ex-cop has consumed today, he remains functional.

Ash seats himself on the ledge of the stone hearth, facing Noah.

"You lied, Haugen."

"Excuse me?"

Noah goes oddly still as his gaze once again locks with Ash's. He looks almost calculating, even. A glimmer of wariness goes through Ash.

He senses something coming. He reaches down and scratches his dog's neck, waiting for Noah to explain himself.

Noah points his glass toward the folder on the coffee table. "Open it, take a look."

Ash frowns.

"Go on."

He opens the folder. On the top of the pile of papers inside the folder is a photocopy of a December issue of the Clinton Sentinel *from twenty years ago. The headline reads:* Mother fears worst for missing daughter.

Below the headline is a photo of Whitney Gagnon. Dark memories seep like ink through Ash's brain. He swallows, then looks slowly up to meet Noah's gaze. "What is this about?"

"How did you really get that scar down your face?"

"You know how." He moves the photocopy aside. Beneath it is a photo of him. Taken not long after the gash on his face. He's holding the reins of a mare at a cattle auction. It was in the newspaper.

Next in the pile is an old photo of himself and Becca standing beside the old red pickup truck he used more than twenty years ago for work. Another memory hits him. Throwing Whitney's suitcase into the back of that dusty old truck, the anger and rage he felt that day. Things begin to go dark in his mind. His head begins to buzz.

"You gonna tell me what this is about, Noah?" he asks.

"You lied, Haugen," he says again. "About the gash."

Ash can't seem to think for a moment. There's a dark thing locked deep inside a vault in the basement of his soul, and he cannot open it or else he won't be able to function. He learned a long time ago that the only way to survive was to throw away the key to what was locked in the vault.

"Fuck me, Haugen, you lied! Becca lied. And I want to know why."

"I don't know what you are talking about," Ash says quietly. But he fears the rage beginning to simmer under his skin at just the faintest hint of a bad memory. "What are you doing with all this?"

"I dropped the ball on those kids." He points his glass at the material on the coffee table, his drink sloshing about inside. "Whitney and Trevor. I dropped the ball because people in this town—especially you—were hiding something. I treated you like my own son. I wanted you to marry my daughter. But you lied, Haugen. And I dropped the case. But now—now I owe those kids. I owe them justice."

"Noah," Ash says coolly, coming to his feet, "I've got chores. I'm leaving. I'll see you again when you're sober and not so full of shit."

"Why no hospital?"

Ash clicks his fingers to summon his dog and goes into the kitchen to fetch his coat.

Noah's voice chases him, growing louder. "Have you been inside my house, Ash, when I wasn't here? Did you take papers from my case notes I made?"

Ash shrugs angrily into his coat.

"Someone saw you, Haugen! At the Renegade Lines bus stop. With Whitney and Trevor. They saw you get into a knife fight with Trevor."

Shock slams through Ash. He returns to the entrance of the living room in his coat.

"Who saw?" he asks quietly, very quietly. "Who saw me that day?"

"Get outta here, you bloody Judas. Go, go on. Come back when you're ready to talk the truth, boy. You and Becca. My ass."

CHAPTER 15

Rebecca's heart jackhammered. For a second she'd thought she'd been hit.

She held rigid, her rifle still aimed at the animal on the snow, her body drenched with sweat in spite of the cold. The noise from the gunshot resounded in her ears.

The shooter had fired a shotgun slug into the snowpack right in front of the left toe of her boot, exploding ice shrapnel up into her masked face. The dog lay flat a few feet from her, growling low in its throat, saliva glistening around bared teeth. Like a rabid wolf.

A hunting spotlight shone down at her as the shooter carefully picked his way down the icy bank, shotgun still aimed at her.

"Drop the rifle. Now," he commanded.

She couldn't move. Her ears were still ringing, which disoriented and unbalanced her, and she was convinced that if she dared move even an inch, the dog's muscles would uncoil in one deadly leap at her throat. She remained frozen with her loaded rifle still aimed dead between the animal's eyes.

She'd almost killed it a second ago. But he'd fired a nanosecond before she'd pulled the trigger, freezing her.

"Put. The. Gun. Down," he growled. Low. Not unlike the dog. "Because if you shoot my dog, I *will* kill you."

"Get that fucking animal off me," she whispered, voice hoarse and muffled beneath her face mask. "So that I *can* put my weapon down."

He whistled. Sharp. Two short, one long. The animal hesitated.

He whistled the same command again. The dog rose slowly, backed away a few inches, still growling, salivating.

"More, Kibu! Back up some more!"

The dog moved farther back.

"Now lower your rifle and set it down on the snow, nice and slow. Then step away from it."

She hesitated, her gaze, every ounce of her focus, still riveted on the dog.

"Do it. Or I will shoot. You're trespassing. You're armed. This is private land."

Rebecca swallowed. Slowly she bent over and carefully set down her dad's gun on the hard-packed snow. She edged backward, away from the rifle, careful not to fall. She had a sense that if she did go down, her movement would explode the animal. And she'd have no way of defending her face and throat if she were flat on the ice.

Mouth dry, she moved a few more careful steps away from the rifle.

He came forward. A dark shape in dark shadows now, shining his hunting spotlight right into her face. She blinked into the bright glare.

"Take off the cap and the mask," he commanded. "Keep your hands where I can see them."

She blinked again, carefully raising her hands. She removed the trapper's hat and pulled down her mask. Her hair released in a crackle of static around her face and shoulders.

He stilled.

Silence—dead, solid silence fell like a weight around him.

Even the growling dog fell quiet, sensing something in its master.

"*Becca?*" A hoarse whisper.

And she knew. She felt it right through the tiny hairs on her body and in the ripple down her spine and the tightening of her throat.

Ash.

She was looking into the barrel of Ash Haugen's shotgun.

He lied.

What were you protecting him from that day?

"Fuck," he whispered, lowering the weapon but keeping the hunting spotlight on her face, coming closer, as if to ensure it was really her. "Fucking hell, Becca, what in the hell? What's with this outfit?"

Her heart hammered. Her whole body started shaking with the aftershocks of adrenaline. On the back of it all rode a smashing wave of anger.

"Get that animal onto a leash," she demanded. "And then tell me what in the hell *you* are doing on *my* property."

He called his dog over. She remained stone-still as he angled the light away from her eyes. From the pocket of his jacket, he took out a leash. Using one hand, he snapped it onto the animal's collar.

In the angled light she saw him better. He wore a huge padded jacket, snow boots. Gloves. No hat. He appeared taller, bigger than she remembered.

Older.

"Is that weapon on safety?" she said.

"It's safe."

"Show me your face so I can see you," she said.

He angled the light a bit more, and his features shot into shadowed focus. Her breath sort of stopped somewhere in her throat for a moment. He looked harder, craggier, in the oddly angled spotlight. The scar still jagged down the side of his face.

Her cowboy she'd once loved. A broody, rugged Wallander of the Canadian north. Her Heathcliff of the wilderness and of her once-romantic teenage heart. The person who'd played the part in her imagination of every hero in every story her dad had read to her all those nights after her mom died—stories read by the fire from books on her mother's bookshelf. This man who was prone to dark bouts of silence and who often needed to go off into the woods alone.

She'd always thought she'd known him as no one else had. That she understood him. Maybe she hadn't. At all.

Rebecca tried to swallow the tide of shaky, hot emotions boiling up inside her at the sight of him after all these years. But suddenly she felt all of seventeen again, and subject to those same old forces.

"It's been a while, Becca. I didn't think you'd come back now that he's gone."

"What are you doing here?" she snapped. "Stalking me from those trees like that?"

"Same thing I think you are. Following those tracks from the shed."

Surprise coursed through her. It was chased by hot suspicion. "You're telling me that you came here, in the dark, to track boot prints on private property that has just been released by the police—the property of a man you were the last one to see alive?"

"That's exactly what I'm telling you."

CHAPTER 16

"I was tracking a big cat with Kibu when we came across snowmobile tracks that led all the way to the back end of Noah's place," Ash said.

As the wind whipped and the earth grew colder and the sky darkened, Rebecca listened to Ash explain how he hunted or hazed large predators on contract for both the conservation office and private entities—large-predator management, he called it. Bear, cougar, or wolf aversion. And occasionally, if an animal had attacked a human, he'd be tasked by law enforcement with tracking down the dangerous carnivore. He used a team of Karelian bear dogs to do it, and sometimes a bloodhound cross.

"Judging by the depth of the sled tracks, and how they'd set up, they would have been made right around the time of the fire," he said. "It made me curious."

"Why curious?"

"Because, Becca, I don't think your father was in a mood to shoot himself that night."

Her heart stuttered. Very quietly she said, "Go on."

"It looked like the snowmobile was parked behind the grove up there." He pointed to the esker ridge behind him. "Two people then dismounted and came down on that side of the ridge over there." He pointed to the bank above the shed. "But when they came out of the shed, they went to Noah's kitchen door and then ended up behind his cabin, and then they ran up this side of the ridge here." He pointed to the deep prints Rebecca had been following.

"At this point, they were falling and moving erratically. They fell again going through the trees up there. When they got back onto the sled, they fled southwest. So I started following the return tracks— that's when I heard an old diesel engine approaching Noah's place. At this hour, and given the weird tracks, I got additionally suspicious. I came back here to see who it was, and I saw you. Armed. Unidentified. And nosing around. Like you said, in the dark and right after the police had released the scene."

"Where do the return tracks lead?" she said between chattering teeth. She'd drawn up her neck tube and replaced the trapper's hat, but the cold tunneled through all her gear.

"I got as far as the Broken Bar Ranch boundary line. I plan on returning at first light."

Rebecca shivered fiercely as the wind kicked up more and started a howl across the frozen landscape. Stars filled the heavens.

"Look," he said, noticing her shuddering, "this weather is only going to get worse, and fast. I've got guest quarters at Haugen Ranch. Come back where it's warm, and we can talk. I'll show you the tracks in the morning."

She *had* to talk to him.

She had so many questions.

She wanted to see those tracks herself.

She also needed to do this on *her* terms. Rebecca had been totally thrown by meeting him like this, and by his commanding presence, the way he still seemed to wield control over her emotions, her mind. She needed the night to process not only seeing him, but seeing firsthand her dad's razed cabin, his burned body in the morgue. She was too vulnerable right now to sleep in Ash's house after all these years of avoiding him, hating him, loving him.

"No," she said firmly. "I'll be at your door before first light tomorrow morning. You can show me the tracks then."

He was silent for a moment, weighing her.

"You sure?"

"Certain."

"Fine," he said quietly. He turned, hesitated, then said, "Want me to walk you back to your vehicle?"

"No."

"Suit yourself." He whistled for his dog, aimed his spotlight up toward the trees, and made his way back up the bank. His beam darted, then disappeared between the trees.

Darkness closed around Rebecca. She cursed.

By the ambient light of the stars and a rising moon reflecting off the snow, she struggled to pick her way over the ice and get around the fire scene and back to the Silverado, falling hard a few times along the way.

By the time she reached her father's truck, her teeth were chattering so violently she feared they might actually break. Fumbling with fingers that no longer cooperated, she managed after several tries to unlock the frozen driver's-side door. Relief rushed through her when it finally opened.

She clambered inside, placed the rifle in a safe position on the passenger's side, inserted the key into the ignition, and managed to turn it halfway to prime it. The light on the dash came on. She turned the key all the way.

The engine coughed, turned over. Then died. She tried again, first waiting to prime the globe that would fire the diesel fuel in this older machine. Light on the dash showing, she turned fully. It choked and coughed as the engine struggled to turn over. Then nothing.

Raw fear crowded her brain. She tried again. Same.

Teeth clattering, limbs shaking, she tried once more, knowing that each time she primed the globe, she was consuming a chunk of battery power, and she didn't know how good the battery in this truck had been to begin with.

Again the engine died.

With a shuddering hand, she reached up to the cab roof and fumbled to click on the interior light.

Panic reared in her heart when she saw the dash in better light. The fuel needle showed empty.

Rebecca sat stunned for a moment. It wasn't possible. She'd filled the tank in Clinton. This couldn't be. Perhaps the Silverado had a leak, and that's why it had been empty in the police station parking lot in the first place. She groped in the glove compartment, searching for a flashlight. Nothing.

She fumbled around in the back of the truck cab. No flashlight there, either. The interior cab light was dimming and would last only as long as the battery held a charge. No flashlight in the back. No old PowerBars or chocolate or candies or survival blanket or candles. Nothing. Just the old clothes she was already wearing.

On some level Rebecca knew she was already going hypothermic. She'd been outside in the extreme cold for a while already, on top of having sweated under Ash's fire and the dog attack. The moisture on her skin, combined with the cold, had lowered her body temperature even further. Her fine motor coordination was gone.

Her capacity to think rationally was probably fading, too, which frightened her most.

She tried to start the Silverado a few more times, even though the fuel gauge registered empty. She was trying to tell herself she hadn't actually checked the gauge after filling up, so maybe the gauge was faulty and there really *was* fuel. She'd had trouble starting it at the RCMP station before, so perhaps it was just a repeat. She also knew that during unseasonably cold weather, some diesel-powered engines experienced difficulties with starting due to the formation of wax crystals that blocked fuel filters and lines.

100

The interior light faded. And went off.

The battery was dead.

The wind whistled louder around the Silverado. The moon rose higher. The snowscape turned eerie. Rebecca's shudders grew violent. She thought she saw a shadow move across the snow. A hare? Fox?

She checked her phone. Dead.

Even if she did manage to warm it up enough to turn on, there was still no cell reception out here.

And it was too far to walk anywhere for help. Not a soul was likely to head out this way at night, either.

Maybe she shouldn't have been pigheaded and should have gone with Ash.

Maybe she should just start walking and she'd happen across someone.

Or was that her brain telling her stupid things?

Emotion welled in her eyes. Rebecca slumped back in the seat.

Fucking ironic.

I've come back home, come out here into the middle of nowhere at night in record-breaking cold, to die. To follow my dad to his grave. Hey, Dad, is this your idea of amusement? Is it your way to finally get me to spend a decent length of time with you? Like forever? Hey, Pop, maybe we'll see Mom . . .

He lied, Becca. You both did.

Was that your voice, Dad?

An image rose in full color in her mind. Whitney and Ash coming out of the barn.

It wasn't a riding accident that gashed open his face, was it?

As blood left her brain and her extremities in order to warm and protect the vital organs at her body's core, her mind started to play tricks. She thought of the lights of the truck that might have been tailing her. Could someone have sabotaged the Silverado while she was inside the moonshine shed?

Could Ash have done it, before coming up around the back?

Or Buck, in the police parking lot, before she'd driven off?

The Silverado has good studded snow tires. You might want to use it if you plan on heading up there . . .

Or was it just her dad allowing his old fuel tank to rust to pieces?

But the idea of sabotage had taken hold. It rose like a black beast along the periphery of her mind, and it grew bigger and darker as it prowled the circumference of her consciousness, circling in, closer, tighter, drawing more and more darkness in with it, until she felt herself slipping into an icy black ink of nothingness.

CHAPTER 17

There are nights when the wolves are silent and only the moon howls—where had Rebecca heard that? She peered through the frosted truck windows, watching as wolves materialized from the blackness of the forest. Their shadows crept slowly toward the Silverado over the moonlit snow. Or was that the wind making shadows? Rebecca struggled to keep conscious. She was getting hot, so hot. Maybe she should take off her jacket, rip off her clothes? Then out of the darkness, she saw her dad. He was coming across the snow. Her big cop dad. He had a flashlight. And the wolves slipped back into the shadows of the forest, afraid of him.

Dad?

She heard her father's voice.

Becca, Becca, wake up.

She opened her eyes. Her dad vanished. She was still in the truck. Alone. She tried to focus.

A light appeared on the rise. She blinked. It was blurry through the ice patterns that had grown over the windshield.

The light pulsed between trees, grew brighter, changed angle, and headed directly for her truck. As the light bounced and wove, it separated and became two eyes set close together, and she heard the whine of an engine. She realized the eyes were the headlights of a snowmobile.

Fear sank talons into her chest. The saboteur was coming back? Had he been waiting for this moment, when she'd be all alone and incapacitated?

Rebecca fought to shake her mind back into gear. She fumbled with a gloved hand for the loaded rifle she'd placed on the passenger side of the cab, but she couldn't make her fingers grasp it. The metal slipped through her glove, and the butt thudded to the floor. She realized it could have gone off. She could have shot herself in the head like her father . . .

The snowmobile barreled head-on for her truck, coming closer. As it reached her, it slowed and came to a chugging halt facing the Silverado. The bright headlights aimed directly into her face through the filigree of ice ferns on the windshield.

Panic whipped. She battled to open her door. Through the gaps in the frost filigree, she saw a dark, helmeted figure dismount and come toward the truck.

Her door finally opened with a crack as ice broke free. Rebecca had been leaning against the door, and she tumbled out, crashing down to the frozen ground.

"Becca!" The figure pushed up the helmet visor and bent over her. "It's me, Ash."

She felt the strength in his arms as he helped her to her feet and she struggled to stand. Her legs crumpled and he caught her.

"Shruck." Her tongue felt too thick. "Shruck outta gash."

"Jesus, you're hypothermic. Can you try to walk? I'm going to walk you over to my sled, okay? Can you try?"

She nodded. Her feet felt like numb stumps. But moving, just the mental relief of knowing she had help, that she wasn't going to die, fired her with renewed effort. She leaned on Ash as he held her upright and helped her hobble toward his running snowmobile. It was then that she noticed his dog sitting in a carrier on the back. She stilled.

"Kibu is fine," he said firmly. "I promise. The only reason he went for you is because I was watching you like I watch big prey, and he's trained to do that. Plus, I got heated seats. And a survival blanket. And emergency heating pads for your gloves and boots. We'll get you back to my place in one piece as long as you can hang on to me. You good?"

She nodded.

And God, she'd missed that voice. Low, bass, assured. As much as she'd never wanted to hear it again and didn't trust him, right now he was her lifeline, and she was clinging to it.

"Kibu, stay," he commanded as he helped her onto the back seat. He opened his emergency kit, activated the chemical heating pads, and slipped them inside her gloves and boots. He wrapped her in a polar shield survival blanket, then removed her trapper's cap and replaced it with a spare helmet he carried. It was big and solid and insulating. He put the visor down, further cutting the cold.

He straddled the machine in front of her, took her hands, and wrapped her arms around his waist. "Can you hang on to me, like this?" He hooked her right hand over her wrist. "Can you hold on?"

She nodded.

"Cuddle close, okay?"

She nodded.

"Good?"

She nodded again.

He pulled down his visor and gave throttle. The sled surged forward with a roar, and they wound and bounded over the hard-packed snow back into the forest, where she'd first glimpsed his light and thought it was her father with a flashlight chasing away the wolves and coming for her.

CHAPTER 18

Rebecca felt warmth. She was enveloped by it. She heard the crackle and pop of dry logs burning and, in the distance, dogs barking. The smell of . . . *fire* . . .

Her eyes shot open, her heart thumping.

He sat there. Ash. In a chair by the fire, watching her with his ice-blue eyes. She was in his living room, and the lighting had been dimmed. The flickering glow of the flames in the hearth behind him cast his rugged features into sharp relief. The scar down the side of his face looked harsh. An old brown dog with a white muzzle slept on a rug in front of the hearth. It looked like a Chesapeake Bay retriever, a dog like her mom used to have. Kibu was passed out on a chair beside Ash.

Faint yips and howls of dogs outside somewhere reached her again.

Rebecca's brain slotted puzzle pieces into place as she struggled through a mental haze to backtrack and figure out how she'd gotten here: The lights following her. The razed cabin and the clues that someone had been inside the shed and maybe fled the scene. Ash shooting at her. No gas in her truck. Fear of dying. Coming here to Haugen Ranch. Shucking her dad's gear in Ash's mudroom. Him helping her into the living room of his old family home—a great big log house built by his grandfather. Seating her on the sofa.

She sat up slowly, trying to pull her brain into sharper focus. A down duvet was wrapped around her, a heated blanket beneath that. The duvet smelled of fresh laundry. Yes, she recalled, the fire had already been going in the hearth when he'd brought her in—she'd noticed that. Next had come hot tea with honey, warm clothes handed to her—fleece, oversize. More tea.

He'd told her not to talk. Discussion could wait.

She met his eyes now and felt a visceral connection across the darkened room. This was her first proper look at him after all these years.

Her teen lover had aged. As she had. But he'd matured in a way she found attractive. He was neither sweet nor handsome. Rugged, rather. A brooding look. Sun bronzed and weathered. Her attention returned to his scar. So prominent, cutting down the left side of his face from eye to jaw. He could have had plastic surgery over the past decades, but clearly hadn't. Her memory slipped back to the day she'd tried to patch him up with the help of a small medical kit and knowledge she'd gleaned during her part-time job as a veterinary assistant.

He lied . . .

Her attention shifted to his hands. His knuckles were scarred.

What were you protecting him from that day?

She recalled the blood she'd seen on those ragged and bruised knuckles back then. Why *had* she not told her father she didn't know for certain he'd fallen off his horse and been dragged across sharp terrain?

Why *had* she not questioned more firmly, at age sixteen, Ash's refusal to go to the ER facility on that particular day? What deep psychology had driven her to possibly blind herself to a darker truth?

In that tempestuous, hormone-filled year she was sixteen, had she conveniently compartmentalized something that had created cognitive dissonance because she'd just recently started sleeping with Ash and *needed* to believe him? *Needed* to trust him again?

How had her actions that day shaped this present? Could it—she—have possibly played a role in her father's death?

And why—oh dear God, *why*—did Ash still make her feel things? This—*this*—was why she'd stayed away. He held a kind of animal magnetism over her. She felt it now, her gaze locked with his arctic eyes. Her attraction had blinded her to the fact that he was not good for her. He was a liar. A two-timing shit of a liar.

She cleared her throat. "What time is it?"

"Almost midnight. You going to be okay? Do I need to drive you to Clinton?"

From his ranch it would take almost an hour, in the dark, on bad roads. And the ER would be closed. They'd have to call 911 for emergency to open up with an on-call physician. It reminded Rebecca that out here, one looked after one's own.

"I . . . I must have passed out."

A half smile. "Slept like a baby. You must have been tired."

A desire to tell him all rose in Rebecca: How rough her journey home had been with the storms. How seeing her father's body had gutted her. How exhausted she felt, emotionally. But she held back as her mind sharpened and the immediacy of why she was here, with him, in this house, was pulled into clear focus.

"What made you return to my father's place when you did, Ash? How did you come to find me?"

"I go up to the Broken Bar mesa sometimes. The view of the valley on a clear, cold night is surreal." A pause. "I needed to think." *After seeing you.* The unspoken words seemed to simmer between them. "Someplace above it all. Then as the moon rose, I caught light glinting off metal where your father's place was. I thought it might be a vehicle, so I went to check before heading home." He paused. "You could have died out there."

Rebecca swallowed as this fact sank like a stone through her gut. "Have you been sitting there watching me like that all night?"

"You worried me," he said. Then, very quietly, he added, "And I like to look at you." He paused. "It's been so long."

She sat up higher and drew the duvet more tightly around her shoulders, on guard and off-kilter. The sound of dogs had quieted; there was just the wind moaning in the eaves outside.

"I heard you married," Rebecca said, wondering who had started the fire that had been crackling when they'd arrived, who had placed flowers in the vase on the table.

He nodded quietly. Her heart sank oddly, and it struck her—his wife was probably in the house, sleeping in their bed.

He said, "And I heard that you have a partner named Lance. Some big-shot injury insurance lawyer."

Rebecca's pulse quickened at the mention of Lance. His name coming off Ash's lips—this intimate knowledge of her private life—felt invasive. "How did you know about Lance?"

"Your father spoke about you often, Becs, in great detail. Noah was so proud of you." He swallowed. "I'm going to miss him."

"What's her name?"

He crooked a brow quizzically.

"Your wife."

He gave a soft snort. And then a slow nod. "I see . . . I guess while Noah told me all about you, he didn't tell you much about me, did he?"

"I asked him not to. Not after I heard you got married."

Her words hung. He regarded her intently, something indefinable changing in his face. He moistened his lips and looked down at his hands. He rubbed them together, inhaled. "Her name is Shawna. She's an artist. We met when she came out here with a painting group. I guided them for the duration of their painting trip."

He hesitated, as if measuring what more he should tell her. The fire cracked, and a log tumbled against the grate. "It didn't work out," he said. "We split up, then divorced six years ago. Marriage lasted seven."

Rebecca's pulse quickened.

He looked up into her eyes.

"Why?" she asked.

He held her gaze, looking right into her, as if accusing her. As if Rebecca were somehow to blame for the failure of his marriage. "It was me, I guess. I just . . . I didn't give it enough. I was absent in a sense, out in the bush a lot, doing my thing. I know I'm sometimes not easy to be with. And . . . she needed more. She had an affair. So I suppose I asked for it. Our marriage has been over for almost as long as it endured." A glimmer of pain danced in his eyes.

Rebecca knew that pain. That pain of betrayal. He'd inflicted that same pain on her. She glanced at the flowers on the table. He seemed to read her mind—he'd always had a habit of doing that, guessing what she was thinking.

"Housekeeper," he said. "She gets them fresh from a florist in Clinton. She keeps me on track." He offered a smile. It did not quite reach into his eyes. "What about you and Lance the injury lawyer? Is it serious?"

The way he said it, he might just as well have said, *Lance the ambulance chaser.*

She watched him steadily, a soft anger beginning to pulse at the personal dig. Rebecca welcomed the emotion. Anger cleared her focus, brought her back to her goal, the reasons she needed to talk to him.

Brushing aside his question about Lance, she said, "Buck told me you were allegedly the last person to see my father alive before he supposedly shot himself."

Or was killed.

"Tell me what happened during those final hours, Ash. What makes you say that my father was in no mood to kill himself?"

He moistened his lips. "I found him in the PetroGas convenience store earlier that day. He was inebriated, and I figured he'd done a little detour on foot from the Moose and Horn under the pretext of visiting his old buddy Clive Dodd, and that he was going to circle back to his truck parked at the Cariboo Lodge—it was a trick of his to get around Solly's watchful eye—and Noah was in no state to drive. I offered to take him home."

Rebecca heard genuine care in Ash's voice. It threw her.

"What time was that?"

"Noon. Arrived at his place around four."

"The drive takes forty-five minutes to an hour max. What happened in between?"

"You're playing cop—I'm being interrogated."

"I *am* a cop. He's my dad. I need to know what happened."

He watched her for a beat. "A white-collar-crimes cop." He let that hang. "That's a long way from homicide, Becca."

"Is that what that is, then—homicide?"

The word shimmered. The fire crackled.

He looked away, swore softly, and raked his hand through hair that was as thick and dark as it had been the day she'd last seen him, but shot through with strands of silver at the temples, which suited him.

"I don't know what to call it yet, Becs, I really don't know. But it sure as hell wasn't suicide, in my mind."

Rebecca's chest tightened. "Talk to me, Ash—walk me through exactly what happened, then. Please. Step by step."

"On the way up from Clinton, we stopped at the Open Circle Ranch. To drop off feed. Maggie was recently widowed. And"—a shrug—"I help her out where I can. It's no sweat to drop off supplies or pick up things for her on my way in or out. Noah fell asleep on the drive up. He was asleep pretty much as soon as we left town. He woke when we reached his cabin."

She eyed him. "And then?"

"I helped him carry in a load of wood. I started the fire. Had a quick drink with him, which I do—did—from time to time. And then I left. The cold front was coming in, and I had dogs to check on and staff to pay." He leaned forward, resting his forearms on his thighs, and clasped his hands together. "But here's the thing. Noah had put the oven on. He'd set *two* plates on the kitchen table. And a packet of cigarettes. He doesn't smoke. He was expecting someone for dinner, Becca. None of that smacks of someone about to take their own life within the following hour."

Her heart beat faster. "The cigarettes were Denali Plain?"

He leaned back slightly. "How'd you know?"

"I spoke to the Maliks at the gas station. They told me he bought a pack of Denali Plain."

A look of wariness entered his features, as though he realized he was being cross-questioned.

"Does Clive Dodd smoke?" she asked. "Buck told me my dad was on his way to visit Dodd. Could he have been buying the smokes for Dodd?"

"Dodd's on oxygen and dying of emphysema. Noah had to have bought those for someone else."

"Did you inform Buck and Dixie, the coroner, about the cigarettes, the fact that my father was expecting a dinner guest?"

"I told Buck."

"Did he look into it? Did he locate and interview the person who was supposed to arrive for dinner?"

"I can't answer that. I know only that the coroner's office took the lead on the case because Buck found no evidence of a crime."

"Buck never mentioned to me that my father was awaiting a guest. He said all indicators pointed to my dad being depressed and suicidal."

Ash studied her in silence, as if deciding what he should share with her. Outside, the moan of the wind sharpened to an eerie wail across the frozen landscape. He cleared his throat. "I'm not sure that Buck is the right cop for this case."

Surprise rippled through Rebecca. "Why?"

He reached over and scratched Kibu's tummy, turning his face away from her slightly. Rebecca had been trained in interrogation techniques. To her, this was a tell. A sign that Ash might be about to lie.

"I don't trust him," he said.

Rebecca thought of the way Buck had stared out the window at the flag snapping in the cold wind, and the words he'd spoken.

The Silverado has good studded snow tires. You might want to use it if you plan on heading up there.

She thought again of the possibility of her dad's truck being sabotaged.

"Why not?" she asked.

He shook his head. "Just . . . don't."

She waited for him to explain further. He didn't. So she filed it away, intending to circle back later.

"And over drinks with my dad, what was his mood? What did he talk about?"

"He was . . . energized, almost. Enthused about one of his new cold case projects."

A frisson chased through her. "Which case?"

Ash hesitated. A fraction too long.

"The Whitney Gagnon and Trevor Beauchamp mystery."

Her heart whomped. She'd guessed it. But hearing those long-ago names spoken out loud, from *his* mouth—it felt raw. Memories exploded through her mind.

She could almost smell the popcorn that had hung hot in the air that night of the rodeo fair. Again, she saw the look in Ash's eyes when she'd caught him coming out of the barn with Whitney. She swallowed and drew the duvet closer around her body.

"Why that case?" she asked, very quietly. "Why now?"

He ran his tongue over his teeth. "Noah had just found someone who'd witnessed Whitney being dropped off at the bus stop that day."

She frowned. "Why is that even an issue? We *know* Whitney and Trevor were at the Renegade Lines bus stop that day. There was that female witness who came forward in December of that year who said she'd seen both Whitney and Trevor climbing into a white van with Oregon plates at that bus stop, before the bus was scheduled to arrive."

Ash's eyes darkened. His mouth firmed into a straight line. He absently stroked Kibu's tummy. He appeared to be recalibrating, facing a big decision. And a sense of foreboding rose in Rebecca's chest.

He inhaled, and his gaze locked suddenly on to hers.

"Noah felt it was an issue because the person who dropped Whitney off was seen getting into a fight with Trevor, who drew a knife." Another pause. The sense of impending doom increased. A shutter banged outside, and something clattered on the porch.

"And because that person was me, Becca."

BUTTERFAT BUCKY IN THE BARN

Cariboo Country. Clinton rodeo grounds. Saturday, July 11, more than twenty years ago.

The heat is oppressive. It's 10:00 p.m. and still light, but the sky glows an ominous orange-brown, with forest-fire smoke hanging in a low, choking haze over the town.

All I wanna do is live it up . . .
Before I die . . . It's gonna be great.
Party all night, until the sun
Comes up . . .

It's the hot summer of the Hazmat Suits' hit. Bodies gyrate and sweat on the packed-dirt dance floor. Above them lanterns swing in the wildfire wind. Chinese lanterns. Yet the rodeo boasts a western theme. The entire village has turned up for the big annual event. People wear cowboy hats and fringed leather vests, jeans, and pretty summer dresses with cowboy boots. Carnival clowns blow balloons for sticky-faced children, and rodeo clowns dance with the bulls. Hired actors move elegantly on stilts through the crowds eating cotton candy and ice cream. The smell of corn dogs and hot dogs and hot buttered popcorn wafts thick in the close, smoky air. There are false laughs and sexual gropes and hooves thudding in the dirt as adults appear ludicrous jiving away, thinking they look as they did when they were eighteen. Or twenty.

In the big barn that the carnival folk built for their horses, Ash and Whitney—sticky with sex, sweaty with heat, flushed with spent lust—fumble and button and zip back into their clothes.

Ash feels ill.

He's just spilled his sperm into the town tramp's pussy, and while he was damned desperate to do it—to just fuck a woman, any woman, this summer—it's not what he thought it would be.

He wanted that woman to be Becca, but Becca had continually rebuffed his clumsy advances. She was clinging to some harebrained idea that she should wait until she was seventeen and in her final year of high school before having intercourse, like it was some personal marathon of endurance through all the heavy petting that was driving him insane with lust.

Ash tried to go further with Becca in a more aggressive fashion last week. And her rejection once again angered him. He cannot admit to himself why he feels so damn angry. Because the things that drive him are dark. And mostly they are locked down in the basement of his soul, where it's black as devil's pitch and cold as witches' tits. And where he doesn't have to examine them, or reveal them to anyone, even himself.

Whitney is laughing and wiggling her butt as she pulls her panties up over white thighs. He's wiping off his cock and praying to heaven Becca will never find out. Because this . . . can never happen again. It was a mistake.

Whitney suddenly goes still. She's listening to something. She turns sharply and shades her eyes as she peers into the shadows among the bales of hay stacked high along the barn wall.

"Shit," she whispers, grabbing her skirt. Then she calls out loudly, "Bucky! I can seeee you! Come on out from behind the bales, Bucky boy!"

Ash spins around in horror to see Buck Johnstone. Standing in the dark dust-mote shadows. Behind a hay bale, near a horse stall. His fly is open and he's holding his thick dick.

Bile rushes up Ash's throat.

That compartment where bad things are locked away cracks open wide, and everything starts clashing in a smoky roar in his head.

Buck disappears in a wink. Ash stares at the shadows. Was what he saw even real? Had Bucky Johnstone really been there, jerking off while he watched Ash and Whitney fuck?

Whitney is carrying on getting dressed.

Sounds of the fair from outside reach him. So do the smells, the sense of the world going on beyond this dimly lit barn. Panic whips through him as he thinks of Becca, of word getting out.

"Did you see what he was doing?" he demands of Whitney.

"Pervert," Whitney says, fastening the buttons of her western blouse over her large breasts. "He's probably gone to finish off behind another hay bale." She reaches down, cups Ash hard between the legs as she leans up, and gives him an openmouthed kiss. She whispers in his ear, her breath warm and smelling of beer, "You fuck good, Haugen."

To his abject horror, his penis stirs again under the pressure of her palm. She gives a little grunt of pleasure as she registers his response, turns her head, and yells into the dim barn interior, "Wanna see him come inside me again, Bucky Boy, Bucky the Ball, Fat-Belly Buck who can't get a fuck!"

Ash blanches.

She takes his hand.

117

"Come, let's go. They're playing my song. And I need a drink."

"Whitney—"

She stills and examines his face, sees his worry. "Look. Buck Johnstone does that, okay? He's a Peeping Tom. He has a thing for me. A serious thing. And not just for me. Other girls have seen him watching . . . stuff. He looks in their windows at night. He peeps through holes in washroom walls. Come." She tugs.

He resists. "You don't care?"

"That he likes me? Hey, you like me. I like to be liked. Come on. The song's going to be over."

Ash holds back. And it strikes him. Whitney Gagnon is a town tramp for no other reason than she likes to be liked. She needs attention. And she's confusing teenage male horniness for affection.

He feels even worse.

They exit the barn, and Ash stalls dead in his tracks. His heart bottoms clean out as he sees Becca standing there. She's caught him and Whitney coming out of the barn, Whitney holding his hand. Their eyes meet. Shock whitens her face.

He drops Whitney's hand.

> Before I die, have some fun . . . It's gonna be
>   great.
> Party all night, until the sun
> Comes up . . .

She spins around and vanishes into the crowd.

He races after her. "Becca! Becca!"

But she's gone. Absorbed into the hot, dancing, sweaty, gyrating crowd and butter-stinking air.

As Ash searches desperately for her, he feels it—the beginning of the end. Of life as he always thought it would be.

Because he fucked Whitney in the barn.

CHAPTER 19

Ash watched Becca's face. The look in her eyes changed as they hardened into something flat and inscrutable.

He lurched to his feet, paced, fisting and unfisting his hands as he walked. Kibu sat up sharply, alerted to his master's agitation.

"Why?" Her voice was dangerously flat. Calm. "Why did you take Whitney to the bus stop?"

He spun to face Becca, his heart beating hard. Hard as fucking hell.

"Because she said she needed a ride. And I wanted to be sure she left town. I wanted her *gone*."

Her features were tight. They revealed no emotion at all, and her toneless delivery, the lack of any inflection in her voice to clue him in to her feelings—Ash had seen that kind of demeanor in cops before. They trained for it. Becca was suspicious of him. And as he held her unreadable honey-colored eyes, a memory flashed through him. Of Becca at eleven. Baking bread with her mom. She was no less beautiful to him now. He'd never stopped wanting the same things he'd visualized that day.

"Why did you and Trevor fight?"

"Why do you think?"

"Why don't you tell me."

Ash did *not* want to relive this with her. It would just drive a wedge further between them. And moments ago he'd glimpsed a tiny spark of interest in her eyes when he'd told her about Shawna, about his divorce. And it had planted in him a faint glimmer of hope that maybe . . . just maybe, she still cared for him, deep down. That things could perhaps yet work between them.

You idiot. You fucking idiot—there is no way on this planet that it could ever work again with Becca.

She'd soon be returning to Lance the insurance lawyer. To her high-powered white-collar-crime career. She'd never have an occasion to speak to him, let alone visit this place, once she sold off her dad's land.

He shouldn't care about being forced to reawaken this horrible past with her, to live it all over again. He shouldn't worry about being forced to reveal his guilt or his secrets via what was beginning to look like a homicide investigation. It was a road they both had to go down because he had a sick feeling that his betrayal with Whitney was now, twenty years later, somehow central to Noah's death.

I dropped the ball on those kids. Whitney and Trevor. I dropped the ball because people in this town—especially you—were hiding something.

He stopped pacing and faced her square. "We fought because Trevor knew I'd slept with his girl while he was away. That's how it went down, Becca. I'd slept with *his* girl, and I was taking her to the bus, and I didn't expect him to be waiting there to go with her to LA, either."

"And that upset *you*? That she'd gone back to Trevor?"

Fuck. "I don't want to go through all that again."

"You have to. What happened back then could have killed my father now."

He knew it. She knew it. But they didn't know why. They were on opposite, conflicting ends of this thing, yet in it together. And one way or another, the two of them were hurtling unstoppably back into their own pasts.

"Why did you not tell anyone that you took her to the bus stop?"

"What was the point? She'd left a note for her mother. Trevor had told friends he was going to LA with Whitney, leaving shit-town-cow-town for good. Those were his words. And they left. No one worried until December, when Whitney's mom and her best friend, Ariel, had heard nothing at all from her, not even over Christmas. So they pressured your father to look into it. He did, and he learned from the bus company there was no record of Whitney and Trevor ever getting onto that bus. There'd been no sign of them over the US border, either." He sucked air in deep, reliving the stress he'd felt at age seventeen over the whole affair. "That's when Whitney's mother and Ariel started putting up posters asking for information about Whitney's whereabouts. That was late December, and that's when a female witness who saw the posters came forward saying she'd seen Whitney and Trevor getting into a white van."

"You remember the details very well."

"After speaking with Noah before he died, I sure started thinking about the sequence of it all."

"So you could get your story straight."

"Jesus, Becca."

"You didn't come forward and tell my father in December '98, either, after you knew he'd started an inquiry?"

"Again, what was the point if they'd gotten into a white van with Oregon plates? My taking Whitney to the bus before they ended up hitching a ride instead of catching a bus was completely irrelevant. We all knew they were intending to head south across the border, aiming for California."

She glared at him.

He sat down hard on the ottoman, rubbed his face, feeling exhausted. For a moment he just listened to the fire, to the sounds of wind and ice crystals ticking against the windows, trying to absorb and process the fact that Becca North was back and in his house. That they were traveling together down this old road. Slowly he looked up.

"You want the truth, Becca? The fucking stupid truth? I didn't *want* to bring it up because I didn't want to hurt you. I wanted you still—I thought I still had a chance." Emotion snared his voice. He struggled to hold it in. "I wanted that one goddamn last chance. I *couldn't* let you go. You were supposed to be my whole life, and Whitney screwed it up."

"*You* screwed us up." Emotion rode sudden and high in her cheeks. Her eyes flashed like liquid. She couldn't hold it in despite her obvious attempts. "*You* continued seeing her after the night at the fair. Marcy told the whole town. Yet there you were, telling me it was over, begging me to trust you. Telling me that . . . you loved me . . ." Her voice broke. "We made love . . . you . . . fuck."

He felt the blood drain from his head.

She took a moment, rubbed her nose, cleared her throat. "So that's why my father said that you lied, then? Because of the fight you had with Trevor, and the fact you showed up with a cut face later the same day? Did he figure Trevor cut your face?"

"He was fishing."

"But *why* was he fishing? He had to have had something beyond the witness statement that placed you at the bus stop and you getting into a tussle with Trevor. That's not enough to open some . . . some cold case investigation. For all we know, Trevor and Whitney maybe just laid low all these years for some other reason. Maybe they went to ground because they got in trouble with the law stateside. Maybe they're living under assumed names in South America somewhere. Wouldn't be a stretch, knowing Trevor. God knows, maybe they died a natural death in Mexico." She held his gaze, cheeks pinked. "So what was it that triggered my father's interest in this old mystery? What new thing did he learn that sparked his investigation, his fear—because yes, Ash, my dad was scared. He called me the day he died, from the Moose and Horn. Before he went up to the PetroGas and ran into you."

Surprise shot through Ash. "He didn't mention it."

"So what was it he found?"

"I don't know. Noah was being guarded."

She looked at him like he was lying.

Then she said, "So who's the witness who saw you?"

"Again, I don't know. Like I said, he was playing his cards close."

She surged to her feet. Hugging the duvet around her shoulders, she walked to the sliding glass doors and stared out into the dark through her own reflection.

"Obviously he was playing his cards close if he thought you had something to do with the Whitney/Trevor mystery." She faced him. "What is the damn mystery anyway? Because at this point I don't even see how Trevor cutting your face before climbing into a van would change things. They still got into the van."

He shook his head. "Whatever information Noah had, it could have been in that case file of his he had on the coffee table. If it was, it's burned. Or the information could also have gone missing out of the file before the fire, because he asked if I had been inside his cabin and taken anything. And if incriminating information really was stolen, then someone else out there must know whatever it was that Noah knew."

She studied him long and hard from across the room.

"*Did* Trevor cut your face?"

"No. We threw a few punches and it was done. I left."

"So how did you hurt your face?"

Irritation sparked through him. "I told you. A horse."

"Why refuse to go to the ER and get proper stitches? What was the deal with that?"

"Probably concussed. Wasn't thinking straight."

"Right."

"Oh Jesus, Becca." He surged back up to his feet. "I wanted *you*. I *needed* you. Touching me. Your hands in my blood, inside my pain, fuck it. Your care—I wanted your care. Whitney was finally gone. I wanted to drown in you. Just you." Emotion burned back into his eyes. Becca stared at him, utterly motionless.

He turned, paced, swung back. "She'd gone. I was amped up from my fight with Trevor. I needed to burn off a whole lotta steam, get her and him right out of my system. So I went for a ride. But I was unfocused, too angry, wrong frame of mind. And I chose the wrong horse to ride in that mood on the cusp of a thunderstorm. One clap of thunder and it spooked and threw me."

Becca moved slowly back to the sofa and reseated herself. Her hands were trembling, her eyes glistening. She broke eye contact and stared at the fire for a long while. His dog, Bear, stirred and stretched on the mat. Ash's blood was pounding in his ears. He was shaking himself.

"What about you, Becca?" he asked quietly. "If you'd had doubts about my injuries that day, why didn't you tell your father, either?"

Very slowly she looked up and met his gaze. Softly she said, "Because I wanted to believe. I *wanted . . .*" Her voice choked.

Emotion seared through his chest. Every molecule in his body ached to hold her. To go back in time and change that one July night of that wildfire summer. Ash had to fight with every ounce of his being not to go up to her, to touch her. He breathed in a shuddering breath.

"And now," she said. "Now . . . I . . . I still want to believe, Ash. Goddammit, there, I said it. I still want to believe you."

His heart stuttered.

She swallowed. "But I can't. Not now. From what my dad said on the phone, whatever happened to him afterward is somehow connected to what occurred between us. I need to find out what that is before I can trust you. I'm going to have my dad's death investigation reopened. I'm going to talk to Buck to—"

"Not Buck."

"Why not?" she asked him again.

"I don't trust him with this."

"You're going to have to explain, Ash."

Nausea washed up into his belly at the idea of having to conjure it up in his mind again.

"He had a thing for Whitney," he said, voice tight. "He was stalking her. Peeping Tom."

She snorted. "How would you know?"

He felt hot. "She told me."

"Right. And you believed her?"

Wanna see him come inside me again, Bucky Boy, Bucky the Ball, Fat-Belly Buck who can't get a fuck!

Ash fought against telling Becca, but decided it had to be the truth now. All of it. As much as he could bear. If not for Becca, for Noah.

He inhaled deeply and rubbed the back of his neck. "Buck Johnstone was in the barn that night at the rodeo fair. He saw us. Me and Whitney. He was watching. And he was jerking off."

A long pause. Then Rebecca came sharply to her feet.

"I need to go to bed." She left the living room and went down the passage toward the guest bedroom he'd shown her earlier, wrapped in his blanket and duvet, her shoulders slumped. And Ash stood alone. Staring at the space where she had vanished.

He walked slowly to the sliding glass doors and looked out into the white glow of the moon on the snow. Leafless branches bobbed in the wind.

Whatever had started that night at the fair . . . it was not done yet. Not by a long shot.

CHAPTER 20

Cariboo Country. Tuesday, January 15.

The morning had dawned brittle and clear. Wrapped in fleece, Rebecca stood at the floor-to-ceiling windows overlooking a white lawn that rolled down to a small lake. She cupped a mug of fresh coffee in her hands. Behind her the fire crackled. Ash had stoked it up sometime earlier, and he'd left a note for her on the kitchen counter along with a basket of warm croissants and a pot of coffee.

Be back once animals taken care of.

Have sent ranch mechanic to look at Noah's truck. We'll meet him at Noah's place via snowmobile and get his verdict.

Will then follow tracks from shed to Broken Bar boundary and see where they lead from there.

Ash.
X.

Rebecca had stared at the *X* for a while. Her mind and emotions were a mess. It had been a long few days since her father had called. But she'd slept soundly for a few hours and recalibrated somewhat. Her first instinct last night had been to tell Ash to stay the hell away from her investigation into her father's apparent suicide. Because however she looked at the facts, he was a key person of interest in her dad's death.

But she also believed what he'd said about Buck.

She believed a lot of what Ash had said, but sensed he was still hiding something big. It would serve her well, she thought, if she kept him close and used him rather than shutting him out entirely. If she pursued her investigation through him instead of going around him, she might learn more. He might slip. And he had contacts in town, where she had none.

So Rebecca's goal going forward this morning was to work alongside Ash to find something that might warrant her calling in a major crimes team. This would mean going over Buck Johnstone's head, but his purview as a local RCMP officer was not to investigate homicides. If a murder had occurred on his turf, protocol required him to call in a specialized RCMP homicide unit anyway.

She sipped from her mug as she watched Ash's figure appear behind a fenced-off area in the distance. He wore a cowboy hat and ranch coat and carried a pail. His breath clouded in the air around his face. A pack of dogs—all black-and-white Karelian bear dogs—bounded and jumped around him. Sun sparkled on the snow.

It was utterly beautiful. A picture postcard of a ranch. Rebecca's heart squeezed. She had missed this, as much as she had denied it to herself. It was part of her soul, this life. The place of her roots.

She took another sip of coffee, her thoughts returning to the boot prints outside her dad's shed and the fact that they led to snowmobile tracks that—as Ash had said—led to Broken Bar Ranch. Her mind segued to Dot's Donuts and Diner and seeing Olivia West and her daughter, Tori Burton, sitting in the booth below the window. The girl with the long, dark, wavy hair who lived on Broken Bar Ranch.

She thought of the hair strands she'd taken from the shed. The sizes of the handprints and boot impressions. Rebecca had a feeling she knew already who might have been inside that shed.

But if it was Tori Burton, who'd she been with? Why had she and her friend fled? Could they have witnessed something that spooked them? Or worse—could they have been involved in some way? She doubted it. It was more likely that the kids had been stealing booze. But Tori Burton had to be a troubled child. There remained the possibility she was capable of dark deeds like her father. Still, the staged suicide of Rebecca's father spoke to something entirely different.

Rebecca moved into the kitchen. She selected a second croissant out of the basket. Holding it in one hand, coffee in the other, she went over to a bookshelf that showcased framed photographs. She took a bite, chewed, as she studied the images.

One photo showed Ash with a woman in front of a waterfall. She wore a white dress. Rebecca stopped chewing.

Shawna?

Their wedding day?

She swallowed her mouthful along with a complex ball of feelings. There was another image of the same woman. Laughing in a red canoe on a still, turquoise lake.

Ash might be divorced, but he hadn't chucked the memories of his marriage and Shawna out of his life. Curious, Rebecca moved to the next photo. She bit into her croissant as she studied it. Ash and two of his Karelians with a uniformed conservation officer crouched beside a massive tranquilized grizzly bear, the bear's claws as long as the men's fingers. Another image showed Ash with a tranquilized cougar, and again, his dogs hovered close to him. These, she realized, were Ash's versions of hunting trophies. Except he would have released these animals safely away from the human interference that had gotten them into trouble in the first place.

She finished the last sip of coffee and bite of croissant. Chewing as she cradled the empty but still-warm mug, she moved to the next framed photo. Shock arrowed through her.

A photo of Ash and her dad. Fishing. From when Ash was around fourteen. Rebecca had taken that photo. She'd been right there with them both. Blood started to pound in her ears as she stared at her dad. A big crunching hole formed in her gut. Painful. A maw of loss. And it just kept on growing as she gazed into his tanned and craggy face. She blew out air and looked at the next image.

Her father again. Standing proud in full ceremonial uniform— red serge coat, high brown boots, jodhpurs, Sam Browne belt, and Stetson. Behind him flapped a red-and-white Canadian flag. The photo had been shot at one of the many Clinton Canada Day parades.

Ash had kept this? Why?

She set down her mug and picked up the frame. Emotions roiled in a complex, churning mess of pain and guilt and love and loss. Rebecca inhaled deeply and pressed the frame tightly against her chest. She held it there, tears escaping her eyes. She let them come now, in privacy. She couldn't hold it all in anymore. She missed him. She missed her dad so much. Knowing he was gone from the world—

"You can have that one."

She caught her breath and spun around. Ash stood there.

"I . . . I didn't hear you come in." Embarrassed, she hurriedly swiped away the tears. "You . . . you kept it," she said of the framed photo in her hands. It was a stupid thing to say, because here it was. Obviously he'd kept it. Ash was clearly a man who kept memories. Of his life, his wife, her own father. Where she'd kept none. She'd purposefully trashed anything that reminded her of the old Becca North she once had been, that hillbilly tomboy from a rural ranch- ing town who loved to ride and help her mother dig dark earth in the vegetable garden, who'd worked for a veterinarian and believed, always, that she'd marry Ash Haugen and have plenty of animals and a garden of her own.

Instead, she was a cop. Commercial crimes, computers, not even a hands-on, messy cop like her dad. A female detective who lived in a sterile apartment and couldn't commit to a man. Or spend long periods with her own lonely father. What had happened to her?

Ash was weighing her, too, silent questions swelling larger and heavier in the room.

"I've got another like it," he said. "Keep that one."

Her pulse jumped at the idea. But she set it back on the shelf carefully. "It's okay. It's yours. You have it for a reason." She stared at it for a moment longer, her back to him. And she said softly, "But what reason, Ash? Why do you keep these of my dad?"

"I loved him, too. Both your parents."

"I know you did." She faced him. "What about your own—you don't have photos of them here?"

He gave a sad smile. It changed his face and punched her hard in the gut. "I preferred yours."

"Why?" she pushed.

"Ah, you know my mom and dad. Old school. Cold. Disciplinarian." He gave a shrug. "I pretty much wanted to move into your cabin and be adopted by your family when I was little." A wry smile curved his mouth. "I even adopted Bear because he reminded me so much of your mom's old dog when I saw him at the pound—I just couldn't leave him there."

Her heart raced. She looked deep into his eyes. And suddenly she saw the boy she'd once known. And the teen. And she felt all of eleven and twelve and fourteen and sixteen again. Emotion surged back into her face, and she turned away. It was all too much at once.

"Take it, Becs." He picked the frame off the shelf and handed it back to her. "All of Noah's photos went up in the fire. You need something of him. Please, keep this one."

She glanced down at her dad in red serge. He looked so proud. Corporal Noah North. She touched his face with her fingertips. What she'd give just to hug him once again, see his familiar craggy face just one more time. She sucked in a shaky breath.

"Thanks," she whispered. She cleared her throat. "I think I will."

CHAPTER 21

Rebecca yanked a strip of yellow crime scene tape free from the ice. She crunched over to the shed and secured it across the door of her father's moonshine shed using a staple gun Ash had loaned her. Breath misted around her face as she worked, and frost that had grown overnight crackled beneath her boots. The air was sharp against her cheeks, and the sky was brutally clear and bright. Rebecca wore a wool hat pulled low over her ears, yet the morning cold still sliced through.

Ash had loaned her several layers of cold-weather gear and had driven her over to her father's property on his snowmobile.

His mechanic had already been to check her dad's Silverado. He'd returned to the ranch to fetch a tow truck. The tow was expected shortly. Rebecca was using the time while they waited to seal off the shed by repurposing Buck's crime scene tape.

The bright colors and crisp, clean lines of the morning, the sparkling-diamond clarity of the landscape, seemed surreal juxtaposed with the charred-ash horror of the burned cabin encased beneath the thick layer of ice. A bird circled and keened up high.

Ash handed her another length of police tape he'd cut free.

"Thanks." She got down onto her haunches and affixed it to form a cross over the entrance.

"You're not still considering bringing Buck in, are you?" he asked, watching her from behind.

"I just want to secure the shed in case we need to get a forensics ident crew in later. I collected some viable evidence inside, but in order to hold up in court, we'd need to do this officially. Can you free that piece over there?"

His boots crunched as he cut free another length of bright-yellow plastic that had been snapping in the breeze.

"Thanks."

"So you'd go over Buck's head, then?"

She gunned the staple into the wood, securing another piece of tape, working clumsily in thick gloves. "Depends if I find enough evidence to bring in a major crimes team. I mean, Buck would have to do that anyway—bring in a team—if this is in fact a homicide." It felt bizarre even saying that about her father. It was bizarre just thinking about how she and Ash had come to be here together.

She glanced up at him from her crouched position.

His breath steamed from his mouth. His eyes appeared even icier blue in this cold. His Nordic heritage. It suited him. Rebecca realized she was stirring awake again. Physically. It bothered her. This was the risk of working with him on her dad's investigation. She did not want to fall lock, stock, and barrel for Ash Haugen again. Especially if he turned out to be hiding something criminal. Especially since she had Lance waiting back east for her. She had to be careful or she'd get burned. Again.

She wiped the back of her glove across her nose. The cold was making it run. "Considering what you told me about Buck, and about what case my dad was working on, this could conceivably be a conflict of interest for him anyway."

"What about a conflict for you—Noah is your father."

"I'm not doing this in an official capacity. Yet. And if I do find something, like I said, I'll contact an outside unit."

She pushed to her feet, handed him back the staple gun.

"What viable evidence did you find inside the shed?" he said. "Apart from boot prints in yellow paint?"

She hesitated, considering how much of that information she should actually share with him.

"Fingerprints," she said, pulling a warm mitt over the thinner gloves she wore. "And a handprint in some yellow paint spill. And a couple of hair strands."

"What kind of hair?"

"Long, dark, with a slight wave." She paused. "Tori Burton's kind."

His ice-blue eyes locked steadily on hers. "You do know who Tori is?"

"Yeah. The patent prints and the boot size would be right for a kid her age. Plus, you said the sled tracks led right up to the Broken Bar Ranch boundary. My working theory for now is Tori Burton was here, with a friend."

He looked worried now, which struck her as curious.

"Anything else?" he said.

She eyed him for a moment. "A padlock that had been picked. It was lying over there." She pointed. "And I found a tool that might have been used to pick it. There's nothing to say the tool wasn't lying underneath the workbench for a long time before the young intruders entered the shed, but it could have been used."

Sun peeked over the hill, and gold rays rippled across the landscape, casting everything in various soft shades of gold and yellow and making ice everywhere spark and glitter like jewels. The sound of an engine reached them.

Rebecca and Ash watched as a dark-blue tow truck bumped its way along the rutted approach road.

While she watched it, Rebecca said, as if lost in thought, "You didn't mention that you and my father were arguing at Dot's Donuts on the day he died."

"What makes you think we were arguing?"

"Marcy. She said you and him got into it. You dragged him out before your chicken sandwiches arrived and manhandled him into your truck."

"Marcy." He swore softly.

"What do you mean, 'Marcy'?"

"I mean what piece of fake garbage news or gossip has *not* been mangled through Marcy Fossum's foul little plastic-surgeried lips?"

The harshness of his words startled Rebecca.

"Noah and I weren't arguing," he snapped. "Your dad was stumbling about the place. I tried to steady him. He told me to unhand him, and got testy about it. Noah was punch-drunk and irritable at that point, and probably needed food—that's why we stopped in to get him a goddamn sandwich in the first place. He walked out of the place. So I left the order and went to get him into the truck. He promptly fell asleep, and woke at his cabin better for it."

The dark-blue tow truck pulled up, big tires crunching on ice and frost. It was mired with road salt and winter muck, the words CARIBOO BREAKDOWN SERVICES emblazoned in big white italics on the sides.

"Better until he got a gun in his mouth," she said coolly, watching as the truck maneuvered in front of her dad's old Silverado.

CHAPTER 22

"This is Wes Steele." Ash introduced a tall man in his late twenties who'd jumped down from the passenger side of the tow truck and come around the front. "Wes, this is Noah's daughter, Becca North."

"Rebecca," she corrected as she extended a gloved hand.

"I'm sorry for your loss." Wes shook her hand. "I heard Noah's daughter was a detective." He offered a handsome grin. "Noah told everyone, like multiple times over. He was super proud. I confess I wondered if he was making you up since we never laid eyes on you."

Frustration nipped at Rebecca. The whole bloody town must think her an uncaring soul.

Wes jerked his head toward her dad's truck. "Once I get the Silverado back to the ranch shop and up onto the hoist, I'll get a better sense of whether that gas tank can be repaired." He glanced at the truck. "But from what I saw when I looked underneath earlier, you're probably looking at a new fuel tank."

The driver's-side door of the tow vehicle creaked open. A guy in his late fifties or early sixties hopped down to the ice with a groan. Burly in his heavy work gear and bent in his shoulders, he ambled over, leaving the tow truck engine running and puffing giant clouds of white into the air.

"Gonzalo McGuigan," he said, holding out a weathered hand, no gloves. Beneath a trapper's hat with earflaps, his complexion was gray and his chin whiskered. "Everyone calls me Gonz."

"Rebecca." She shook his hand.

"Guess you wouldn't remember me from back in the day, eh, back when I was a good-looking young gun?"

"You were never good-looking or young, Gonz," Ash said.

Gonz grinned and pushed his cap back on his head. Rebecca noticed his index and middle fingers were stained yellow—the kind of stains that came from nicotine when a person smoked cigarettes without filters. She eyed Gonz more closely.

"Noah spoke plenty about you, though." Gonz's voice was like rough gravel in a pipe. "It's a fucking shit deal to go out like that." He glanced at the razed cabin and fell silent a moment. "Maybe we shoulda seen it coming," he said quietly. He cleared his throat and jerked his thumb toward the Silverado. "Well, we should crank this thing up." He started waddling toward his rig.

"Did you know my father well?" Rebecca called after him.

He stopped, turned. "As well as anyone who's been around awhile. Used to throw back a few drinks with Noah from time to time at the Moose and Horn."

"Did you ever visit him here, at his cabin?" she asked, thinking of the Denali Plain cigarette pack and Gonz's nicotine-stained fingers.

He angled his head and squinted against the sun's rays. "Nah," he said. "Not many came out here to see Noah, I don't think."

Gonz returned to his cab, grabbed a pair of heavy-duty work gloves from the driver's seat, and shuffled around to the back of his tow truck. He began to unhook chains with a loud rattle and clank.

"Does it look like wear-and-tear damage to the fuel tank?" Ash asked Wes, who'd stood by in silence.

"Wear and tear? Jeez, no way. The Silverado spilled pretty much its entire load of diesel onto the ice right there in one shot. Probably took a few minutes total. Tank was spiked with a sharp tool from the looks of things. Pretty mean way to steal gas, if you ask me. Some of the kids around here have been doing it and reselling. They punch a hole in a vehicle tank, drain what fuel they need or what fits into a jerrican, and then just let the rest drain out."

Rebecca frowned. "Could the damage have occurred in Clinton and the fuel leaked out along the way? The vehicle was left unattended in the public safety lot for a few days after my father's death."

"Nah, not a chance." Wind blasted, ruffling the sandy-blond hair on Wes's bare head. He clapped his gloved hands together to ward off the cold. "A hole that big? Like I said, you'd have dumped it out pretty much in one go. You wouldn't have made it one klick out of town after you'd filled that tank up at the PetroGas. That damage happened right here."

A chill trickled down Rebecca's spine. Her gaze ticked toward the trees that screened the Silverado from view of the shed. She had to have been inside the shed when it happened. Her father's words snaked through her mind.

I think someone followed me home in the dark. I think he knows what I know.

Once more she thought of the truck lights that had maintained a steady distance behind her on the highway the day before, and the lights that had appeared behind her again before she'd almost struck the deer.

"Good thing Ash found ya when he did." Wes glanced northward, squinting against the bright glare that came off snow and ice. "With this Arctic outflow? You'd have been a frozen popsicle before morning. They'd have had to chip you right outta that Silverado."

"Hoi, Wes! Ready to winch up here!" Gonz yelled, boots squeaking as he returned to the cab. He hauled himself into the driver's seat.

"God summons." Another big smile. White teeth. Nice face. He hesitated. "If you're thinking of selling that Silverado, I'd be happy to off-load it for you. I guess you'll be selling the land, too?"

"Not making any decisions yet," Rebecca said.

Ash glanced at her.

"Well, I'll let you guys know what the repair is going to look like after I get it up on that hoist. Might be worth letting that old beater go."

Wes jogged back to the truck. They all watched as the old Silverado was winched up and free of the ice with metallic groans and creaks of protest.

Wes secured the chains and climbed back into the tow cab.

Gonz gave a wave and began to turn the rig around. As it turned, Rebecca noticed a decal on the rear window of the tow cab with the words SCOTT'S MOTORSPORTS.

"What's Scott's MotorSports?" she said.

"A specialty auto shop up in Devil's Butte." Ash tilted his chin toward the now-departing caravan of tow truck and Silverado. "Wes's uncle owns the place. Wes works for him part-time, or anytime he can, frankly. It's his passion, tricking out trucks, doing snowmobile or motorbike foil design, decals, that kind of thing. His work on our ranch vehicles is his bread and butter. The other stuff—it's what he does for fun."

"Has he worked for you long?"

He glanced at her, a slight frown in his brow. "For the Haugen-Douglas ranch partnership business, maybe three years."

"What is the Haugen-Douglas partnership?"

"I lease almost two-thirds of my land to the Douglas Cattle Enterprise, mostly for grazing. It's good pay and leaves me to focus on the conservation end of my business." He paused. "Wes is a good guy. Why do you ask?"

"Did you tell Wes that I filled up at PetroGas before coming out here?"

The frown deepened. "No . . . but he would have guessed, given it's the only station at the north end of town."

"He also would've had to guess that I'd needed to fill up at all." She shaded her eyes as she watched her dad's crippled old beater being dragged toward the distant bend in the road. It made Rebecca's heart hurt, the finality of it.

The tow rounded the bend and disappeared. An explosion of blackbirds burst into the clear sky and started swarming in twisting shapes. A raven, disturbed by their flight, swooped down from a snag high in a tree. It landed atop the stone chimney that pointed out of the frozen ashes into the sky.

Craack.

Rebecca shivered as the sound of the tow truck died into the distance and a quiet descended with a sense of menace.

CHAPTER 23

Rebecca tucked in close behind Ash on his snowmobile as they roared across the snowpack, thudding hard against ice. He felt solid. The wind was sharp, clean. The fields sparkled and the sun painted soft oranges and yellows and peaches and pinks across the snow, and deeper blues lurked in shadows. It was like sensory pathways were reawakening in her. She was in touch once more with a young part of herself, her world back east blurring into an alternate reality as a bead of wild freedom built down deep in her belly and gathered density with the g-forces collecting at her core.

Ash slowed, still steering alongside the frozen tracks that led from her father's land. They had reached the Broken Bar Ranch fence. The tracks turned here, ran along the fence for a short way, then headed through a gap onto Broken Bar land. Ash brought the snowmobile to a stop at the gap in the fence. Rebecca lifted her visor and shaded her eyes as she scanned the trail onto the neighboring property. She could see where the tracks joined the hard-packed snow of the approach road to the Broken Bar Lodge.

He shoved up his own visor and said, "You want to go talk to them? It's Tuesday. Tori will be at school."

"Yeah," she said loudly over the purring engine. "Might be best to speak with her mom first."

They came to a stop in front of a big covered porch. A carved bear statue coated in ice stood guard at the base of the porch stairs. Rebecca pulled off her helmet along with the wool balaclava she was wearing beneath. Static crackled in her hair as it caught the wind coming off the lake. She dismounted, trying to recall the last time she'd visited this lodge. It must have been a party for Cole's birthday when she was in tenth grade. Her father and Myron McDonough—Cole's father—hadn't exactly been on speaking terms. From her dad's account, Myron hadn't exactly been on speaking terms with *anyone* since his wife died.

Ash dismounted, tugged off his helmet. A dog could be heard barking inside in the lodge. Ash had left Kibu at home today since they'd planned on coming to Broken Bar. He'd told Rebecca that Kibu didn't play nice with many other dogs. It was a hallmark of his breed and something Ash needed to manage. But Ace in particular had proved a problem for the young bear dog, he'd said.

Ash knocked on the big old wooden door. A swing chair without pillows creaked in the wind on the porch. Several pairs of snow boots lined the wall next to the door.

Ash knocked again with the knocker, louder. Rebecca touched Ash's shoulder and pointed to a pair of Sorels near her feet. "Those boots look about the right size," she said quietly. She bent down and lifted the Sorels to examine the tread pattern on the soles. *Yellow paint.*

She held the soles out for Ash to see. "Matching tread," she said quietly.

The door swung open. Rebecca came sharply to her feet, the boots still in her hands.

Olivia West, the woman from Dot's Donuts and Diner, stared at Rebecca; then her gaze dropped to the boots in Rebecca's grip. Olivia was dressed in fitted jeans and a fleece jacket. Her hair was thick and lustrous and hung below her shoulders. A ropy scar was visible around her neck. It looked like a terrible, permanent neck choker.

Rebecca blinked instinctively at the sight of the scar, the horror of it suddenly vivid against the context of all the news articles she'd read about how Eugene George had used a rope around Olivia's neck to tie her naked in his shed with nothing but animal skins for warmth.

Olivia's gaze shot to Ash.

"Ash?" she said. "What's going on here?"

"Liv, this is Rebecca North, Noah's daughter."

A dog—the German shepherd Ash had mentioned—came to the door, struggling to move on his hind legs but obviously eager to see who was visiting.

Olivia reached down and touched the German shepherd's head as if grounding herself. She turned to Rebecca. "I saw you at Dot's." Her voice was measured. "This must be hard for you—I'm sorry about Noah. But . . . what's going on here?" Her gaze went back to the paint-marked Sorels, then shifted to Ash's snowmobile parked beyond the porch. A man appeared behind her, and a frisson of recognition coursed through Rebecca. Cole McDonough.

She hadn't seen him in decades, but it was unmistakably Cole. Tall, muscular. Prominent brow, strong chin. Thick brown hair. A virile genetic echo of his father.

"*Becca?*" he said. "Holy . . . Is that *you?*"

"Cole."

"Wow, it's been a crazy-long time." His gaze ticked to Ash, then Olivia, then to the boots in Rebecca's hands. His features changed as he assessed the situation quickly. And something about his reaction—by the way neither he nor Olivia mentioned the boots—told Rebecca they'd expected this, or at least anticipated something.

"Come . . . come inside," Cole said. "We can talk by the fire."

They stepped inside. Olivia quietly removed the Sorels from Rebecca's hands and went to put them in a closet. Rebecca and Ash exchanged a glance as they removed their own boots. Cole took their coats and hung them on hooks made from antlers.

A massive moose's head peered down at them from an archway that opened into a living room and dining and bar area clearly designed for lodge guests.

Cole led them toward the seats in the living room.

Surprise washed through Rebecca, and she stilled momentarily as she saw Tori Burton seated on an ottoman in front of the fire. The child was playing a game of chess with a ruddy-faced man in his thirties. Both the man and Tori glanced up. Tori's face blanched. She shot to her feet, instantly wild-eyed. Olivia hastened up to her daughter, placed a hand gently on her shoulder, and said quietly, "Go upstairs, Tori."

"Actually," said Rebecca, coming forward, "I'd really like to ask Tori some questions. We hadn't expected to find her home. I—"

"I kept her from school today," Olivia said crisply. "She wasn't feeling well. Tori—upstairs."

Tori hesitated, a deer caught in bright headlights. She seemed incapable of moving.

Rebecca regarded the child. She'd come here to learn if Tori had been inside her dad's moonshine shed. She believed she already had that answer now, given the yellow paint on the boots outside the door, and the Sorel tread that matched the prints in the shed. Plus, there was the hair, the small handprints. Her goal now was to learn whom Tori had been with, when exactly she'd been inside the shed, why she and her companion had fled, and what they might have witnessed.

"Take a seat," Cole said smoothly, but his eyes had turned grave. "This is Dave Brannigan, our ranch hand." He motioned to Tori's chess partner. "He's the one who alerted everyone to the blaze and got the volunteers out there."

The ranch hand rose and shook Rebecca's hand.

"Dave, good to meet you," she said. "And thank you."

"Call me Brannigan. Everyone does. I wish there was more we could have done. But the fire was so fully engaged all we could do is wait for the pumper truck to come from Clinton. It's been devastating to us all. I can't imagine your sense of loss."

"I really appreciate your efforts, truly," Rebecca said, suddenly sideswiped by emotion again. This grief thing was a roller coaster.

Brannigan dug his hands deep into the front pockets of his pants. "Was there something suspicious about the fire, then? I thought the investigator said it was accidental, caused by a toppled lantern, but I heard around town you had some concerns."

Small towns. I need to be more careful.

"Just trying to piece it all together as my own way of coping." Rebecca cleared her throat.

"Could you give us a moment?" Cole said to Brannigan.

"No worries. I . . . I was about to go help Roshan with that load of laundry, anyway." He nodded to Rebecca. "I really am sorry. If there's anything we can do—"

"Thank you."

"Please, sit," Cole said again, taking a seat on the sofa near the fire. His was a casual but commanding presence. Not unlike the Myron McDonough Rebecca remembered from her youth.

"Tori, take a seat," Cole said firmly.

Olivia's gaze flared to Cole. He gave her a loaded look.

She moistened her lips, and she and Tori seated themselves side by side on the large ottoman. Ace was already snoring on the faded Persian rug in front of the hearth. Rebecca and Ash followed suit, taking seats next to each other on a sofa.

"Tori," Cole said, "you know Ash, right?"

Tori nodded, looked down, fiddled with her fingers.

"And this is Becca North. Noah's daughter. She's also a cop."

Tori went rigor mortis rigid, still looking down, hands clenched now.

"Becca, what did you want to ask Tori about?" Cole prompted.

Rebecca leaned forward. She measured her tone, keeping it gentle.

"Tori, could you tell us about the snowmobile tracks that led from my father's cabin to this lodge? Ash here is an expert tracker, and he can tell from snow and weather conditions that those tracks were made right around the time the blaze broke out." Rebecca paused, watching the child, who seemed as though she might faint.

"Ash can also tell that two small people—kids—came fleeing out of my dad's moonshine shed. They went to my dad's kitchen door. Then they ran up the bank behind the cabin. They fell a few times in deep snow while running through the aspens that grow on top of the esker ridge behind my dad's cabin, and then they jumped onto a snowmobile that drove right here, to this door." She was fudging it, but only slightly, for reaction.

She got none. Tori remained frozen, refusing to meet her eyes.

Olivia, however, paled visibly.

"So you *are* treating the fire as suspicious now?" she said.

"So far there's been no evidence to indicate arson," Rebecca said. "Or anything other than death by a self-inflicted gunshot wound. But I do have some questions, like who was in my dad's shed with Tori around the time of the fire, and why Tori and her friend fled." Rebecca hesitated, feeling bad for the kid. "Thing is, Tori, I *need* to know exactly what happened to my dad. And I believe you or your friend might have seen something that could help me." She paused for several beats. "I *can* prove it was you in that shed. But it would really be much easier if you just told us what you saw."

Tori's gaze flared up to Rebecca. "I wasn't there!" Her cheeks flushed dark red. "I was not in there! I didn't see anything!"

Olivia placed her hand on Tori's knee.

Rebecca reached into her pocket and took out her cell phone followed by three brown envelopes. She placed them all on the coffee table in front of her.

"In this envelope here"—Rebecca placed her hand on one—"there are some strands of long, dark, wavy hair. It looks like your hair, Tori. And we have technology that can prove these things." Rebecca touched the second envelope, the one with a bulge.

"And in this envelope is a padlock that was picked to gain access to the moonshine shed." Rebecca picked up the third envelope. She held it open so Tori could see inside. "And this in here is a bone pocketknife I believe was used to open the lock."

Tori swallowed. Ash leaned forward to see the knife inside the envelope. Rebecca felt him tense beside her at the sight of the translucent handle.

"Do you recognize this knife, Tori?"

"No." The denial came too fast, without Tori even looking. The kid began to rock slightly, clutching her knees. "I wasn't there."

"Forensic science is good at matching tool marks to metal, so we can probably prove it either way," Rebecca said. "I also have these."

She picked up her phone and selected from her photo app a clear image of one of the boot prints in the dried, yellow paint. She showed it to Tori, then to Olivia. Cole leaned over to see it, too. He exchanged a glance with Olivia.

"The paint matches the paint on your boots that were outside the front door, Tori. And the Sorel tread is also a match. So is the size of the prints."

She swiped to the next pic. "And this—" She showed Tori, then Olivia, an image of the handprints. "They're called patent prints when pressed into a medium like this paint and easily visible. Every human has uniquely individual patterns of ridges on their hands and fingers that can be matched to prints like these." Another pause. "Thing is, everywhere someone goes, they leave a trace. It might not be immediately visible to the naked eye, but those who are trained know what to look for. Science can prove you were there, Tori. It's called Locard's exchange principle."

Tori's gaze shot like a bullet to a set of framed photographs on the wall near the bar.

Rebecca followed her gaze. Tori appeared fixated by a large portrait-style image of a Mountie in full regalia. And bang, it hit her. The kid already knew about Locard's principle. Her adoptive father, Sergeant Gage Burton, had worked as a top homicide detective. Tori was no stranger to the basics of forensic science. And that was a portrait of Gage Burton.

Rebecca came to her feet and went over to study the portrait, along with smaller images that had been hung around the focal piece.

The smaller studies all showed scenes from Sergeant Gage Burton's full regimental funeral—RCMP members in "review order" dress of traditional red serge with Stetsons and Sam Browne belts, medals and mourning ribbons. The traditional eight bearers carrying the casket in procession, followed by a sea of officers in red. A firing party discharging three rounds of blanks in the classic salute at the graveside. And a haunting image of Tori seated and being presented with a perfectly folded Canadian flag in her adoptive father's honor. Olivia's German shepherd sat alert at Tori's boots. Olivia and Cole were seated on either side of the child. Another image showed a Mountie playing pipes in swirling mist.

Emotion balled in Rebecca's throat. She thought of Ash's photo of her own father in his review order uniform—the pride in her dad's expression, in his stance. And it suddenly pained her intensely that he'd died in the ignoble way he had.

That he'd never be buried with full military honors like Sergeant Gage Burton had. A ferocity exploded in Rebecca's chest.

She was going to prove it—that her dad had *not* taken his own life. She was going to prove without a doubt that he had perished in pursuit of a cold case, one that he had never given up. That he had, in effect, been killed in the line of doing his duty. And damned if she wasn't going to give him a memorial ceremony that he would be proud of. A hero's send-off. Because he *was* a hero in her eyes, even if she'd never told him. And bagpipes—she would hire a pipe player. She remembered clearly how the strains of "Amazing Grace" played by a solitary piper had once moved her father to tears.

She sucked in a deep, shaky breath, almost afraid now to look around and face the room. Afraid they'd all see the rawness of her love for her dad. Her vulnerability. Her pain.

Still facing the portrait of Gage Burton, Rebecca said carefully, "Is this your father, Tori?"

Silence.

Rebecca turned. "It looks like a truly beautiful ceremony. You must be so proud."

Tori's lip wobbled.

Rebecca returned to take her seat next to Ash. "I wish my father could also have a service he would be proud of. He was a Mountie, like your dad."

"Gage wasn't really my dad," she mumbled.

"Of course he was. There are many different ways to be a parent, or a child."

Tori stared at her.

"I'd like to know if my father shot himself, or if he died in pursuit of some case that he was working on. Sort of like in the line of duty." Rebecca cleared her throat. "My father can never have a full regimental funeral like Sergeant Gage Burton did, but I'd like to honor him in a way that he would be proud of, and part of that will be to find out exactly how and why he died."

Olivia and Cole exchanged a sharp glance.

"I wasn't there," Tori said softly, tears leaking out of the corners of her eyes.

Rebecca nodded. "It's tough to lose a parent at your age. I know because I lost my mom when I was twelve. She died of cancer suddenly, and I think it changed me forever. And now that my dad has also gone, my biggest regret—because we always have regrets about people in our lives—is that I didn't come home often enough, and I didn't tell him I loved him. I . . ." Her voice caught on the huskiness of emotion. "I didn't hug him enough. Or realize he was lonely and maybe struggling, too."

Ash placed his hand on her knee. Warm. Comforting. And Rebecca did not push it away. Instead, almost reflexively, needing his comfort on some subliminal level, she covered his hand with her own. A silent thank-you.

"I'm not blaming anyone for anything, Tori," Rebecca said softly. "I know you were there. I just want to know what you saw."

Tori lurched up. "I *wasn't* there!"

"Who was with you?"

The kid began to shake, her face as white as a ghost. "No one. I told you. No one. I wasn't there."

Olivia shot to her feet. "You need to leave. You're upsetting my daughter."

"Liv," Cole said.

"No, Cole, they need to leave. Now. If they do have any more questions for Tori, they can come back with official warrants or something. Tori, go upstairs. At once." Olivia regarded Rebecca, her eyes crackling with ferocity. "I'm not having her go through this. Not now. Not after everything she's been through. Please, leave."

They got up.

But as they took their leave, Rebecca held back and said quietly to Olivia, "I know you want to protect her. I understand that. Really, I do. But if Tori was there, hiding from it is not the best way to handle it. There is evidence. You need to help her find a way to come forward with this."

Olivia did not reply. Mouth set in a firm and resolute line, she simply waited in silence for Rebecca and Ash to exit. She shut the door behind them with a firm click.

CHAPTER 24

Rebecca grabbed her helmet off Ash's snowmobile seat and raised it to put on her head. Ash stopped her by placing his hand on her arm.

"You okay?" he said.

"No, I am not okay," she snapped. Wind gusted hair across her face.

"I know what you're going through, Becca. I know, grief is—"

"You know shit. Really, Ash . . . he . . . my dad . . . he might have been working a case that he had never been able to solve back in the day, when a desperate mother came to him and said, *Where is my daughter?* It bugged him. All these years. It might have been one of the million little things that made him sad with his life, that made him tell people in the pub he felt like a failure. My mother left him in death. He struggled to raise me on his own, to make me feel okay about things, but I just hurt at the time, so badly that I didn't *see* my father. I didn't understand the man—the real person he was deep down inside. The boy he once was, the dreams he might have still had. I didn't think how terribly he had to have been hurting, too, because he always put a smile on his face, for me, and—" She turned away, blinking tears into the blades of icy wind coming off the lake as she struggled to marshal her emotions.

"And now . . . this . . . an ignoble death—"

"You can't say that about suicide. It's—"

"It's not what happened! He *didn't* take his own life—I won't believe it. He was shot—it had to have been staged. Then he and his case evidence were burned in a fire. All alone in his little cabin. Afraid. No military honors. No brotherhood of cops in red serge to bear his casket. I—" She looked up at the sky, as if gravity might hold back the tears. She heaved out a chestful of air in a cloud of condensation. "I never came home because of you, Ash."

She met his gaze.

"Because of you and what happened with Whitney. And now he's dead. He's gone. And it *still* looks like it's all about you and Whitney. And me. And it killed him. Somehow it ended his life."

"Hey." He took her hand. "That's not—"

"Don't." She shook herself free of his hold. "Do not tell me I'm not being fair. It's the bottom line. You know it. I know it. I—"

Ash grasped hold of her by the shoulders and forcibly pulled her to him. He wrapped his big arms around her and held tight. So tight. Just held as the wind gusted around them. And he did it because he knew that they'd crossed a line already when he'd placed his hand on her knee, and she'd allowed it. And she'd covered it with her own.

Ash could see that everything that hurt Rebecca about her father somehow revolved around him. And the fact that she still clearly cared about him. And probably always had. And she didn't know what to do about it because this thing that had driven them apart was now forcing them together to solve the mystery of her father's murder, and it came with a mushrooming sense of doom. Because Rebecca also knew in her heart that Ash was still keeping something fundamental from her. And when she learned what it was, it would probably break her in two all over again.

Because the past writes the present, and the present writes the future, and sometimes the loop just cannot be broken.

"It's okay," he said, his rough-stubbled cheek pressing against hers in the cold. He stroked her hair. "It's going to be okay."

Rebecca leaned in to him, and she wished it were true. But deep down she knew nothing about this could end well.

———

Olivia watched them from the window. Ash comforting Rebecca. Anger, anxiety thumped through her chest.

Ever since she'd escaped depraved captivity—after enduring every dehumanizing thing that bastard sadist Eugene George had thrown at her—she had *not* allowed herself to be labeled, to carry the banner of a victim, to be shamed as something disgusting and tainted and broken. Her own family had tried to force her into that role, shunning her. Her own husband—once she'd returned home—would no longer touch her. She'd almost cracked. Almost killed herself. But she'd found Ace. And she had pulled herself up by her own bootstraps and left town. And changed her name. And then she'd found this ranch, and Myron McDonough, who gave her a job that allowed her to keep her dog with her at all times. Which in turn had led her to find a wonderful man in Myron's son, Cole. And then she'd gotten her child back.

She now refused to let her child be labeled. She'd be a mother cougar. She'd show her daughter a female role model in the face of social adversity. Damned if Tori would feel compelled to leave this town—assumed to be bad blood because of her father.

If Tori had been inside that shed, Olivia would find a way to allow Tori to tell her about it on her own terms, when she was ready.

Cole came up to her side as Ash and Rebecca finally departed on the snowmobile. He placed his hand on her shoulder.

"First thing they jump to is the serial killer's kid," Olivia said, watching them disappear into a cloud of dry snow blowing off the lake.

"Easy, Liv. First thing Rebecca jumped to was tracks that led here. Complete with all the other evidence she mentioned."

Silence.

"She has her own grief," Cole said. "You saw what happened to her when she looked at those photos of Gage's funeral."

"She came down too hard on Tori. That's not fair. I should have stepped in earlier."

"You're not thinking straight right now. You're knee-jerk wanting to protect something you thought you'd lost twelve years ago. And that you can't bear losing again." Cole glanced over his shoulder to ensure that Tori was out of earshot, and he said quietly near Olivia's ear, "You *know* something happened with Tori that night. We *both* know she was with Ricky right before the cabin fire." A pause. "We need to figure out how to handle this proactively before there's an official investigation and uniformed officers come banging on our door because *we* didn't do right by either Tori or Noah."

She swung to face him. "You think it wasn't an accident? You really think Tori was involved?" Her fear was raw and real. "You think she saw something?"

You think she has her father's bad blood in her veins?

"You said she's been having nightmares, Liv. There's the moonshine bottle you found in her room."

Olivia dragged her hands over her hair. "I never want to consider that her father's genes might drive her, too, one day. Never. And that's what's happening here, Cole. I'm being forced to doubt, to question the unquestionable."

"Go upstairs, try to talk to her again."

Olivia made her way upstairs. Tori's door was closed. She hesitated outside, then knocked gently.

"Tori?"

"Go away," came the muffled voice inside.

"Tori, I need to speak to you."

Silence.

She tried the knob. Relief sliced through her—it wasn't locked. Small, small steps. She sucked in a deep breath and measured her voice. "I'm coming in, okay?"

Silence.

She entered.

Tori was on the carpet at the foot of her bed, balled up around Ace. She looked up, and Olivia saw that she'd been crying into Ace's fur. Her heart clutched. She knew exactly what that felt like, what solace a dog could offer.

She sat on the floor next to them, stroked Ace. "They have evidence you were there, Tori."

A sniffle.

"And I do know you had a bottle of Noah's moonshine."

Tori's body stiffened.

"And we know you were with Ricky on his snowmobile, and that you came home just after the fire had broken out, and that ever since you've been deeply upset and worried about something, and not sleeping well."

Silence.

"Talk to me, Tori. Let me help you before this goes too wrong. But in order to help, I do need to know the whole story. Why did you flee? What did you and Ricky see that night?"

"I . . . I wasn't there. I wasn't." Her voice was thick with emotion. "It's all lies." Tears sheened down her cheeks. She stuck her face back into Ace's fur. "It's not true," she mumbled into the dog. "It *can't* be true. It's all lies."

———

After Olivia had left her bedroom, Tori sat there holding Ace for a long time. She was going to throw up, she was certain of it. She didn't know what to do. Ricky would be taken away. Forever. And if she confessed that she'd been the one inside Noah's shed stealing from him, and that she'd gone into his house and started that fire and then had run away without helping, would she also have to go into some system like Ricky? Would they take her away, too?

She was scared. Really scared. She was not a bad kid. She *wanted* to confide in Olivia. She felt terrible for the cop woman—Becca—losing her own dad. She hadn't thought of the old man having a daughter. Or being a proper RCMP officer like Gage. Or that he should also have some honor at his memorial service with Mounties in red serge, and maybe Becca should also get a folded flag.

Tori knew exactly what it felt like to lose a father she loved with all her heart. And she'd grown up with other detectives and beat cops around the house—Tori's default was to trust law enforcement officers. Because cops put away bad guys. Like her dad had. Like he'd hunted down Eugene George even when no one believed he was still out there. But she also loved Ricky. He was everything. Was Ricky a bad guy?

She rocked, hugging her knees. It wasn't so simple, was it? Good and bad. She'd always thought it was so simple.

She missed Melody, her adoptive mom. Missed her like a hole was in the place of her heart. Because Melody would have answers for things like this. Melody always did.

THE GUARDIAN

Cariboo Country. Eighteen months ago.

Ash sits side by side with Running Wind Simon atop a mesa. The valley and lakes below have been carved smooth by glaciers. From this vantage point, Ash can sense the curvature of the earth, the endlessness of space.

But it's the sense of time that Ash always feels most acutely up here. Time and timelessness. How men are like little ants on the crust of the earth, busying themselves with all that is so important, but their lives and industry are just a blink in geological time, really. Borrowed time at that. Mother Earth has only to shrug a shoulder in her sleep, and all the little men and houses go tumbling and scattering, and the men go fleeing for safer sanctuary.

As he and Running Wind contemplate the vista below, there is a sense of utter peace—not a word passes between them.

Running Wind whittles a piece of silver birch. The rhythmic movement of the blade is meditative. He uses a pocketknife crafted of translucent bone inlaid with a tiny gold horse's head. The knife has several fold-out tools, including a hoof pick.

Ash watches his hands. His skin is walnut brown. His black hair is long and shot through with strands of silver. His nose is patrician. Like an eagle's beak. The ledge of his brow is prominent over deep-set eyes.

Despite his age, the man shows few wrinkles, yet his years of knowledge and sorrows and joys show in his eyes. And the whites of the old man's eyes are yellow these days.

Ash feels time slipping away.

The sun starts to set, and the change in temperature stirs a breeze.

"Snow will fly soon," Running Wind says without looking at Ash.

Ash nods. He's growing impatient waiting for the reason Running Wind has invited him to climb up here this evening. But he's learned not to rush the old man or get hung up on his methods of delivering information.

Ash and Running Wind have shared a bond ever since Ash encountered the First Nations trapper working one of his lines in the forest. Ash was eleven that day. He'd stuffed his little duffel bag full with clothes, some comics, sandwiches, and he was off to live alone in the wild, he told Running Wind.

The trapper just nodded. He didn't stop him, or try to turn Ash around. Or even ask where he was going.

Feeling scared and a bit lost at that point, Ash followed the trapper as he worked his line and field-dressed and skinned his catches. At night the trapper slept under the trees without shelter, but he did not allow Ash to sleep too close by. Nor did he offer the young Ash any of his food. And when Ash's sandwiches ran out and his clothes grew wet and the weather turned colder, Ash asked for some food.

Running Wind told him to go hunt for some. Because that's what people who live in the wilderness need to do, he said. He explained that if Ash really wanted to run away from home, he should plan better, learn some skills, be better prepared. The wilderness did not tolerate a boy unprepared, he said. And if Ash really wanted to go on a vision quest and become a real man, Running Wind said, then he not only had to learn the language of the wild, but he would have to ready his mind. And only then would he be able to hunt the great bear.

In the end, survival instinct got the better of eleven-year-old Ash, and he found his way home. But after that encounter he regularly sought out the mysterious Running Wind and went trapping and hunting with him. It was Running Wind Simon who taught Ash how to watch and listen and talk to the wilderness. And to track. He became an expert tracker of both animal and man.

Running Wind dusts shavings off his birch stick. "That scar, Asbjorn"—he hasn't called Ash by his full name since the time in the woods when he was eleven—"you could have had surgery, tidied it up a bit, hid it better."

Tension tightens through Ash.

"Yet you haven't. You choose to wear it like the mark of the young warrior who faced down the great bear. Like you face bears for a living now."

Ash laughs. But it sounds hollow. Anxiety whispers. He picks up a small pebble, throws it down the ridge. It clatters and clacks its way down. He throws another stone after it, this time with increased urgency.

"Why do you hunt predators—the bears and big cats and wolves? Why do you need to keep the ranchers' calves and lambs safe at night, Haugen?"

Silence. Tension winds tighter. Ash feels as if black ink is leaking between the separate boxes in his mind.

Running Wind looks at him. "Why do you wear that scar?"

He throws one more stone. Hard. It clicks and clacks and sets a small avalanche of stones and gravel skittering below.

"To remember? Like a brand of punishment? A label? Like a brand of ownership on a cow—showing you're owned by a deed of your past? Or because it proves you can conquer the bear?"

Goddamn him and his riddles, his metaphors. Ash surges to his feet before the boxes and compartments in his brain can collapse and ooze together into a black and toxic morass that will mess with his head and with his ability to control his life.

"Sit," Running Wind orders.

Ash blinks at his tone.

"I have something to ask of you. I need your help. With my grandson."

Surprise washes through Ash.

"Ricky?" he says.

"Sit."

Ash reseats himself cautiously.

Running Wind points his birch stick at Ash's face. "I don't want Ricky to wear a label like you wear that scar, Asbjorn. I need you to watch over him for me. Ricky is going to be thirteen next winter. A rough patch lies ahead. I've gotten him into that restorative justice program. But . . . it's a fine line now. That cusp between youth and adulthood. The people in his neighborhood . . . They have a strong influence. He has another strike, he's out. He's going to end up far from home behind concrete walls and razor wire with the big bad boys, and it's going to be over. Like it was with his father. But if we can keep him on track for a few years . . ." His voice fades.

"What's this about?"

Running Wind breaks eye contact and stares out over the eskers and lakes toward the white mountains beyond. Quietly he says, "I think you know what it's about, Asbjorn."

Ash's pulse beats faster. He studies Running Wind's profile. The aggressive angle of his nose, the sharp ledge of his brow. Wide mouth. Skin the color of polished walnut. And he does know. The time is close. Running Wind is about to die.

"You've got family," Ash says. "Other friends."

"I also think you know why I need it to be you."

Because Running Wind once looked into the eyes of an eleven-year-old boy and saw a truth no one else had seen. Or one they'd refused to see because it was too uncomfortable. Because if they acknowledged the truth, they might then have to confront their own dark faces in the mirror, and see monsters looking back into their eyes.

A sick, bitter taste fills his mouth at these thoughts. All he can say to Running Wind is, "Yeah."

"Yeah?"

"I'll look out for him."

Running Wind studies his eyes.

"I will. I vow it. I'll see Ricky through that rough patch. I'll die on that hill for you, okay?"

Running Wind's old and yellowed eyes crinkle at the edges as he smiles.

He points his white birch stick out over the sweeping valley. "Once that whole valley was sage scrub. Nothing more. Until one little beaver dammed a small stream." Silence. Wind rustles through autumn grasses. "A small act," he says quietly, "that reshaped the future." He looks at Ash. "The past doesn't always have to write the future."

———

Ash receives a call two weeks after the day he met with Running Wind atop the mesa. The remains of his old mentor have been found in fresh snow in a remote part of the woods along one of Running Wind's traditional traplines.

It appears the old trapper passed just three days after asking Ash to watch over his grandson, but his remains were only discovered ten days later.

He was found by a hunter who noticed corvids and eagles circling high above a clearing. Wolves had been at his body, as had foxes, martens, birds, rodents, and other smaller creatures. There was not much left of him. Running Wind would have thought this fitting—being quietly recycled and fed back into the animals and forest and the ground of his people.

He'd slipped away with the peace of knowing Ash's promise was ironclad. It was the best Running Wind could do for Ricky Simon.

Now it was up to Ash.

CHAPTER 25

"Do you know anyone who smokes these?" Rebecca placed a packet of Denali Plain cigarettes on the coffee table.

Opposite her sat Clive Dodd in his wheelchair, linked to his portable oxygen machine, small tubes creeping around his wrinkled cheeks and feeding into his nostrils. Ash had driven her into town after they'd returned to Haugen Ranch and picked up the truck and Kibu. Rebecca needed to buy some clothes. She wanted a hot shower. She wanted to call Lance and ground herself. She needed some distance from Ash in order to clearly formulate her next steps.

Being in his presence—the way his aura sucked her in—had thrown her way too far off center. She had to step away and recalibrate.

But as they'd approached PetroGas, she'd asked him to pull into the convenience store first. She'd bought the cigarettes, and they'd gone around the gas station to the back lane and found Dodd's house, allegedly her father's original destination on that fateful afternoon before Ash stepped in and took him home.

Outside Dodd's frosted windows the winter shadows had already grown long and dark. A bone-chilling wind howled from the north, rattling at his shutters, lifting crystals off snow in clouds and skittering debris along sidewalks, making Clinton resemble a ghost town where instead of heat and tumbleweed, there was cold and ice.

Ash sat on an overstuffed chair beside her with Kibu at his feet. Rebecca felt his eyes on her. She felt the weight of his thoughts. She forced her focus back onto Dodd, onto the reason she was here. Her dad.

"Oh, you are cruel, Rebecca North," Dodd said as he gazed upon the blue packet of cigarettes emblazoned with health warnings. He opened his mouth to speak again, but hacked and wheezed instead. He dabbed the corners of his mouth with a handkerchief, and Rebecca noticed his nicotine-stained fingers.

Dodd gave a weak smile. "Denali Plain used to be my pack-a-day vice." Another spasm of coughing. "And look at me now. Emphysema. Lungs are shot. You really are awful tempting me like that."

"But you still sneak one, right? I mean, maybe once in a while?" she prompted. "Maybe my dad occasionally bought them for you when he came over?"

He laughed, then dissolved into another bout of wheezing that tensed both Rebecca and Ash. Spittle frothed at the corners of his mouth. He wadded his handkerchief to his lips while a spark of mirth still fought its way into his rheumy eyes. For a brief moment Rebecca glimpsed an echo of the man Clive Dodd had once been.

"Maybe." He raised an index finger and wagged it at her. "But if you tell Thora, I shall have to kill you."

"Who is Thora?"

"Thoraline Battersby? My home care nurse—bloody tyrant. You know the movie *One Flew Over the Cuckoo's Nest*? Well, she's Nurse Ratched. Used to work at the Clinton health-care center before retiring, then, like most of us, had to return to work part-time in order to make the ends of her pension meet. Works for a home care outfit now. In her late sixties and she's still cracking the whip on us old men. You don't remember her?"

"I . . . Maybe." Rebecca racked her brain but couldn't place the woman. She glanced at Ash. "Do you?"

"I know who she is," he said with a suddenly shuttered look that gave Rebecca a moment's pause. She filed it and made a mental note to circle back later.

"Yeah, well," Dodd said, "I always maintained you were one of the lucky ones, Beccy. You got outta Dodge. Place is getting smaller, going downhill faster than ever now. People selling land out to the Germans, foreign investors, the Chinese, numbered companies from the Lower Mainland, that's who's buying up the place. And you think they come and spend their money in town? Not a snowball's chance. Small businesses are dying. Even got refugees running the old store over at the gas station now. Next thing there'll be ranchers wearing bloody turbans. Not the same. Us old folk are being displaced before we've got one toe in the grave, I tell you. Every time your dad bemoaned your absence, I told him you—you were smart, one of the lucky ones. It was good that you got away." He fell silent a moment, apart from his wheezing.

"But he missed you, Becs. He sure as hell missed you." He faded into his own mind, a sadness taking hold and shaping his body. He nodded his head, as if agreeing with something he'd thought, or remembered. "You know, if Noah had one big regret in life, it was not earning your love."

"He has my love," Rebecca said crisply with a flick of a glance to Ash. "That's why I'm here now. And I'm not leaving until I'm done."

Clive Dodd dissolved into a paroxysm of coughing. Ash hurriedly poured him water from a jug on the table and handed him the glass. He drank with a trembling hand, then set his glass carefully down.

"God, I'm gonna miss Noah like all hell. Who else is going to come by here now apart from Ratched? Hah—" He reached for his water again, sipped. "Maybe I'll meet him down there soon enough, because I sure ain't going up to heaven." He stilled. "I'm sorry, Beccy. I'm so sorry. I really did believe I'd check out before he did."

She breathed in slowly. "When did you last see him, Clive?"

"Maybe two weeks ago."

"How did he seem?"

"You mean, did he seem like he was gonna go off and eat his gun? No bloody way. No."

"Were you expecting to see him the day he died?"

"That's the thing. I was. He'd called from the Moose and Horn. Sounded ramped up and right fussed about some case. He did that. Picked an old case, or it picked him, and it bored away at his old gray cells. And we'd brainstorm. Noah said he wanted to do that again, he needed input, he said, and I was pleased because his attention had been elsewhere of late, and I don't get out much, 'specially in the winter. So I waited and he never came. I waited some more, then thought, okay, so maybe he's passed out drunk somewhere again. But . . . then I heard the news."

"So he was going to bring you cigarettes?"

"Nah. Moonshine, yeah, but he didn't bring smokes." He eyed the packet. "You gonna leave me those?"

"I can't do that. Can I?"

He shrugged, opened his hands, palms up. Trembling. "Dying anyway, right? Figure I got maybe a few days or weeks or months left. If I had my druthers, I'd check out now. Like, where are my pleasures? *He went out doing what he loved*—I always liked hearing that when someone kicked the bucket. Bloody robs your dignity when you can't get around yourself."

She glanced at Ash. He shrugged. Rebecca hesitated, then slid the Denali Plain across the coffee table toward him.

"Oh, you are an angel." He leaned forward and reached out his shaking hand like an arthritic claw. He clasped the blue packet with government death warnings printed all over the packaging.

"I'll have to hide them from her," he said, clutching them close. "She confiscates them if she finds them. Bloody hypocrite. Probably confiscates mine so she doesn't have to buy her own." A laugh that degenerated into a cough. "Don't know what your father saw in her, honestly."

"My father? Thora?"

A look of surprise. Then a nod, as if it made perfect sense that she knew nothing about her own dad. "Noah was dating her. Thoraline *Ratched*."

Rebecca's heart kicked. She shot a look at Ash. He looked just as surprised.

"Just to be clear," she said, "you're saying that my father was seeing Thora Battersby, as in—"

"Dating. Yup. Your dad and her had a thing going for maybe four weeks now. He met her right here in my house. Noah had known her from way back when, of course, but at that time she was married. Then she and her husband left town for some years on contract work. But Thora returned after she was widowed, Lord knows why. Some places have a grip on people for no sensible reason."

The shocker zinged through Rebecca's brain, tilting everything she thought she knew sideways. Her dad was dating again? She'd never thought of him in that context—a man in need of a woman's love. A woman apart from her mother. Chastised, sad for her father, she said quietly, "How long had my father been excited about his new case, Clive?"

He pursed his lips while lovingly fingering his blue packet of Denali Plain. "Coupla weeks. Three or four."

"And he told you what case it was?"

"That missing-kids case from over twenty years ago. He'd learned something new about it."

"Did he say what?"

"Not a word. That's what he was coming to talk about that day."

CHAPTER 26

Ricky's little sister yelled to him from the small living room. "Ricky! Phone!"

He got off his bed and padded into the living room on socked feet.

"Your *girlfriend*," she teased, dangling the receiver just out of his reach.

He snatched the receiver from her.

"Yeah?" he said into the receiver.

"It's Tori," came a whisper so soft that he leaned forward as if it might help him hear better.

"Tori? You okay?"

"I need to see you—I really need to see you. I don't know what to do. They *know*."

Worry sparked through Ricky. He glanced at his sister. She was supposedly concentrating on a giant puzzle in front of the TV, but Ricky knew she was listening intently to his side of the conversation. Because she was his little sister. It was what she did.

Ricky's mother was busy making dinner in the kitchen with her new baby on her hip—the kid spawned by that drunk loser two trailers down. She'd taken one lover after another ever since his dad had gone and gotten himself beaten to death in prison. But this one worried Ricky. He'd struck Ricky in the face when he refused to put up with the asshole's shit.

He turned his back to the room, lowered his voice.

"Can you get out?"

"Yeah, I think. Maybe later, after dinner, when they go into the library."

"Meet me at the northwest end of the lake around eight thirty behind the barn, near the campsite entrance, can you do that? I'll be waiting for you there. We can go over to those abandoned cabins on the back end of Haugen Ranch. No one ever goes there. We can talk."

"Okay," she whispered.

"Dress warm, 'kay? It's friggin' freezing to death out there."

He hung up. In the tiny bedroom he shared with his little sister, Patience, Ricky geared up in his thermals. He carried his boots through the living room and put his finger to his lips when Patience saw him.

"Where ya going?" she whispered.

He was about to say, *None of your stupid business.* But as he looked at her little dark eyes peering at him above the puzzle pieces of Paris on the coffee table, something in his heart cracked. Patty was probably never going to see the Paris pictured in her puzzle. Her face was maturing, and life was about to get real tough. He was realizing that shit took care of you unless you took care of the shit and yourself in this world. And Patty . . . she needed someone, too. Maybe being Tori's friend and seeing into the girl world from a different angle was making him soft. Or hard. Depending on how you looked at it.

"I'm going to see a friend. Shh. Be good."

"What friend—Tori?"

"Yeah." He sat on the edge of the sofa and pulled on his boots.

"I like Tori."

"Me too," he whispered.

She smiled. He and his little sister shared a dad. Their father had been arrested for drug trafficking two days after Patience was born. Ricky never saw him again. But he could see the echoes of himself in Patty's face, in her dark and slanted eyes, her high cheekbones and dusky, smooth skin. Something surged inside Ricky. It was more a physical reaction than a thought. Like an urge. To protect her.

"You going to the old summer camp buildings?"

He frowned and gave her a fake-stern look. "Our secret, right?"

She nodded.

As he shrugged into his jacket and pulled on his balaclava, she whispered, "When you coming back?"

He grabbed his gloves. "None of your business. Be good."

Outside it was fully dark. It had been so for a while. Darkness usually fell around 4:00 p.m. this time of year. But tonight, because of the clear sky, the moon and stars painted everything with a blue-white glow. Bare tree fingers wagged in the wind. He smelled dope in the air. Probably that loser fuck of his mom's. All freaking losers here. Except Ricky didn't know how to get out. And he was scared. About what Tori had said.

In the carport he climbed onto his old sled, put on his helmet. Tense, he checked the shadows. He saw no one. He fired his engine, and it coughed and choked, then roared loud into the night with a cloud of fumes. His heart kicked with adrenaline. He shot a last glance at his little broken-down mobile home with its peeling siding and insulation paper sticking out and one window plasticked over because the pane had cracked. And he saw Patty's little face watching him.

He roared off into the night, bumping over ice and coughing blue smoke in white clouds into the dark. He made for the back trails that would take him through the woods, up into the higher elevation and ranches of Broken Bar country.

News traveled on the wind in places like these. News like there'd been two witnesses in Noah North's shed when the fire broke out. Kids. And that they'd fled on a snowmobile. One of the kids was Tori Burton, who did not have a sled. The other, it was figured by those doing figuring, was Ricky Simon. Because everyone who knew Ricky knew he had a crush on Tori.

The rumor on the wind was also that Noah's detective daughter had visited Tori at Broken Bar. Both Brannigan and Roshan knew this, and they knew what Rebecca North had said. Brannigan had told his mates at the pub, some of whom had tried to help fight Noah North's fire. Roshan had mentioned it to one of her friends, who had mentioned it to another.

Which was why he now sat in shadow on a snowmobile outside Ricky Simon's house.

He watched Ricky Simon roar off on his crappy old two-stroke engine sled, headlight beams bounding in the dark as he left a stinking wake of fumes.

He watched the headlights heading off over the back fields behind the trailer park, took another drag on his smoke, flicked the butt into the snow. He exhaled and pulled down the visor on his helmet. He'd been waiting in this tit-freezing cold for Ricky to leave on his machine. Had to happen at some point. The goal was to get the kid alone, in an isolated spot, and get him to have an accident. *Contain the damage.*

So far, from what people were saying, the kids were not talking. No one seemed to know what they had seen, or why they had fled. The key was to keep it that way.

He started his engine. It purred smooth and quiet. A nice juiced-up four-stroke sled with some serious power. He took off after the headlight beams, bouncing among trees up the back hills behind the trailer park village. It looked like the little Simon shit was going up into the old cross-country ski trails. Beyond which lay wilderness and

Broken Bar Ranch. Luck was shining with the moon tonight. If it all played his way, the little shit-ass was going to meet the serial-killer kid. Two birds. One stone.

———

The snowmobiler stopped on the ridge, in front of a line of marching spruce. He kept his lights off.

Down below, near the Broken Bar Lake campsite entrance, Ricky Simon sat on his sled, engine running, headlights on. The kid was waiting for something.

A little shadow with a flashlight came running out of the cover of the trees. *Tori Burton.*

He watched as the figure he believed was Tori straddled the snowmobile behind Ricky. The snowmobiler unzipped his jacket. He got out his phone. Cold bit into his hands as he took off his helmet and heavy gloves to place a call. There was reception in this area near the ranch. Lady Luck was with him on this frigid night.

The wind blew and he watched the moon shadows over the cold landscape as the phone rang.

"They're together. On the kid's sled," he said when the phone was picked up.

"Where?"

"Northwest end of Big Bar Lake. Looks like he's heading up to the south road. There's one way he's likely to head on the south road, and that's east. Nothing but wilderness the other way."

"Don't lose them. But stay back. Keep me posted. Coming in from the east."

The snowmobiler tucked the phone away and drew down his visor. He revved the engine, thinking how ironic it would be if those kids were heading into the abandoned summer camp area. Private property. But never used. Fucking ironic.

And disturbing, he thought as he came down the fall line of the bank. That old place was witched. She'd just fucking vanished there. Into clean air. Or she'd morphed into a fucking deer—that's what it had seemed like.

He'd always harbored a secret fear that she still lay there. Her dark bones. In wait. To rise.

To get them.

So it was with a tiny beading fear, a whisper of foreboding building in his chest, that he followed Ricky Simon, carefully holding back a steady distance, his headlights off, driving down the faintly moonlit track through the frozen white forest. Trees like guardians closing in and growing taller on either side.

It was like she was calling them all to her.

He shook the feeling. It was this weird-shit forest at night. It gave him the creeps.

CHAPTER 27

Ash pulled up outside the Cariboo Lodge. It was early afternoon and already the sky was sulky and dark. A torn banner flapped in the wind, and a small group of men huddled outside on the patio smoking under a heat lamp. Lights glowed yellow in the general store next door.

Clive Dodd had given them Thora Battersby's address. Ash and Becca had gone in search of Thora, but there'd been no one home at her apartment above the hardware store.

Becca sat for a moment staring at the general store windows. It was warm inside his GMC cab, and she appeared to be bracing herself to step out into the cold once more. She looked tired. His heart swelled. Grief was a tricky demon. Ash figured she was only just beginning to absorb the reality of her father's death. Trying to solve the mystery around it was serving as a way of escaping the pain, he reckoned. Keeping her busy. But her guilt over not being there for Noah was compounding things. The worst was probably yet to come.

She reached into the back, gathered up her things, and clasped the door handle.

"I'll let you know about the Silverado when Wes calls," he said. "Whether he can fix it or not. Either way I'll pick you up here tomorrow morning."

"There's no need, Ash. I still have the Prius rental parked out back."

"Those rentals don't come with proper snow tires."

"I'll get something else if and when I need to head onto unpaved roads."

His pulse quickened. He could feel her slipping away from him. They'd crossed a Rubicon back at Broken Bar Ranch. They'd touched each other. She'd allowed him to hold her, and now everything felt as delicate and tremulous as fine crystals, and he did not want to shatter things, because a tiny spark of hope now burned deep and secret in his belly.

"It's only a matter of time before Tori will talk," he said, shifting the subject, not quite ready to let her go. "I suspect Olivia and Cole just need to find a way to help her handle it. I'll head out there tomorrow, try to talk to Olivia again."

"Let me do that."

He held her gaze. She still didn't trust him.

"Ash, did you recognize that knife when I showed it to Tori?" she said suddenly.

His gut clenched. He hesitated a moment too long, and she saw it. "Looks like a Trappersfrost brand," he said. "Older kind."

"But you haven't seen it before, have you? You don't know who it belongs to?"

Shit.

"There are a lot like that out there, Becs. Various iterations over the years."

She regarded him steadily. Wind rocked the truck. Pressure built in his chest. He *had* to speak to Ricky before handing him over to Becca and the cops, had to get his side of the story. The kid would be toast if he went back into the system. Ash had no doubt after seeing that bone knife that Ricky had been with Tori in Noah's moonshine shed.

"Call me if you learn anything else." She opened the door.

"Becca—"

She turned.

Several conflicting options warred inside him.

"What is it?"

"I think I know who witnessed me taking Whitney to the bus stop that day."

She closed the door. She waited.

He rubbed the back of his neck, resisting.

"Ash?"

He cleared his throat. "Thora used to live with her husband, Jake Battersby, on the same street where Whitney used to live with her mother. Right across the road from each other."

She blinked. Her body went unnaturally still.

He broke eye contact and stared ahead through the windshield. He watched two people huddled in coats cross the street. They ran up the stairs to the warmth of the lodge. He took in a deep breath.

"That morning when I went to pick Whitney up to drive her to the bus stop, Jake was packing his truck for a stint up north on one of his logging-contract jobs. He saw me pull up outside Whitney's place, where she was waiting with her bags. It was early. Really quiet in the street. I put Whitney's suitcase in the back of my truck, and he saw her climbing into the cab. He waved at me, and I waved back. Then I drove to the bus stop. Presumably, given that Jake faced a long drive north, he'd have gone to the PetroGas to fill up. The gas station is diagonally across from where the Renegade Lines bus stop used to be in that undeveloped lot beside Dot's Donuts and Diner."

He glanced at her. Her eyes were narrowed, and the suspicion in them made his heart sink. He knew that by the time all the truth came out, the little spark of hope that burned in his gut would be long dead.

"Go on," she said, voice flat.

"Given that Clive Dodd said Noah only started dating Thora three or four weeks ago, I figure it had to have been her who told Noah about Jake having witnessed me that day. Heaven knows why, or how it might have come up between Noah and Thora." He inhaled deeply. "But it makes sense."

She appeared to search for words. But after a moment all she said was, "Right. I need to speak to her."

"Don't do it without me, okay?"

Her eyes flared hot now as her gaze locked with his.

"Please," he said. "Don't go anywhere, don't go interviewing anyone, without me. Not until we know if your truck was sabotaged. If it was a malicious act, whoever did it knew you would likely have died out there last night . . . It might not be safe."

"I'm a big girl, Ash. I know how to look after myself if I need to."

"Someone could have tried to kill you, Becca. They could try again."

She turned away, moistened her lips. Another blast of wind rocked the truck, and cold fingered in through cracks and crevices.

"I *want* to trust you, Ash. But I can't help feeling you're holding things back from me."

His face heated. He reached to touch her gloved hand, but she moved it away and opened the door. The wind grabbed the door, and she had to hold tight to it as she climbed out with her things.

Urgency slammed through Ash. He leaned over the passenger seat. "Becca, wait—"

She hesitated, looking into the cab. Wind, icy, swirled into the interior. Her eyes turned watery and her nose pinked.

"What?" she said.

"I . . . Tomorrow."

"What tomorrow?"

He wavered. It was so deeply personal, and it probably bore no relevance at all to Noah's death, and he could see that it would hurt her more profoundly than everything he'd hurt her with before. But it had come to a point where not telling Becca what else had happened between him and Whitney would probably be as damaging as telling her. Still, his whole being resisted. The idea of voicing it, bringing it out into the open, was painful for him—he'd kept it secret for the last twenty years.

"We'll talk tomorrow," he said.

She eyed him, then banged the heavy door shut. Through the frosted passenger window she held his gaze a moment longer, then turned and walked toward the general store.

Ash watched her hesitate outside the general store entrance, look up at the sign, then enter the establishment. The glass door swung shut behind her. He could see her inside, moving toward the clothing section.

Fuck. He dragged his hands over his hair.

This was not going to end well. No matter how he looked at it.

CHAPTER 28

Rebecca toweled off her hair as she stood in a lodge robe in front of her motel-room window. Frost feathered the panes, crystals multiplying upon crystals as she watched. A similar pattern of chill grew and spread through her chest as she looked down into the darkening main street.

The new gear she'd bought at the general store lay across the bed. She hadn't expected to find much in the way of fashion in the all-purpose outfitters that had stood on that street corner since she could remember. And she hadn't. But what she had bought would suffice—thermal underwear, neck tube, mitts, gloves, socks, fleece, hat, down jacket, and boots. She was after function and warmth at this point.

She tossed the towel over the back of the chair, cranked up the room heat, and began cutting the tags off the new garments.

She pulled on a pair of woolen socks that were thick and gray and trimmed at the top with a stripe of red, followed by a pair of lined Carhartt pants that felt stiff and clunky. Over a long-sleeved thermal top, she donned a fleece jacket. She blow-dried her hair, then packaged her dirty clothes in the bag provided for motel laundry. As she moved, she caught sight of herself in the mirror and did a sharp double take. The old Becca looked back at her. An echo of the kid she had once been. No makeup. Ranch clothes designed for outdoor work. It shook her. Feeling cast adrift suddenly, she reached for her phone and called Lance.

Hearing his voice would serve as a touchstone.

Rebecca returned to the window as the phone rang. She felt a smile curve her mouth as she pictured him in his high-end apartment, legal papers spread all over his desk and coffee table.

He answered. "Rebecca?"

Noise drowned out his voice—he was in a crowded, public space. He spoke louder. "Rebecca—hey, hang on a sec. It's loud in here. I'm going to find somewhere I can talk."

She waited while he went in search of a quieter location. Then she heard a single voice talking to him in the background. Female. Distinct. She recognized it. Heather Whitehall. A junior associate at his law firm.

He came back on. "Sorry about that. Got a bit of a celebration going. Firm won the case today."

She heard the woman again.

"I'll be right in," she heard him say quietly through what she presumed was his hand over his phone. A sort of sinking, distancing feeling unspooled inside her. She felt her link across the country thinning like a thread about to break.

"Was that Heather?" she asked.

A slight pause, but it was too long. And Rebecca knew. She knew in the way a woman who has been ignoring the signs for too long knows.

"Yeah. Yeah, we're all here," he said lightly. "So, I've been wondering how it's all going. You holding up? When will you be back? Set a date for the memorial service yet?"

She felt herself close up. As if her father's world—this landscape of her youth and her complicated feelings about it all—did not belong to him and his glib expressions of interest. The Becca part of

Rebecca—it was here. In the Cariboo. And it was reclaiming her. And Becca needed to do good by her dad. Atone. Alone.

"Not sure yet. There are some complications."

"Such as?"

"I . . . Just some things I need to look into. His death wasn't straightforward."

He detected the note in her mood. "Do you need me to come, Rebecca? Do you need—"

"No," she said, surprising herself with the sudden conviction she felt. She did *not* want Lance out here. "I'm fine. Really."

She heard Heather's voice again in the background. That familiar sensation of betrayal sank into her belly like a cold stone.

"I'll call when I have news, dates," she said crisply. "Congrats on the case."

"Rebecca—"

She hung up. Numbed. Distanced. Rebecca stood for a moment looking at her own reflection distorted in the frosted pane. It was darkening outside. Maybe inside herself, too.

Her on-off Lance was sleeping with another woman. She shouldn't be—wasn't—surprised. He'd asked for commitment, and she'd dragged her heels. And now the relationship she should have bothered to nourish was withering, and Lance was sending out feelers, seeking sustenance elsewhere. Rebecca was being shown the hard way, once again, that without care and attention, without proper love, things disintegrated. They withered and died.

She ran her hand over her hair. What was wrong with her? How had she gotten this way? Become incapable of fully committing?

But deep down she figured she knew.

Something had broken inside her that hot summer long ago. Perhaps it had broken even before that, when her mother left this world. When she was twelve. And she'd never been able to make herself vulnerable to that kind of pain again. Which was dumb. Other people had lost parents at a young age. And they'd been betrayed by young lovers who were also their best friends. They seemed fine.

She checked her watch. She needed food and figured she might get lucky and find Solly Meacham on duty at the bar.

Rebecca looped her hair back into a messy and still slightly damp bun and pulled on her new boots. She tucked her wallet and phone and key card into her jacket pockets and left her room. She made her way down toward the noise coming from the Moose and Horn.

She couldn't go back now—so she was going all the way to the end. She would solve this thing. She would bury her father in a way that would make him proud. And the clues forward could lie in the pub downstairs, where her father had hung out drinking the morning before he called her and then ended up dead with a gun in his mouth.

CHAPTER 29

Rebecca entered the Moose and Horn through dark wooden saloon doors. It was warm inside and smelled boozy, and was surprisingly busy—a hub of congeniality away from the bleak, dark, and frozen streets outside.

It had been renovated since she'd last been inside the old pub. A retro theme now dominated, with photographs of the gold rush and ranching pioneer days adorning the paneled walls. A long, copper-topped bar stretched the length of the room on one side.

A guy in his late twenties wearing a retro white shirt with a bow tie and suspenders worked the bar behind an antique-looking cash register.

Rebecca made her way toward the middle of the long bar counter. She drew up a stool and seated herself.

Behind the bar, above rows of bottles, faded color photographs depicted the more recent history of the town. She realized with a start that one image showed her father and mother and herself as a tiny baby at a town ceremony from days past. Her dad was in uniform. Her mother wore a pretty summer dress and balanced baby Rebecca on her hip.

Rebecca's heart quickened as she stared at the image. A part of her was here, in this bar, with the rest of the town's past. Even as she'd been trying to run from it.

The bartender came over and handed her a pub menu and list of drink specials.

"I'll be right with you," he said. Rebecca took the menu and turned on her seat to better survey the establishment.

From her vantage point she could see the entrance of the adjacent Red Steer Steakhouse. The loud clack of billiard balls, followed by cheers and laughter, pulled Rebecca's attention to a pool table near the rear of the establishment. A group of men was gathered around the table. With them was a statuesque Amazon of a woman sporting a bleached-blonde Mohawk. She wore tight-ass jeans and black biker boots. Rebecca watched as the woman leaned across the table, took careful aim, and hit her target. Cheers erupted again. The guy beside her placed his hand on her rump and whispered in her ear as he squeezed her ass. The woman threw back her head and laughed.

But as if sensing her scrutiny, the male stilled, turned. Rebecca was struck with a bolt of recognition.

Buck Johnstone.

Out of uniform.

Buck eyed her for a long moment. Those around him glanced her way to see what had snared his interest. Surprise whispered through Rebecca as she identified the ripped bald guy with Buck as the biker from the PetroGas convenience store. And she realized the other players were Wes Steele and Dave Brannigan plus a dark-haired male she didn't know. She nodded to the group.

Buck gave her an odd little two-finger salute, and Wes raised his beer bottle as if to say cheers. She wondered again about the damage to her dad's truck. They turned back to their game, but the men leaned closer as if in earnest conversation, and Buck must have said something about Rebecca, because the blonde turned to stare brazenly.

A strange coolness filtered through Rebecca. She felt like an outsider who was purposefully being isolated from the herd.

"Can I get you anything?" She jumped. It was the smooth voice of the barkeep. She turned on her stool to face the counter—she could still glimpse the pool-table guys in a mirror.

He smiled. "Didn't mean to startle you. New in town? Or just visiting?"

"Sort of old and back in town."

He grinned. She liked his face. Had she and her peers all appeared so young and fresh-faced and earnest once? She quickly scanned the menu and realized she was ravenous. "I'll have the moose burger with yam fries," she said. "And a Guinness."

For her dad. He used to like Guinness. Usually followed by a shot of whiskey.

"Is Solly on tonight?" she said as she handed back the menu.

"Yeah—you know Soll?" He drew stout from a tap.

Rebecca smiled and immediately felt better for it. "If you come from this town, you know Solly. Thanks," she said as he set the creamy-topped drink on a coaster in front of her.

"Soll!" he called through a hatch that led into the kitchen as he placed her meal order through.

She came out wearing a Moose and Horn apron over faded jeans, a western-style shirt, and a leather vest. She'd tucked the bottoms of her jeans into distressed cowboy boots.

Rebecca felt a sharp punch of familiarity. Solly Meacham was the same but different. She had about eight years on Rebecca, but she'd aged faster in appearance than Rebecca liked to believe she herself had. But wasn't it always like that? You saw yourself in the mirror daily, and came to accept the small changes over time. But someone who hadn't seen you in a long while registered the changes all at once, and it came as a shock. Soll had the weathered complexion of a smoker. Her once-thick, sandy-blonde hair looked dry and overprocessed and had been cut short.

Her smile, though, was huge.

"Well, shit me," she said, wiping her hands on her apron as she came over. "Look who's in my bar. Becca North! The prodigal daughter returned."

"Ouch," said Rebecca.

Solly laughed. The sound husky, warm.

"How you doing, Soll?" Rebecca said. Solly's mom had been all about nature and the moon and stars and had named her Solstice Summer. But she'd been called Solly as long as Rebecca had known her.

She looked Rebecca up and down, taking in the Carhartts and work gear, her hair scraped back in an untidy bun.

"Ha, well, look at you. You can take the girl outta cow town, but you can't take the ranch outta the girl, eh, Becs? And there I was thinking you were some slick big-city high-rise detective. What they call it? White-collar-crimes cop?"

Rebecca snorted. "Commercial crimes. But I guess this place has a way of reminding someone what they came from."

Solly's smile faded as the reason for Rebecca's return rose between them. "I am so sad about Noah, Becs. We all are. Shit, what a thing. You okay? Will you be organizing a memorial now? Because a couple of us were talking about doing something if you didn't . . ." Her face changed as she realized what she was saying. "I . . . God, I'm sorry. It's just that Ash had told some folk you were involved in some big trial that was in the national media and really busy testifying, and maybe you couldn't come, like legally, technically, I mean, if you'd been subpoenaed. At least not right away."

"Ash told you this?"

Soll looked like she'd stepped on a land mine. "He . . . I guess he kept up on you. I mean, he visited Noah a lot, and obviously Noah always spoke about what you were up to."

The barkeep brought her food. Solly looked relieved.

Rebecca had lost her appetite.

185

Another clack of scattering billiard balls sounded, and a cheer rose from the back. The musician ended his song, and a few patrons clapped. He started a k.d. lang number.

"I will be organizing a memorial once my dad's body is released."

"Problem?"

"Just . . . tying things up."

Solly frowned.

"Great photos," Rebecca said, taking a bite of her burger followed by a sip of stout to wash it down. "I see you even have one of me and my mom and dad up there."

Solly turned to look.

"Oh yeah, from that old July first parade." She nodded toward the photograph. "Can't believe how much more like your mom you're looking these days."

The notion blindsided Rebecca. Faded memories of her mother crowded suddenly into her mind, gaining life. Color. She had never thought of herself as resembling her mom. It imbued her with warmth and a sudden odd sense of belonging, of place.

"But yeah, I got prints made from the museum and archives society. Lewis's idea. He's been wanting to do it for years. Renovate with a history theme. And that there is still the poster from the movie *Hunt for the Wild*, based on Cole McDonough's book. That was some day. Myron sprang for beers and moose burgers, and he brought a DVD for us to watch and copies of the book for door prizes. We all watched on a big screen here in the bar." She met Rebecca's gaze. "Myron even invited your dad, can you picture it?" She laughed. "Lasted maybe thirty minutes before the two of them had a spat. A record, if there was one."

Rebecca couldn't help but smile. "How is Lewis doing?" she asked about Solly's husband. "Is he still so hands-on with the hotel, or has he stepped back a bit?"

Lewis used to manage the Cariboo Lodge Motel for his father, and Solstice Summer Hobson had been a waitress at the Red Steer back when Rebecca was in high school. It was how the two had met. At the time Lewis Meacham was considered a damn fine catch for easygoing Soll, who had been raised by her divorced mom in a run-down apartment in Devil's Butte. The Meacham family were huge cattle ranchers in the region and had been big money since the 1800s, when a Meacham forebear had struck gold on the Horsefly River. Lewis Meacham's dad had at one point owned half the businesses on Main Street, and he'd built the Cariboo Lodge. A micromanager and notoriously tightfisted even with his own kids, he'd finally passed it all on to Lewis and his younger brother, Mikey, when he died.

"Oh yeah, we both still like the dig-in, face-to-face management gig. Hell, look at me." She held her hands out to display her apron and gave a throaty chuckle. Rebecca noticed the packet of cigarettes in the apron pocket. "Lewis pretty much leaves Mikey to run the ranching side of the Meacham enterprise, but it's all in the family, one way or another. Your burger okay?"

"Yeah, just not very hungry." She picked at a yam fry. The Guinness was going to her head on an empty stomach and days of inadequate sleep—plus shock, grief, stress, and plenty of burgeoning feelings of guilt and inadequacy. Feeling slightly ill suddenly, Rebecca pushed aside her plate.

"Tell me about my dad, Soll. Buck said he was in here the morning of his death."

Solly reached for a cloth and wiped a spot she'd noticed on the counter. "Yeah. Noah never passed through town without stopping in here. On that day, he was at the door from opening."

"That was unusual, I presume?"

With the back of her wrist, Solly wiped a stray strand of hair from her brow and nodded to some patrons who'd come in rubbing their hands from the cold.

"Kinda." She hesitated. "Why don't we go sit in that booth over there? Quieter. Hey, Hank, bring me a coffee, will you?"

Rebecca took her beer and plate, and they moved into a small booth. A mug of coffee was placed in front of Solly. She sipped as Rebecca asked her questions.

"Did you speak to him that day?"

"Sure, yeah. I was doing inventory at the bar. He sat at the counter, watching TV. We chatted some."

"Did he say why he'd come into town that morning?"

"He said he'd driven super early to Cache Creek to see someone about a cold case he was investigating. He didn't say who, though. Or what the case was, but word around town was that he was looking into that old Whitney Gagnon and Trevor Beauchamp missing-persons thing, and I got a sense it was a woman he'd gone to see. But he was rattled, I think. The person he went to see had had a terrible accident the evening before. Hit black ice, it seems, on a bad stretch of that highway. Went over the canyon into the river."

Rebecca's pulse quickened. "Is this person all right? Did my dad say?"

"She died at the scene, apparently. Single-vehicle accident. No witnesses. Notoriously bad spot, that. Noah didn't know that she was dead until he got out there. So he came back and stopped in here, probably to calm his nerves or something, and then just got too far into his cups, as he usually did."

Energy coursed hot through Rebecca's veins. She recalled Dixie's words at the morgue.

Noah had publicly expressed dissatisfaction with his life . . . at the Moose and Horn pub. Over the last few months. This was revealed by police interviews. Patrons and friends reported him saying that he felt he'd been a failure as both a cop and a father.

"Did he seem depressed by what had happened?"

"On the contrary. He seemed . . . agitated, jumpy. Or . . . it could've just been a hangover, because he settled a bit after a couple of drinks." A pause. "He was a good guy, Becca. He just drank a helluva lot, and it was messing with his head, you know? Full of these weird theories, and worries, and always obsessed with some case that probably wasn't even a case to begin with."

Rebecca frowned, her mind racing as she watched Solly's face intently. Who might her father have gone to see in Cache Creek, and what did it have to do with his case? And why had he needed to drive out so early to speak to this person? A deeper, darker thread snaked through her questions.

He's been inside my cabin, took some papers from my case file . . . I think someone followed me home.

Was this Cache Creek person's death right before her father's visit a coincidence? Or something more sinister?

"So you told this to Buck?" Rebecca said. "About the Cache Creek witness."

"Yeah, sure." She took a sip from her mug. "But like I said, your dad was often weird about his projects and increasingly paranoid and confused about shit. And he ended up really out of it by noon that day. There's a bunch of people in town who said we all should have seen this coming. I guess we did. I'm just sorry I never did anything personally. But look at half the guys who come in here. I sell booze to them. Their lives revolve around that pleasure. What am I going to say? 'Hey, get your life together, buddy, and stop coming to spend your money here'?"

"Who else did he speak to in the Moose and Horn that morning?"

"Ah jeez, I don't recall who all was in and out. He spoke to anyone who came up to the bar."

"So everyone knew he was looking into the Whitney and Trevor mystery?"

"Pretty much. He'd asked me specifically about Whitney because she used to work here part-time in housekeeping. On weekends and over that last summer she was still in town."

"Specific questions?"

Solly made a moue and thought. "More like, did I remember seeing her much with Trevor over the summer before they left." Another pause. "Or if I'd seen her with any other guy. And he asked if I'd seen her with Ash specifically."

Rebecca inhaled slowly and nodded. "Anything else?"

"Questions like, had Whitney appeared worried about anyone in particular at the time. It was like he was sort of trying to get a picture of her life that year. He asked if she'd spoken to us about going to LA, and whether I'd gotten the sense at any point that there was something bad going on in her life."

"Was there anything you told him that piqued his interest?"

She snorted softly. "Twenty years is a long time ago, and I told him so. The only thing I can specifically recall from that year with respect to Whit was that she took some time off to go on one of those camping trips organized for problem youth. You know the ones started by Dr. Miller?"

Rebecca frowned. "I don't think so."

"Anyway, that was about it. Oh, and I did tell him I knew Whit had been seen with Ash at that biker bar up in Devil's Butte in the months before she and Trev left."

"Yeah," Rebecca said quietly. She knew all about that.

I wanted her gone.

It appeared that was the angle her father had been pursuing. Ash. But whether he'd found substance to it—that's what niggled at Rebecca.

"And yeah, I told Noah that Whit had started talking about going to LA. She'd said she could *finally* afford it. I didn't think she would just up and do it with Trev, though."

"What do you mean, afford it?"

A shrug. "Like I said, Becs, it was way back. Lewis and I had gotten married two years before, and my head was full of planning, building the new house. I wasn't focused on one of the housekeeping staff's boyfriend woes. That said, I do recall that for some reason I was under the impression she'd come into a fair bit of cash."

"Like how much?"

"Don't know. But quite a bit."

"She said 'cash,' like actual cash?"

"I really don't know. It could have been Trevor's money. He was always working on contracts up north, and in the oil sands. You can earn real big there. Plus, Trev dabbled in selling small-time recreational drugs, dope, that kind of thing. All I can say from the hotel perspective is one minute she was here, next she walked out and never came back to work. And then we heard she'd left her mom a note, and Trevor had told his friends he was leaving town."

"Which friends?"

"Jesus, this is like twenty years ago. I have no freaking idea."

While Solly was talking, Rebecca saw a party arriving for dinner in the restaurant area next door. She recognized Dixie among the group. The coroner was with her husband, a much older-looking Dr. Bob McCracken than Rebecca remembered. Dixie noticed her and gave a wave. Becca nodded, a sense of small-town claustrophobia closing around her. Everyone and everything here was knitted into a web, and it felt like it was tightening.

Solly glanced over her shoulder to see what had caught Rebecca's attention.

"Oh, I should go. McCracken's got a big birthday celebration happening, and we've got a special menu I want to oversee. You know he was elected mayor last year? Thank heavens Clayton Forbes was taken out of the picture. Forbes was arrested and charged with fraud right before Christmas. Will be a while till that case goes to trial, but he hasn't been seen around town since." She slid to the edge of her booth seat.

Rebecca's attention was still on the group entering the Red Steer Steakhouse. She was thinking how Bob McCracken had been their family doc, and how, as a kid, she hadn't liked him, although she couldn't say why.

"Is McCracken still practicing as a GP now that he's mayor?"

"Reduced his hours to a few patients. He's got a new doc working for his practice and some specialists who come in from time to time. Gone are the days where he was everyone's doc."

Solly made to get up, but hesitated. "You don't think Noah did it, do you—killed himself?"

A ripple of wariness brought Rebecca's focus back onto Solly. "What makes you say that?"

"Your questions. The scuttlebutt starting to go around." She nodded toward the pool-table group—they were busy leaving. "And those guys. Wes mentioned he towed Noah's truck, and that you appeared to be investigating the fire scene, had taped off the shed. Brannigan said you were at the Broken Bar Ranch asking about witnesses."

Cold tightened through Rebecca. It came with a hit of fear. The last thing she wanted was to put that kid in the spotlight, or in jeopardy. A sense of urgency began to tick inside her. She needed to be more careful.

She watched as Buck and his friends exited the bar. Solly got to her feet. "You going to be okay? Can I get Hank to bring you anything else?"

"Wait, Soll, one more question, please, quick. Did you know my father was in a relationship?"

"With Thora Battersby? Yeah. She's down at the end of the bar there, with Don Barton and Jerry Phibbs."

Rebecca shot a look across the room. A woman in her late sixties sat drinking wine with two men around the same age. The television screen in front of them was tuned to an ice hockey game. They all looked up and cheered as a player scored.

"*That's* Thora?"

Solly made a wry face. "A good drunk needs a good drinking buddy," she said gently. "Thora was Noah's."

CHAPTER 30

Ash drew up outside Ricky Simon's house, studded tires crunching on glinting ice. He killed the engine. Moon shadows stretched between derelict mobile homes, and crystals hung suspended in the air, forming eerie halos around lights. He noted Ricky's sled was gone from under the carport.

He got out of his truck, leaving Kibu curled on his sheepskin on the back seat. He made his way to the door. A piece of plastic taped over a window waved in the breeze like a ghost arm. Some creature scuttled under the porch, claws skittering on ice.

Ash shone his flashlight under the porch. Glass bottles winked in his beam. An animal growled, and his light caught the glow of eyes. A stray dog. He hoped it would find a warmer place for the night. He picked up a bottle, upended it, and shone his flashlight on the bottom. *NN/06-18*. It was the coding system Noah had used to date his batches of moonshine. *NN* for Noah North, plus the date he'd bottled the stuff.

This confirmed what Ash had already known. Ricky Simon stole hooch from Noah. Ash also knew that Running Wind Simon had given his grandson, Ricky, his old Trappersfrost knife before he went off into the wilderness to die. There was no doubt in Ash's mind that the kid had been inside that shed with Tori Burton around the time of the fire.

And instead of calling for help, alerting everyone to the blaze, Ricky and Tori had fled.

Ash figured he knew why, too. He heard Running Wind's words on the sibilant night breeze.

He has another strike, he's out. He's going to end up far from home behind concrete walls and razor wire with the big bad boys, and it's going to be over. Like it was with his father.

Ash's concern was that if Becca found hard evidence and brought in a provincial major crimes unit, Ricky would be taken in as a key witness, and this would be out of his hands. Not for a moment did he think Ricky had shot Noah. But the kid might have seen something, and information might help Ash ameliorate the situation with Becca before things spiraled out of control.

I vow it. I'll see Ricky through that rough patch. I'll die on that hill for you.

Ash clumped up the wooden steps and thumped his gloved fist against the peeling door.

The door opened, spilling yellow light into the night. Ricky's mother stood there, one hand on the door, the other on her hip. Dark hair hung in a ponytail down her back. Her eyes were bloodshot and unclear. His gaze went to the kitchen table behind her. A child sat in a high chair with a plastic bowl of orange-colored pasta. Orange ringed the baby's mouth like clown makeup gone wrong. On the table was another one of Noah's distinctive bottles. And a glass half-full of the contents. His heart tightened. Ricky's mother was drinking the hooch that Ricky stole. Rather than admonishing her kid, she was using him to feed her addictions. He cursed inwardly.

"Where's Ricky?" he asked her.

"Whaddya want him for?"

"Need to speak to him. It's urgent. Where'd he go?"

"Man, I don't know with that kid. Uses this place like a fucking hotel. Maybe he should quit school and get a job so he can pay rent at least."

Ash saw a young girl in the living room area. Patty. The kid was watching his exchange with her mother with intense dark eyes. Behind her a car-chase-and-gunfire scene played on the television screen.

"Can I ask Patty some questions?" Ash said. Ricky was close to his little sister—maybe Patty knew something her drunk mother had failed to notice in her addled state.

"Hey, fill your snow boots, ranchman. Come inside and close that door behind ya before we all go dying of cold on your account." She sauntered back into the kitchen, grabbed her glass, took a swig, and went to stir a pot of something bubbling on the stove.

Ash entered and shut the door. He took off his boots and went through to the tiny living room.

"Hey, Patty." He crouched down next to her. "Cool puzzle."

"Thanks."

"Is that the Eiffel Tower?"

"Uh-huh."

"You must have been busy on that for weeks."

A shy smile. "Just a few days. After school and stuff."

A pot banged in the kitchen, and Patty shot a nervous glance in that direction.

"You know where Ricky went, don't you?" He was fishing, but he had a gut sense she at least knew more than her mother.

"He got a phone call," she said quietly.

"From who?" Ash asked.

"I don't know." She stared at her puzzle.

"Patty, I know that you know. I can tell. It's okay, Ricky is not in trouble, never from me, you got that? I just need to tell him something."

She glanced toward the kitchen.

He reached out, moved a puzzle piece into place. "Bingo," he said.

She grinned. He waited until her mother moved behind the partial wall dividing the living room and the kitchen, out of view, and he said quietly, while moving another puzzle piece, "Do you know if he went to meet a friend? Like Tori, maybe?"

Her eyes flickered and her mouth firmed into a tight line, as if she were afraid the answer would pop right out without her bidding.

"I'll tell you something, Patty. You know your granddad asked me to watch over Ricky, right? Kinda like a big guardian angel out there."

She glanced up. Dark liquid eyes met Ash's gaze. She had Ricky's chiseled cheekbones and smooth skin. She was a beautiful little thing. What chance did she stand in a place like this? He thought of Whitney and felt remorse. Whitney's upbringing had not been dissimilar. And every young, testosterone-charged male in want of an easy fuck had fed right into her silent cry for attention. Whit had obliged and opened her legs because she'd been needy, and then she'd been labeled a slut. And she'd had to wear that label because the past wrote the present and the future. And Ash hated himself for feeding into that, too. It had lost him Becca. If there had been anything he could do to turn it around, atone fully, he would have done it a long, long time ago.

He lowered his voice. "And to tell you the truth, I think your big brother could be getting himself into trouble tonight. I need to make sure that doesn't happen," he said softly, moving another piece. Her gaze followed his fingers as he slotted a corner into the base of the Eiffel Tower. He had her attention.

"But I need to know where he went in order to keep my promise to Running Wind, and to keep Ricky out of trouble with the police, okay?"

Her eyes flared to his. She examined him, searching for sincerity, then nodded quickly. "He took the sled." Another sharp glance to the kitchen. He noticed bruises on the side of her neck. Anger rose hot in him. He told himself he'd come back here, keep an eye on this situation, too. Before she ended up a Whitney, bearing a label she would never shake.

"Is there a special place he likes to go meet Tori?"

"Patience!" came a screech from the kitchen. "Supper!"

Patty spoke quickly. "There . . . there's some abandoned summer camp buildings. They go there sometimes."

Ash felt a black chill. He swallowed. The back end of his own ranch? What sick, twisted irony was this? He never went there. He'd mentally fenced that section right off his acreage, and he'd allowed the ruins to be swallowed by forest.

"Thanks, Patty. You're a good kid." He dug out his wallet and extracted a twenty-buck note. He placed it on the table next to the puzzle. "Go get yourself something nice, okay? Shh." He put his finger to his lips. "This is between you and me."

Heart wrenched, he took his leave.

Ash and Kibu drove back up into ranch country. He guessed Ricky had headed up into the hills behind the trailer park, but he had to go the long way around in the truck. As he drove, he felt a dark sentience closing in like a suffocating, cold black smoke, as if a force outside of them all, some evil, were sucking them all back to one point in that hot wildfire summer where they would be forced to face it all again. Because it hadn't been done right the first time, and the wrong was festering.

CHAPTER 31

"Thora Battersby?" Rebecca said.

The woman looked around in surprise. Her complexion was flushed, eyes bright and slightly unfocused. The two men with her, Don Barton and Jerry Phibbs, fell silent. Thora looked Rebecca up and down. She was clearly tipsy, a full glass of white wine in front of her. A pack of Denali Plain lay on the counter between her wineglass and the men's beers. A Zippo lighter had been set atop the pack. Jerry Phibbs's fingers showed the yellowed stain of a heavy smoker. The cop in Rebecca quickly registered details. She wondered who in this rural town did *not* smoke.

"I'm Rebecca North, Noah's daughter."

"Oh my goodness, love, I should have recognized you from photos he had." Definitely tipsy. "I . . . This is Jerry and Don. They knew your father, too. We're all old friends."

Rebecca nodded. This woman did not come across as grieving a lost loved one.

"Could we have a word in private, maybe at that booth over there?" Rebecca motioned to where she'd left her beer and uneaten food, and where Solly's coffee mug still sat.

Thora exchanged a quick and unreadable glance with the men. "Sure, of course." She came down off her stool and swayed almost imperceptibly on her feet. She wore jeans, cowboy boots. Sweater. Thora grabbed her wine, but left the cigarettes with the men. She followed Rebecca to the booth.

They seated themselves, and Rebecca pushed the plate of food to one side.

"I'm sorry for your loss, Rebecca," Thora said as she got comfortable and took a quick gulp of wine.

"Likewise, Thora. I didn't know my father was seeing anyone."

Thora flicked a glance at the men. Nervous? Or perhaps just discomfited in the presence of her dead lover's daughter?

"Must have been an awful shock," Rebecca said.

"Killing himself like that? God, yes. But then . . . maybe I *should* have seen it. I do ask myself over and over if there were signs." She hesitated, as if deciding where to start, or just a little slow on too much wine. "But I didn't know him *that* well. We hadn't been together long," she said. "Just a month, really. And I have to confess, Rebecca, it was usually in a social, drinking environment. Never anything too, too personal. It was just nice to have . . . a friend, you know? Someone to cuddle with in front of a fire on cold nights. Life gets lonely. We filled a need for each other."

So a drinking buddy with extras on the side, thought Rebecca. She glanced at the two men. Replacement auditions, possibly?

"Was my father any more depressed than usual? I mean, *were* there any signs, in retrospect?"

"Not really, no. He was actually kind of excited by his new case, but these things can be deceptive. I've worked years as a nurse, some of that time in ER. And . . . often it's the ones you least expect, the ones who *don't* talk about taking their lives. The dark horses. Those are the ones who surprise you." She lifted her glass, held it up as if making a toast. "Alcohol doesn't help." She took a sip. Set her glass down. "But Lord, one needs it every now and then."

"Was my dad perhaps expecting you for dinner the night he died, Thora?"

Emotion suddenly reddened her nose. She stilled, glanced down. "Yes," she said. "I feel that maybe if I had gone, I . . . that things would have worked out differently."

"You *canceled*?"

"I called to take a rain check, yes. About four forty-five p.m. is when I phoned."

Just after Ash left, and shortly before Brannigan reported the blaze.

"Why did you cancel?"

"I wasn't feeling that well."

Rebecca regarded her, weighing, taking a measure. "Was he upset that you canceled?"

"I don't think so. He sounded like he'd had a few drinks and would probably settle into a few more happily on his own."

"Do you smoke, Thora?"

A flicker of surprise. "I do."

"Did he ever buy you cigarettes?"

A sad smile. "Yeah. Sometimes. Money is tight. I retired, but my pension only goes so far. I had to go back to work. Home care. I have a few clients, but not enough." She inhaled deeply. "It's a small town."

"Clients like Dodd?"

She gave a soft snort. "Yes, like Clive Dodd. I met your father, or I should say became better acquainted with him, through Clive."

"Did my father discuss details of his recent investigation with you?"

A leeriness entered her eyes. "What is this about? Do you think there was something suspicious with his death?"

"I just need to know exactly what happened, Thora. Otherwise I'll never rest. You know what I mean?"

She nodded. "I understand. And if you mean did he discuss the Whitney and Trevor missing-persons thing with me—yes, he spoke to me about that."

Anticipation pinged through Rebecca. She leaned forward. "Thora, did you know that he drove to Cache Creek to see someone in relation to his investigation the morning he died?"

"I knew he was going to. I didn't see him that day. As I said, we were going to catch up over dinner, and I was going to stay over, but I canceled."

"Do you know that the person he went to see in Cache Creek was killed in a single-vehicle accident the evening before he got there?"

She paled, an inscrutable look reshaping her features. "You're not serious?" she said quietly.

"Who was he going to see?"

She rubbed her brow, swallowed, made no eye contact for a moment. Then she looked up. "He was going to talk to the woman who witnessed Whitney Gagnon and Trevor Beauchamp getting into a white van with Oregon plates at the Renegade Lines bus stop on September twenty-seventh just over twenty years ago."

Excitement chased through Rebecca. She recalled the witness coming forward at the time, but not who she was.

"What was her name?"

"I can't remember—I'm not sure he actually mentioned the name," Thora said. "It was in the papers at the time, though. Noah had located her and reached her by phone." She paused, a seriousness darkening her eyes. "The witness told Noah on the phone that she'd lied to him all those years ago."

Rebecca blinked. *"What?"*

"She never saw them being picked up."

"What do you mean?"

"The witness never saw Whitney Gagnon and Trevor Beauchamp hitching a ride with a van from Oregon."

Stunned, Rebecca stared at Thora. "She *lied*?"

"Seems so."

"Did she say *why* she'd lied?"

"Because someone asked her to. She got some deal—money, I think. Or drugs. She was using heavily at the time, she told Noah. She said she'd have done anything to score."

"Who asked her to lie? Who paid her back then?"

"I don't know. Noah was going out to see her to get the details on record."

"Why now?" Rebecca asked, her brain reeling. "Why confess suddenly now?"

"Because Noah found her and reached out. He said it happens sometimes with cold cases. Circumstances and people change, and where they wouldn't speak before, they might finally come forward. She told him that she'd turned her life around. Gone clean. Found religion. Part of some whole atoning thing, like a twelve-step program, was to make amends with people in her life who she'd wronged."

Rebecca's heart whomped. "Who else knew this?" she asked very softly. "Was Buck told?"

Thora fiddled with the stem of her wineglass. "No, I don't think so." She looked up, a raw pain now in her eyes. "Noah thought he was onto something, and it seemed like he suddenly didn't want to tell Buck everything, or even me. He seemed to be holding his cards really close to his chest." She breathed in a deep and shaky breath. "I wrote it off to his conspiracy stuff, his paranoia, his need to make a difference or to find some kind of worth by solving an old crime after he'd felt all washed up for so long. I . . . It was like there was a big hole inside his chest that he was always trying to fill by trying to 'fix' some aspect of the past." Thora fell silent for a beat.

The music in the room changed to an up-tempo western song.

"The old nurse in me thought it was some subterranean psychological thing, but harmless." She held Rebecca's gaze. "Do you think there was more to it?" She looked worried. "Do you think he really was onto something?"

"Like I said, I'm just trying to piece things together for myself." But her heart was galloping. This changed everything. "Thora," she said quietly, "did my dad tell anyone else about this Cache Creek witness recanting?"

She pursed her lips, thinking. "Maybe Rennie Price at the *Clinton Sentinel* newspaper? Rennie has physical copies of the *Sentinel* going back thirty years or so in his morgue. Or that's what he calls it. Your dad got the witness's name from the newspapers in the morgue, since the old missing-persons files were long gone. I mean, it wasn't considered a crime when those teens left town. Whitney had left a note for her mother, and she'd told her friend she was catching the bus that day. And Trevor had told friends he was leaving, from what I understand."

"Did *you* tell anyone that this witness lied?"

She broke eye contact, and Rebecca knew she had.

"Who did you tell, Thora?"

"I . . . I might have mentioned it in the bar."

"When?"

"Maybe two days before Noah drove out there."

"Who was in the bar?"

"The usual. I was sitting over there with Don and Jerry, same place. The place was packed. Anyone could have heard, I suppose, and told anyone else."

Rebecca felt tense.

"So it was your husband, Jake, who saw Ash deliver Whitney to the bus stop that day?"

She nodded. "That's what got Noah looking into the case in the first place. We were drinking, making merry, shooting the breeze. I was telling him about the logging work Jake used to do, and how Jake was away from home for long stretches. And it came up—our old neighborhood, Whit and her mom living across the road from us."

"And it was Jake who saw Ash and Trevor fighting at the bus stop?"

"Yes. Jake was filling up at the PetroGas when he saw the two getting into it. He could see them down the street. Trevor had a knife out. But by the time Jake was done gassing up, Ash had driven off already, and Whitney and Trevor looked fine, just standing there waiting for the bus with their bags. So he drove on."

Rebecca's blood beat hotter, tension torquing as she was thrust emotionally back to that time.

Thora broke eye contact and twirled her glass of wine in a wet circle it had made on the table. Rebecca could feel something else coming.

"What is it, Thora? What are you not telling me?"

"I . . . I know it was not my place to tell your father—" She looked up and met Rebecca's gaze. "But I was tipsy, and in the context of what we were talking about—Ash, Whitney, Trevor, the fight at the bus stop—I mentioned that I had been working at the health-care center at the time. And a few weeks earlier, Whitney had come in for an ultrasound."

Blood drained from Rebecca's head. Sound turned tinny in her ears. "You mean—"

"Whitney was pregnant."

Nausea washed through Rebecca's stomach. "How . . . how far along?" It came out a whisper.

"I don't remember exactly. I only recall thinking that Trevor had been away on the oil sands for six months prior, so it couldn't have been his. I didn't ask Whitney, of course, and she didn't offer. But when Ash picked her up across the road that morning twenty years ago, I'd been saying goodbye to Jake, and I saw them through the kitchen window, and I wondered . . ."

THERE BE MONSTERS AMONG US

Cariboo Country. Sunday, September 27,
just over twenty years ago.

Ash doubles over and barrels like an enraged bull at Trevor.

"Asshole!" Whitney flings open the truck door and comes running after Ash.

But Trevor is streetwise and steps aside fast, sending Ash spinning and flailing wildly forward through the force of his own momentum. As Ash staggers sideways in the dust, trying to keep upright, Whitney latches on to his shirt with both hands.

"Stop it!" she screams, trying to pull him back from Trevor.

But Ash's focus remains on Trevor—the guy has a knife out. Trevor flicks the blade open. Metal glints in the early-morning sun. He drops into a crouch. Holding his flick knife forward, blade tilted upward, he sways his body from side to side, ready for another lunge from Ash.

Ash shakes Whitney off him and barrels at Trevor again. Trevor swipes the knife. Ash ducks sideways, comes up, and lands a crack of *knuckles against cheekbone. Trevor grunts. He tries to spin and stab at Ash again, but he appears dazed from the blow to his face.*

Ash lands another punch. His fist meets bone and gristle with a crunch. Trevor's head is flung sideways. Blood spurts from his nose. His knife clatters to the dirt and sends up a small puff of dust.

"Ash! Stop it! Now!" Whitney's voice is hysterical. She leaps onto Ash's back, wrapping her arms around his neck and her legs around his hips. It handicaps Ash. Trevor uses the gap to deliver a punch to Ash's sternum. Ash crumples, winded, and he goes down hard under the weight of Whitney. She lands beside him with a thud in the dust.

The three are stunned into a lull. A car goes by.

"Jesus, Ash." Tears streak down the dirt on Whitney's face.

Ash fears she might be hurt. He holds up his palm to halt Trevor. Trevor stumbles backward, wiping blood from his face and cursing.

"You okay, Whit?" Ash gets onto his hands and knees. He comes up to his feet, wobbling a bit from dizziness. He holds out a hand to help her up.

"Fuck you!" She refuses his offer of assistance and clambers to her feet. "What in the hell? You fucking loser!"

"What's he doing here?" Ash says again, jerking his chin at Trevor.

"He's coming with me to LA, that's what he's doing here!"

She marches around to the back of his truck and struggles by herself to haul her suitcase out. Red dirt stains the side of her T-shirt. Her jeans are covered in dust. Her hair is a mess. She manages to maneuver her suitcase up over the edge of the truck bed, and it thuds hard to the ground. "And I'm serious. What's it to you? Nothing. So fucking get real, Ash Haugen." She fetches her purse and her CD player from the passenger seat of the cab. She opens her purse and hands Trevor a wad of Kleenex.

He dabs at his bloody nose, his gaze shooting daggers at Ash, but he holds off. Whit is now in control of the boys.

"Who's paying for his ticket?" Ash demands. "Me?"

"How I spend my money is not your worry."

"It's my money, Whitney. It's all of my fucking money! Everything I've worked for to save for college. Did you know that? My paying you to get out of town means I get stuck here for the rest of my fucking life, running my father's ranch, just like he wanted." His emotions run high. He's shaking. "Every penny I earned on jobs ever since I was twelve is what you got, and you got it for one goddamn reason. To take care of things."

She eyes him. Something hardens in her face. She stands straighter and places a hand on a cocked hip. The yellow rays of the morning sun catch her long, gold hair and make it glow about her face like an angel halo. He can see the shape of her nipples beneath her white T-shirt.

"Well, maybe I won't take care of things."

"What do you mean?"

"Maybe I'll keep it."

"Whitney," Trevor says, his voice low, quiet, dangerous, "quit it, now."

A frustration, a fury Ash can't bear or even articulate, balloons inside him. He is compelled by an urge to put his hands around her pale neck and squeeze her to death in anger. Just to make it all stop, make her go away.

Trevor's eyes watch him over the wad of Kleenex clutched to his nose. "She'll take care of it," he says.

Ash shoots a glance at him. "What's it to you?"

He says again, "Don't fucking worry, man, she'll do it, she'll take care of it."

CHAPTER 32

Rebecca sat on the edge of the motel bed and stared at the makeshift crime scene board she'd taped to the wall. Thora's words whirled in a repetitive loop through her brain.

Whitney had come in for an ultrasound . . . When Ash picked her up across the road that morning twenty years ago, I'd been saying goodbye to Jake, and I saw them through the kitchen window, and I wondered . . .

After leaving the Moose and Horn, Rebecca had hightailed it back to the general store, where she'd hurriedly bought sheets of white paper, tape, and permanent markers in different colors. She was a visual person. She still liked to use an old-school "whiteboard" to map out her investigative links, and she wanted to put things down on paper now.

But before taping the paper in connecting sheets onto the wall, Rebecca had done an internet search on the Cache Creek car accident. She'd come across a tiny article in the online version of a newspaper that covered the Ashcroft–Cache Creek region. The single-vehicle accident victim's name was Oona Ferris. Her next of kin was an aunt named Chloe Kennedy. The aunt was quoted in the article as saying she didn't know how she would live without her niece, and that it was her niece who'd supported her financially since she was disabled.

Rebecca planned on contacting and visiting the aunt tomorrow.

She replayed her conversation with Thora again in her mind.

Did my dad tell anyone else about this Cache Creek witness recanting?

Maybe Rennie Price at the Clinton Sentinel *newspaper? Rennie has physical copies of the* Sentinel *going back thirty years or so in his morgue . . . Your dad got the witness's name from the newspapers in the morgue.*

Rebecca wondered if there'd been something else in those old newspapers that might have caught her father's attention in connection with Oona Ferris and her statement twenty years ago. She'd visit Rennie Price and the offices of the *Clinton Sentinel* tomorrow as well.

At the top of her chart, in black marker, Rebecca had written and underlined the names of the victims:

Whitney Gagnon, Trevor Beauchamp, Sergeant Noah North.

Beneath Whitney's name she'd listed:

- *Pregnant.*
- *Had come into substantial amount of cash before vanishing?*
- *How? Where from? Why?*

She'd made another column headed PERSONS OF INTEREST. Under that heading she'd listed several names.

Ash Haugen:

- *Slept with Whitney July 11 (Clinton Rodeo Fair—always held on second Saturday of July).*
- *Father of Whitney's baby?*
- *Seen with Whitney several times after July 11 in Devil's Butte bar until the day she vanished—Sept. 27.*

- *Ash took Whitney to bus stop early on Sept. 27.*
- *Ash confessed he wanted her gone.*
- *Ash fought with Trevor. Trevor pulled knife. Ash found later that day barefoot on a logging road in a storm. Dazed state, covered in blood plus other injuries.*

Rebecca reached for the motel-room coffee cup and sipped the brew she'd made earlier. She didn't want to dwell on her feelings. She was focusing on the questions now. It was her way of blocking it out, coping with the fact that Whitney could have been carrying Ash's baby.

And there was a much more sinister question. If Renegade Bus Lines had no record of Whitney and Trevor getting onto the bus that day, and if the pair had not left town in a white van—where had they gone? How?

Had they even left?

Was it remotely possible that someone had done something terrible to them and they could still be here? Somewhere in the area?

Was *that* what her father had been digging at?

As Rebecca studied her crime scene board, there was no way she could lie to herself—Ash Haugen was pivotal in all this. He had motive. He'd probably gotten Whitney pregnant. He'd wanted her gone. The pregnancy information potentially gave new context to his fight with Trevor.

Had Trevor known about the baby?

She sipped from her cup again. Her coffee had gone cold, but she barely noticed. She had to think it—if Ash had hurt Whitney and Trevor, and then her father had started poking deep into the past, asking Ash worrisome questions, it gave Ash serious motive to hurt her dad as well. In order to shut him up. Ash was also the last person to have seen her father alive.

Motive, opportunity, and means. MOM. He had them all.

This was not looking good. Rebecca felt ill. She set down her cup and ran her hands over her hair.

No wonder her father had called her in Ottawa asking her those questions. All the pieces slotted together now. And her dad had been puzzled over why she'd backed Ash's story about the riding accident.

Rebecca had wanted to believe Ash that day. That was all. As stupid and simple as that.

Sometimes those closest are the most blind to the Monster who lives among them.

She *still* wanted to believe in him.

She *still* found it near impossible to think Ash would kill her father. He loved her father—she truly believed that. Those framed photos in his house told her that. Or could he have kept them out of guilt? People were complex that way. She'd learned this many times over during her years of police work.

And what if exposure, conviction, imprisonment were too great a price to pay for love?

Would fear of the consequences of truth trump the other—yes, it would. It usually did.

And she had to entertain the possibility that whoever had killed her father had also learned—or known about—the false witness in Cache Creek who'd been ready to recant.

Rebecca surged to her feet and paced her room.

What other possibilities could there be?

She spun, grabbed her black marker, and scrawled another name on her sheet in the PERSONS OF INTEREST column.

Corporal Buck Johnstone:

- *Peeping Tom.*
- *Stalked Whitney Gagnon?*

- *Stalked others?*
- *Watched Whitney and Ash having sex at the carnival.*
- *Bullied at school.*
- *Had early access to crime scene.*

She stepped back and stared at Buck's name, her brain wheeling. Buck had had initial control of the investigation into her father's death. He could easily have staged a suicide—he was a cop, he knew how, and he knew what a coroner and pathologist might look for. He could have passed the investigation quickly over to the coroner's office without presenting certain incriminating or circumstantial evidence to Dixie. Which would in turn have hampered Dixie's investigation. For example, had Buck followed up on Ash's statement that there'd been two plates and a pack of cigarettes on her dad's table? Why had Buck not mentioned an anticipated dinner guest to Rebecca?

Perhaps, twenty years ago, Buck had driven past Whitney and Trevor at the bus stop after Ash had left. Perhaps Buck had offered them a ride somewhere? Buck could have coerced the Cache Creek woman into lying about a white van two decades ago.

What would his motive have been for hurting Whitney that September? Revenge for rejection? For having been mocked by her? A sexual infatuation that had festered into something dark and dangerous?

It was possible.

And Buck's life—the way he knew it—would have been seriously threatened if Rebecca's father, his mentor, had told him he was reopening that cold case with new leads.

Buck, too, had motive, opportunity, and means. Both in Whitney and Trevor's disappearance and in her father's death.

On her chart she wrote:

Tori Burton:

- *Was in moonshine shed around time of fire.*
- *Who with?*
- *Why did she flee?*
- *Did she witness something?*

She chewed the back of her Sharpie. Tori was pivotal. Rebecca could no longer play nice in trying to unlock the kid. She needed to know who she had been with and what she had seen. She'd pay Broken Bar another visit and play harder ball with Olivia and Cole tomorrow.

As she focused her thinking via her chart, something Solly Meacham had said filtered to the top of her mind.

The only thing I can specifically recall from that year with respect to Whit was that she took some time off to go on one of those camping trips organized for problem youth. You know the ones started by Dr. Miller?

Dr. Miller. Why did that name sound familiar? It hit her. Dixie had mentioned a Dr. Miller when talking about her father's depression.

Bob had referred him to a therapist, yes, Dr. Rio Miller in Clinton. Additionally, he'd recently publicly expressed dissatisfaction with his life . . . at the Moose and Horn pub . . . He felt he'd been a failure as both a cop and a father.

Could there be a connection between Dr. Rio Miller—who'd accompanied a troubled Whitney on a camping trip twenty years ago—and her father, a patient who might have told Dr. Miller what was going on in his life, including details of his investigation?

It was a stretch—Rebecca didn't know enough—but she added Dr. Rio Miller to her list as a person who knew and had interacted with Whitney, and who was still present in the area now. And who was also linked in some way to her father.

Rebecca leaned forward and wrote a question under Dr. Miller's name.

- *Why had Whitney needed to go camping with Dr. Rio Miller?*

If Rebecca questioned this therapist, it was unlikely the doc would divulge privileged patient information. But she could try.

She tapped the Sharpie against the palm of her hand.

Who all had known that her father had found the false witness? And who had known he was going out to see her that morning?

Thora Battersby, for one, had known her dad was driving out to Cache Creek. Thora also knew a lot of other things about the case. Thora was the trigger that had caused her dad to reopen his old investigation into the vanished teens.

Rebecca added her name to the board.

Thora Battersby:

- *The trigger for Noah to reopen old investigation by mentioning she and her husband, Jake, had witnessed Ash taking Whitney to the bus stop the day she disappeared.*
- *Knew witness in Cache Creek lied and had been paid to do so.*
- *Knew Noah was going to meet with witness.*
- *Knew Whitney was pregnant.*
- *Lived with husband, Jake, across the road from Whitney.*
- *Was expected for dinner on the night Noah died. Claimed she called to cancel. Could she have been to the cabin and lied about canceling?*

There would be phone records. Rebecca could always try to obtain those to determine whether Thora had called the cabin to cancel.

But what motive might Thora have to kill her dad?

Rebecca stilled as a dark tendril of thought threaded into her brain. A nurse like Thora would have access to drugs, like benzodiazepines. Ash had also said her dad appeared focused, fairly sharp in mind, when he'd left the cabin. Could someone have arrived and spiked her father's drink with some kind of tranquilizer so that he passed out in his recliner? Making it easier to stage a suicide?

She checked her watch. It was late. Pathologist Bert Spiker would be long gone from work. Rebecca contemplated calling Dixie at home, but she suddenly felt paranoid. Like her father had, she now felt compelled to play her cards very, very close to her chest in this town where everyone was connected and rumors traveled on the wind.

Wind gusted and ticked ice against the panes. Rebecca jumped. Adrenaline thrummed. She stared at her reflected image in the black windowpanes, and fear—like distant wolves lurking at the edge of a forest—began to take hold of her.

If her father really had been murdered, if the Cache Creek witness had also been murdered, it placed the punctured gas tank of her dad's Silverado into chilling context. Someone really had tried to kill her. Maybe because she was picking up where her father had left off.

Ash was correct. She might not be safe. They might try again.

Could she even trust Dr. Bert Spiker?

Rebecca paced, rubbing her arms, feeling a chill deep in her bones. Or was she simply falling victim to neuroses, like her father had, in this frozen place trapped under a Stephen King–like Arctic dome of pressure that was locking in the frigid cold and isolating her from her grounded sense of self back east?

She *had* to ask Bert about the toxicology panel he'd run. From what she understood, he was newer in the area. He had not been around back in the Whitney days.

She reached for her phone. She had his cell number, and maybe he'd pick up at home. Rebecca placed the call. While the phone rang, she considered her options.

She had theories. She had circumstances. She had possible motives, means, opportunities. But still no solid proof. Even so, perhaps it was time to contact the RCMP's regional major crimes unit, just to open an avenue of communication with a detective over her concerns.

And for her own safety.

Her call was picked up.

"Rebecca?" came Bert Spiker's high, nasal voice. "Everything all right?"

"Sorry about the hour, Bert, but I have a question about the possibility of other drugs in my father's system. I know you probably ran a routine tox panel, but would something like, say, ketamine or benzodiazepines have shown up in your tests? Something that could have exacerbated the effects of the alcohol already in his system?"

Some medication a nurse might have access to . . .

Bert explained that he hadn't received all the results from the lab yet. "Obviously the report will not be finalized until we do. But while additional medication might have been a contributing factor, I'm confident at this point that cause of death is consistent with an intraoral, self-inflicted gunshot wound."

"Can you expedite those tox results?"

"I . . . Is there a problem, Rebecca?" asked the pathologist.

"Things are just not sitting easy with me for various reasons. I know it's asking a lot, but if you wouldn't mind, could you give me the results as soon as possible? And keep quiet that I asked, for now?"

Silence.

Wind banged, howled. "Rebecca, this is not something that I am—"

"Bert," she said, "I'm asking you in an official law enforcement capacity to keep my interest in the tox panel between you and me.

Look, it's not my jurisdiction or purview, but I am making contact with major crimes tomorrow for reasons I can't divulge yet. I need those test results, and if you don't *have* to mention them to anyone until we have conclusive results, it'll make things easier for the investigative team that takes over. I'm sure the major crimes guys would appreciate that," she said in an attempt to strong-arm him.

He cleared his throat, then said in his strange voice, "Not a problem. I will do my best."

She killed the call.

Outside, a moon hung over the distant snow-covered hills, tinting the landscape a haunting, eerie silver. Wind dervishes twisted down the now-deserted main street, swinging signs and the hanging traffic lights.

Somewhere out there, perhaps, the remains of two teens lay buried. And possibly, with them, a baby. Ash's baby.

Rebecca hugged her arms over her chest. Heartbroken, angry. And more fiercely determined than ever to fix this in the name of her father.

CHAPTER 33

Tori wrapped her arms tightly around Ricky's waist as they sped along the south lake road under the moon. He'd brought her a helmet that was hot pink. He said he'd "acquired" it for her. She didn't want to ponder the meaning of that, other than that it thrilled her in a way, the illicitness of a hot-pink acquisition. And that he'd done it for her. He was solid and bulky in his gear and felt good. She'd been careful to dress warmly, too. Lots of thermals and layers and a face mask under the helmet.

The old snowmobile engine coughed and spewed choking fumes. The rutted ice on the road was hard, making them slam and rattle and slide and judder where the snowplow tracks had set into ridges. She clenched her teeth against the jolts as speed gathered deliciously in her gut. She felt exhilarated. Free, even if just for this moment, with her arms around Ricky Simon, the skull pattern on his badass helmet glowing in the silvery moonlight.

The forest grew thicker along either side of the road. Like soldiers carrying black spears that stabbed into the moonlit night, the trees became taller, pressing in closer and closer as the road narrowed. Purple shadows swallowed the track ahead. The logging road turned suddenly away from the lake to follow high above a twisting river as it led toward the turnoff that would take them to the abandoned summer camp at the back end of the Haugen Ranch.

Tori and Ricky had been there several times before. Someone before them had hammered pieces of plywood onto the old ruins to fashion a little hideaway. Not much snow reached the ground through the dense canopy in that spot. It was like a protected haven, and always warmer in foul weather because it was insulated from the wind, as if the trees linked arms around the place and watched over it.

Ricky had candles stashed in the hideout. He had a lighter in his pocket. And Tori could detect the hard shape of a moonshine bottle under his jacket.

Suddenly the trees were gone, and they hit a stretch with rocky banks that reared up to their left with a sheer drop down to the river on their right. Fear cut through Tori's exhilaration, and she held more tightly on to Ricky. This bit of road always made her edgy.

Ricky loved it. He kept the pace as the road swerved in a wide bend. But he slowed abruptly as they rounded the curve. Headlights were coming directly toward them. Worry sparked through Tori.

The lights were bright. As they neared, Tori saw they belonged to a big truck and included a row of hunting spotlights that blazed blindingly along the top of the cab.

Instead of slowing upon sight of their little snowmobile, the truck seemed to speed up and veer right into the center of the snowy road. Surely the driver had seen them? Ricky slowed further.

The vehicle kept coming.

It was now on their side of the road. The cliff fell to nothingness at their right. No barrier. Her throat went dry. She blinked like a mole into the lights, feeling the tension hardening Ricky's body.

Surely whoever was driving that big-ass truck could see them now?

But no, it kept coming. Fast. The road narrowed some more. Ricky tried to go closer to the edge.

No, no, no . . .

The hunting spotlights dimmed suddenly. Relief rushed through Tori. The driver had seen them!

The truck came up alongside them. Big. Shiny. Black. A sticker on the side. Everything seemed to move in slow motion. The truck swerved sideways and hit the front of their snowmobile. Hard. The jolt cracked through Tori's spine, through her jaw, reverberated through her skull.

Shock exploded through her body.

Their machine spun. Her leg hit the truck. Pain slammed through her knee. She heard the engine. She smelled it. She felt the warmth of the exhaust. Screaming filled her ears. Was it Ricky? Was it her screaming?

The snowmobile skis hit a rock, and they flipped up high into the air and went over the edge. Tori felt herself flying free. She hit the ice bank with a smash and began to tumble down. She grabbed wildly for something to arrest her jolting slide down the cliff toward the frozen river far below.

Her gloved hands found purchase on a thick sapling that grew out of the bank between rocks. Tori held tight, breathing hard. She heard the heavy bangs and crash and breaking of Ricky's snowmobile as it cartwheeled and bounced down the embankment to slam with a final loud bang as it shattered ice at the bottom. Everything went still.

Dead silence descended.

It pressed in with the cold. Tori's limbs shook. A ringing sounded in her ears, along with the dull thud of her own blood. She could taste blood in her mouth. Ricky?

"Ricky!" she yelled. Her helmet muffled the sound. *"Ricky!"*

Silence.

Tears filled her eyes as she clutched her sapling. Was Ricky dead? Had he gone to the bottom?

Time stretched. Up above, stars streaked the heavens. It grew colder. Her hands and feet had gone numb. She didn't know how much longer she could hold on. Her whole body hurt.

The sound of an engine reached her. Tori's pulse kicked back into a jackhammer. A vehicle was coming. It sounded like the big truck returning.

Maybe they were coming back to make sure she and Ricky were dead. Because that truck had purposefully tried to kill them. She was certain of it. And she was sure it was because of what they'd seen at Noah North's cabin.

She should have told Olivia. She should have told Noah's cop daughter.

The vehicle came to a stop somewhere high on the road above her. The engine kept running. Carefully, so as not to slip farther down the ice bank, Tori tried to move her head so she could look up. But the edge of her helmet obscured her view. She could see only lights. She heard a truck door slam.

A spotlight began to dart and bounce across the incline. Fear spiked through Tori's heart. They were looking for her and Ricky.

She heard a man's voice. Yelling. Sound was muffled inside her helmet. Her ears were still ringing loudly.

More light played across the embankment. The beam settled on her for a brief moment, and she squeezed her eyes shut tight, willing them not to see her.

Please, no. No, no, no.

More yells. Snatches of words reached through to her. *Find them! Get them! Do it . . . Find them!*

Lights bounced closer. Rocks and pieces of ice skittered and clattered around her as someone began moving above her.

Tori began to pass out. She fought to keep present, to keep holding on.

Find them!

She passed out again. Or did she?

Ricky?

Where was Ricky?

Oh God. She'd do anything to make this right, *anything*. To get him back, to know that he was okay.

Time slowed further and distorted, and Tori felt her vision going black again, closing in from the sides.

The movement of a shadow snapped her back. Her eyes flared open. She heard skittering and snuffling. And she was terrified and held dead still . . . heard more yelling, another command. More sniffing, snuffling, getting closer.

"Find it!"

They were using a dog. To track them down! Oh God, she and Ricky should have told someone about the old man and the fire, because now they were dead, and no one would know why.

The dog reached her. Huffing, it went for her neck. She felt the lick of a tongue under the collar of her jacket. Warm. Wet. Then the dog started to bark wildly, angrily, louder. It licked her again. Tori started to cry. She heard a man's voice.

"Kibu! Kibu, what is it? What you got there, Kibu?"

More loud barking, another lick.

CHAPTER 34

"Okay, you guys, this isn't a game now," Ash said to Ricky and Tori, who were huddled in his living room by the fire. "This is life-and-death stuff. You *both* need to fess up everything that has happened from that day you were at the cabin. *Everything.*"

Tori was on his sofa, her leg elevated, with an ice compress on her knee. It was badly swollen. Both kids were battered and bruised and sore, but otherwise Ash hadn't detected anything broken. They'd been lucky to have both been flung free of the snowmobile before it could mangle and smash them on its tumble down to the river.

Ricky had been flung off right near the road, and had managed to pull himself up by the time Ash arrived. Tori was farther down the bank, clinging to a tree that grew out of some rocks. Kibu had located her, and Ash had managed to drag her up the bank, then help her up onto the road.

He'd assessed the injuries as best he could with a flashlight at the scene, then bundled them into survival blankets and cranked the heat up in his truck. His home was closer than Broken Bar Ranch, so he'd come straight here, where he'd further assessed their condition and determined he didn't need to dial 911. He'd called Olivia and Cole instead. Olivia had told him on the phone that Cole was in town giving a talk at the library on his books, but she was on her way over. Ash had then tried to phone Rebecca. Several times. But she was either out of range or not taking his calls. This unsettled him on both counts.

The kids were, however, in shock. Ricky's complexion was bloodless, his face bruised, his eyes like saucers. He couldn't take his eyes off Tori. He seemed terrified she might have been more seriously hurt, and that it was all his fault. Tori kept tearing up and stroking Kibu. Bear curled next to Ricky. The animals were helping them settle.

"It was just an accident," Ricky said, his wide-eyed gaze still fixated on Tori.

"Then I need to call the cops," Ash said. "Because when I came up that road, I saw lights from a stationary truck *and* a snowmobile at the accident scene. And I saw shadows of more than one person moving in front of those lights. Those people had hunting spotlights and appeared to be looking down the bank. And when they saw me, they fled the scene. That's a criminal offense."

Ricky's attention flared to Ash. He stared. Teeth clenched.

Ash pulled his cell out of his pocket. He began to dial.

"Wait!" Ricky said.

Ash halted. "Why?"

Silence. The fire crackled.

"Does this accident have anything to do with you guys being in Noah North's shed at the time of the fire?" Ash said.

Tori started to cry. Panic cut across Ricky's face.

"Look, Ricky," Ash said, "if this is connected to that fire, this is the real shit now. And it's not just the cops you need to worry about. Both of you almost died. You're damn lucky you were flung free of that wreck. You could have gone all the way down and through the ice, into what is a very fast-flowing river."

Ricky seemed unable to speak. Ash glanced at Tori. "Tori—does this have to do with the fire?"

She started to sob and slobber loudly. Ash's heart wrenched. That kid had been through so much, he didn't want to push her. He knew zip about child psychology, but he figured maybe he should just let Olivia handle the questioning and decide whether to seek medical attention in the morning. But hard-ass little Ricky Simon was another matter.

"Did you see anything distinctive about the truck, Ricky?" Ash said.

"Just a fucking truck," Ricky snapped.

"Color?"

"Maybe it didn't see us," Ricky said. "Maybe the driver was drunk or texting or something. And it was just a stupid accident."

"It was shiny black," Tori blurted out suddenly. "And it had a sticker above the back wheel hub."

Ricky's gaze flashed to her, his eyes burning hot, his body tight.

"And it saw us. It had all the hunting lights on along the top. It saw us, and it came straight for us on our side of the road, and it hit us *on purpose.*"

Ash's pulse quickened. "What kind of sticker above the hub, Tori?"

"Like a wolf-head design. A wolf with angry teeth." She wiped the tears from her cheeks. "And the truck had those silver things covering the wheels, with those bolts that stick out. And it had a big, shiny silver grille with one of those bar things in front."

"A bull bar," Ash said. "Ricky, could you determine the make of the truck?"

"No. I . . . I didn't." He seemed unsure now, less defiant in the wake of Tori's confession. "I was focused on not going over the edge, and the lights were blinding."

"Do you also feel it came for you on purpose?"

He looked down at his hands and nodded.

"Did you make out any numbers or letters on the plate?"

"No," he said softly.

Ash waited a few beats, allowing the kids to process. Then he said, "Now, tell me what happened at Noah's cabin."

Both tensed. Ricky glowered at Tori, as if in warning. She broke eye contact with Ricky and picked at a loose thread in the blanket covering her.

"Listen to me, guys, the driver of that truck attempted to kill you. And he was not alone, because when I arrived, like I said, there was a snowmobile with that truck. I saw at least two people. This looks like a coordinated effort, like it was planned. For some reason, some people want the two of you dead, do you understand this?"

Tori made a small noise. Ricky's gaze remained fierce and locked with Ash's.

"Those drivers stuck around to finish the job, because if they were trying to rescue you, they would not have fled when they saw my truck coming." He paused, his gaze still warring with Ricky's. "The *only* reason you and your friend are alive now, Ricky Simon, is because your grandfather was looking out for you."

He blinked. Tori glanced up.

"Running Wind asked me to watch over you so that you don't end up like your father. Which is why I went to look for you at your house after I saw that knife Rebecca North found in her dad's shed. The knife used to pick the lock on the shed door. And if I hadn't come looking for you, you'd both be long gone in that isolated area, and in these temperatures."

"Patty squealed." Ricky spat out the words.

"Damn right she did. She cares for you. Like your grandfather did."

His eyes glittered. His mouth quivered. "I *will* end up like my dad if you tell the cops I was in that shed," he snapped.

"Bullshit!"

He blinked.

Ash leaned forward. "If you don't deal with this like a man now, head-on, accept the consequences for your actions, you're not only going to end up *just* like your father, you're going to hurt people who love you, and you're going to get people you care about killed. Now think about that, you little shit." He dragged his hand down hard over his mouth, then pointed his finger at Ricky. "This is not just about you. This is about Tori. About Noah North. About Rebecca, a cop's daughter, who is grieving her father. This is about a Mountie who needs justice and a decent and honorable funeral. It's about someone out there who maybe shot and killed Noah, and who could kill again if you protect him with your silence. You have no right to silence any longer, Ricky Simon."

Ricky reeled visibly. Then recoiled like an angry, loaded spring.

"Running Wind went and fucking died on *me!*" His eyes gleamed with tears. "He went and killed himself out there on his traplines. He didn't have to do that."

"He was sick, Ricky. He was dying. He needed to go meet his maker on his own terms because his time had come. Do you think being hooked up to machines was a better way for Running Wind? Stuck in some sterile hospital for months, costing your family money it doesn't have? He went out there in part for himself, and in part for *you*, Ricky. You and your mom and Patty." He paused.

Tears began to leak down Ricky's cheeks.

Tori sat in dead silence, hands fisting the blanket into knots.

"Running Wind entrusted that knife to you as a totem, something to remember him by. Not to go picking locks to steal some poor old man's hooch."

Ricky sniffed and swiped at his snotty nose with his sleeve.

"What's in it for you anyway, ranchman?" he said, slipping into his mother's lingo and wielding it like a shield.

"Your grandfather, that's what." Ash glanced away, took a moment. Then said simply, "I loved him. Like a father."

Ricky stilled.

"When I was eleven, he sort of rescued me. And when he knew he was going to die, I made him a vow. I promised him I would not let the shit in your life take you. And that, my boy, is a promise I will keep. No matter what."

Tears welled again in Ricky's eyes. He glanced at Tori.

Tori said, "We were in the shed. Ricky saw a man."

Ricky lurched to his feet. "Tori!"

"Listen to Ash, Ricky! The bad guy *knows*—everyone knows we were there. Rebecca, too. And she's got proof. And Olivia and Cole know."

"Fuck this." Ricky marched for the exit. Ash grabbed his arm, stopping him. "Let me go, you asshole."

"You sit down. I'm going to help you with this. I'm all you've got, Ricky. Me and Running Wind's spirit is all that stands between you and a one-way street to hell."

Ricky swallowed.

"Sit."

Slowly, he acquiesced.

"Tori?" Ash said. "Talk to me."

She sniffed away her tears and said, "We were inside the shed when we heard someone outside, going into Noah's cabin. We got scared thinking it was Noah coming, so we hid behind the work-bench. We waited. And just when I thought it was safe to go, we heard a gunshot. Then sounds of someone running through the slush away from the house."

Ash tensed.

"The person ran through the aspens behind the shed. We heard brush breaking. And then he got onto a snowmobile and drove away fast."

"Did you see him?"

"Ricky saw him."

"Ricky?"

The kid glared sullenly at the flames in the fireplace. Time stretched. Wind whistled in the eaves outside and around the chimney.

He finally turned to face Ash. "He was wearing padded, waterproof snow gear, all black," he said quietly, broken like a wild young stallion in a corral. "He had a helmet on. It was blaze orange with a great black spider design over it." He swallowed. "His visor was down, so I didn't see his face."

"Height? Build?"

He shook his head. "All bulky snow gear. But not short. He moved fast, like he was fit. And the wrap design on his machine was the same design as on his helmet. Bright orange, with a big, black, fanged spider, and web lines. It was a newer machine. Two-stroke. Real smooth engine." He looked like he was going to throw up.

The mood in the room shifted.

"What happened then?" Ash asked.

"Tori wanted to run away, but we'd heard the shot, and I was worried about the old man. I wanted to check on him."

Ash studied the kid, a bead of hope forming in his chest. Ricky was a good person. Running Wind had known that.

"So we went to look in the back window of his cabin. I saw his slippers, and a drink had spilled on the floor. He wasn't moving, and I got a real bad feeling and told Tori we needed to go look inside." He cleared his throat. "The kitchen door was open, which was weird. There was a lit lantern on the table. I went into the living room and . . ." He fell quiet, struggling now. "And he was there. In his recliner with his shotgun between his legs and the back of his head blown out. He was dead."

"And then?"

"Then I panicked. I tried to grab Tori so she wouldn't see, and I knocked over the lantern and it caught fire."

"That's not true," Tori said.

Ash looked at her. She glowered at Ricky.

"It was me," she said. "My arm. It flung out when Ricky tried to stop me from seeing the dead man. It was me who set the cabin on fire."

That bead of hope in Ash's heart pulsed and grew. Ricky Simon, even now, was trying to protect his little friend at what could be great cost to a kid who'd been busted for minor arson before.

"The whole place started to burn really fast," Tori said. "We ran away."

"Why did you not go for help?" Ash said.

"Because then they'd know we were stealing," Tori said. "And that we had caused the fire and burned Noah, and Ricky would go to real prison this time." Her voice caught. "And he wouldn't ever come back."

Ash nodded slowly. His brain raced.

"Who knew you were going to be on that road tonight?" he said. "Apart from Patty."

"I didn't tell anyone, Ricky, I promise," Tori said.

"I only told Patty. But I did think at one point on my way over to Broken Bar that someone could have been following me," Ricky said. "I saw lights through the trees for a while. I took a side trail, and the lights disappeared."

Made sense, thought Ash. Word could have gotten out that he and Rebecca had visited Tori at Broken Bar. Brannigan had likely heard. There had also been a housekeeper hovering around. Either of them could have mentioned it to any number of people.

He rubbed his brow, pressure building inside him. "Why were you going to the old camp on my property?"

"Because no one goes there, and there's buildings and a place to hide and hang out," Ricky said.

"That's all?"

"Yeah, that's all."

Ash weighed the kid, heat prickling over his skin as he thought of the camp ruins, and his mind fought itself deep inside.

They heard a vehicle drawing up outside, tires crackling and crunching on ice.

Ash got up. "Here." He handed Ricky his phone. "Call your mom. Tell her you're okay and staying with me for a while. If she needs you, she can call me. Give her my cell number. Tell her she can call anytime."

He went to let Olivia in.

CHAPTER 35

Ash opened the door, and Olivia entered, shrugging out of her coat, the scar around her neck visible for all to see. "Where is she?" She tugged off her toque, and her hair flew up in a mass of static. Her cheeks were flushed and her eyes bright with urgency.

"In the living room. She's okay physically, Liv. Just a little beat up, with a wrenched knee that might require a medical eye. I've got an ice compress on it."

Olivia swept through into the living room. She stalled at the sight of her daughter on the sofa. "Tori?" she said, as if suddenly unsure.

"Mom!"

Tears sprang into Olivia's eyes. She hurried over to her child, and Tori flung her arms around her mother. Olivia hugged her tightly back. Neither spoke. They just held each other. Ash felt himself choke up—he'd bet his bottom dollar that this was the first time Olivia had heard Tori call her *Mom*.

He made a sign at Ricky, indicating for him to follow so that Tori and her mom could have a moment. Ricky hesitated, glanced at Tori, then Olivia, and got up and followed Ash through to a bedroom door.

Ash opened the door. "This is yours for now. There's a bathroom through that other door there. Soap, shampoo—everything you need is in there."

Ricky stared at the big king bed. The fluffy duvet. The television on the wall. He glanced up at Ash with disbelief in his eyes.

Something fisted in Ash's chest. He looked like a child. He *was* a child, thought Ash. A child only a few days into his teens, one who needed a father. A kid as old as he had been when he knew he would marry Rebecca North. This thought put Ash squarely into the mind of a twelve- or thirteen-year-old, because he could suddenly—so very clearly—remember being there himself.

"I'll find you some pj's," Ash said gently. "Go take a nice warm bath or shower. You'll feel better. And you can sleep in—we're going to keep you out of school for a few days. I'll put the pj's on the bed for you."

Ricky broke eye contact. He looked down at his feet. "Thanks, Ash," he said, very quietly.

"You can thank your grandfather."

He nodded and entered the room.

Ricky Simon was crying, and he did not want Ash to see.

———

When Ash reentered the living room, Olivia had Tori all bundled up and ready to go. She led her limping daughter into the mudroom. While Tori put on her boots, Olivia took Ash aside.

Quietly, she said, "What do you think this was? An accident?"

"No," he said. "Not from their description of events, and from what I saw. Keep her close. Keep an eye on her. Keep her out of school for a while, okay? Until we know more for sure."

"You think this is because she could have witnessed something in connection with the Noah fire?"

"Yeah. They witnessed someone at Noah's place. I'll let her give you the details. It doesn't look good."

"You going to the police?"

He hesitated. "I'm going to try and call Becca again. She was talking about bringing in an outside RCMP team because of the small-town interconnectedness and potential conflicts of interest."

"You mean *Buck* has a conflict of interest?"

He gave a shrug. "Who knows? Either way, he'd have to hand a homicide over to a major incident team anyway. So maybe just lay low on talking to the local cops, if possible? Until Becs gets a team in. We can let them handle it. All I'm going to do with Ricky in the morning is report a hit-and-run. There is a chance it could be unrelated to Noah." But he doubted it. "The kids gave a description of the truck."

She frowned.

"Look, if it was connected, it's unlikely whoever went after the kids tonight will do it again in full view, Liv. *Especially* if we do report it. They've lost their window of anonymity. Now that we know they're out there, I figure they're more likely to lay low. Or go on the run. They'll be worried the kids have already talked now anyway."

"There's more than one?"

"I saw at least two."

She cursed softly, then gave a wry smile. "At least she'll be home laid up with that knee awhile, so I can keep an eye on her. I suppose it's a blessing in a way." She paused. "You'll let me know what happens?"

"I'll keep you and Cole in the loop, I promise."

"What about Ricky?"

"I'm keeping him here, in my home. With me at all times."

She placed her hand on his arm. "Thank you, Ash. For being a good neighbor, a friend."

He smiled and saw them out. He stood at the door and watched them go, their brake lights flaring briefly at the end of his driveway. And as he faced out into the frigid cold of the night with the warmth of his home at his back, Ash felt worth. He felt protective and paternal instincts awakening in him. But with those feelings also came the deeper, more complex pangs of regret. And the stirrings of dark memory.

He shut and locked the door and tried once more to call Rebecca. No answer.

He went to the window and looked out into the dark, turning his phone over and over in his hand. He dialed again.

This time he left a message.

"Becca, there've been some developments. I need to speak to you—it's urgent." He wavered. "There's . . . also something I've been needing to tell you." He cleared his throat. "Call me. If I don't hear from you, I'll be at the hotel first thing in the morning."

CHAPTER 36

Cariboo Country. Wednesday, January 16.

It was 7:35 a.m. when Ash brought Ricky into the dining area of the Moose and Horn. Only a few patrons huddled in the booths over breakfast—mostly construction types en route to jobs and getting an early start. The gas fire was flickering, and the place smelled of good coffee and bacon. One server was on duty, a woman Ash didn't know. Solly was behind the bar checking stocks.

She looked up as Ash and Ricky entered.

"Hey, guys, what's up? In for breakfast before school today?"

"Ricky's hanging with me for the day," Ash said. "Can you keep an eye on him for me, Soll? I need to go up and talk to Rebecca."

She frowned. "Everything okay?"

"All good. I just need to make sure he stays put. You got a menu for us?"

She smiled, but it didn't quite meet her eyes. She could read Ash's mood and was naturally curious. She reached over the counter for a menu and handed it to Ash.

Ash showed Ricky a booth in front of frosted windowpanes. It was visible from all angles of the room and easy for Solly to see.

"Sit here," Ash said, placing the menu on the table. "Order whatever you like."

"Serious?" he said, opening the menu. "Anything?"

Ash met his gaze. Ricky's features were oddly earnest. And although it shouldn't, it shocked him a little that this was a big deal for Ricky Simon, being able to order whatever he liked off a full breakfast menu.

Ash smiled. "Yeah, kid. But make sure you get some protein."

Ricky grinned.

Ash returned to the bar and asked Solly for two coffees to go. While she fixed them, he tried once more to call Rebecca on his cell.

Still no reply.

Anxiety edged into him as he killed the call. She had to have received his voice mail by now, surely?

"Here ya go." Solly handed him the coffees.

"Do you know which room Rebecca is in?" he asked casually as he accepted the coffees.

She eyed him and angled her head.

He grinned and held up the two cups. "I'd like to surprise her with room service."

Solly gave him Becca's room number.

———

Balancing one coffee cup atop the other in his left hand, Ash knocked on the door with his right.

Silence.

He banged again. "Room service!" he called.

The door opened a crack.

Becca peeped out. She was wrapped in a hotel robe, her hair mussed. She looked unnaturally pale. And she'd clearly been fast asleep. Warmth, desire, surged unbidden into Ash's chest at the sight of her vulnerable and unguarded like this.

But her face changed as she registered him. She glanced at the coffees, pushing a fall of hair back off her face, but said nothing. Something was wrong.

Anxiety braided deeper into Ash's chest. He was already on edge, given what he'd come to confess to her. Now he felt he was treading on eggshells. He considered backing away. Almost.

But he also had to update her about Ricky and Tori's narrow escape last night.

"Can I come in?"

"Ash, I—"

"It's urgent. Did you get my message?"

"Look—"

He pushed past her, entered the room. But he stopped dead at the sight of the papers plastering the wall.

She'd taped together sheets of white paper on the wall space above the desk. On the sheets were lists of names and questions scrawled in black and red and green ink, and lines joining them.

He stared, coffees in hand. She shut the door quietly behind him and went to pull the bed linens straight.

At the top of the board were Noah's, Whitney's, and Trevor's names under the title VICTIMS.

But all Ash could seem to focus on was his own name. And what Becca had scrawled under it.

- *Father of Whitney's baby?*

"You know." His voice came out in a hoarse whisper.

Silence.

He turned.

She stood there. White as a ghost. And so beautiful to him. And yes, she knew. It was written all over her face in the raw way she looked at him. And Ash's heart crumbled into a million little pieces.

CHAPTER 37

"How?" Ash asked. "How did you find out?"

She pulled her robe more tightly across her body and folded her arms over her chest. "Thora. She worked as a nurse at the Clinton health-care center when Whitney went in for an ultrasound."

Blood drained from his head. "And Thora told Noah? That's what triggered him with all this?" He waved a coffee cup at her crime chart.

"It came up between them. Add to that the fact you were seen taking Whitney and her suitcase to the bus stop, and then fighting with Trevor, it apparently renewed my father's interest in a mystery he'd been unable to solve."

Her eyes were inscrutable. Her mouth flat.

He set the coffees down and lowered himself slowly to the edge of the bed, his legs suddenly refusing to support him.

"Why, Ash?" she said. "Why hide it? Why not tell me?"

"Why do you think? As far as I knew, Whitney and Trevor got into that van and left. Why on earth would I have chosen to bring this up after they'd gone? She was going to have an abortion in California. She asked me for money so she could make it happen. I gave her everything I had. I had nothing left, Becca, apart from maybe one last chance with you. Then Marcy Fossum screwed that up."

"*You* screwed it up. *You* were meeting with Whitney after you told me it was over."

"Because she told me she was carrying my child. I *had* to see her. I didn't know what to do about it. I even offered to 'do the right thing' and marry her."

Becca turned her back sharply and stared out the window. He dragged his hand down over his mouth, blood booming in his ears, skin hot.

"She said yes at first," he said quietly. "And I thought that was it. My life was over. But then she suddenly changed her mind and said she wanted to get rid of it, and she needed money in order to do it. So I had to meet with her a few more times to arrange things."

Becca kept her back to him.

Ash inhaled deeply. This was it. The endgame. He and Rebecca were finally hashing this through, and she'd be out of his life forever.

"It was a mistake, Becca," he said softly. "I've been paying for it for years."

She turned slowly. Her features were strained, and deep shadows underscored her eyes. "And in December twenty years ago? When my father started looking for Whitney at the request of her mom? You didn't tell him then."

"The fact Whitney was pregnant did not change the fact she left town of her own accord with Trevor. It didn't make any difference whether she showed up stateside or in Mexico or Nicaragua, or God knows where."

She regarded him steadily.

"You could have told me sooner than now, Ash. You could have told me after my father died. After he'd been raising questions. After the possibility of homicide was raised."

"I was going to. I called you last night, dammit, I wanted—*needed*—to talk to you about this now. I knew I had to."

Becca swallowed. "You said you gave her money?"

"Everything I had. Every penny I had worked for and saved from the time I was twelve. My whole college fund. My parents were certainly never going to fund an education. My dad didn't believe I needed one when I had the ranch waiting for me. Dead against it. Why do you think I never did go to school in the end? Why do you think I never followed through on that agricultural management degree I always told you I wanted? I wanted out of this town, too. I wanted to expand my horizons and build opportunities for *us*, Becca. I had dreams—big, beautiful dreams. And then I made one terrible mistake on one terrible night. And my whole life blew up in my face." He swallowed. "And in your face. And I am so sorry."

Emotion, raw, twisted her features. Her eyes glistened. "Are . . . are you certain it was yours?"

"She said it was. Trevor had been away for the prior months. I believed her."

"You believed *Whitney*, who probably at one point or another screwed half the boys in her grade?"

"That's harsh, Becca, and you know it. She was a mess. And we were both scared. Neither of us wanted this. I was seventeen. She was still only sixteen, just turning seventeen. My father would have . . . I didn't know what to do." He scrubbed his hands over his face, sat in silence for several beats. A horn sounded outside. He looked up. "I didn't want *her*. That life. I wanted you. I wanted to die, Becs, when you left."

Coolly, Becca said, "She could have gotten an abortion here."

"Not here. She would have had to go to the Lower Mainland. It wasn't so simple back then. And she wanted to go to LA anyway. But she needed money to get there. Trevor had returned, and now, in retrospect, given that Trevor was waiting to meet her at the bus stop, it was maybe his idea to get rid of the 'Ash problem' and take my money to boot. Believe me, the irony is not lost on me, and I'm sure he got off on it—me funding *his* new life in LA."

"That's why you fought?"

"That's why we fought. I wanted to kill him."

Her eyes narrowed.

"Not *kill* him kill him."

"But you were mad enough. You *could* have killed him."

He stared.

"It doesn't look good, Ash. Whatever light you hold it under. You wanted Whitney gone, and you wanted to kill Trevor." She paused. "How much money did you give her?"

"Almost eleven grand. That's all I had."

She nodded, and he could see her brain working, and it worried him. He had a sense she knew more than she was letting on.

"It might not look good, Becca, but I'm being straight with you. I was angry, yeah. Filled with rage—an urge to kill them both, honestly. I hit Trevor twice, I think, before I came to my senses. Then I left. And that's the truth of it. And however bad it looks, they got into that van and left town of their own accord. And I tried to bury my shit and move on."

She weighed him in silence for several long, ominous beats, then seated herself slowly on a chair, facing him.

"Ash," she said quietly, leaning forward and clasping her hands. "I've got to ask you again, because it was the key question my father had for me . . . how *did* you hurt your face? And your hands?"

He swore softly. "Like I told you. Many times over. I was wrecked by what had just happened with Whitney and Trevor. I rode a horse too recently broken, and in the wrong frame of mind. The animal wanted nothing to do with what it sensed in me. And I paid for it. End of story." He looked away, then swung sharply back.

"You know what cuts me—and I don't expect sympathy—part of me always wondered what if . . . what *if* she kept my baby? She made some stupid-ass comment at the bus stop that morning, and I thought it was just to wound me, and it did. Because I never stopped wondering. What if I *do* have a child out there, somewhere in the world? A daughter. A son. Who doesn't know who his or her real father is. Who'd be of college age by now. A whole life lived and lost to us both. And when your father started looking again . . . I almost *wanted* him to find her, so I could learn the truth for certain."

"Ash. I don't think you have a child out there somewhere."

He stilled at the tone in her voice. His gaze locked on hers. Tension rose in the room.

"I don't think Whitney and Trevor ever left town. I think they're still here."

CHAPTER 38

"What do you mean, they never left town?" Ash stared at Becca.

"Whitney and Trevor never got into that white van with Oregon plates. The witness who came forward in December lied," Becca said.

"I . . . don't understand."

She assessed him, her eyes cool. She was searching his face for a tell, some sign he'd known this already. His skin was hot.

She reached for a hair tie next to the bed and pulled back her dark hair as if needing to tighten her face—the front she was showing him. She hooked her hair through the tie to form a tight bun and said, "My father looked up the witness as part of reopening his investigation. He found her living in Cache Creek. The woman used to be a drug addict and apparently had a come-to-Jesus event in her life. She'd cleaned up and was on a mission to tell the truth. So when my father asked about Whitney and Trevor and the van, she confessed she'd lied to him all those years ago. Someone had coerced her into doing it, allegedly in exchange for either drugs or money to buy drugs."

"*Who* coerced her? *Why?*"

"That's the big question. It seems she didn't tell my dad over the phone. He drove out to meet her the morning of the day he died." Becca watched him. Again he got a sense she was waiting for him to slip, to reveal that he'd had prior knowledge of this.

"But when my father got to Cache Creek, he learned she'd been killed in a car accident the night before—skidded on black ice and went over an embankment. That's what I've been told. I intend to follow it up and confirm the details today."

"What's the name of this witness?"

"Oona Ferris."

"The cops said it was an accident?"

She held his gaze. "I plan to look into that, also."

Ash felt light-headed. All this time he'd been 100 percent convinced Whitney and Trevor had left town. And now . . . this blew apart everything he'd thought was true, everything he'd built his life on over the past twenty years.

Becca picked up one of the coffees he'd brought and went to the window. She sipped while she looked out into the bleak morning, her back to him. He took in the shape of her shoulders, her waist, the line of her neck. His heart squeezed. He loved her. She was acting bold, but he could see she was hurting. On so many levels. She was as fucked up about all of this as he was.

"If they never left town," she said quietly, still with her back to him, "it means their remains could be out there somewhere. They could have been right here, all this time." A pause. "Them and the remains of a fetus."

Ash felt sick.

"Maybe Trevor did something to her," he said. "Maybe he hurt Whitney, took my money."

"Because she'd been unfaithful and was carrying *your* child?" Becca faced him. "And then what? He went dark, changed his name, is living in hiding somewhere? I thought about that. But Trevor is not around now to have staged my dad's suicide."

Ash heard a vacuum cleaner start up down the hall. He scrubbed his hands harder over the stubble on his face. "I can't believe it—that they're still here," he said.

"Can't? Or won't?"

"They *had* to have left, Becca. And maybe changed their names, anything, but not . . . not this."

She took another sip of the coffee, steam rising about the cup. "Yeah," she said quietly. "Anything but this would be more convenient. Better that than to think of your progeny rotting away in the ground somewhere close to home."

Anger surged and hit like white-hot fire. He held her glare, his heart thumping. He could hear the vacuum cleaner of the housekeeper coming closer outside the door. Claustrophobia began to choke his throat. A thread of panic raced through his chest along with a need to escape. Before he spoke harsh words to Becca that he could never take back. Then he thought of Ricky waiting downstairs.

His vow.

He thought of Running Wind sitting calmly beside him atop that mesa with the wind in his dark hair and his nose like a regal bird's beak as he whittled his birch stick. And it calmed him.

The damage was done.

It had been done the night he'd swallowed too much beer and fallen for a stupid fumble in the hay at the carnival because the woman he really loved had refused to sleep with him, and it had threatened his tremulous sense of masculinity for reasons he was not ready to admit even to himself.

And now the collateral damage from that hot, awful night was still spiraling outward all these years later. He couldn't go back and undo that moment, much as he would if he could. And he had to forgive Becca her sharp tongue because looking at those comments she'd scrawled on the chart on the wall, he'd think he looked guilty as sin, too.

He could only go forward. Sort this out for Noah. Get him justice. For Becca, as best he could.

For Ricky. And Tori and Cole and Olivia. So that the kids would stay safe.

He blew out a lungful of air.

"I don't know how to explain what this latest news does to me now, to learn that my baby could have been—" His voice cracked. He looked away. Swallowed. Tried again. But he couldn't voice it.

"All I know, Becca, the one true thing, the one constant, solid thing in my life"—he held her eyes, those honey-colored eyes he'd seen in the kitchen that day when Mrs. North was baking bread—"has been my love for you. Always."

She tensed. "Ash, please, please don't—"

"I must. What else can I say? I'm stripped bare here. What you see is this." He opened his hands. "I couldn't even make my marriage with Shawna work because there was always this specter. This unresolved past. You. This sense of something that was not allowed to come to its natural conclusion."

"I . . . I can't do this, Ash. Not now. Not ever."

"I'm not asking you to. That's it. I've said it. I love you. And my guilt over Whitney is now tenfold because I'm sure whatever I did led to the murder of your father—a man I cared deeply for. And now, possibly, it's also led to the death of this witness."

She stilled at his tone. "Why are you so sure it was murder?"

"Because someone *was* inside your father's cabin at the time of the gunshot," he said. "A man who fled on a snowmobile. Ricky saw him—just his suit and his helmet, and the machine. The kids finally spoke after someone tried to kill them both last night."

"*What?*"

"I tried to call you. Several times. A truck ran Ricky's snowmobile off the road and down a steep bank last night. Just like your witness went over a steep bank. Same MO. The kids are lucky they were cast free of the wreck before it went down. And that I arrived when I did.

If the fall didn't kill them, they'd have frozen to death before help came their way on that remote section."

Becca slowly reseated herself.

She stared at him in silence, blood draining from her complexion. "This is why you tried to call?"

"This is why."

"Are they injured?"

"Bruised, shaken. Okay. But it rattled them into telling what happened at the shed."

He told Becca what had transpired when he arrived on scene. He relayed Tori's description of the truck and the decal of the wolf on the side, and what the kids claimed Ricky had witnessed from the shed window.

Her eyes narrowed when he mentioned the wolf decal.

"You reported the hit-and-run?" she said.

"Not yet. Ricky is downstairs with Solly. I thought he should come with me to tell Buck."

CHAPTER 39

Rebecca's blood raced. She finally had witnesses. A description of a suspect who'd fled her dad's cabin in a snowmobile. And if the kids' accident *was* linked, she also had a description of a truck, plus an indication there had been more than one person involved. But she still couldn't shake her suspicion Ash was holding something back.

"How did you come to be there just after the kids went over the bank?" she asked, probing.

"I went to look for Ricky after I dropped you off. You were right, I did recognize the knife you found in the shed. Ricky's grandfather, Running Wind Simon, gave it to Ricky before he died."

"Fuck, Ash." She set her coffee down abruptly, her emotions churning like a bloody roller coaster in her chest. "Why in the hell didn't you tell me—what is going *on* with you?"

"Because I had to speak to Ricky first. Look, Becca, it was going to come out that Ricky was there, either from Tori or me, but I needed to hear Ricky's story first, because the kid needs help. If he'd been reported straight to Buck for theft and connection with possible arson, he'd have been pulled out of his restorative justice program and gone into the system. I knew he hadn't killed your father—"

"Oh, did you now?"

"For heaven's sake. He didn't stick a Mossberg in your father's mouth and stage a suicide. He was stealing booze. And—"

She opened her mouth to speak.

He raised his hand. "No, hear me out. Before Running Wind passed, I made him a vow—that I would watch over Ricky and get him through this rough patch of his early teens. He lives in a tough environment, and he's not a bad person. Just done some stuff that's going to label him for life if he's not pulled out now. And come hell or high water, I intend to honor that vow. All I wanted was to speak to him, understand, and help show him the best way to come forward. Think about it. You. Buck. RCMP. You want to keep your jobs, you follow the rules, the law by the letter. Not a helluva lot of room for all the gray areas in between. I didn't want to put you into a position where you knew about Ricky and then I maybe had to ask you to pretend you didn't."

She stared at him. This man. This confounding man. This person her whole life seemed wrapped around, who was moody at times, and passionate, and not at all straightforward, and she had no idea whether she could trust him when he kept things from her like this. But the emotion in his voice, the fierce light in his eyes, the way he was trying to father some punk-ass kid because of a promise to the kid's grandfather—it piqued her curiosity. It clutched her heart.

"Why such passion, Ash? For this vow, for this kid? Why did Running Wind ask *you*?"

A look passed through his face that chilled her, but it was so quickly gone she wondered if she'd even glimpsed it.

"He . . . helped me once. When I was eleven."

"How?"

Ash gave a slight shrug, broke his gaze, and appeared to study the makeshift whiteboard on her wall. When he spoke again, he seemed distant.

"I ran away from home once. Running Wind found me in the woods, and . . . like some damn wizard he led me home with his words. Became a sort of mentor ever since. Taught me bush craft. It's why I'm good at what I do now. Tracking. Predator hunting."

"You never told me."

"It was guy stuff."

She studied his profile, saw the lines of sadness and tension around his mouth. "Does this have any bearing at all on the Whitney thing?" she said.

"None." He hesitated, breathed in deep, then faced her. "You want to come with us to report the hit-and-run to Buck?"

She bit her lip. He was changing the subject.

It was guy stuff.

She let it go and considered his question. Reporting the hit-and-run, just the accident, could play into her hands. How Buck handled it could tell her a lot. If there was any connection between Buck and the crimes, this could tip his hand.

"Okay," she said quietly. "We report it, but I want to keep what Tori and Ricky saw on my father's property apart from this. We keep that for an outside investigative team. They'll want to hear it straight from the kids. And you personally need to step back from this now, Ash. Way, way back. If we're looking at homicides here, you have to understand that it doesn't look good for you. You're up to your neck in this. From Whitney and Trevor to my dad to potentially the Cache Creek witness. Detectives *will* look at you first, and they'll go at you hard. And God, I hope you're not hiding anything else because . . ." Emotion washed hot and sharp into her chest, catching her off guard. She turned away from him and tried to breathe, to compose herself.

He got up and came behind her, touched her shoulder. She tensed.

"Don't," she whispered. "Please. Just . . . don't."

He removed his hand. She cleared her throat. "Statistically, when a female disappears under suspicious circumstances like Whitney did, it's the boyfriend, the husband, the lover who did it. And that's going to be their first angle in." She turned to face him. "It's going to be rough, Ash."

"Yeah."

"And we're over—you and me—you do know that. We were over a long, long time ago."

His eyes darkened and glittered, and the expression on his face made her heart hurt. He said nothing.

"Until a team gets in, you look after Ricky. Cole and Olivia can watch over Tori. And you and I will cut ties and not communicate. I'll take Ricky to report the hit-and-run to Buck. I want to watch Buck's reaction, see how he handles this."

"Ricky won't go. Not unless I go with."

"Ash—"

"I'm sorry, Becs. That's where I draw my line. I promised I'd have his back, be there for him. He's scared of Buck, of police. This is a big deal to get him this far. Besides, I was at the scene. I also need to report what I saw and did."

She studied him.

"Get dressed," he said coolly. "We'll be waiting for you downstairs in the Moose and Horn. We all go together." He hesitated, cast a quick glance at the board where his name was circled in red. And left.

The door shut with a cold click behind him.

CHAPTER 40

Rebecca entered the Moose and Horn and saw Ash sitting in a window booth next to a wiry kid with walnut-colored skin, high cheekbones, and smooth blue-black hair. The kid wore a black hoodie with a white skull design. Solly stood in her apron chatting to them.

The kid stilled and stared at Rebecca as she approached. She could read apprehension in his eyes.

"Hey, guys," she said with a smile. It did not come without effort, but she wanted to put Ricky Simon at ease. She was going to need his full cooperation.

In front of Ricky was a plate of half-finished flapjacks with a piece of sausage and some bacon, all smothered in syrup. A bottle of maple syrup stood next to the plate.

"Mornin', Becca," Solly said, appraising her. "Can I get you something—Ash here has ordered the full Clinton ranchers' special."

She realized she was famished. "I'll have the same, thanks, Soll. And a large coffee."

"Sure thing." Solly went off, and Rebecca slid into the booth opposite Ash and Ricky. Through the frosted windows the wind blew skiffs of snow through the morning traffic—if one could call it that—moving through the main street.

Rebecca took her notebook, pen, and colored Sharpies out of her bag as Ash said to Ricky, "This is Sergeant Becca North, Noah's daughter."

Rebecca glanced up from her bag, offered another smile. "Hey, Ricky, Ash told me you and Tori can help us with some information."

He studied her with the wariness of a small, wild animal. His body was tight, as if primed to bolt at a nanosecond's notice.

She opened her notebook. "I'm going to help you through this, okay? This is not about getting you into trouble. If you can tell me everything you know, it will help me keep you *out* of any trouble. Do you understand this?"

Ricky's gaze ticked to Ash. His big, dark eyes seemed to say, *Is she for real? Can I believe her?*

Ash nodded.

Rebecca was struck by the quiet bond between Ash and this kid. For a sharp moment she saw Ash in the context of a father figure. Ash who'd lost a baby, and who'd been eaten by a lack of closure around that for the past two decades. She stilled inside and regarded him for a moment, her paradigm shifting yet again. He might be implicated up to the neck in whatever crimes had been committed around Whitney Gagnon, but he hadn't been trying to kill Ricky Simon and Tori Burton last night. No way. He'd been trying to save Ricky, and was still trying to save him right now.

Warmth, compassion, crushed through her chest. She cleared her throat, clicked the back of her pen, glanced around the establishment. The seats of the booths all had high backs, and no patrons were seated on either side of theirs. Noisy chatter down at the far end of the restaurant would prevent their conversation from being overheard. It was private enough.

"Ricky," she said quietly, "can you walk me through, step by step, what happened the night my father's cabin burned down?"

He fidgeted with a knife and nodded.

"Start at the beginning. When you decided to go to my dad's place."

Another nervous glance at Ash. "We—Tori and I—wanted to go get some of the old man—Noah's—moonshine from his shed. I knew his habits. How he fetched wood in the evening, and then didn't come out again. So we were waiting up on the ridge for him to do that." A pause as he watched Rebecca writing this down in her notebook.

"Go on," she said neutrally. But her pulse raced.

Ricky proceeded to recount the series of events and what he and Tori had seen.

"You sure it was a shotgun?"

"Yeah. It sounded like a shotgun."

She noted this in her book. "And you're sure the snowmobile had a four-stroke engine?"

"Hell yeah. I can tell the difference. It was a nice new engine, from the sounds of things—deep pitch, good silencer."

"Have you ever seen that helmet or snowmobile before?"

He shook his head.

Solly arrived with the food and they fell silent. Solly eyed them, sensing something. "Everything okay?"

"All good," said Ash with a false smile.

"Holler if you need anything." Solly glanced at Becca's book and markers on the table, but said nothing and left.

Rebecca reached for her coffee, took a sip. Ash started eating his breakfast, but she wanted to get this down while the kid was talking.

"Why didn't you go for help, Ricky?"

"I was too scared. He—your dad—was dead already. I had no doubt. And I'd been busted before. I . . . I didn't, I . . ."

She nodded. "It's okay. I understand. Ash explained your situation to me."

His shoulders sagged in relief. Tears pooled in his eyes. He swiped them away fast, embarrassed. Rebecca got the sense Ricky Simon never cried. At least not in front of people. This was hard on him.

"You're doing great, Ricky," she said. "Thank you."

He swallowed and rubbed an invisible spot on the table.

She placed some blank sheets of paper and colored markers in front of him.

"Pretend the red Sharpie is an orange one," she said. "Can you draw the helmet design and snowmobile foil design?"

He worried his lip with his teeth, then picked up the black marker.

Rebecca and Ash ate while watching Ricky make swift movements with the markers across the paper. She exchanged a glance with Ash. The kid was good. Damn good. Talented, in fact.

He pushed his finished work toward her.

A tarantula-like spider with fangs and a web covered the orange helmet. The design matched the hood of the sled he'd drawn.

"This is good, Ricky, very good. Do you draw a lot?"

He shook his head.

"You should."

He looked shy for a moment. "Patty's the one who likes to draw," he said very quietly. "I think my dad was good at it. He used to draw comic stories for me. When I was little. Before he went away."

Ash pushed his empty plate aside and reached for his mug. "The machine you think might have followed you last night—did it look like this one, perhaps?" He nodded at the drawing.

"Can't say. I just saw glimpses of the headlights through the trees."

Rebecca inserted Ricky's rendition of the helmet and sled into her notebook and shut the cover. She put the book and pens in her bag.

"What happens now?" Ricky asked.

"I'm going to be contacting homicide investigators in the Lower Mainland," she said. "The RCMP has a special unit that handles murder investigations in other jurisdictions. They'll probably open a case file, start an investigation, maybe send someone out here to start with, followed by a team, depending on how this plays out." She held his eyes. "You can't speak about this to anyone, okay?"

He nodded.

"You and Tori are going to need to cooperate with the investigators fully. When they question you, they'll advise that you have a parent or guardian present. Your mother—"

"I want Ash."

She glanced at Ash. "We could probably arrange that," she said. "And it would be a good idea for both you and Ash to speak with a lawyer, also. And remember, the fact you were in the shed is not something that is going to get you into trouble, not in this case. The fact that you were in there is going to help. It will help solve my father's murder."

And that's what it was going to become now—an official homicide investigation. She'd make the call as soon as she'd verified the Oona Ferris–Cache Creek witness story, which she planned to attack right after they filed a hit-and-run report with Buck.

"Now, we're all going over to the RCMP station to file that report," she said.

Ricky tensed.

"It'll be fine, Ricky. Just the facts of the accident. Because at this point there is no proof that the accident was linked to the cabin fire or shooting."

CHAPTER 41

Rebecca observed Buck closely, watching for any tic, any clue he'd already known of the incident. But the cop remained guarded, sitting behind his metal desk and taking notes as he listened to what Ricky and Ash had to say.

When they'd finished, he closed his notebook and said, "Thanks for coming in. I'll look into it. Probably some guys driving under the influence and didn't want to stick around when they saw someone coming."

"Still a crime," Ash said. "Hit-and-run. Drunk driving."

"Yeah, like I said, I'll look into it." He checked his watch and came to his feet. "Impaired guys in a big truck with a bull bar like that? Probably thought they'd hit a deer out there along that quiet stretch. Not many drivers along there at this time of year, especially at that hour."

"Exactly," said Rebecca, also coming to her feet.

Ash and Ricky followed suit, metal chair legs scraping on the flooring.

Buck looked at Ash. "What were all you guys doing out there at that hour anyway?"

"And what's that question got to do with a hit-and-run?" Ash said darkly, tension rising between the two. Ricky backed toward the door. "It's an approach to my land," Ash added.

"Unused land." Buck went to his office door, opened it for them to leave. "I'll let you know if I find anything."

Ash and Ricky made their way through the station to the front exit, but Rebecca held back.

"What do you drive when you're not in an RCMP vehicle, Buck?"

His gaze flared hotly to hers. She could feel the energy pulsing off him. He was riled—there was no love lost between Bucky Johnstone and Ash Haugen. Given what Ash had told her about Buck's sexual fixation on Whitney, and his having watched Whitney and Ash fornicating in the barn, it was understandable. Buck knew that Ash knew he was watching and jerking off. They were locked together in the dark memory of that night, and bound together by an unspoken pact to keep the silence.

Oh, the mutual secrets we keep for personal benefit, she thought, looking up into Corporal Buck Johnstone's clear blue-green eyes.

"I drive a Ford F-350 pickup," he replied. "Like half the guys in town. Other half drive GMCs or Dodges or Silverados."

"Yours black?"

His eyes narrowed. "What are you insinuating, Becca?"

"Was it parked in the lot outside, next to my dad's Silverado, when I first came to see you and picked up my dad's vehicle?"

Silence.

Outside his window the red-and-white maple leaf flag snapped clean and bright against the brittle blue sky. Just like it had when her father held this office.

"That's the public safety lot out there," Buck said as he followed Rebecca's gaze out the window. "It's used by the municipality's public works personnel, and by firefighters. And yeah, I used my Ford to come to work that day."

The image of the truck parked next to her father's Silverado rose in her mind—shiny-new black Ford F-350 with big-ass wheel simulators, a fancy chrome grille, bull bars, and other bling, including a decal on the back window that depicted a snarling wolf.

She thought of Ash's description of the wolf decal Tori had seen on the truck that ran her and Ricky off the road.

"The wolf sticker on the back window of your truck—what does it denote?" she said.

His eyes flickered and his jaw firmed. "A hunting club. The Wolf Pack."

"Based where?"

His eyes narrowed further. "Nowhere. We just meet to hunt. Have online groups and an email loop. What is this about?"

"Who all is in the club?"

His gaze locked with hers. "Some of the guys like their privacy. It's not for me to say."

"Who's the main contact?"

"Look it up. If you'll excuse me"—he checked his watch again—"I have a presentation to prep for council."

"Your truck isn't parked out there this morning," she said as she exited his office.

"Because I came to work in the cruiser. Becca—"

She stilled, turned.

"Remember something. Ricky Simon is full of shit. A compulsive liar. There's more to this, and I can smell it—there's something he's still not telling me, or telling us. Or *you* are not being totally straight with me." His eyes held hers. "Be careful."

"Of who?"

He said nothing. He closed the door in her face.

——

Ash and Ricky were waiting in Ash's truck—a big, dark-gray, almost-black GMC with hunting spotlights across the top. It was true, Rebecca thought, half the people in town did drive big, dark trucks, as Buck had said. But there was no wolf sticker on Ash's truck.

She climbed into the passenger seat. Ricky was in back. The engine was running and the cab interior warm.

"What was that about?" Ash said as he put his GMC in gear.

"I asked Buck about his truck. I think it has the same decal Tori saw, and it's black. With hunting spots." Her cell rang as she spoke. "Bert Spiker," she said as she checked the caller ID. "I asked him to have some toxicology tests expedited."

She connected the call and put the phone to her ear as Ash pulled out of the public safety parking lot.

"Bert? You got something already?"

"I managed to put a rush on the tests, like you asked, given your concerns over a homicide." He paused. "You were right."

Her pulse quickened as she listened to Bert explain the results. Ash shot her an inquiring look as he drove.

She killed the call and sat for a moment, her heart racing.

"What'd he say?" Ash asked, turning onto the main road.

"Ketamine," she said quietly, her brain scrambling and rearranging pieces like a Rubik's Cube. "The lab found high levels of ketamine in both my father's femoral and heart blood samples. The concentration in the heart blood was higher. He said the difference in the concentrations observed was consistent with incomplete distribution through my father's body. Which is what would happen if the drug was administered either intravenously or via intramuscular injection."

She turned in her seat to face Ash. "He said injected ketamine—as opposed to orally administered ketamine—takes effect within mere seconds to a minute." Rebecca looked at him. "The gunshot wound killed my dad very soon after the injection, hence the uneven distribution in blood. The drug has a quick half-life. Which means it usually works pretty fast through a living body and wears off, which would leave little to no tox trace. But in this case, the drug was still in his blood because his heart ceased beating, and the samples were extracted within a narrow-enough time frame and properly preserved."

"That fits with Ricky's account of the timing," Ash said as he stopped at a traffic light. "Whoever went into Noah's cabin acted fast. The killer came prepared."

"Perhaps my father knew the person and didn't see the injection coming. On top of the alcohol, the drug would have seriously incapacitated him. Whoever injected him could have then easily staged him in a suicide position and pulled the trigger."

"Not Thora?" he said quietly.

She leaned back in her seat. "As a nurse, Thora could have access to something like ketamine. I don't know that she'd have arrived on a snowmobile, though. She didn't strike me as someone athletic or agile, or who moved fast enough to match Ricky's description." Rebecca mulled over the possibilities. "Whoever killed him had to have known about the gun in his safe, and given my dad's history, they knew everyone would easily buy into the idea of suicide."

Ash drew up outside the Cariboo Lodge Motel.

"And now?" he asked.

"Now you stay the hell away from all this while I visit Oona Ferris's aunt in Cache Creek, and check with the police there for more details on her accident. And then I call a detective with the district homicide unit. What's the verdict with my dad's Silverado?"

"Wes says you need a new truck. He reckons patching that rusted old beater up is not a safe option. Becca, if you're thinking of driving out to Cache Creek in the Prius rental, let me drive you rather. Roads are still icy—"

"No. You need to back off, Ash. I don't want you part of this now."

"The tires on those rentals are not—"

"They're all-season. The road is well salted. I'm not heading into unpaved areas, don't worry."

And it hung. Ash worried for her. Their gazes locked. She recalled his hand on her shoulder this morning, his words.

All I know, Becca, the one true thing, the one constant, solid thing in my life, has been my love for you.

Somewhere, somehow, they'd slipped over a line.

She moistened her lips, anxiety of a different kind twisting through her. As much as she was trying to push him away, his words, his touch, had cracked a carapace around her. Emotions, feelings, were seeping out. Unarticulated possibilities were surfacing. She couldn't allow that. But she was also unable to stuff it all back into those cracks. And she was afraid—that Ash just might have done something terrible, because she still sensed he was hiding something very dark and fundamental from her.

She swallowed. "Thanks," she said simply, and got out of the truck.

CHAPTER 42

Ricky sat in the back seat and watched Sergeant Rebecca North go up the stairs to the Cariboo Lodge entrance.

He liked her. Even though she was a cop. He'd never met law enforcement like her. He'd figured they were all more or less like Buck and were therefore the enemy.

She was pretty and tough and sort of untouchable. Not like some of the women he'd been raised around—females who acted like they wanted to be twenty when in truth they were old mothers who did drugs and drank and swore and passed out while their kids were playing with wires behind television sets. Like that time Patty almost got electrocuted when she was two.

Rebecca spoke nicely and had kind gold eyes, and thick hair the color of dark chocolate. And she made Ricky feel important, as though he had worth. As if she maybe even respected him. Which was kind of unreal. No one treated Ricky with respect.

"Wanna sit up front, bud?" Ash said.

He climbed over into the front passenger seat next to Ash and buckled up. They both sat awhile in the truck and watched her go inside. The lodge doors swung shut behind her.

"She's nice," he said to Ash.

"She is nice," Ash said.

"Is she your girlfriend?"

"Was. A long time ago."

"And not now?"

"Not a chance, bud." He put the truck in gear.

"What happened?"

He glanced at Ricky. Ash Haugen's eyes sometimes looked like glacier ice—the sort you see when you look through a hole in the snow into a crevasse. And they were intimidating sometimes. They cut right into you like they had a superpower.

"I fucked up," he said.

Ricky held the man's gaze, wondering whether he should ask how, then decided he better not.

Ash pulled into the road and did a U-turn across the main street so they could head back north to Haugen Ranch.

"What was that stuff about Special K and Noah North?" Ricky asked.

"Special K?"

"Ketamine."

Ash cast him a glance. Ricky could see he was figuring what to share with him, if anything. Resistance rose in him because he knew he was going to be treated like a shit little kid again who couldn't be trusted.

"You know ketamine?"

"Shit man, yeah, I know Special K. It's used by vets and doctors, and they sell it on the rez sometimes as a party drug."

"Who sells it?"

He felt himself tighten up. Those rez dealer guys scared him. If he spoke about them, he was toast. They'd beaten him up twice before when he wouldn't give them some of the moonshine he'd nicked. One had threatened to come after Patty once. They'd probably even kill him.

"Just a bunch of guys who deal with those biker sled-necks up in Devil's Butte."

Ash came to a stop at a red light. "What biker sled-necks?"

"I dunno, man. They just . . . sell drugs. I'm not sure who they are." His heart was beating fast. He didn't want to lie to Ash, but he really didn't want to talk about those guys, either. To his relief, Ash didn't push it.

The light turned green, and they drove awhile in silence, the radio playing softly. It was a nice interior, he thought. He'd like to own wheels like this someday. Heated leather seats and everything. He fiddled with the controls, making his seat tilt backward, then forward.

"Is Sergeant North going to stay in town after this?" He moved his seat up, then down.

A beat of silence.

He looked at Ash's profile. A little muscle at Ash's jaw pulsed. And it struck Ricky that Ash Haugen was really hung up on Sergeant North. Like seriously.

"Nah," Ash said finally. "She's got a life elsewhere."

"Back east?"

"Yeah."

"She's a detective there?"

Ash nodded.

And as they drove, Ricky wished he could find a way make Sergeant North stay. For Ash. He had an urge to help make Ash feel better. To fix things. A lot of things. He sat back for the remainder of the return trip to Haugen Ranch mulling over this.

But when Ash took the turnoff that led to Broken Bar Ranch instead of taking the fork to Haugen Ranch, Ricky sat up sharply.

"Where are we going?"

"Tori's place. You can hang out there awhile, see how she's doing."

Tension whipped through him. "But—"

"Olivia called earlier to invite you."

"She *called*?"

"Yeah. She and Cole figured you might want to stay and have dinner with them. I can pick you up after. It'll give me a chance to catch up on some ranch work."

Ricky's pulse worked in double time. "Olivia wants me there?" he said again.

Ash ticked a glance his way. "Yeah, bud. She figures since you and Tori are so close, it's time to get to know you better."

"Shit," he whispered as he sat back in his seat. Part of him was scared. Part of him wanted to cry. No one invited Ricky Simon anywhere. Let alone to a fancy-ass ranch.

CHAPTER 43

"Noah often came in here over the years looking for one thing or another," Rennie Price said as he watched Rebecca paging through a bound volume of weekly newspapers from the end of 1998 through early 1999. The *Clinton Sentinel* publisher had brought the archived volume out from his morgue to a table in a small, windowless conference room. He watched Rebecca from the doorway, overtly curious.

After visiting the police station with Ash and Ricky, Rebecca had returned to the lodge, picked up the Prius, and driven to the old newspaper offices. She'd found Rennie hunched over his desk and jabbing away at his keyboard, hunt-and-peck style.

"So this is the volume he was interested in the last time he was here?" she asked.

Rennie nodded. "Yeah. Noah was searching for the name of that witness from twenty years ago, in connection with that Whitney Gagnon and Trevor Beauchamp missing-persons mystery."

Rebecca glanced up. "My dad told you that?"

He nodded.

"What else did he say?"

Rennie scratched his big beard and frowned. He was in his early sixties, sported a thatch of thick white hair, and had an open and friendly face with laugh lines around blue eyes. He clearly loved his

job running a community newspaper even though it was a dying—
or dead—enterprise. He'd been editor, then publisher, of the *Clinton
Sentinel* as long as Rebecca had been aware there even was a town
newspaper.

"Well, Noah explained he was looking into that old mystery
again—he often did that with one cold case or another." He smiled
sadly. "It kept him busy, I think. I'm gonna miss him coming in. We'd
usually have a coffee and chat while I photocopied whatever articles
he was interested in at the time."

"Do you perhaps recall which articles he asked to have photocopied when he was in here last?"

"Oh yeah, sure. He asked for a copy of the front-page article we
ran on the two teens in the Christmas-week issue, the one where we
covered the Santa Parade."

Rebecca hurriedly flipped back through the pages until she found
the Christmas issue Rennie was referring to. The headline was printed
below the fold—under a color photograph of Santa on a float.

Clinton Mother Searches for Daughter Missing
Since Fall

Embedded in the text was a high school photograph of Whitney
Gagnon—long golden-blonde hair and a sweet smile that belied the
complexities of her life. She wore a snug white T-shirt and long silver
earrings in the shape of narrow leaves. Rebecca scanned the article.

Witness Oona Ferris, 18, of Devil's Butte, upon hearing that Janet Gagnon was worried about her daughter's whereabouts, reported that she was driving
by the Renegade Bus lines early on the morning of
September 27 when she saw Whitney Gagnon and

Trevor Beauchamp hitching a ride. As she passed by them, a white van with Oregon plates pulled off the road and stopped for them. Ferris said the teens ran up to the vehicle with their bags and climbed in.

Rennie tilted his bearded chin toward the page and said, "Your dad asked for copies of that article; plus, he was interested in another one from September of that year."

"Do you know which one?"

"Yeah, matter of fact I do. Although I'm not sure what it was that interested him specifically about that one." He reached across Rebecca and paged back through the copies to find a small story buried on page seven alongside the weekly Clinton police report.

"That one." He tapped the piece with his index finger.

She leaned forward and read the article closely.

It was a conservation-office report about shots fired in an area that had been closed to hunting for the season. According to the article, Clinton resident Barnaby "Barnes" Hatfield was driving his truck along the Main Line logging road when a bullet came through the passenger-side window and lodged in the seat's headrest. His son, Frank Hatfield, was in the passenger seat at the time and miraculously escaped the close call unhurt. Rebecca read further:

> Hatfield said he slammed on the brakes. Both he and his son glimpsed something running in the woods. They thought it was a deer, but the bush was dense so they couldn't be sure.
>
> "We were both shaken up," said Hatfield senior. "We got out of the truck and saw quite a bit of blood by the side of the road. Something had been injured pretty good, but we stayed out of the bush for fear of

another stray bullet coming our way. Friggin' dangerous, hunting out of season like that."

Rebecca checked the date of the incident. Sunday, September 27.
Same day the teens disappeared.

She frowned. The article continued to say that a conservation officer had investigated the following day, but a heavy storm had blown
in right after the incident, and any blood trace that had been seen by
the Hatfields had been washed away. The bullet that had lodged in
the headrest was a .30-30 caliber. Typical ammunition used to hunt
game. Like deer.

"Could I get photocopies of these as well?" Rebecca asked.

"Sure thing." Rennie reached over and hefted the bound volume
up into his arms with a grunt. He carted it over to his photocopy
machine. Rebecca followed and watched as he made duplicates.

"Do you know Barnaby Hatfield?" she asked.

"I did. He died two years back. He was eighty when he passed.
Fine hunter he was, right to the end."

"Thanks," Rebecca said as Rennie handed her the copies.

"His son, Frank, is still around, though," said Rennie. "Frank's
in his late fifties now. He and his wife run Hatfield's Hardware up in
Devil's Butte. Took it over from his old man some years back."

———

Using speakerphone, Rebecca called the RCMP detachment in
Ashcroft as she drove her Prius rental to Cache Creek, a small town
about thirty minutes south of Clinton. Cache Creek fell under
Ashcroft police jurisdiction, hence her call to that station.

Undulating white fields of snow-covered scrub rolled by on either
side of her vehicle as she waited to be put through to the officer handling the Oona Ferris file.

Before leaving Clinton, Rebecca had looked up and made contact with Chloe Kennedy, the aunt of Oona Ferris. She had arranged to meet with Chloe and was headed there now. Rebecca had also placed a call to the southeast district major crimes unit based out of Kelowna and explained her situation. She was told that Sergeant Grace Parker, a homicide detective, would call back later.

"Hello, Corporal Jay Mohammad here," came a voice as her call was connected.

Rebecca explained who she was and asked about the accident involving Oona the previous Monday night.

Mohammad consulted his files and said, "Single-vehicle accident involving a white 2016 Subaru Outback. Evidence on scene was consistent with the vehicle having hit black ice. It lost control, spun, and left the paved road, going onto the gravel shoulder, where it went through the barrier and down into the river. Accident appears to have happened around six fifteen p.m. That's when the decedent's watch stopped. The timing is consistent with the pathologist's estimated time of death. The decedent was the sole occupant of the vehicle."

"So there's no sign that another vehicle might have been involved?" Rebecca said. "No indication she might have been hit and forced off the road?"

"Looks like an unfortunate accident. It's a notorious stretch. The Subaru took a beating on the way down that cliff," Mohammad said. "But our investigators found no evidence of another vehicle's involvement—no paint marks, no other tire marks."

Rebecca considered this. Perhaps it really was just an unfortunate coincidence. But her gut was screaming otherwise. Maybe Oona Ferris wasn't hit by another vehicle, but she could have been terrorized into driving beyond her safety level on a notoriously icy and twisty stretch of highway. It might not be something that could be proved.

"So no witnesses?"

"Negative. A couple called the accident in around two a.m. Tuesday morning."

Mere hours before her dad was due to meet with Oona Ferris.

"The couple had stopped at a viewpoint along that stretch of highway to photograph a display or aurora. They saw something glistening in the river ice below, and then they saw the damage to the barrier. They made a 911 call. Oona Ferris was pronounced dead on scene. Her vehicle was pulled up later that morning."

Rebecca thanked Mohammad and killed the call as she pulled into the historic town of Cache Creek.

CHAPTER 44

The woman who opened the door was bent forward at a sixty-degree angle and leaned heavily on a walker. Her steel-gray hair was scraped back into a severe bun, and her features were drawn. Rebecca judged Chloe Kennedy to be in her early seventies, and in pain.

"I'm Sergeant Rebecca North," she explained. "Thank you for agreeing to see me."

"Come on in," Chloe said, shuffling backward to make room for Rebecca to enter the tiny home. She winced as she moved. "Damn arthritis," she said.

"I'm so sorry for your loss," Rebecca said as she removed her coat and boots. And the words felt trite. It was the same refrain she'd been hearing herself in Clinton since she'd arrived home.

"And for yours."

Rebecca nodded and thanked Chloe. She'd already explained in her phone call about her father's death, and why she wanted to meet in his absence.

"I still can't quite believe it," Chloe said, leading the way into a tiny, dim living room with outdated furniture. From all appearances, money was tight for Chloe Kennedy.

Chloe eased herself down into a brown chair and motioned for Rebecca to take a seat on the matching sofa opposite. Lace sheers draped over a window with a view into the service entrance of a Dairy Queen restaurant.

"I suspect I will process it all in due time, but it was so sudden. You mentioned you had some questions."

Rebecca took a seat. "As I explained on the phone, my father was due to meet with Oona in person last Tuesday morning. I'm not sure how much your niece told you about what he wanted to speak to her about?" Rebecca said.

"Oona said Corporal North had called and asked about that old missing-persons case. Oona told me she'd lied to him twenty years ago about seeing that young woman and her boyfriend getting into a white van, and that she'd confessed this to Corporal North over the phone. She wanted to cooperate fully with him, and was actually really pleased to be meeting with him and getting this off her chest. She said she'd forgotten all about it until his call. Oona was in a real bad way back then, on drugs and all." Chloe fell silent and stared absently at the sheers hanging across the window.

Rebecca felt a swell of emotion. She identified with Chloe, with the way grief waxed and waned and sideswiped and numbed.

Chloe reached for a tissue from the box on the table beside her and blew her nose. "I'm sorry."

"Don't be," Rebecca said.

Clearing her throat, Chloe said, "Oona cleaned up about seven years ago after a bad health scare. She went through rehab and committed her life to religion and to atoning for all the wrongs she felt she'd done through her addicted years. And she moved in with me. She . . ." The woman faltered. She blew her nose again, wiped tears from her eyes. When she spoke again, her voice was husky and thick.

"Oona dedicated herself to caring for me as my own health deteriorated. She made me her mission. She's all I have. I mean . . . had. I . . . I don't know what I will do without her."

Rebecca's heart hurt for the crippled senior. She discreetly checked her watch, giving Chloe time to compose herself. But urgency nipped at her for answers, and she wondered when the homicide detective would call back.

"Did Oona tell you why she lied?" Rebecca asked gently.

"Drugs. Someone knew her weakness and used it. They asked her to say she saw those teens getting into that van with US plates."

"Who asked her?"

"I don't know. I got the sense it was a guy, though—someone who moved in her circles back then. Oona was going to tell Corporal North everything when she saw him."

"Did she say this person specifically asked her to report US plates?"

"Oregon, yes."

"Did Oona inform anyone else—apart from you—about the planned meeting with my father, about the fact she was going to officially recant her statement?"

"I don't know. I don't imagine so."

"Who were Oona's friends back then, do you know?"

"She was estranged from us—her family—during that period, so no, I don't know. She was acquainted with Whitney Gagnon and Trevor Beauchamp, though, that much I am aware of."

"She didn't attend school in Clinton, did she?" Rebecca couldn't recall anyone named Oona Ferris at school.

"She went to high school up in Devil's Butte, but dropped out early."

"The newspaper article in the *Clinton Sentinel* from the time said Oona was eighteen when she claimed to have witnessed the van."

"Yes. She'd just turned eighteen, which is how come she could start working in bars."

"Do you have any idea which bars? Where she was staying?"

"Odd waitressing jobs at several establishments, I believe. One name that did come up in passing was the Devil's Butt."

Rebecca glanced up sharply from her note-taking. That was the same bar in which Ash had been meeting Whitney after he'd claimed it was over with her—the bar where Marcy Fossum had also worked. It had changed names since, but she didn't know what it was called now, or if it was even still there.

"It stuck in my mind because it felt ironic with how she'd turned to God and the church once she got clean," Chloe said. "At the time she was living in Devil's Butte with some guy, but I don't know who." She blew her nose again. "I'm sorry, I'm not much help. What do you think really happened to those missing teens?"

"It's a mystery," said Rebecca. "One my father was trying to solve."

"But why would someone want Oona to say they got into a US van?"

"To misdirect, I imagine. To make us think they did leave town for California." Which was why Becca had a strong feeling the opposite was true. And they were still here. She believed her father had also come to this conclusion, and someone had found out about it. And killed him before he could prove it.

"You think something awful happened to them? And that this man who coerced Oona into lying was responsible?"

"I don't know. But I'd be interested to know who Oona was living with at the time." Rebecca's phone buzzed in her pocket. She discreetly checked the incoming caller ID. Detective Grace Parker from major crimes. "I really must take this," she said, coming to her feet. "It's a homicide investigator from Kelowna who is going to help out with this."

"Go ahead." She waved a veined hand at Rebecca. "And please, let yourself out, if that's okay. I just don't have the strength right now."

Rebecca thanked the woman, and she connected the call as she made her way to Chloe's mudroom.

"Rebecca North," she said into the phone, reaching for her parka and boots.

———

Rebecca sat in the Prius rental, heaters blasting, while she listened to Detective Grace Parker, who said her unit had been given the okay to take the case, and she was opening an investigation. She'd managed to have Rebecca seconded to the team—basically assigned to the case, primarily in an advisory and liaison capacity.

"I've had it cleared it with your superiors," Grace said. "And I've informed Corporal Buck Johnstone we've taken the lead on the Corporal Noah North death investigation. And that we've advised the coroner's office we're now the lead agency on this case. I've also asked to be copied on all their files to date. I've got ident guys heading out there now to re-secure the fire scene. ETA sometime tomorrow morning. I don't know how much they can do until the freeze lets up, but I don't want anyone compromising what has not already been compromised. I've also advised that Corporal North's body be held pending further instruction. The Ashcroft detachment will be forwarding us their files on the Oona Ferris vehicle fatality and holding the Subaru wreck pending possible further forensic investigation on our part." Sergeant Grace Parker's delivery was clipped in the manner of an efficient cop focused on the job without emotion. Rebecca knew officers like her well. They weren't out to make friends but to solve cases, and to put another notch in their clearance-rate belts.

"I'll be familiarizing myself with the files as they come in," Grace said. "I'll be up there myself either tomorrow or the following day. I can pull in more members as needed. I'll personally be working out of the Clinton detachment, and yes, I'm aware of your concern that Corporal Johnstone might have a conflict of interest in this case, but he will not be involved in the investigation. So far, we have no evidence that Corporal Johnstone has not done due diligence to the best of his ability up until this point."

"I understand. I look forward to meeting you," Rebecca said as she put the Prius in gear. The windows had defrosted enough for her to drive.

As she pulled out of the parking space in front of Chloe's home, she briefed Grace on her meeting with Oona Ferris's aunt.

"I'm heading back to Clinton now to interview Whitney Gagnon's mother, Janet Gagnon, to see if she can provide any leads as to who Oona Ferris lived with. Apparently Ferris was acquainted with Gagnon. I will also check out the bar where Oona Ferris used to work—if it's still there. It was called the Devil's Butt; however, that establishment changed its name some years back." She turned onto the highway.

"While in Devil's Butte, I'd also like to interview Frank Hatfield of Hatfield's Hardware. According to a newspaper article my father photocopied from the *Clinton Sentinel*, on the same day that Gagnon and Beauchamp disappeared, Hatfield and his father came across shooting in the woods during a period when hunting season was closed for that area. They narrowly missed being hit by a stray .30-30-caliber bullet. And they reported seeing a lot of blood along the side of the Main Line logging road. I want to know if my father had already spoken with Hatfield. I'd also like to know where along the logging road this incident happened, and why my father might have been so interested in it. Hatfield might be able to tell me."

Parker instructed Rebecca to run with what she had going so far, and to brief her when she arrived in Clinton.

CHAPTER 45

Rebecca watched Janet Gagnon pour coffee into two mugs in her tiny kitchen in the trailer-park home where Whitney had grown up. From the rear, Whitney's mother looked frail. Her hair had thinned and was shot through with gray she hadn't cared to color.

She set the mugs on a table, one in front of Rebecca, and drew up a chair for herself. "I guess I never moved because it felt like I'd be abandoning Whitney in case she wanted to come home. It's silly, I know. Cream?" She held up a small carton.

"No, thanks." Rebecca nodded to the window and the house across the street. "Was that Thora and Jake Battersby's place?"

"Yeah." Janet picked up her mug and cradled it in her hands. From the front she looked even more haggard. Dark rings scooped hollows under her eyes, and her skin was lined and papery. She looked like a woman who'd suffered too long and who lived on too little sleep. Even her voice had grown thin. Nothing robust at all about Janet Gagnon.

"The Battersbys were good neighbors. I could always count on Jake to help when things like the dishwasher or washing machine broke, or if I had plumbing issues. That kind of thing. A real old-school handyman type. Always had a smile, too."

"He was around here often, then?"

She offered a wan smile of her own. "When things broke—but I guess my old crap tended to go on the blink more often than not." She cleared her throat, took a sip of coffee. "So, you've officially opened my Whitney's case? After all these years? That's what you came to tell me?"

Rebecca nodded. "A major crimes team out of the Lower Mainland is taking the lead. They'll be sending officers up."

"But why? Why now?"

Rebecca considered how best to frame the narrative and decided Janet deserved straight-up transparency. "My father's death might not have been suicide."

Janet's eyes widened. "As in . . . *murder*?"

"The evidence has raised some questions. At the time of his death, he was looking into Whitney's case again because he'd happened across some new information. There's a chance his death is related to what he learned about Whitney and Trevor through his investigation."

She set her mug down abruptly. "What new information?"

"The witness who saw Whitney and Trevor getting into a white van lied."

"What?"

"No one saw them leaving town."

She stared. Processing. "You mean . . . Oona Ferris? She *didn't* see them?"

"No."

"Why did she lie?"

"That's part of the investigation. I understand Whitney knew Oona. Did she know her well?"

"I . . . I don't know. She originally met Oona at a bar in Devil's Butte."

"The Devil's Butt?"

"Yeah. It riffed off the town name. Oona worked there. Her boyfriend was a manager there at the time Whit went missing," Janet said.

Rebecca's pulse quickened. "Do you recall his name?"

She shook her head. "I'm sorry." She lifted her mug, hesitated. "Why don't you ask Oona?"

"Oona was killed in a vehicle accident the evening before my father died."

Janet stared. Slowly she lowered her mug. "Is it connected?"

"It's part of the investigation."

She fell silent. Emotion pooled in her eyes. "Something terrible happened to Whitney, didn't it? I know it did."

"We don't know yet, Janet," Rebecca said gently. "And it would help if you didn't talk to anyone about this. I know it'll be tough, but it's a very small town. Everyone is connected, and it could hinder the investigation at this point to have too much information floating around out there."

"I understand."

"Is Ariel MacAdam still in town?" Rebecca asked of Whitney's best friend.

"She left some years ago. Moved to Kamloops." A sadness fell over her features. "If it wasn't for Ariel, I might not have gone to your father that December to ask for his help. I was so worried when I had heard nothing, especially approaching Christmas. But I thought . . . maybe my own daughter just hated me. I . . . I'd let my baby down, and I knew it. As a single mom, working two jobs with no support from her deadbeat dad, I struggled to get through a day, let alone deal with someone like Whit." She wiped away a tear. "She was a challenging child. In retrospect, her acting out, her sleeping around, it was a cry for my attention, and I heard it too late. And then she was gone. I . . . I tried, Rebecca. I did my best at the time. The best I could."

"I know." Rebecca covered Janet's veined hand with her own. "If there is something to find, I will do my best to find it. I promise." She paused. "Is Whitney's father still around?"

She shook her head. "Lung cancer. He was a heavy smoker and drinker. He died just over ten years ago." She got up and fetched a small wooden box off a shelf in the adjacent living room.

She set it on the table, reseated herself, opened the lid, and took out a photo of a baby on a young woman's lap. "That's me and Whit." She wiped her nose and smiled sadly.

Rebecca studied the photo. Janet looked beautiful. Young. With the promise of a future in her eyes, and in the child she held so lovingly. The baby was laughing and reaching for whoever shot the image.

"Who took it?"

"Her father. Before things started to go wrong. And I still have this." She opened a tiny silver box and unwrapped the cotton wool inside. "One of her baby teeth." Janet's chin wobbled, and she pressed her lips together. "So . . . small." She held it out for Rebecca to see.

DNA, thought Rebecca as she examined the tiny tooth. They might be able to extract some for a comparison if human remains were ever found.

"And this." Janet opened a folded piece of tissue paper and revealed a lock of gold-blonde hair tied with a tiny piece of red thread. "From her first proper haircut. In a salon."

Rebecca nodded, uncomfortable at the rawness of Janet's emotions, and with this little shrine-in-a-box—the way it was all shaping Whitney into a real human being in her mind. As a teen, Rebecca had detested Whitney Gagnon, the promiscuous classmate who'd fucked her boyfriend in the barn. But this mother held memories of a beautiful baby girl, a first lost tooth, a first haircut, of struggling to work two jobs in order to support a daughter left lonely and neglected at home. She thought of what Ash had said—that Whitney was not a bad kid. And it struck Rebecca that Ash was a way better person than she was, even for all his secrets. His mistake with Whitney had ruined his life and her own, yet he still found room for empathy for the young woman. Guilt fired Rebecca's resolve. She would do right by this mother. She would find her daughter. She'd do it for her dad.

Gently, Rebecca said, "What was your perception of Trevor, Janet? Did he love Whitney? Was he good to her?"

Janet carefully wrapped up the tooth and replaced it and the lock of hair in their respective containers. "It was more a codependent kind of relationship, I think," she said as she closed the lid on the box shrine. "They had a need for each other but weren't always kind to each other. I suppose in their maladjusted ways they maybe really did care for one another. Trevor had his issues. He basically had absent parents. Got into some trouble with the cops from time to time at an early age, and he ended up living up to his own reputation."

Rebecca thought of Ricky, and how Ash had stepped up and was trying to stop exactly that from happening with Running Wind's grandson. A wave of unbidden affection for Ash surged through her. A sense of kinship. Old feelings she really didn't want to feel again.

"Trevor probably thought he could kick his rep, start afresh in LA like Whit wanted to," Janet said.

"Could Trevor have hurt Whitney? I mean, if he felt she'd betrayed or wronged him?"

"Trev? I don't think so." A pause. "But then one never knows, does one, what monsters might lurk in a man?" She studied the box abstractedly. "I thought Whitney's father would never raise a hand to me."

"And he did?"

She nodded.

"It's why you left him?"

She nodded again, biting her lip. And Rebecca's heart ached for this mother. For all her dreams that had died.

"Who were Trevor's friends, do you know?"

"Mostly transient sorts. He worked on the oil sands, and other contracts up north. Sometimes his contract connections came through town and would hang with him and Whit. But no one special that I can recall."

"Before Whitney left that goodbye note, did she give you any idea she might have come into some money?"

Janet glanced up sharply. "It's funny you say that. Ariel, her friend, mentioned this to me much later, well after your father had sort of given up on locating Trev and Whit. It made me wonder. It . . . I mean, Ariel said she'd gotten the sense it was a substantial amount. She just figured it was Trevor's money."

Everything I had. Every penny I had worked for and saved from the time I was twelve. My whole college fund.

"When you say substantial—like how much?"

"Like fifty grand. Maybe more."

Surprise rippled through Rebecca.

"You can make some really serious money on the oil sands," Janet offered. "The trick is to hold on to it. Most of those guys blow through it as fast they earn it. One trip into the city and it's gone. Huge, crazy spenders. Then again, maybe it wasn't saved contract money. Trevor did run with some dark sorts. I had a sense he dealt in minor drugs from time to time. Maybe he ran some drug trade or something up in the oil sands. Most of those guys were into cocaine at the time."

Rebecca filed this away. And now she faced the question she'd been dreading.

"Janet . . ." She cleared her throat. "Did you know that your daughter was pregnant?"

Janet's hands fell flat to the table. They lay there as if the nerves controlling them had been severed. Her jaw slackened and her mouth opened. When she spoke, it was barely a whisper. "*Was* she?"

"It appears so."

Silence. A clock ticked. Wind rustled outside the windows.

"A grandchild. I . . . I could have had a grandbaby?"

Rebecca gave her a moment to process.

"Whose baby?" she asked.

"Whitney told Ash Haugen it was his."

Janet closed her eyes. Swallowed. Inhaled. "Ash—he's a good sort."

"Is he?"

She opened her eyes and met Rebecca's gaze. "Isn't he?"

"I don't know," she said quietly.

"You don't think Ash could have hurt Whitney?"

"No. I don't think so."

But he was hiding something. And Rebecca knew firsthand from her years as a cop that sometimes those closest to us could be the worst monsters of all. Statistics proved it, too.

———

After taking her leave, while warming up her car again, Rebecca phoned Ash.

When he answered, she said simply, "How much money did you say you gave Whitney?"

A hesitation. "I told you. About eleven thousand dollars. It was all I had—I was paid very little as a kid back in the day."

My whole college fund.

Rebecca killed the call and sat while two holes formed in the fog on her windshield above the blasting heater vents. It might have been everything Ash had to put toward his college education, but it was a far cry from fifty grand or more.

Was this about money? A drug deal gone wrong? Some sort of revenge? Could this be more about Trevor than Whitney, and have nothing to do with Ash? Could the young couple have scored the cash illegally and escaped town and gone into hiding somewhere in the world?

But then why would Oona Ferris have been coerced into leading law enforcement to believe they'd left town in a van from Oregon? And who might have coerced her? It *had* to be someone who was still in town. Especially if Rebecca's father's death was tied to this.

What am I missing?

And . . . if Whitney and Trevor had actually been in possession of more than fifty grand—possibly in cash, as Solly had intimated—and if something bad had happened to the kids, where had the money gone?

Who might suddenly have come into a lump of cash in late 1998?

Who out there still had a secret worth killing for?

CHAPTER 46

"No, I had not met with your father yet," Frank Hatfield said as he led Rebecca into the back room of Hatfield's Hardware in Devil's Butte.

Hatfield, in his late fifties, was a gaunt and pale beanstalk of a man who stood around six feet four with a fringe of brown hair that ran in a trimmed half-moon shape around the back of his shiny pate.

He offered Rebecca a plastic chair, which she took, and he perched himself on the edge of a metal desk piled high with a mess of papers. A coffee machine, fridge, and microwave took up space along one wall. On another hung various hardware gadgets and keys to be cut.

"Noah called to say he wanted to speak with me about that shooting incident twenty years back, but he didn't say why." He fiddled with a stapler from his desk as he spoke. His eyes were such a dark brown that they were almost black. They reminded Rebecca of a beetle.

"Do you recall the incident well?" she asked.

"Heavens, who doesn't remember a .30-30 coming through your window and smashing into the headrest behind your head? It's imprinted on my brain for all time. I figured God was looking out for me that day. Had the bullet gone a few inches this way or that, or had my dad been driving just a fraction faster or slower, I'd be stone-cold dead and six feet under."

"What happened after you realized you'd near-missed the stray bullet?"

"My dad stopped the truck. We stared at each other; then we both looked into the woods. We saw something. Running, moving fast. Thought it was probably a whitetail deer fleeing some hunters, even though hunting was closed in that area."

"Could it have been something other than a deer?"

His heavy brows knitted together in a sharp V above his nose. "You mean like some other game?"

Rebecca leaned forward, holding his piercing beetle gaze. "Or maybe . . . it was one of the hunters running?" she suggested to open his mind to the possibility that it might not have been an animal at all.

"A *person*?" He fell silent, his brain computing where she was going. "Jesus, you mean . . . like could it have been someone running *away* from the shooters?"

"I think maybe that's what my father wanted to ask you. If it was possible."

"Why? I mean, why would he even think that?"

"I'm not sure at this point." Rebecca offered him a smile along with her lie. "I'm just trying to piece together what my dad was up to in the days that led to his death."

He smoothed a pale, long-fingered hand over his pate. "Wow. I mean . . . now that you mention it. I suppose it *could* have been a person."

"So you're not one hundred percent certain it was a deer?"

He rubbed his mouth. "I guess . . . the color was a bit off for the deer in this area."

"How so?"

"More . . . pale, I guess. More gold than gray-brown."

Rebecca felt energy thump into her veins. She thought of Whitney's photograph, the long gold-blonde hair. "What happened next?"

"We got out of the truck, went to the edge of the forest to see."

"Why did you do that if there'd just been a stray bullet flying—you weren't concerned about another?"

"I'm not sure. It was . . . All I can think is that something was off. We got out because something wasn't right. Felt wrong."

"How so?"

He shook his head. "I don't know. I can't recall exactly."

"And then?"

"Then we saw the blood on the side of the road. In the ditch. On the grass and stones. A lot of it. We went a little deeper into the forest, and then the thunder started crashing and rain started. Lots of wind. Lightning. We hurried back to the safety of the truck for fear of a lightning strike—my grandfather was killed by lightning on his ranch back in the day. We drove off and called the incident in to the conservation office when we got home."

"Frank, can you close your eyes, relax, try to go back in your mind, and picture it as it happened, blow by blow, and describe to me what you're seeing, feeling, smelling as you and your father stop, get out of the car, look into the shadows between the trees, that sort of thing?"

"I can try." He closed his eyes and breathed in deep, exhaled, and breathed in again. "I was shaking," he said. "In shock. Still sort of trying to assimilate what had just happened, what had hit the headrest." He paused. Rebecca could see his eyeballs moving back and forth beneath his thin blue-veined lids.

"We peered into the shadows. It was dark between the trees. It's a dense old-growth part of the forest in that spot. Branches were moving wildly because the storm wind was just hitting. Very heavy wind. Hot. There was a sense of electrical pressure. We saw movement."

"What color?"

"I . . ." His eyes opened. "Definitely pale, more . . . golden colored than a deer. I . . . I always thought it had to have been a deer."

"Sometimes the brain works that way. We see what we expect to see. We see the thing that is most logical under the circumstances," Rebecca said. "Especially when under stress, or in shock."

He exhaled heavily and looked even more bloodless than before, his eyes seeming to sink deeper into their cavities beneath his brows. "You think it was a person, a woman?"

"Why did you say 'woman'?"

"I . . . Maybe it was long hair." He looked ill. "Maybe that's what our brains were saying when we thought deer, but felt something was off."

"And the blood?"

"Something had been injured bad. Dark blood, arterial, heart kind of blood that makes you think something has been fatally wounded and just on borrowed time until the animal bleeds out."

Rebecca's nerves thrummed, her blood pumped, and her skin tingled—the reaction she got when pieces of a case started slamming together. But she still couldn't see the whole picture.

"We might need you to come in to make an official statement when some of my colleagues arrive in town, if that's okay," Rebecca said as she came to her feet and dug a card out of her wallet. She handed it to Frank Hatfield. "If you remember anything else, please call me. Anytime."

He studied the card, looking as though he might throw up.

"Before I go, Frank, could you show me on a map exactly where this incident occurred?"

"Yeah, yeah, for sure." He opened a drawer in his metal desk, rummaged around, and took out a waterproof map, the kind used by hunters and other outdoor enthusiasts who were well aware that modern tech could let a person down in the wilderness, and that could mean death.

He shoved aside some papers on his desk and laid the map out on the surface. He grabbed a pen. With his long, spiderlike finger he traced the curves of the Main Line logging road. "We were driving along this road here. And the bullet hit us there." He marked the spot with an X and tapped it.

"Right there. I know because it's almost on the boundary of the provincial park on the south side, and Crown land—government land—here on the east. And that line there—that's the property line at the back end of Haugen Ranch."

Rebecca felt as if a small, cold stone had just dropped clean through her gut.

"And over there"—Hatfield pointed with his long finger—"that's the abandoned summer camp that Olav Haugen's father used to lease to an outdoor outfit for nature education and stuff for schoolkids. Olav never renewed the old lease when he took over the ranch, and that part of the Haugen land hasn't been used for decades."

Olav Haugen—Ash's father. Ash's ranch. *Shit.* Every which way this thing turned, Ash Haugen was still at the center.

As Rebecca took her leave, Frank called after her, "Oh wait!"

She turned.

"I forgot. It's here somewhere."

"What is?"

"Souvenir. I kept it as a souvenir." He opened and closed several drawers, scrabbling around in each. Finally he stood up and held something out toward her with a flourish. "Got it! I *knew* it was in one of these drawers. Not every day one gets one of these puppies slamming into their headrest."

He was holding a spent .30-30 bullet—the point squashed into a palm-tree shape around the nose.

"Dug it out of the headrest," he said, a smile cutting across his face and crinkling his eyes.

CHAPTER 47

Rebecca slowed her Prius. It was getting dark now, and the road was icy. She peered through the windshield at the buildings, looking for the old Devil's Butt bar property. This part of town had not changed much in the past twenty years. If anything, it had decayed and gone downhill. Or perhaps it was just the bleak effect of winter—the bare-branched trees like gnarled fingers reaching for the sky, the whiteness of the salted roads with blowing drifts of dried snow, the weathered siding on buildings without the softening effect of flowerbeds. Or maybe it was just the fact that the new stretch of highway had been built around this section, cutting off traffic and strangling businesses.

The Devil's Butt had once been a pull-in for long-haul truckers, logging rig drivers, and summer bikers as well as other motorists. It had at various points offered adult entertainment late at night. There'd been drug busts that Rebecca had heard about in her youth. A regular dive bar, basically. A place where people like Ash and Whitney could meet and sit in a dark back booth and no one would ask questions. Or talk.

Unless it was Marcy Fossum.

Now you'd have to pull off the highway and make a specific detour with intent to visit the place. If it was still here.

As she drove, she considered Frank Hatfield's words. She'd head out to the shooting location tomorrow, but first she'd need to find a vehicle with proper winter tires. And preferably studded. Circling like prowling wolves around the periphery of her thoughts was the fact that the shooting incident had happened at the back end of Haugen land. A place, she knew from when she was a teen, where Ash refused to go, even when she'd expressed interest and specifically asked him to take her to see the summer-camp ruins.

She turned a corner and instantly saw the giant sign above where the old bar used to be. Neon-pink letters declared the new venue to be the Sled-Nex Bar and Grille. With an *e*. The neon flickered eerily against the indigo northern sky. Wind whipped down the streets and darted among the squat warehouse-style buildings, casting old newspapers and other garbage adrift.

She pulled into the icy parking lot and studied the place for a moment. Several large trucks with sleds on the back were parked outside, as was a motorbike that had navigated the ice. A Harley. It looked like the one she'd seen outside the PetroGas. Uneasiness crawled under her skin.

She told herself she had nothing to worry about. She was just going in there to ask about the history of the place, and to see if the new owner or manager could tell her who might have managed the bar back in late 1998 when Oona Ferris worked here, or where she might find that information.

She locked the Prius and entered the bar.

It took a moment for her eyes to adjust to the dimness inside. Nothing fancy about this place. Bare decor, round tables, a long bar counter, and pool tables. The music was rock.

Three men gathered around one of the tables. Two dressed in black snow gear. One in the Devil's Butte redneck uniform of Carhartt jeans and a padded plaid shirt. Two guys played pool near the back.

Surprise spiked through Rebecca when she saw who was working the bar—the statuesque Amazonian Mohawk blonde. The woman whose ass Buck Johnstone had been feeling up at the Moose and Horn.

The men at the table turned to look at her. The "redneck," she realized, was Gonz the tow-truck driver. The second man was the bald biker she'd seen at the gas station. The third she did not recognize. He looked First Nations—glossy, shoulder-length black hair.

She nodded to Gonz.

He did not smile, but he raised his beer as if in a slight toast.

Uneasy, self-conscious, aware of where the exits lay, which pocket her cell was in, the fact that she was unarmed, Rebecca made her way to the bar. They all watched.

Mohawk placed her hands apart on the counter and leaned forward as she waited for Rebecca to reach her. She wore a black T-shirt that revealed the tats on her arms. Nose and eyebrow piercings winked in the light.

Six feet tall at least, Rebecca figured. Ripped body. Not someone she'd want to tangle with in a dark alley.

"Sergeant North," the woman said. Her accent was German.

Rebecca feigned a smile and drew up a stool. "You have the advantage," she said as she seated herself atop the stool, waiting for the woman to share her name.

"I like it that way."

Her words hung. The music segued to something smooth and country.

Mohawk grinned sharply. The suddenness of it, the pointed eyeteeth, the way it changed her face, was a shock to Rebecca. The woman knew it, too. Her smile had been wielded as a fanged weapon, because it faded almost instantly. "So what can I get for you?"

Rebecca asked for whiskey, sensing this would weigh more heavily in her favor than sparkling water or juice. And frankly, she could use a stiff drink about now.

Mohawk slapped a thick glass on the bar counter, poured a shot. She set the drink on a coaster and slid it toward Rebecca.

"So what do you really want at the Sled-Nex?"

"You're a friend of Buck Johnstone's," Rebecca said, taking a sip.

"So?"

"A name would be nice." Rebecca smiled. As warm as she could fake it. And took another sip. The burn down her gullet was good.

"Zinn."

"Zinn who?"

A snort. "Zinn Guttmann. You going to write that down, Detective? As part of your investigation?"

Rebecca's gaze locked on the woman's. "And what investigation might that be?"

"Into your father's death. Everyone's saying you don't believe he did it."

"I don't."

Zinn regarded Rebecca steadily. Billiard balls clattered as a cue sent them scattering. Rebecca felt a heavy sense that all three dudes at the table were watching, carefully, her interaction with the barkeep. The song changed. Someone else entered the bar behind her. Tension whispered. Rebecca forced herself not to turn around to see who had come in. She took another sip and said, "And neither does the major crimes unit out of Kelowna. They're opening an official investigation." While Rebecca had asked Janet Gagnon to keep details of the investigation to herself, this much would be public as soon as Parker's team started arriving tomorrow. And Rebecca wanted to see the reaction of Zinn Guttmann—friend of Buck's—to this revelation.

The woman's body stiffened. An eyebrow crooked up. Her eyes showed keen interest, then flicked toward the table where the men sat. "On what grounds is it being reopened?" she said in her German accent.

"I'm not at liberty to say. But I'd like to speak to the owner of the bar. Is he around?"

Another tick of her gaze toward the table, then she turned her head and yelled, "Wally! There's someone to see you!"

A door behind the bar swung open. Out stepped a small and wiry man in his mid- to late forties with a wizened face and close-set eyes.

"This woman here, Sergeant Rebecca North, wants a word with you. She's the cop daughter of Noah, you know, the old guy who burned in that fire?"

Rebecca flinched inwardly, but she kept her features impassive as Wally weighed her in silence for a moment from his office doorway, then came forward.

Rebecca explained to Wally she was looking for information on the old Devil's Butt bar. Zinn Guttman listened closely while wiping down the counter. Rebecca had a sense that whatever she said would be relayed to the guys at the table within minutes of her departure. And perhaps to Buck, too.

"Can we talk somewhere private?" she asked.

"We can talk right here," Wally said.

Her gaze warred with his. She felt a shift in energy from the men at the table.

"Fine," she said quietly. "Do you know who the manager was here in late 1998, when the place was called the Devil's Butt? Or who the owner was back then?"

"Yeah. Owner was Bart Tucker. I was the manager. Why is this of interest?"

Energy quickened through her. *Go easy,* she told herself. She could always return with backup, or Grace Parker could have Wally brought in for official questioning. But this basic information would help her move the investigation forward.

"What is your last name?"

He ran the tip of his tongue across the inside seam of his lips. The movement reminded Rebecca of a reptile. Something with cold blood.

"Fowler," he said.

"Was there more than one manager?"

"Just the one, just me. And an assistant manager. Bart was here most of the time until he sold the place to me."

"So you bought it?"

"Yeah. And renamed it." He gave a shrug. "Needed a bit of a change. Most of the guys coming in here are big into hunting, and into sledding in the winter and their bikes in the summer, hence the name, Sled-Nex."

"So a lot of the patrons are hunters?"

A wariness entered his eyes. "Most people who live in Devil's Butte hunt. Why?"

She thought of the wolf logo on Buck's truck, and the logo Tori had described as being on the truck that had run her and Ricky off the road.

"Is the Sled-Nex Bar and Grille perhaps affiliated with any particular hunting club?"

He said nothing. His walls were going up. She changed tack.

"So you'd have known Oona Ferris?"

He blinked. "Oona? What in the hell has *she* got to do with anything?"

"You dated her?"

"Fuck yeah. We lived together awhile. She did some of the adult-entertainment stuff when we still had it."

"So you knew she'd witnessed Trevor Beauchamp and Whitney Gagnon getting into a white van?"

"Yeah." His posture was even more guarded now. His eyes, too.

"Apparently she was driving by that day," Rebecca prompted.

Silence.

"Do you know if she doing the driving herself? What vehicle she was in? Or whether she was with someone else who was driving?"

"Jesus, I don't recall. It's twenty fucking years ago."

"When did you last see Oona?"

"Probably twenty fucking years ago."

"Do you know where she is now?"

"No. What is this?"

"What about Marcy Fossum? Did she work here at the same time as Oona?"

"Marcy? Yeah. Far better employee, too, I'll give her that. She's doing good with Dot's Donuts and Diner now. Really turned herself around. But Oona? She went on a one-way downhill. We broke up not long after that time she was a witness."

"Why did she suddenly come forward at that time?"

"Christ, I don't know. Maybe because Whitney's mother was putting posters up all over the place and that cop—your father—started looking."

"Did you know Trevor Beauchamp?" Rebecca asked. "Did he ever frequent this place?"

"When he was in town, yeah. He was a regular."

"The buzz back in the day was the Devil's Butt was a place you could score."

"Score?"

"Oh come, Wally." She offered a false smile. "Drugs. It was common knowledge. There'd been a couple of busts here. Bikers arrested. And one or two truckers."

"Whatever happened here among the patrons, or outside in the parking lot, it happened outside of my knowledge or control."

"Right. So when exactly did you take over this place, Wally?"

He rubbed his brow. "Probably 2000, or maybe the year or so before. Bart's health wasn't good. He'd been wanting to sell."

Rebecca thought of the more than $50,000 in cash that had allegedly been in Whitney's possession.

"And an opportunity to secure financing suddenly came your way?" she said.

"Look, I don't like your tone, and I don't know what any of this has to do with your father's unfortunate death. I'm sorry about that, I am, but I'm done here. I've got a delivery coming in." He swaggered back into his office and slammed the door behind him. Rebecca stared at the door.

"Anything else, hon?" the Mohawk woman said.

Rebecca released the pent-up air in her chest and asked quietly, "Who's the bald guy at the table behind me?"

Zinn Guttman glanced over Rebecca's shoulder, hesitated. "Jesse Scott. Why?"

"He a local?"

"Yeah."

"What does he do?"

"He drinks beer in my bar, that's what." She glowered at Rebecca. "Beyond that, ask him yourself."

Rebecca pushed back her stool. She plunked cash on the counter. "Thanks. Keep the change."

She left the bar, the men watching her brazenly as she pushed through the old saloon doors.

Outside, the wind cut with blades of cold. Rebecca's body hummed with adrenaline, and her brain raced as she made her way carefully over the ice toward her Prius.

It was completely dark out now. But she saw light coming from beneath a garage door in a warehouse building next to the bar. A sign above the garage door was illuminated. SCOTT'S MOTORSPORTS AND REPAIR SHOP.

Rebecca hesitated—where had she heard that name before? Then it struck her—the decal on the side of Gonz's tow truck.

She thought of the look Gonz had given her inside the Sled-Nex bar. And of the way he'd regarded her father's cabin when he'd arrived to tow the Silverado. And of his nicotine-stained fingers. Gonz who was sitting with a bald man named Jesse Scott.

Ash's words came to mind.

A specialty auto shop up in Devil's Butte. Wes's uncle owns the place. Wes works for him part-time, or anytime he can . . .

Rebecca studied the sign for a moment, her gut instincts rustling. There was a smaller entrance door beside the garage bay door.

Rebecca went and knocked with her gloved hand on the small side door.

CHAPTER 48

There was no answer at the door of Scott's MotorSports and Repair Shop. Rebecca surveyed the lot behind her. The wind howled. She shivered, tried the door. It opened.

"Hello?" Her voice echoed into the interior.

She was answered by silence and the rattle of the Arctic wind outside.

Tentatively, she stepped inside. "Hello? Anyone here?"

Silence.

She entered the garage bay area. It was heated, warm. A black pickup truck was up on the hoist. No one around.

She walked around the truck. A Ford F-350 with a shiny chrome grille, a bull bar, chrome wheel covers. Just like Buck's. And it sported a row of hunting spotlights across the top of the cab. But there was no howling wolf decal on the rear window. Rebecca took note of the plate, Buck's words going through her mind.

I drive a Ford F-350 pickup. Like half the guys in town. Other half drive GMCs or Dodges or Silverados.

Someone was in the process of applying flame decals along the flanks of the vehicle. Tongues of orange-and-yellow flame licked along the doors and over the rear wheel hubs. If there had been a sticker on the left hub, as Tori had described, it was gone now.

Rebecca walked to the left front of the truck, took off her glove, and ran her palm over the panel, searching for signs that it might have hit Ricky Simon's snowmobile, and wondering if it was possible that this truck had just had some panel beating work done to fix any damage.

"Hey!"

She jumped. Spun. Heart hammering.

Wes stood in a doorway that led to an adjacent store, wiping his hands on a rag. He wore orange coveralls.

"Becca?" Surprise raced across his face as he registered who she was. His gaze shot to the Ford on the hoist, then back to her. "What are you doing here?"

"Passing by. I saw the sign—Scott's MotorSports." She fudged it. "Ash told me you worked here sometimes. For your uncle. He's Jesse Scott, right?"

Wes frowned. A leeriness entered his eyes. "Yeah, so?"

"I just saw him in the bar next door. I . . . I've decided I want to sell my dad's Silverado if it can't be easily patched up. So when I saw the sign, I thought I'd stop by, see if you were here, and whether you were still interested?"

His frown deepened. "Yeah, I'm still interested." He shot another look at the vehicle up on the hoist. Clearly something about Rebecca's presence in conjunction with that Ford truck was worrying him.

"I can offer a fair price," he said. "Can you give me some time to come up with a number? I'll call you."

He wants me out of here.

"Sure." She smiled and jerked her thumb toward the Ford. "Nice decal detail. It's your work?"

He nodded. "My part-time passion."

"Some panel beating as well, up front here?" She smoothed her hand over the body.

He tensed.

Silence.

She pulled her glove back on, letting the silence drill deeper.

"What's this about?" he asked.

"Oh, nothing, really. Just that when I came in here, I thought I recognized this vehicle as one I saw in town the other day, same plate," she lied. "But that one had damage to the left front, and a hunting-club sticker above the rear left wheel hub. You know, the one with a wolf logo? Wolf Pack hunt club, I think it's called."

He swallowed and paled a little. "I wouldn't know what truck you saw."

So, not a denial. A misdirect. His demeanor further piqued her interest.

"Whose truck is it?" she asked.

"Look, I'll call you with an offer for the Silverado, but I got work to finish in back."

"Wait," she said, hurriedly digging into her pocket. She took out the folded pages upon which Ricky had drawn the helmet and sled foil design.

"Do you recognize this work, but in orange?"

He studied it. Something about his body went very still.

"Why?" He looked up. "Is this something to do with your investigation?"

"I just have some questions. Do you recognize it?"

He winced and shook his head. "Hard to say. Maybe. But I can't recall where."

"It's very distinctive," she said. "Someone in your field would recall, surely? At least if it was done locally."

He shook his head again, not meeting her eyes now. He was lying. She was certain of it. Wes Steele knew the person this design belonged to.

"Thanks." She handed him a card. "If you do remember, please call me."

As she made to leave, she turned abruptly to face him once more and said, "You didn't say whose truck this is."

"Not for me to say."

Her gaze locked with his. "Do you perhaps know about the hunting club called the Wolf Pack?"

He moistened his lips. "Yeah."

She waited.

He pocketed her card, then recommenced wiping his hands, concentrating pointedly on the task. "It was something that started way back, apparently. Extreme hunting."

"Which is what?"

"Remote environments. Kept secret and announced at the last moment so guys can't really prepare with prior knowledge of terrain or weather conditions, stuff like that. The guys also kind of put handicaps on each other—draw lots to decide. Like a contest, a game. Hold several hunts a year. Sounds cool to me." He hesitated, met her eyes, frowned, then said, "Why do you ask?"

"I'd seen the sticker. Wondered, that's all. Do you know any of the members?" Like Buck, for example, whom Rebecca had seen Wes playing pool with at the Moose and Horn the day she'd interviewed Solly Meacham. Along with Jesse Scott and Zinn Guttman.

His mouth settled into a tight line. His eyes darted back and forth between the truck and the door behind him to the adjacent store. "Can't say that I recall who all is a member."

"'Kay, thanks." Rebecca smiled and pocketed Ricky's drawing. Wes watched her gloved hands. "Call me about the Silverado. I need to get a more robust vehicle to navigate these roads."

"Talk to you later," he said.

Rebecca exited the garage. It was even colder out now. A gibbous moon hung in the sky with a pale halo around it. Fingers of trees formed haunting silhouettes, bobbing in the wind. A tin clattered unseen over ice.

As she started toward her Prius, yellow light spilled suddenly from a storefront adjacent to the garage. Rebecca stopped, frowned, then made her way back to the wall of the building. Staying close against the wall, she huddled deeper into her parka against the wind and peered carefully into the window. Around the side of the window display she could see a corkboard with photos—a brag board, or portfolio of sorts, that showed various vehicles with design work. She caught sight of an image pinned in the top right corner. A photo of the snowmobile design that Ricky had rendered—a giant black spider with fangs and a web against a background of blaze orange. Her pulse quickened.

More lights suddenly blazed on inside the store.

Rebecca stepped back into shadow.

She saw movement inside. Wes. He'd entered and flicked on the lights. He went to the counter and picked up a phone's handset. She watched him dial someone, then talk, gesturing.

He hung up abruptly and came toward the board. Rebecca leaned farther back into shadow as she watched Wes unpin the photo of the orange machine with the spider. He moved out of sight.

Shivering, Rebecca waited awhile longer in shadow. The shop lights went off.

She hurried back to her Prius, got into the vehicle, and fired up the engine and heater and fan. She made a note of the Ford F-350 plate number on a piece of paper before she forgot it. When her Prius was defrosted enough to see through melted holes on the windshield, she put her vehicle in gear and reversed out of the lot.

Things were connecting. Circles were tightening. Somehow Scott's MotorSports and a member—or members—of a hunting club were tied to her dad's death. She just wasn't sure how.

Or why.

Or what these people had to do with Whitney and Trevor's disappearance—extreme hunting gone wrong?

CHAPTER 49

Ricky sat with Tori by the fire in the living room of Broken Bar Lodge. She was teaching him how to play chess. Olivia and Cole had gone up to the library, giving them some time alone. Which boggled his mind. They'd left Ace downstairs with them, and he snored in front of the fire.

This place was huge. His whole house could probably fit into this open-plan living room area with its log beams and wood paneling and ginormous table for guests and big dinners. They'd shared a meal at that long table—he, Tori, Olivia, and Cole. Cooked by an employee named Roshan. A venison pie with proper pastry plus dessert and everything. Olivia and Cole had chatted with him about whether he was going to think of getting a new snowmobile, and if he worked summer jobs. They'd asked how many siblings he had. What movies and books he liked. What he thought about the proposed pipeline up north, because some of the members of Ricky's First Nations community were involved in the political protests around that.

It kind of shocked him that people cared what he thought about abstract things like that. Like it mattered what his opinion was. Like they were really interested because it helped shape their own decisions. It made him think. Hard. Because he hadn't really considered the pipeline and its ramifications for First Nations communities like his, and what would happen to the forests and rivers and game if there was a spill.

It turned his thoughts to Running Wind because his grandfather had felt strongly about all kinds of things like that. And remembering Running Wind made his chest sore. Ash's words curled through Ricky's memory as he moved a pawn.

Running Wind entrusted that knife to you as a totem, something to remember him by. Not to go picking locks to steal some poor old man's hooch . . . He went out there in part for himself, and in part for you, Ricky. You and your mom and Patty . . . Do you think being hooked up to machines was a better way for Running Wind? Stuck in some sterile hospital for months, costing your family money it doesn't have?

Ash's words filled him with guilt. But they'd also started a tiny fire deep down in his belly. A desire to try to live his life in a way his granddad would approve of. Like Running Wind was a compass, and maybe if Ricky steered by that compass, he could have things like this ranch house. Delicious food at a big table. People around him who cared what he thought. Maybe if he got a nice house, he could get Patty to come live with him, and she'd be safe from that shit-ass boyfriend of his mother's. Ricky worried about that dude. And he worried about the asshole's little baby getting hurt, too. His mind sifted to what Rebecca had said in Ash's truck about ketamine, and his thoughts turned darker.

Tori leaned forward suddenly and snatched one of his pawns off the board, leaving an avenue for her bishop to his queen.

"Hey!"

She chuckled and waved the dead pawn at him. "You're doomed, buddy. I got this one."

He frowned and studied the board, hunting for a way out. Ace shifted in front of the fire. The wind whistled outside, and Ricky felt, yeah, he wanted this warmth. This safety, this comfort in his life. He glanced up at Tori and met her eyes. His heart did a funny squeeze. Maybe one day—just maybe—he could marry a girl like Tori.

CHAPTER 50

Cariboo Country. Thursday, January 17.

The bank clerk left Rebecca alone in a small, airless room with her father's safe-deposit box. Now that Grace Parker and her team were officially on the case, Rebecca felt she needed to turn some attention to sorting out her father's affairs.

Duddy Rawlinson of Rawlinson & Diamond Attorneys had given her the key and a copy of her dad's will. She knew her father had used Duddy as his lawyer in the past, and she had called him early this morning to see if he'd perhaps handled a will for her dad.

He had. And it surprised Rebecca a little that her father had been this organized. He'd left everything he owned to her—the razed cabin, the uncultivated acres of land, the broken-down paddocks. The old Silverado. A small amount in savings and stocks and bonds. And a key to this box on the table in front of her.

She steadied her mind and opened it. Inside, on the top, was a map showing the property lines of his farm. Now *her* farm. It was far bigger than she'd realized. Land just lying there. Everything that had been left to crumble upon the death of her mother. As if part of her father had gone with her, and the only energy and drive that remained he'd put toward his job and toward Rebecca. Her chest tightened.

Beneath the map were an architect's plans for a cabin renovation that had never happened. Rebecca smiled wryly to herself. No chance of renovating that cabin now. She set the map and unused plans aside. Next in the box was a stack of old photographs. The top one was a faded image of a young, dark-haired woman in a yellow summer dress. She wore a huge smile and a strand of pearls.

Surprise washed through Rebecca. She turned over the photo. In neat cursive writing on the back was her mother's maiden name, Paige Richmond, and a date. The photo had been shot two years before her mom and dad had married. Three years before Rebecca had come into their lives.

A wave of emotion crashed through her, and tears blurred the image. The thought of this young, beautiful woman with so much of the future glowing in her smile so many years ago . . . She couldn't even begin to articulate to herself what it meant to see this. Solly was right. Rebecca could see an echo of herself in the features of this young woman, in the way her mother held her head for the camera.

Beneath this photograph there were others. Her father as a newly minted rookie in uniform. He looked so proud. Another image showed her dad holding a chubby Rebecca of around six months up like an airplane against a blue sky.

She touched the image gently. And she felt a whisper. His memory. Shimmering around her like a presence conjured from this box. Just as Whitney's mother kept a shrine of keepsakes to conjure her daughter to life in her mind, this box had been her father's shrine to his married life. And he'd left it for Rebecca. Not every memory of their lives had gone up in flames.

She removed the photos. At the bottom of the box lay a midnight-blue velvet pouch with a drawstring.

She untied the string, opened the pouch. Out slid a strand of creamy pearls.

Rebecca's heart stalled.

Her mother's. The same pearls the young Paige Richmond was wearing in the photo taken two summers before she married.

Oh God. I can't handle this right now . . .

Tears sheened down Rebecca's cheeks. She found a tissue in her pocket, blew her nose. Then she picked up the strand of pearls and clasped it around her neck. She slid the pearls under her sweater, cold and foreign against her skin before they started to warm. She placed her hand flat over them. And somehow, as trite as it might have seemed, she felt as if she'd just been welcomed home. She remembered that warm feeling of her mother's arms around her. She could feel her father spinning her like an airplane up high in the sky. She could hear his voice in her mind—him reading her stories. She could smell bread baking in the kitchen, and she could recall the sensation of her mother's horse under her, and the sun upon her back as her mom taught her to ride. She could smell the loamy earth of the old vegetable garden, and see the smudge of dirt on her mother's face that had made her laugh. She remembered the feeling of her mother's dog's fur beneath her palm, and how the old dog would lie at her mom's feet while her mom sat at her sewing machine at that table now in the moonshine shed.

Rebecca had a sudden urge to sand that old table down, oil it up. Bring it back to life and put it in a big farm kitchen. The thought shocked her. But it was there. A bright color image.

Her gaze fell on the map of the land. And Rebecca knew with sudden and utter conviction she was not going to sell that land. Not now. Not right away. It was still her home. This place—her people, her family—were still here in spirit, and she wasn't going to leave until she'd felt their memories dissipate, the spirits of them leave. A proper goodbye might take some time. It might mean facing painful feelings and working through them as opposed to running away from something that hurt. As she had as a teen. As she'd always run since.

And maybe—she thought as she packed the photos and map and plans back into the safe-deposit box—maybe the thing she'd been unable to face back when she was sixteen, seventeen, eighteen, was the thing she'd craved the most. This connection. The love. The sense of roots. Because she'd become terrified on some subterranean level of being abandoned. Betrayed. As her mother had abandoned her in death, as Ash, her rock, had betrayed her in life. So she'd pushed her father away, too, when he'd been suffering the loss of his wife and needed his daughter's love. She'd abandoned him in her own attempts to armor herself for survival.

She shut the box, thinking life was messy and complex.

I miss you, Dad. I'm so very sorry I came back too late.

CHAPTER 51

Rebecca parked her new SUV rental along the edge of the logging road. After visiting the bank, she'd traded the Prius for an upgrade that came with solid winter tires. Engine running, she checked the map that Hatfield had marked against her vehicle's GPS. This was the spot where the .30-30 rifle bullet had come through the Hatfields' truck window.

She killed the engine and got out.

Cold and the quiet of endless forest descended. Crystals sparkled on trees and on the ground and on the road. She crunched over to the side of the road where Hatfield had described a ditch with blood.

A raven cawed. She jerked her head up. A scattering of blackbirds exploded into the pale northern sky. She watched them, her pulse beating a little too fast as the giant flock folded and re-formed in patterns across the sky. As she watched, a wan sun peeked over the tips of the trees, spilling pale color over the forest. No warmth.

She turned and surveyed the area. The forest was dense here. Old-growth trees encased in frozen snow. Dead snags poked ominously above the canopy. A bird of prey with something wriggling in its beak watched her from one. A chill trickled down her spine when she realized just how close to Haugen Ranch land she stood. Through those trees, she knew, lay a clearing. Then, on the other side of the clearing, the ruins of an abandoned summer camp—an overgrown, densely treed area at the back end of Haugen property that had been neglected and allowed to grow wild.

She remembered this area because when she was in tenth grade she'd asked Ash to show her the camp ruins, but he'd acted so oddly in refusing that it had stuck in her mind. He'd said he never went there, no one did. He'd told her the ruins weren't safe, but she hadn't believed him.

The winter chill seemed to sink deeper into her bones along with unbidden and darker questions that didn't butt up well against logic— why had Ash avoided this place? Why had he lied?

Sometimes we see what we think we should be seeing. Like a cop sees a gun in a hand that holds a cell phone. Like the Hatfields, perhaps, had seen a deer fleeing, and not a young woman with long gold hair, because it created too much dissonance in their brains.

Like I, perhaps, refused to see things about Ash?

But, Rebecca argued with herself, Ash had avoided this place *before* Whitney and Trevor had vanished, and *before* the Hatfields had caught a stray bullet in their headrest and seen that blood and something running through the woods.

She crunched over hoarfrost layering the ditch and entered the forest. She stood where she believed the Hatfields might have stood on that hot Indian summer day just over twenty years ago, right on the cusp of a tremendous thunderstorm. The same storm in which she'd seen Ash wandering dazed and bloody.

She moved a little deeper into the white trees. The tall sentinels surrounded her, stiff, watchful. As if sentient beings. The wind soughed through their frozen branches, the ice crackling and whispering. They were magnificent old trees. They'd stood here for well over two decades and watched whatever had played out beneath their branches. The memory of the event the Hatfields had witnessed was recorded in their fabric. The blood that had spilled had been absorbed by their roots, the nutrients denoted in their rings.

A crack split the silence.

Rebecca inhaled sharply. She stilled and listened, trying to ascertain where the noise had come from.

Ice?

Another sharp report cracked through the forest.

Gunshot.

A bullet slammed into the trunk of a tree near her head. She flung herself down to the frozen snow. Her heart jackhammered. She lay listening to the echo dying into the distant hills, trying to figure out which direction the shots had come from.

Silence descended.

The wind, sharp and sibilant, hushed through the forest. A bird cried.

Then she heard it, a crunch of movement on snow. It came from deeper inside the woods.

She edged up slightly and scanned the area. She could discern no shape moving between the trunks or in the shadows. Rebecca scuttled in a careful leopard crawl over the ice toward her vehicle.

She crawled onto the road and around the far side of her vehicle. She reached up for the driver's door handle. Crack. A bullet pinged off the bumper from the opposite direction. Heart pounding in her throat, she yanked open the door and clambered into the vehicle, staying low below the windshield. She reached for her father's rifle, which she'd put into the back. She loaded it and edged into position. She peeked up through the windshield.

A bullet thunked into the side of her SUV.

She ducked, started the engine, then opened the driver's-side window. Edging up cautiously, she inched the rifle muzzle out the window. She curled her gloved finger around the trigger, waited. Another shot slammed into the side of the SUV. She fired.

The sound blasted through the SUV interior, slamming into her eardrums. Her eyes watered. She could hear nothing apart from the boom deafening her ears.

She saw a movement among the trees. She opened the driver's-side door. Using it as cover, she got out, fired again.

Over the deafening booming in her ears, she thought she heard an engine start up. Snowmobile. It roared somewhere behind the cover of the trees on the Haugen side. And disappeared into the distance.

Dizzy from the sound against her eardrums, she got back into the car. Reloaded. Waited.

Silence.

The swarm of blackbirds murmured above the forest canopy.

The pale lemon of a sun eked higher over the tips of trees. It was all calm again, as if nothing had happened. Witnessed only by her and these frozen conifer sentinels. Much the same as it might have seemed for the Hatfields twenty years ago on the cusp of a storm that had washed everything, including the blood, away. But not the bullet. She now had that bullet.

And she now knew that someone did not want her here, in this very spot. Because this was where something had gone very wrong that Indian summer so long ago, on that day Whitney and Trevor seemingly vanished from the face of this earth. This was it—ground zero. That blood of the wounded animal could have been the blood of a young woman who was pregnant. And possibly being hunted.

She felt ill.

Rebecca checked her phone. Her hand was trembling.

No cell reception.

She got out of the SUV and checked the vehicle for damage. The bullets had slammed into the left rear passenger door. They were lodged somewhere inside. Now she had those bullets, too. Still shaking from the aftershocks of adrenaline, she got back into the driver's seat and engaged her gears.

When she finally hit the paved highway at the top of the escarpment and found cell reception, she pulled over and called Detective Grace Parker. She told Parker she wanted a cadaver dog team. She explained why.

"There's an abandoned summer camp on the back end of Haugen Ranch. We should search that area first."

"It's private property?"

"Belongs to Ash Haugen." She felt a wave of nausea at the words coming off her tongue, at the ramifications for Ash of what she was setting in motion. She felt she was betraying him. But something was off about the back end of his property. There was still something he was hiding. Regardless, she was doing her duty, and this was her commitment to her father.

Grace informed Rebecca she was just pulling into town. She instructed Rebecca to head directly to the Clinton RCMP detachment and meet her there. They were setting up an incident room.

"I'll put in a call to the K9 cadaver crew," Grace said. "Meanwhile, I'll get work rolling on a search warrant for Haugen's property."

CHAPTER 52

Rebecca perched on the corner of a metal desk in the small incident room that Sergeant Grace Parker had commandeered in the Clinton RCMP detachment.

The major crimes investigator had brought a detective from Kelowna with her. Also in the room with them was Corporal Jay Mohammad, the officer from Ashcroft who'd been tasked with the Oona Ferris incident. Plus, Grace had brought with her a tech who would handle comms and liaise with the southeastern district major crimes HQ.

"So, what have we got so far?" Grace stood in front of what was now a crime scene board on one wall of the room.

She'd stipulated that this room was to be kept locked and was off-limits to anyone not directly involved in the case, unless they had specific authorization from her personally.

Which meant Buck was sidelined, and he was seething about it.

Grace pointed a slender finger to a photo on the board. She wore a steel-gray suit over a polo-neck sweater that fitted her gym-honed body like a glove. Parker stood around five feet four and was in her midfifties. She carried an air of experience and unfettered efficiency. Her voice was clear and clipped. Her hair was cut convenience short, and her movements were sharp, like her piercing gray eyes.

No wedding band, or any other jewelry for that matter. Her makeup was subtle, but she did wear some. A tiny nod to vanity, Rebecca suspected.

She wondered briefly if Grace Parker had always been this way, or if her exterior was a carapace hardened over years of fighting her way through a competitive environment for a coveted top spot in major crimes in what was still, unfortunately, a fairly misogynistic and paramilitary federal and regional law enforcement agency.

Rebecca had wanted to be a cop like Sergeant Grace Parker. She was on her way to getting there. But watching Grace now, in this detachment that had been her father's, Rebecca wasn't so sure it was still what she wanted.

"Whitney Gagnon and Trevor Beauchamp"—Grace moved her finger over an image of Whitney, then Trevor—"last seen here." She tapped a spot on the map mounted to the wall. "The Renegade Lines bus stop, in what was a vacant lot next to Dot's Donuts and Diner. No record of them since that Sunday morning of September twenty-seventh when Ash Haugen dropped Gagnon off and fought with Beauchamp, who allegedly drew a flick knife."

She met the eyes of everyone on her team, one by one.

"Corporal Noah North was investigating this case on his own time. His interest seems to have been sparked by Thora Battersby." Grace ran through everything Rebecca had given her to date, including the details from her visit to the Sled-Nex Bar and Grille and Scott's MotorSports last night.

"The Ford F-350 that was up on the hoist is registered to Jesse Scott. He's also the owner on record of the auto shop; plus, he's a part owner of the Sled-Nex bar in partnership with Wallace 'Wally' Fowler. According to records, he acquired the business in November 1998. Jesse Scott is known to police."

Rebecca sat up. This was news to her. The timing of the business takeover was also interesting—November 1998 was just more than a month after Whitney and Trevor disappeared with cash possibly totaling over fifty grand.

Grace consulted her notes. "Scott has done time for possession of narcotics with intent to distribute, and for assault and battery. Has known connections to bikers and the drug trade in the north." She looked up.

"In order to determine whether his Ford F-350 was involved in the snowmobile accident with Ricky Simon and Tori Burton, we'll need a warrant. We don't have enough evidence to secure one. Yet."

She pointed to another photo on the board. "Oona Ferris. Deceased in a single-motor-vehicle incident hours before she was due to tell Noah North who coerced her into lying about seeing Whitney Gagnon and Trevor Beauchamp climbing into a white van with Oregon plates." She gave a nod toward Corporal Jay Mohammad.

"Jay's Ashcroft colleagues are reopening the Oona Ferris accident investigation with assistance from our Kelowna team. Ferris used to live with and work for Wally Fowler. We'll presume she also knew Jesse Scott. We already know she was acquainted with Whitney Gagnon, and presumably also with Trevor Beauchamp because Fowler claims Beauchamp was a regular in the bar at the time."

Grace strode across the room. "Allegedly the teens went missing with around fifty thousand dollars in cash. Allegedly Whitney Gagnon was around twelve weeks pregnant with Ash Haugen's child." She stopped pacing and faced the team.

"In full disclosure," she said, "Rebecca here is not only Noah North's daughter, but she was in an intimate relationship with Ash Haugen at the time of the teens' disappearance. Rebecca's role from here on out is for background information and to function in an advisory capacity." She addressed Rebecca specifically. "Thank you for your work to date."

Rebecca swallowed, nodded. She'd come clean with Grace. Every last detail. She could no longer protect Ash from whatever secrets he was holding, or lie to herself. She needed the truth—they all did. However it came.

"It's a small town," Rebecca offered. "You're not going to find anyone *not* connected to someone. And Ash Haugen and I did break up right after he initiated a relationship with Whitney Gagnon."

"Haugen remains a key person of interest at this juncture," Grace said. "Our working theory is Noah North and Oona Ferris were killed because someone involved with the disappearance of Gagnon and Beauchamp was worried about being exposed for what we're going to assume might be the double homicide of Gagnon and Beauchamp."

She strode once more across the room in her low heels, turned to face the team, and folded her arms across her chest. "This might be about money—where did the alleged cash go? It might be about passion, revenge for a perceived wrong. Could Ash Haugen or Trevor Beauchamp have hurt Whitney Gagnon? Could she have been pursued by a stalker, a Peeping Tom?"

Rebecca noted that Grace did not mention Buck specifically. She was respecting his office, for now, but keeping that avenue of investigation open.

"It might be that the teens were picked up hitching at the bus stop and taken on a sick joy hunt near the back end of Haugen's land. It could be a combination of any of those angles. Whatever it is, someone in this town knows. Someone who was in the area twenty years ago and is still in the area now. Either this suspect has been living here all that time, or has returned." She paused. "Or perhaps it's more than one suspect. Whoever it is, they've proved they are prepared to kill not once to keep it quiet, but several times. And might try again."

"Have you got an ETA on the K9 cadaver unit?" Rebecca asked, checking her watch, feeling tense.

"The K9 team landed by helicopter twenty minutes ago," Grace said. "They're already on their way out to the Main Line logging road location described by Frank Hatfield. They will be joined there by a civilian SAR team presently setting up a command post. Before we can go onto Haugen's land, however, we will need a warrant. I'm waiting on that now. As soon as it's cleared, we go in. The bullet from Hatfield's truck has been sent for ballistics analysis, along with the bullets from Rebecca's rental. The ident team has lifted prints from North's moonshine shed and is working on the cabin fire site as we speak, looking specifically at the gun cabinet and North's weapon for additional latents. Autopsy results have gone for secondary analysis, including the tox reports."

Grace's phone buzzed. She checked it and repocketed it.

"I've got an officer posted outside the Sled-Nex bar and Scott's MotorSports. He will watch for any suspicious activity. We've got officers in Devil's Butte inquiring about the orange snowmobile and helmet. We'll be bringing in Thora Battersby for questioning, and Frank Hatfield for an official statement. We'll also bring in Solly Meacham, who spoke in some detail to North on the day he died, and we'll bring in Ash Haugen." She cleared her throat.

Rebecca's mouth felt dry. She shifted her position on the metal desk, uncomfortable. Tense.

A knock sounded on the door. A young female officer Rebecca had not yet seen entered. She held up papers.

"Got the search warrant," she said.

Grace addressed the officer from Kelowna. "Get the warrant to Haugen. Stat. Go in at the front entrance of his ranch. Stay in contact. As soon as it's delivered, notify me, and we'll move the crews in on the back end."

Rebecca came sharply to her feet. "I'll do it."

Grace Parker studied her. The fluorescent lighting from above glanced off the lenses of her small wire-rimmed glasses, rendering her eyes inscrutable.

"Why?" Grace asked quietly.

"I know him," Rebecca said. "I can read him. I might be able to get something out of his reaction. He might be more cooperative and tell me something he wouldn't tell an unknown officer."

I owe it to Ash. I need to do this myself. I need to see his face when he learns a cadaver dog is searching that piece of property he never wanted to visit.

Grace weighed her for a moment.

"Fine." She nodded to the female officer to hand Rebecca the warrant, and Rebecca got an uneasy sense Grace Parker might be playing her. Watching. Waiting, possibly, for Rebecca to slip up. Because if Ash had wanted Whitney Gagnon gone from his life, Rebecca had also wanted her gone.

CHAPTER 53

It was around lunchtime and the weather was finally showing signs of breaking when Rebecca made her way down to the lake on Ash's ranch. His housekeeper had said she'd find him on the ice with Ricky.

Black clouds boiled and muscled together above the distant Marble Mountains, and a warmer wind twisted conifer branches into a frenzy, cracking ice and dislodging chunks of frozen snow that landed with thuds as temperatures rose. She heard a dog yapping and the sharp clack of hockey sticks and the scrape of blades on ice. She crested a rise and stilled as she saw them below.

Man, boy, and dog playing ice hockey on the lake in front of a goal net.

For a moment Rebecca stood and watched, besieged by a sense of past and of future. Of playful and devastating. A father figure and an accidental son.

The warrant in her pocket burned a hole in her chest as her stomach shrank with anxiety.

Ash *thwocked* the puck, sending the black disk skittering over the lake surface. Ricky chased after it with wild strides. Ash followed, agile but bigger. Kibu slipped and slid, barking, after them. Ricky fell and went sliding a distance on his stomach. She heard the boy's laughter.

Ash skated up to him and held out a hand, the wind ruffling his dark hair. Ricky's gloved hand clasped Ash's. Even over this distance, Rebecca felt the lock of a bond in that clasp. Her heart went tight. Ricky would have to leave, return to his mother. Grace wanted to separate the young witness from a person of interest who held coercive power over the kid.

Part of Rebecca just wanted to walk away, right now, make it all go away. She didn't want to be party to this search, this violation of his private land, and what was to follow for Ash. But one way or another, she and Ash had been locked together in this from that hot July night twenty years ago at the annual Clinton Rodeo Fair, as had Bucky Johnstone, jerking off as he watched Ash and Whitney in the barn.

Once Ricky had been righted on the ice, Ash slapped him hard on the shoulder; then he stilled, as if sensing her presence up on the rise. He glanced her way.

Time stalled.

It was a moment from which there could be no turning back. He waved. She raised her hand. And he started to skate slowly toward the shore, his movements changed, as if he'd read the gravity in her salute. Ricky and Kibu followed behind him.

They came off the ice as Rebecca made her way down to the lake edge.

They took off their skates on a small bench that had been cleaned of snow and pulled on their boots. She waited a tiny distance away.

"Give us a moment," Ash said to Ricky. "Take Kibu up to the house."

Ricky eyed Rebecca, then looked deeply at Ash.

"Go," he said.

Ricky carried his skates over his shoulder and called Kibu. The dog followed him up toward the house. Ricky hesitated, stopped, looked back.

Ash nodded, as if to say, *Go on. It'll be fine.* But Ricky could see it wasn't fine.

Ash came up to her, cheeks ruddy from cold and exercise, his ice-blue eyes hauntingly pale, his black hair mussed.

"This doesn't look like a social visit," he said quietly.

"I'm sorry, Ash." She reached into the breast pocket of her parka, took out the warrant. She handed it to him.

He read it. His face, his body, tightening as the wind whipped his hair.

His eyes met hers. He said nothing.

The unspoken hung between them.

"You could have just asked." His voice was low, quiet. Dangerous. His eyes crackled with fury.

"Sergeant Parker needs it done by the book."

"What? You think you're going to find human remains? Whitney? Trevor? Why there? Why on my land? Why *that* place?"

"What is it about 'that place,' Ash?"

He turned abruptly and strode up toward the house in Ricky's wake.

"Ash!"

"I'm going out there," he yelled over his shoulder.

She hurried after him. "It's not a good idea."

He spun. Ice fire burned in his eyes. His jaw jutted out, aggressive, rigid. The shape of his body was fierce. "It's my land, my property. I am entitled to see that they don't overstep the bounds of this fucking warrant." He waved the paper in her face.

"Then I'm coming with you."

"No, you're not. I'm taking my sled. Heading across the land. It's faster." He started back toward his house. She grabbed his arm.

"No, Ash. If you want to go out there, you're coming with me. My vehicle." She'd been given use of a police SUV because her rental had gone into evidence. She'd also been issued a service weapon, which was in a holster at her hip. "We go the long way around, by road. I can't have you interfering with a K9 search coming in on a sled from the other end."

He paused, his back to her, simmering.

Clouds churned across the sky, darkening the pale disk of the sun. Wind gusted sharply, and the first few tiny flecks of snow floated into the air. They settled white on his dark hair.

She saw the moment in his body when he conceded. A subtle dip of his shoulders. And he recommenced his stride toward the house.

She hurried after him, heart racing.

I know him. I can read him . . .

And she didn't like what she'd seen. A glimpse of raw fear beneath rage. The dangerous combination of a predator cornered.

CHAPTER 54

The road had been cordoned off.

Rebecca showed her badge to the officer parked in his cruiser at the barrier. He offered her a clipboard with a sign-in sheet. As she signed, he told her where she could park. She handed the board back to him, and he waved her through.

She drove her black, unmarked Chevy Tahoe to the designated parking area. Ash sat stoic and sullen at her side. He'd spoken no words on the trip over, and the tension in the Chevrolet was heavy. A sense of foreboding simmered between them. Rebecca parked, feeling time overlap. It felt as if everything back then had led to this moment.

They exited the vehicle and walked in silence toward the SAR command van and an assortment of police and civilian vehicles with search and rescue designations on their plates. They were all parked close to where Rebecca had been shot at earlier, including the ident van.

Police tape cordoned off the area where she'd been fired upon. The tape flapped in the wind. Crime scene techs in white Tyvek suits combed the ground looking for shell casings and other evidence.

A demarcated path led in and out of the search area. Rebecca and Ash followed it to the clearing. What would be scrub and fire-weed and berry bushes in the summer was covered in snow that was softening as the front moved in. All around them chunks of snow melted and slid from branches, bombing to the ground. The branches, released from their weight, sprang back and waved in the storm wind. It felt as though the forest around them was alive, agitated. Tiny flecks of snow mocked and danced in the wind, growing fatter and fatter.

Rebecca and Ash crossed the clearing along the demarcated path and entered the forest on the opposite end. They were now on the back end of Ash's property. A SAR member in a heavy red jacket with CARIBOO SEARCH AND RESCUE emblazoned in white down the arms halted them.

"Sorry, you can't go further," she said. "Cadaver team is working the area."

She was tall, fit-looking, with a clean face devoid of makeup and her blonde hair pulled back in an efficient ponytail.

Rebecca held out her police ID. "Sergeant Rebecca North," she said. "And this is Ash Haugen, the property owner."

The woman eyed Ash. Direct. Unflinching. "Kat Morgan." She offered a gloved hand. In her other she held an insulated mug of what smelled like coffee. "Search manager."

"Found anything?" Rebecca asked.

"Not yet." Kat sipped her coffee as she watched the woods. Rebecca could hear snatches of voices and calls coming through the trees from where she presumed the abandoned summer-camp ruins lay. Snow thumped to the ground from higher up in the canopy. Even the smell of the air was different in the warming temperatures, more rounded. Softer.

"This change in weather is good for the K9's nose," Kat offered, tilting her chin toward the sounds of the search. "Warmer. Wetter. Smell carries better."

They waited as Kat finished her coffee and intermittent broadcasts stuttered through the radio in a pouch on her chest.

Her radio crackled again. "Unit one for Kat. Unit one for Kat." She stepped aside to answer a request from the field.

Rebecca glanced at Ash. Everything about him looked wrong. Tight. Black. Dangerous. He refused to meet her eyes. Instead, he stared fixedly into the trees, listening to the calls of the searchers. An ill feeling seeped and settled into the pit of her stomach.

"Why did you never want to show me this area of the ranch, Ash?"

His mouth tightened. He was too angry to talk to her. Or worse, he was afraid.

"What happened here? Something happened here, didn't it? And you know what it is."

Now he met her gaze. His eyes locked onto hers. Anxiety sank talons into her chest at the look on his features.

"Ash," she whispered. "Talk to me, *please.*"

"You asking me as a cop, or an old friend?"

She swallowed, holding his gaze.

He turned, but as he did, loud barking came through the trees. It changed quickly to wild yipping. Kat exploded into action and moved fast into the trees. Rebecca took off after her.

Ash followed. The yipping grew louder, sharper, increasingly urgent. A voice reached them. Male.

"Got something! Got an alert here!" Ahead of Rebecca, Kat's radio crackled.

They broke through brush and came upon the scene.

A slender black Labrador was rearing up and down as it yapped at a massive, toppled old-growth cedar log that was decaying in a small clearing where the cabin ruins poked out from snow and vegetation.

One of the cabins, Rebecca noted, had been sealed off with plywood boards upon which graffiti was scrawled. The place felt eerie. Hallowed. Watched over by tall trees that seemed to gather arms around the place.

"Something inside this log deadfall!" called the male dog handler.

Kat hurried over to assist a SAR member who was trying to clear old snow and other detritus from the hollow opening of the log.

Once they'd cleared a hole, Kat got down on hands and knees and shone a flashlight in. "Can't see anything from this end."

"It's way down on this end," the handler called, tapping the log. "Spirit is alerting down here."

A police officer came through the trees with a crowbar. Excitement shimmered as the cop and a SAR volunteer worked to crack open the top of the decaying tree trunk. Rebecca and Ash stared in simmering silence as one of the officers used the crowbar to crack open a curved slab of bark like it was the lid of a chest. Or coffin. Spirit was trained to alert only on cadaver scent.

A hush fell over the group. Even Spirit became quiet.

A few flakes of snow wafted through the canopy. Everyone moved forward. Kat shone her flashlight into the cavity.

"Shit," she whispered.

Rebecca moved forward to see.

Inside, under the glow of Kat's flashlight, was a whole skeleton curled into a fetal position. The bones were stained dark brown. Bits of decayed fabric clung to the ribs, but the rest of the bones were exposed. It appeared they'd been perfectly preserved in their cedar coffin, no dirt or detritus covering them.

Kat moved her light closer. Rebecca leaned in farther. And her heart stopped.

Cradled by the pelvic bones was a rounded shape. Maybe the size of a tennis ball. And what looked like more tiny bones.

She couldn't breathe.

No one spoke.

The officer clicked on his flashlight and added more illumination. His beam glanced off a piece of oxidized metal near the skull. It was about an inch long. Shape of a leaf.

An image flooded Rebecca's brain—the school photograph in the *Clinton Sentinel* article from the last days of 1998, showing a bright and vital young woman with gold hair and the light and smile of the future in her eyes. And leaf-shaped earrings glimmering from her ears. *Whitney Gagnon.*

They'd found her.

And her baby.

She'd been sleeping here, curled around her fetus and protected by the ancient cedar log, for the last two decades, right here on Ash's land.

"Looks like that could be a bullet." The cop pointed his flashlight at a darkened piece of metal near the skeleton's shoulder.

"Everybody back, move back. Now!" called Grace Parker as she came marching through the trees followed by two crime scene techs in white boiler suits, one carrying a camera. "I want this entire area sealed off," she barked at her officer. "Now! Everybody back! And I want a cover brought in—a tent that can cover this whole log. This snow is forecast to turn to rain before dark. And I want lights. Get a portable system and generator brought out here. Stat."

The K9 handler had stepped aside and was playing a reward game of tug with his Lab.

Rebecca glanced at Ash. He had come up the log and was standing beside her.

He was white. Absolutely bloodless. Staring at the little skull and bones cradled in the skeleton's pelvis. His baby.

"Get him out of here!" Grace called when she caught sight of him, her face furious.

Ash lurched over to the bushes. He bent double, retched twice, and threw up, a hand bracing on the trunk of a tree for support.

Grace Parker addressed another RCMP officer. "You. Take Mr. Haugen there down to the Clinton detachment. Give him his rights and hold him for questioning until I get there."

CHAPTER 55

Cariboo Country. Friday, January 18.

Rebecca watched through the two-way mirror as Grace Parker and her homicide colleague from district HQ seated themselves at a table opposite Ash in the interview room.

They'd detained him for investigative purposes for almost twenty-four hours now. Grace and her partner had taken a break and were coming back for another shot at him. Rebecca checked her watch. They needed to release him within the next thirty minutes or charge him.

Ash had asked for counsel. His lawyer—who reminded Rebecca uncomfortably of a young version of Lance—sat beside him. Ash had so far been cooperative. He'd voluntarily given a DNA sample and been fingerprinted. He looked aged. Tired. Beaten but not bowed. A powerful and caged animal who did not belong in there.

Or did he?

Conflict, pain, anxiety churned through Rebecca. She wanted answers as badly as any of them, but her gut, every instinct, believed that while he would prove to be innocent, there was still something that did not meet the eye. Ash was withholding something, and Grace sensed it, too.

Rebecca's fear was that Ash was so committed to keeping whatever dark secret he held that he could end up going down for this if he and his lawyer weren't careful.

"He's guilty," said an RCMP officer, who stood beside Rebecca. "He's fucking guilty as sin. You can see it."

She looked at him, a hot hatred erupting though her. "What happened to innocent until proven otherwise?" she said.

"What—you don't think he did it?" He snorted. "After everything you heard in that interrogation?" He held out his hand and began to tick points off on his fingers.

"Haugen admitted he'd fathered that fetus found in that log. He admitted he wanted Whitney Gagnon gone. *He* took her to the bus. *He* was angry with Trevor Beauchamp for taking his money and his pregnant girl, and *he* got into a fight. Witness saw him. Witness saw a knife drawn. And Haugen sure as hell is lying about that scar down his face. Says it was a horse. Funny, eh, how it happened on the very same day? And there's your own testimony that he was wandering down the road in the storm, bloodied and beaten up and dazed. He was also the last person to see Noah North alive. Haugen made a statement that he'd noticed the key in North's gun safe on the wall. He knew there was ammo in there. He could have returned on his snow machine. He has access to veterinary supplies like ketamine on the part of his ranch rented by Douglas Cattle Farms. Their large-animal vet keeps supplies there. He admits North spoke to him about the case—North could have told him about the witness in Cache Creek."

"So where's the snowmobile and helmet that Ricky Simon witnessed?" Rebecca countered. "Those weren't found on his property."

"He'd have dumped them when he saw from the tracks that the kids had been in the moonshine shed and maybe seen his helmet and machine. *He* could have tried to run them off the road."

"His truck doesn't have the sticker Tori Burton described."

"Could have removed it."

"And then he rescued them?"

A shrug. "It's possible. When he saw they were still alive. Misdirect the investigation."

He lied . . . It wasn't a riding accident that gashed open his face . . .

That was the thing that had bugged her father. Enough that he'd phoned her and asked her about it.

It bugged Rebecca now.

Focus. Consider just the facts. Just the facts.

A forensic anthropologist had been brought in. The anthropologist and her team were out on-site now, working on documenting the grave and remains in situ; then they'd be removing the bones and transporting them to a specialized room that had been set up next to the morgue in Devil's Butte.

DNA from the female skeleton would be analyzed and compared to DNA that had now been extracted from Whitney's baby tooth, which her mother had surrendered to the team. DNA from the fetal remains would also be sent for analysis and would be compared against Ash's sample for confirmation of a paternal match. These tests would be expedited, Grace had said, given that a killer or killers were still presumed to be at large.

The team was also awaiting ballistics results from the Hatfield bullet, and from the bullets extracted from Rebecca's rental. Grace was additionally encouraged by the discovery of some yet-to-be-identified partial latents that techs had managed to lift from her father's gun safe.

Inside the interview room, Grace opened her notepad and commenced questioning Ash again.

"Where is Trevor Beauchamp's body?" she asked.

"I told you, the last I saw of either Whitney or Trevor was at the Renegade Lines bus stop on the Sunday morning, September twenty-seventh."

"You remember the date?"

"I remember the date."

"Why?"

Ash sipped from a plastic cup of water. "Because I would be free to pursue my relationship with Rebecca North." A pause. "It was a big deal for me."

Emotion swelled and formed a hard basketball in Rebecca's chest. She felt the cop beside her staring at her.

"And your injury was incurred later that same day?"

"I told you. Riding accident."

"Why refuse to be taken to the ER?" Grace's partner asked.

"Can't say. Wasn't thinking clearly."

"Did you know Oona Ferris?" Grace asked.

"I'd been introduced to her at what was the Devil's Butt bar in Devil's Butte. And I saw her there on a few other occasions."

"When you met with Whitney there?"

"Yes."

"Did you coerce Oona Ferris into lying about the white van?"

"No."

"Did you give Whitney cash?"

"I told you, yes. Around eleven grand."

"Where is that money now?"

"I don't know what happened to that money."

"Where are the orange snowmobile and spider helmet?"

"I have no orange snowmobile or spider helmet."

"Did your employee, Wes Steele, design that spider and web foil for you at—"

"Look," said Ash's legal counsel as he leaned forward. He overtly checked his watch. "We've covered this ground. My client has answered all these questions more than once. You either need to release him or bring him in front of a magistrate and charge him."

Grace checked her own watch. By her expression Rebecca could see she was frustrated. There'd been a seismic shift in attitude among the investigative team after the human remains and little fetal skeleton had been found. This case was serious—a meaty one. It had all the feels. It was suddenly no longer about an old drunk and mentally addled small-town retired cop eating his shotgun. It was about one of their own who had not given up on a cold case more than twenty years later.

And it was about an unborn baby.

It was exactly what Rebecca had wanted—for her dad to be taken seriously. To be shown to have gone down while pursuing a case.

Her goal had been won. She'd exonerated her father. She'd given him back his pride.

But now she had this—Ash being interrogated for her dad's murder and facing possible charges for the double homicide of two teens—one of them carrying his baby—and for the possible murder of Oona Ferris.

She got up, grabbed her coat off the back of a chair, and left the observation room.

Rebecca punched her arms into her parka as she marched through the building. She exited into late-afternoon darkness hung low with black clouds. She walked bareheaded through softly falling snow, aiming for the place down the street where her father used to go to find warmth and friendship. The Moose and Horn in the old Cariboo Lodge Motel.

She needed a drink.

She needed some familiar faces.

She needed friends.

CHAPTER 56

Cariboo Country. Friday, January 25.

Rebecca sat at a table in the Moose and Horn with Solly and Dixie and their husbands, Lewis Meacham and Dr. Bob McCracken. They were enjoying a new pub menu item of beef-and-Guinness potpie; Solly had invited them to be guinea pigs for a meal on the house.

The establishment was filled with music, laughter, voices, the clack of cutlery and crockery, and the scents of good, hearty winter fare. Outside, snow fell softly and consistently, and the temperature hovered just above freezing.

She reached for her beer glass and said to Solly, "This place is crazy busy—is it always like this on a Friday?"

Solly grinned. "Happens when you're the only watering hole in a one-horse town."

"That, plus the dark of midwinter," Lewis added. "Cabin fever— folk need a place to get out and gather." Lewis was looking good. In his forties and fit with a head of thick brown hair and dancing brown eyes.

"Like the village living room," added Bob, delivering a forkful of steaming, dark Guinness pie to his mouth. The man who had been the village doctor had widened in girth and thinned in hair, but the doc carried his new mantle of mayor with obvious pride and pleasure. Rebecca liked him a lot more now than she had as a kid.

She smiled and felt better for it. These people were good company.

"You guys have enjoyed it—the hospitality industry?" she asked Solly and Lewis.

"We've had a good run since my dad died," Lewis said, breaking off a hunk of soda bread and sopping up the rich gravy on his plate. "God bless his soul, but things sure got a lot nicer after he passed."

"Lewis." Solly punched his arm.

"It's true," he said around his mouthful, his dark eyes playful. A scoundrel, Rebecca thought. Lewis was charming, seductive, nice to be around.

Solly reached for her glass of stout. "I guess old man Meacham was a control freak, a micromanager. Bitter by nature. Just born that way."

"Ah," said Bob McCracken. "Give the man's ghost a break."

Dixie placed her small hand over Bob's large one. And as Rebecca observed these two couples—each person so different, yet each complementing his or her partner—she felt a pang of emptiness. She'd officially broken it off with Lance on Monday. Or, rather, Lance had dumped her. He'd informed her over the phone that he'd asked Heather Whitehall, his junior associate, to move in with him. She'd taken a position with another firm to avoid complications. It was serious. He'd been terribly apologetic about delivering this news while she was struggling with the loss of her father, but Rebecca had cut him off and said, "It's fine, Lance. I'm happy for you. Enjoy your relationship."

She took a gulp of her cold beer, recalling with a wash of shame the way she'd ugly-cried alone in her hotel room after hanging up. She'd sobbed over the loss of something she hadn't really wanted, but maybe thought she had, and now she was adrift, not knowing what she *did* want.

"You doing okay, Becs?" Dixie asked, watching her.

"Yeah. Yeah, I'm fine." She took another sip followed by a forkful of pie. "It's just being sidelined from the investigation," she said around her mouthful. "Feel a bit at a loose end."

"I know how you feel." She gave a wry smile. "Having my work second-guessed is no fun, either."

"The case would have gone back to the RCMP either way, Dix, once the ketamine and other subsequent evidence showed up."

Dixie reached for her glass. "Still." She raised her drink. "Here's to answers, and finding who did it."

They made a toast, but the mood had shifted.

"How is Buck handling it all?" Solly asked, forking up the last bit of pie on her plate.

"I don't know," Rebecca said. "He wasn't happy to see Grace and her team arrive, that's for sure. But from what I last heard, it seems his work was pretty much by the book. So far. Someone did a good job of faking a suicide—enough to throw off the initial investigation. If it wasn't for my dad's phone call to me, it all might have ended right there."

The group fell silent for a moment. The elephant among them was Ash. No one asked about him, or mentioned his name, even though Rebecca knew the whole village was abuzz with news of the skeleton-in-the-log discovery and the tiny baby bones. Everyone in town seemed to be waiting, suspended on tenterhooks, for the case to break as Grace Parker's team meticulously worked through its investigation.

Ash's property had been searched in more detail for the orange snowmobile and helmet. As far as Rebecca knew, nothing had been found of the sled anywhere. Neither had evidence been found to secure a warrant to search Jesse Scott's business, or his truck, to see whether his vehicle had recently been involved in an accident.

A second cadaver dog team had been flown in, and the search area around the abandoned cabins had been expanded in a quest to locate the remains of Trevor Beauchamp. But as far as Rebecca knew, not a sign of Trevor had been found.

Grace's team had questioned Wes Steele, but he'd come across as afraid and uncooperative, which had only further piqued Grace's interest. Wallace Fowler and Jesse Scott were not cooperating with police, either.

Wallace, it turned out, also had a record. For possession of narcotics with intent to traffic. He'd served a small amount of time years back for that. Grace had Devil's Butte cops looking into other links—bikers, truckers, dealers. Wallace Fowler and Jesse Scott hung loosely with known members of organized-crime groups who fed drugs northward, and onto and through the local reserve. But whether they had anything to do with the teens' disappearance, or the cash Whitney had allegedly been carrying, or the coercion of Oona Ferris to obstruct justice, or the supply of ketamine . . . remained a mystery.

Grace had also questioned the large-animal vet who worked on Haugen Ranch about ketamine supplies, probing the Ash angle simultaneously.

And while Ricky had been returned to his mom, Tori remained safely tucked away at Broken Bar Ranch.

"You been keeping busy, Becca?" Bob asked. "Dix told me you bought a new truck."

She smiled. "Yeah, well, my dad's was toast. I've been sorting through his affairs, getting things lined up for when his body is finally released." She reached for her glass. "I think he'd like to be buried here in town, in the little cemetery where my mom was laid to rest. This was his community—he loved to serve. I thought it would be nice if they were back together."

Silence fell around the table once more.

Bob cleared his throat and said, "About the memorial, his celebration of life, you should hold it at our ranch. We'd love to host everyone. Noah was not only my patient, but also a friend."

"Absolutely," Dixie said, wiping her mouth with her napkin. "We'd be honored to host a celebration of Noah's life, Becs. Our place is huge. We could invite everyone in town."

"You know what I think," Solly said, leaning forward. "We should do it right here. In the Moose and Horn. *This* was Noah's place. His social hangout away from home. He was always in here. His photos are on the wall. Everyone in here knew him. These are his people. We could shut the whole place down in Noah's memory. First round of drinks on us. Good music, good food. We can make some rooms available upstairs for those who'd like to crash here. He'd have liked it that way."

Emotion swelled in Rebecca's chest. Her gaze went to Thora Battersby, who was sitting at the end of the bar with her mates Don Barton and Jerry Phibbs. She could almost see the spirit of her dad sitting there with them, chatting, laughing. Feeling a little less alone. She met Solly's gaze. "I think he would, Solly. Thank you. And thanks for the offer, Dix and Bob, I—" Emotion stole her words for a moment. "I think he really would love to know we were gathering here at the Moose and Horn in his name."

Solly gave her a quick hug, and Rebecca felt a sense of belonging. Of kinship. It was a relief to share grief rather than bottle it all up and face it solo.

As she hugged Solly, Rebecca saw Marcy Fossum entering the pub with a male friend.

"Hey, guys, how's it going?" Marcy said as she sauntered up to the table while her man went to the bar. She wore tight black pants and a sweater with tiny flecks of sparkle. "Any word on the ID of the body? Or if they've found another one yet?"

Solly hooted with laughter. "You'd be the last person to tell, Marcy!"

Marcy pouted, but her eyes smiled. "You know how to spoil a girl's fun. They brought me in and questioned me, you know? That Grace Parker woman. Cold as steel. Bet she hasn't gotten laid in ten years. They wanted to know if I remembered Oona Ferris, God knows why. I heard Oona was killed recently in a car accident. Black ice."

"*Did* you know her?" Lewis asked.

"Yeah, well, we both worked up at the old Devil's Butt bar in Devil's Butte." She cast a side-eye at Rebecca. "Same time Ash and Whitney used to come in. And Trev, too. Oona was dating Wally, who owns the place now. Terrible about that little baby of Ash's—that totally guts me. When I heard about those little fetus bones, I looked up on the internet what that must look like. Holy. Rough. Ash must be just slayed to think of it lying there the whole time, those tiny little bones. Wonder if it was a boy or a girl? I heard from Buck about it being Ash's kid. You think you know people." She shook her head.

"Innocent until proven otherwise, Marcy," Bob said, seeing Rebecca about to blow.

"And Buck shouldn't be talking about the case, either," added Dixie.

"He's been sidelined." Marcy cast another glance at Rebecca, like it was her fault. "He's not impressed. They even questioned *him* on the fact he's friends with the barkeep up there—Zinn Guttman—and with Wally. And he plays pool with Scott and Wes. And they were all questioned, but Jesus, who doesn't know everyone in a town like this? It's what makes Buck the right cop for this town. He's friendly with everyone."

"That's also why the RCMP likes to rotate officers out of a community after five years," Dixie said. "You can lose objectivity. You become vulnerable to coercion, don't see things you don't want to see."

"Still, why they questioned those guys, I have no idea. It makes no sense . . ." Marcy's voice faded as she caught sight of someone entering the bar.

They all turned to look.

Ash.

He hesitated in the entrance, saw Rebecca at the table, and stilled. Rebecca's heart kicked into a stutter.

He looked terrible. Pale. Thinner. Still big, but something about him was utterly broken.

A hush fell over the table.

Everyone looked at him. His presence seemed to rush like a whisper through the patrons as others in the pub turned to stare. As though he were a pariah.

He gave a nod to Rebecca and went to the bar.

"I think he did it," Marcy whispered, watching him. Her partner came toward the table carrying two beers. "I should go." Marcy took her leave.

But the mood at Rebecca's table had turned sober. They finished their meal, conscious of Ash sitting at the bar, his back to them all.

Rebecca's phone rang. She checked the caller ID. Sergeant Grace Parker. At this time on a Friday evening?

"I need to take this," she said, and excused herself.

Rebecca stepped into the lobby. She stood near the phone her father had used to call her at the beginning of the month. It seemed like an age ago. She connected the call.

"Rebecca North."

"Rebecca, I thought you'd like to know." No inflection in Grace's voice, nothing to foreshadow what she might be about to say. The consummate cop. "We got results. DNA."

Rebecca's hand tightened on the phone. Through the saloon doors she could see Ash's profile at the bar.

"What have you got?"

"It is Whitney Gagnon. DNA from the skeletal remains is a match to the tooth DNA provided by Janet Gagnon." A pause. "And the paternal test for the fetus . . ." Rebecca tensed. "It's not a match to Ash Haugen."

Her world stalled, tilted, tipped.

"*What?*"

"Haugen is not the father of the infant remains."

CHAPTER 57

"Where does he get it?" Ricky demanded of his mother.

She stood in the kitchen, looking like a wreck. The baby slept in a cot in her bedroom. Patty was doing her homework in the adjacent living room, television on loud as usual, mostly to drown out the yelling.

"Get outta here, Ricky. I don't have to answer shit like that. You'll wake the baby."

"Special K," he insisted. "I heard Louie and his shit-faced loser cousin talking about it. Ketamine—how they got it from somewhere to sell. He was talking about it right in this house. Where Patty could hear—screw waking his baby. Who does he get it from? Who do they sell it to?"

The TV went louder.

He felt bad, but he was mad. At his mother. At the entire world. At Becca for bringing that warrant that had made them find that skeleton and take Ash away. For the past week he hadn't gone to school, and there'd been a stupid uniformed rookie sitting in a cruiser outside the house. He was terrified they'd put Ash in prison now, far away, like they'd done to his father, who'd gone in and never come out. It was like Ricky's worst nightmare all over again—the new father figure he trusted, who had his back, once more being ripped from his life. It burned like hell. It enraged him, this powerless feeling in the face of government authority. On top of that, he was sure Ash wouldn't have killed somebody. Ash needed help.

"Tell me!"

"Fuck off, Ricky."

"Don't you talk to me like that! You shouldn't let Patty hear shit like that."

"Listen to *yourself.*" She pointed her finger at him, hot spots forming on her face.

"*You're* the one who brings that loser Louie in here," he snapped. "You had his baby. My dad would eat that loser fuck for breakfast." He marched to the little mudroom, pulled on his snow boots, and rammed his arms into his jacket. He left the house, slamming the door behind him.

Snow fell thick and quiet outside. It was dark. He was shaking. He had to help Ash. Someone had injected old man Noah with ketamine, and Ricky had a gut feeling it had come from the same place Louie the loser—his mom's stupid-ass, drugged-up boyfriend—got it.

He saw the cop cruiser sitting across the road behind the veil of falling snow, engine puffing and windows misted as the officer inside kept warm. He ducked through the carport at the side of the house and went around the back of his residence. He cut through a snowy alley between houses.

On more than one occasion he'd seen some First Nations–looking dude he didn't know going to visit Louie's place. One time he'd seen that long-haired dude in town with a big, bald biker guy who was rumored to be a fixer for the bikers and sled-head hunters up in Devil's Butte. There was a club up there where they all hung out. Ricky wanted the name of the Indian dude.

If he could tell the cops where the ketamine had come from, if he could find whoever was on that snowmobile with the orange-and-black markings, he could maybe get Ash outta there. They'd see he had nothing to do with Noah North's death.

He banged on Louie's door.

"Louie!"

Nothing.

He thumped harder with the base of his gloved fist.

"Louie! Open up!"

No answer.

Ricky tried the door. It opened. He stepped inside. Louie lay half passed out on the sofa, beer cans on the floor everywhere.

"What's his name?" Ricky demanded, clumping farther into the house in his boots, trailing clots of snow behind him.

"What?" Louie struggled into a sitting position and rubbed his face. "What you doing here, you little prick?"

"I want the name of the guy who brings you drugs to sell."

He laughed, then dissolved into coughs.

"What's his name, Louie? Tell me or I'm going to the cops. Now. With this." He snagged two baggies of white powder off the coffee table, knocking over an empty beer can as he did. "What's this?" He dangled the packets in front of Louie. "Worth some time in the slammer?"

Louie lurched to his feet and snatched for the baggies. Ricky stepped back. Louie stumbled forward and fell on his face. He swore.

Ricky pocketed the stash and turned to go.

"Hey! Wait. Give that back to me." Louie dragged himself back into a sitting position on the sofa. He was shaking and sweating, and Ricky figured he needed a fix bad.

"They'll kill me if I don't get money for it," Louie said. "They'll kill me and then go for your mother and kid sister, you shit."

"You lie. You *need* this, don't you?" Ricky had learned at a tender age via his father what people would do, and give, for a fix once they were addicted. Anything. So he stood his ground.

"Tell me, Louie."

Louie rubbed his face. Ricky went to the door, opened it.

"Stu!" Louie called out behind him. "His name is Stu fucking Henry."

Ricky returned to the sofa and waggled the baggies just out of Louie's reach.

"Where will I find Stu Henry?"

"Give me that."

Ricky stepped back as Louie lunged again.

Louie breathed heavily. He looked sweaty-hot in his dirty white muscle shirt. Skinny brown arms. He stank. He was shaking hard now.

"Where?" Ricky said again.

"Stu and his cousins got a piece of land halfway between Broken Bar and Devil's Butte."

"What's this place called?"

"Ain't got no name. It's just north of Blue Lake—that little trout lake where the old mine used to be. Property is fenced. Archway entrance with antlers. Can't miss it. Rottweiler on a chain."

Ricky dumped the baggies of powder back on the table. "Where's your snowmobile key?"

"Stu and those guys will eat you for breakfast, you little shit," Louie said, grabbing up the baggies like a desperate man. "Don't say I didn't warn you."

"Snowmobile key?"

"You can't—"

"Where are the keys?"

Louie glanced at the kitchen counter.

Ricky turned, following his gaze. He saw the keys. He grabbed the fob and slammed out of the house.

Louie's sled was parked around the back and was a lot nicer than the one Ricky had lost down that canyon. He straddled and started the machine. Relief washed through him as the needle registered a full tank of gas.

He revved the machine, clicked on the headlights, and gunned down the road through the soft layer of new snow as he made for the back hills beyond the trailer homes.

Behind him falling snow filled his tracks.

Soft and silent.

CHAPTER 58

"Whose baby is it?" Rebecca said, her heart racing, her skin hot.

"We haven't found a match yet. It's not Trevor Beauchamp's, either. We were able to obtain DNA samples from a blood relative of Beauchamp's living in William's Lake to see if we could make a familial match. It was negative. The anthropologist puts the fetal age at around twenty weeks." Grace hesitated. "I just thought you'd like to know."

Rebecca ended the call and lowered the phone. She stared at Ash's figure at the bar. The barkeep set a plate of food and a pint in front of him. He reached for the pint and sipped.

So Grace was human, after all. She'd chosen to inform Rebecca for personal reasons, as a gesture of solidarity to a fellow cop. Because she hadn't needed to do that. Rebecca's brain churned over the facts.

Ash had slept with Whitney—allegedly for the first time—at the rodeo fair on July 11 that year. For the fetus to have been his—if Whitney and her baby died on September 27—it would have to have been almost twelve weeks old.

But twenty weeks? Who had Whitney slept with in May of that year, if it wasn't Trevor? Why had she lied to Ash? Had Trevor known whose baby it really was?

This flipped everything completely on its head.

The image of Ash's face at the scene of the log grave when he'd seen evidence of the tiny skull and bones rammed through her mind. All these years he'd wondered if he might have a child out there in the world. He'd given his money, all his savings, to Whitney. He'd lost out on his college degree. It had cost both him and Rebecca their relationship. It had irreversibly changed the course of their lives. Whitney's one lie. Because if she hadn't lied, Ash would not have been meeting with Whitney in the Devil's Butt bar.

Marcy would have had no gossip.

Rebecca would have forgiven Ash—they'd been trying to work through it all until Marcy revealed Ash was still "cheating" behind her back with Whitney.

And her father might still be alive.

Pain washed over her, through her. For him. For everything they'd all lost.

Rebecca reentered the pub. She walked slowly up to him. Hesitated. The noise around them was loud. She placed her hand gently on his shoulder. His solid shoulder. He tensed, looked around sharply.

She drew up a stool and sat beside him. Suddenly the words seemed too big and she was unable to voice them. They felt like a mounting avalanche inside her that was going to shatter and smother everything that had grown in its path since Whitney's lie. And what would be left, then?

"I thought Grace ordered you not to talk to me," he said. "Or see me."

"Not supposed to."

He sensed something coming—she could tell by the obvious tension in his muscles. He waited, his ice eyes holding hers. The knowledge grew bigger inside her chest as she battled for a way to deliver it.

"Ash . . ." A wave of emotion slapped her upside the head. She struggled to hold it in, looked away.

He placed a hand over hers. Solid, warm. So . . . Ash.

She swallowed, inhaled, faced him. "Grace Parker called." She cleared her throat. "It's not yours."

"What?"

She looked deep into those glacier-blue eyes. "The fetus—the child Whitney was carrying when she died—it's not your baby."

He stared. "What?"

"It's not your baby, Ash. The DNA is not a paternal match to yours. You're not the father."

He went white. He looked blankly into her eyes. Time stretched, and the pub activity morphed into a blur around them.

"You sure?"

She nodded.

His shoulders sagged inward as if the punch of the information were visceral, a blow to his solar plexus. His features slackened. His eyes—those beautiful, haunting Nordic eyes she'd always loved—pooled with emotion. His complexion changed, color shifting, draining.

He opened his mouth to speak, but said nothing, as if all the words needed to articulate the crashing maelstrom defied him.

"Whose?" he managed to ask.

"Don't know," she said quietly. "If the father's DNA is not already in the system, they're not likely to get a hit against a profile. Unless they get a hit on a family member, maybe." She paused. "We might never know."

Tears formed at the corners of his eyes. They leaked into the creases. One tracked down the scar on the side of his face.

Her heart cracked. She reached up, wiped the tear away, and ran her palm gently down the scarred side of his face.

"Why did she lie?" he whispered.

"Money, maybe? I don't know."

"I almost married her. I almost did the 'right thing.'"

Rebecca said nothing.

"Trevor?"

"Not his, either."

He turned away. Stared ahead.

"All this time," he said. And then again, quieter: "All this time. So much lost. I . . . All the wondering if my baby had been born, if my child was out there. And then when I saw those little bones, that tiny skull that could fit in the palm of my hand . . ." Another tear slid down the side of his face.

The barkeep glanced at him and exchanged a look with a patron.

Rebecca put her arm around him and said near his ear, "Come. Come up to my room. Let's get you out of here."

A PLAN

Cariboo Country. Sunday, August 30,
more than twenty years ago.

"Sorry, Whit. I'm so sorry," Trevor says as he settles back into the driver's seat of the cube van with HIGH COUNTRY LAUNDRY emblazoned on the sides. He shuts the driver's door and hands Whitney a can of ice-cold lemonade. The same laundry company name is written across the back of the shirt Trevor wears. The fabric is crinkled and sticks to his torso with sweat. It's sweltering outside, but the air-con in the laundry truck makes it cool.

Whitney presses the lemonade can to her cheek where he hit her with the flat of his hand.

"Look . . ." He leans forward, moves a damp strand of hair off her brow. "I . . . You gotta understand. I go north, work my ass off for six months. My girl is here, and I look forward to coming back, and then I find you been fucking around like a little bitch in heat and you're pregnant? Jesus." He sits back irritably and rakes his hand through his damp, dark hair. He remains silent for a long while. Almost vibrating. Whitney knows better than to say anything right now. It'll trigger another blow. Better to let his rage and adrenaline simmer down.

"*You know,*" *he says suddenly, still staring straight ahead,* "*it's not just the baby, the pregnancy thing. I can deal. I swear. I can handle that easier than you going and fucking Haugen in that barn.*" *He turns sharply in his seat and faces her square. The heat in his eyes frightens her.* "*Haugen? For Chrissake.*" *He glares at her. She can see his temper starting to rise again.*

Easy. Easy . . . Don't say anything that will trip his trigger . . .

"*I'm sorry,*" *she says quietly, breaking eye contact, looking down. Submissive like she's learned helps.*

"*Why him?*" *He's picking at the scab, opening the wound, rubbing salt inside.*

Because he's nice. Because he's handsome. Because he's a guy I never thought would even look at me, and he did for that brief moment. And he's so much better than you. Because he goes for girls like Becca, and I am jealous of what girls like Becca have, and I wanted to take it away from her. Because he said he'd do the right thing, and me and my baby would have some security in a life that is offering me nothing else right now. Because I don't want to end up like my mom . . .

Trevor's fists open, close, open, close. Very darkly, quietly, he asks, "*Why are you still seeing him? If it's not his kid?*"

Whitney just met with Ash in the bar. Trevor was waiting outside the Devil's Butt when they came out. Ash went one way, but Trevor startled her in the alley between the auto shop and the bar. That's where he hit her in the face, demanding to know why she'd been in the bar with Ash, what they'd been doing. Marcy Fossum had tipped him off that she and Ash had been meeting there. He'd come to ambush her, catch her in the act.

Whitney picks nervously at the hem of her summer dress. The sun hits her face through the passenger window as the angle changes. The sky is still filled with a smoky haze, a sort of brown-orange in color.

"*I was scared,*" *she says quietly.* "*I thought I'd just skipped a cycle. Then I did a test.*"

"*Should have just gotten rid of it,*" he says.

"*I didn't know how. I have no money. I . . . I thought if I told Ash that it was his . . . he'd have to help.*"

"*Why?*"

"*Because.*" He's nice. He's like that.

"*Fuck it, Whit—why?*"

"*He did fucking help, okay! He made sure I went to the clinic for a scan to be sure I was okay.*" A hiccup of emotion catches her voice as she thinks of the little thing growing inside her. She both hates and is intrigued by it. It gives her a weird feeling of specialness. Part of her wants to keep it, love it. Part of her wants it dead. Gone.

"*Did they ask at the health-care center whose kid it was?*"

"*No. And I didn't say.*"

An ugly laugh issues from his throat. "*Fucking loser.*" He laughs again. "*It's not even his kid and he wants to 'do the right thing.' How long did you think you could pull this one off?*"

"*I'd say the baby came early.*"

"*Yeah?*"

"*Yeah. These things happen.*"

He looks at her, seeing her seriousness—she'd marry Ash Haugen. Have a life.

"*He works with cows, Whitney. A guy like him knows all about things like gestation periods. He'll figure out you were shitting him.*"

She turns her face away, looks out of the window.

"*And what if you tell the real father?*"

"*I did. He said no one will believe me that it's his. He said I'm a slut.*" And she is one. The father of her baby makes her feel small. Ugly. Like a piece of garbage.

Trevor sits. A long time. The engine runs. The vents blast cool air. Through them comes the lingering scent of wildfire smoke. She can also smell cigarette smoke on Trevor.

"Here's what we do." He turns to face her. "Listen carefully. You go to Haugen and tell him you don't want to have his baby. You want to get rid of it, and you need money to go to Vancouver or Seattle to do it. And I fucking guarantee he will cough up and be too happy to bail, because he doesn't want to care for you and have a millstone around his neck. I mean, seriously, you?"

Tears well in her eyes. She knows Trevor is right. Why was she even thinking it could work?

"And that baby-daddy a-hole—you tell him you're gonna give birth to his kid. And when it's born, you will be able to prove that he's the father. Paternal DNA and all that shit. Tell him you will do that, get tests. Unless . . . unless he gives you fifty K in cash and then you will leave town and get rid of it."

"Fifty K! Christ! He'll never—"

"Oh, he will."

"Cash? Are you fucking serious?"

"Dead serious. He'll find a way to scrounge it up. Mark my words." His eyes glitter with excitement as his idea grabs him by the throat and begins to consume him.

"Think about it, Whitney. You get his money, plus the money from Ash. We take it all and go to LA. You get the abortion, we both start over."

"We?"

"Yeah, babe, 'we.' You always said you wanted to go to LA, didn't you? Start over, you said. It would be cool, you said. You don't think you'll manage on your own in Cali, do you? A kid like you from a redneck trailer park in interior BC? What do you know? You need me, babe."

Something about the way he says it scares her.

He leans forward and puts the cube van in gear. Hot energy rolls off him in waves.

"Where are we going?"

"I gotta deliver this load of clean sheets to the Cariboo Lodge. And you're going to talk to baby-daddy. After that, you go find Ash Haugen again, and you tell him what you want."

"Now? Today?"

"Right now. Soon as I've dumped my load for this shit-end job. When we get the money, I quit. I won't need to work these in-between-contract jobs anymore. We're fucking outta cow town, babe. We get on a bus to Cali, and we're good." He grins broadly at her. His muscles—his neck, his arms—are tight with adrenaline. He's overexcited.

"I don't know why you need to drive for the laundry if you make as much as you say on the contracts, anyway."

"Yeah, well. I had a bad run on a deal I invested in." He shoots another glance her way. Whitney is uneasy about what she sees in Trev's eyes. It's shiny and manic. "It'll be good to get away. Start over."

She gets the sense he wants to flee from something. She wonders if it was a drug deal gone bad.

By the time they reach Clinton, music blaring in the truck, Trev drinking a cold Molson's as he drives and in excellent spirits now, the idea is actually growing on Whitney. Trev is right. She always wanted to see LA—try to make a go of it there. Hollywood Boulevard. Sunshine. Warmth. Bikinis and shorts. Maybe a waitress job to start, near a beach. Where movie stars and beautiful people can be seen. It'll be good to have Trev at her side. No baby to worry about. Freedom beckons.

She leans back, takes his beer can from him, and swallows deep, relishing the cold explosion of beery froth in her mouth.

"Hey." He snags it back.

She smiles. "Don't have to worry about the baby now, do I? Can drink as much as I like."

He grins. "Fuck yeah." He bobs his head up and down at the idea. "And we can always hit your baby-daddy for more cash again," he says.

She stills. "What?"

"*Once we're over the border, like when we get down to LA or something. We could say we need more money before we go through with the abortion. We could hit him for another payment.*"

A dark, inky feeling seeps into her belly.

Trev flashes her another hot grin. White teeth. Black hair. Shiny eyes. "We can tell him to wire it direct into our new account, or something." He nods again, in time to the music blasting from the laundry-truck radio. "We can buy our own truck. How about that, Whit? You. Me. Drive down Big Sur, into Mexico, South America . . . Cancún . . . Big-time, baby." He laughs, head thrown back. More than a little wild. "Baby, baby, thank you, baby-daddy baby."

Whitney falls silent.

"Huh?" He looks at her. "Right, huh?"

"Right," she says softly, her hand going to her stomach.

CHAPTER 59

Rebecca cranked up the heat and made motel-room coffee. Ash sat on the side of the bed looking physically crushed. She handed him a cup. He took it and absently set it down on the nightstand.

"She lied to me and I bought it." He scrubbed his hands hard over his face. "It was my guilt. The fact I'd cheated on you. It made me feel I somehow deserved what Whitney was selling me, and that I had to accept the blowback." He snorted. "She used me. If you say the fetus is around twenty weeks, she *knew* it wasn't mine."

Rebecca drew a chair up and sat opposite him, leaning forward, her forearms resting on her thighs, hands clasped.

"And you're sure it's not Trevor's?" he asked, meeting her eyes. "Because I can see that playing out. Him milking me for it."

She shook her head. "Grace said no. She'd obtained DNA from a close family member of Trevor's."

"Those times we met in the bar, after she told me, I read her wrong, Becca. She sold me on the idea she was terrified. Of raising a child alone. Of tackling the world as a single mom on a low income, like her own mother. I hated the idea of my son, or daughter . . . of *me* doing nothing to help my own child." He swore softly. "She seemed so genuine, so vulnerable, mortified by the idea of an abortion."

He surged up, paced. A caged bear in the tiny motel room, the energy radiating off him palpable.

"Do you have *any* idea whose baby it could be?" Rebecca asked.

He stopped pacing, faced her. "No. Not apart from Trevor's. She never mentioned being with anyone else. But then she had a reputation for sleeping around." He hesitated. "There was the way she sometimes exchanged brief looks with Wally Fowler and Jesse Scott when we were in the Devil's Butt. I mean, Wally was bedding Oona at the time, but I think he probably could have gotten into Whitney's skirt one time or another. And Jesse Scott—women didn't say no to Jesse. Especially the young female biker groupies. They pretty much lined up to be screwed by Jesse like it was a patch of acceptance, like he was vetting for membership to the sled-neck biker bunch. I suppose I wouldn't be surprised if he'd been with Whitney, too."

"What about Buck?"

He rubbed his face again, as if trying to irritably scrub the whole mess away so he could see more clearly.

"I don't know." He met her gaze. "She might have let Buck have his way with her at some point."

"It could explain his obsession with her," Rebecca offered. "It could have given Buck a sense of entitlement, ownership. It could have enraged him when he saw her with you in that barn, especially if he'd been given the idea, somehow, that he was the one who'd made her pregnant." She paused. "It would have given Buck additional motive to hurt both her and Trevor." She thought of Buck's truck, and the sticker. "He also has a black truck with hunting spots."

Ash slumped down onto the bed again. He sat silent for a few moments. "All this time," he said again, quietly.

"Ash, when did Whitney change her mind and ask for abortion money?"

"End of August that year. She came to my house, which was weird."

"How'd she get to your ranch?"

"She said she'd been dropped off down the road and walked the rest of the way."

"Someone drove her and wanted to stay out of sight?"

"Maybe, in retrospect. She knocked on the door. We spoke outside. It was hurried. She said she'd been doing some research and knew where to get rid of the baby in California." He inhaled deeply, rubbed his knee. "But she needed money. She said she would stay in California afterward, start afresh."

"She seemed different—no longer afraid?"

"Yeah. Confident in her decision. To tell you the truth, I heaved a sigh of relief. It was my get-out-of-jail-free card. Until I handed over all my savings and it hit me, I really was stuck in this town, on my dad's ranch." His gaze locked with Rebecca's.

She wanted to touch him. But she held back.

"Where might Whitney have gotten another forty or fifty thousand dollars?"

"I have no idea. Maybe Trevor pulled some scam. Maybe it was his drug money."

Rebecca worried her lip with her teeth.

"Ash?" she whispered, holding his gaze. "It was something that really bugged my father, and it's still eating at me. And I have to ask you, just one more time, the scar on your face—was it really from a riding accident?"

Something shuttered instantly in his eyes. Rebecca could see him pulling up emotional drawbridges, bars going over windows as he withdrew behind the walls of his stone castle, the truth burrowing down into the deep, dark, wet dungeons of his psyche.

"I told you." His voice came out flat. His muscle tension said he was angry.

Frustration fired a spear through Rebecca's chest. "I *know* what you told me, Ash."

"Then quit asking."

"Look at yourself. Your change in mood, how you get angry about this question. There's stuff, Ash, that you are not telling me, and that's okay on one level, but not as far as this Whitney case goes, because it's going to get you charged for murder if you don't open up. Jesus." She came to her feet and dragged her hands over her hair. "You're being so damn pigheaded. Why . . . why are you hiding this from me? What can *possibly* be so bad?"

He glowered at her.

She reseated herself directly in front of him. "Look at this from a homicide investigator's perspective, from the point of view of a person who doesn't know you. You have the most motive in Whitney's death, for all the reasons already mentioned. You've also been really weird about that land, that abandoned summer camp on the back end of your property. You never took me there, even when I asked. And when I watched you observing that K9 cadaver search, you looked like someone going into severe stress." She paused, watching his face.

"It was like you knew, Ash. You *knew* what we were going to find in that log. My father said it on the phone just before he died—'He knows,' 'He lied.' What did my dad mean by that?"

Ash sat mute, staring at the wall above her crime scene chart now.

Frustration mushroomed into anger inside Rebecca. "You're not helping yourself, do you know that?"

He shot abruptly to his feet, snagged his jacket off the back of the chair, made for the door.

Rebecca's stomach fell. If she let him out that door, the years of life that had unraveled around Whitney's lie would continue to unspool, then be gone forever.

He reached for the door handle.

She lunged to her feet and grabbed his arm, suddenly furious, all the years of hurt and pain crashing in a monstrous tidal wave through her.

"Don't, Ash. Do *not* do this to me. Not now. You said you wanted me, wanted *us*—you even said you still loved me, for Chrissake. Yet you're trying your damnedest to push me—everything we ever shared—away. *Why?*"

She could feel his body vibrating under her hand.

"What is it about that place, Ash?" she whispered. "Why did you refuse to go to the clinic?"

"Because I wanted you to treat me, Becca."

She swallowed, her stomach falling further. "That's a pretty pathetic excuse, and you know it."

His eyes narrowed. He suddenly released the door handle and faced her square, toe to toe, a dark and terrifying passion glinting in his eyes, in the furious set of his jaw, in the raw energy radiating off him like a cold, black smoke that was filling, choking the room.

She released his arm, suddenly leery of his energy. She took a step backward.

"You want to know why I fucked Whitney?" His words came out of his mouth like hard bullets.

Rebecca flinched. He took a step forward.

"Because she had big breasts, and she was all pussy, all female, Becca, and she *wanted* it. She wanted my cock inside her!"

She blinked. Her eyes watered. Her heart started to stammer. She became aware he was blocking the door, her exit route.

"She thrust herself at me," he spat in disgust, "and . . . and . . . I wanted it to be you, and . . ." His voice broke. He turned his back on her. His shoulders slumped forward. When he spoke again, his voice came out quiet, defeated. "And I'd never been with a woman. I was eighteen and had never slept with a female. I . . . I needed to know that . . . that I could. Especially that summer." His words died on a whisper.

He stood there, back to her, suddenly as still as stone. His hands clenched. His neck muscles corded tight.

Something about his tone, his stillness, his tightness, scared Rebecca. She'd made him crack. Her mouth went dry. Her pulse pounded. She was fearful of what was coming next, but she had to know.

She waited. The wind outside gusted, swirling snow against the window. "Why, Ash?" she asked quietly. "Why that summer?"

"Because that summer I tried to sleep with you."

She tried to swallow. "I wanted to wait."

He spun around. The look in his face was raw. "When you said no, I became afraid. That it was me—something *wrong* with me." He opened his mouth, closed it, swallowed. Then he tried again. "I . . . I'd only ever been with a man."

Shock. Confusion raced through her.

"I'd only ever been with my father."

She shook her head, as if to process, but couldn't.

"He abused me since I was little, Becca. Very young—before I even knew it was wrong. He made it normal, and as I grew older, I became aware that it wasn't, and he used it like a weapon my whole life. He controlled me with it."

"The cabins," she whispered, her eyes beginning to burn.

He nodded.

He stood there. Stripped bare. This big man. This man Rebecca knew she'd always loved and tried not to.

"He would rape me there, at the old cabins, when he was angry. Coerce me, cajole me. Hurt me. Then he'd give me special gifts. A new horse. My first rifle. A puppy. Other things. Mess with my head."

"Ash, Ash—" She reached out. He stepped back.

"The worst was when I'd get an erection when he touched me." Emotion surged into his eyes. "Becca . . . I needed you. I needed you that summer with my heart, soul, and my body. I was always terrified you'd find out and be disgusted, tell everyone. I was terrified you wouldn't see me as . . . as man enough, and when you—"

"Come, come here." She reached out, took his hands in hers, drew him close. She wrapped her arms around his big body and rested her cheek against his chest, and just held him. Tight. So tight. She wanted to say, *Shh. Don't talk about it, don't say anything else.* But she also knew she had to listen now. She had to. To this horrible, horrible thing.

She led him to the bed, sat beside him, thigh to thigh. Close. Holding his hand. He was so masculine. So big. So vital. Everything she'd thought she'd known about this man, this teen inside, this boy inside, this Ash Haugen she'd loved, had been mistaken. So very wrong.

And now that she knew, things about him suddenly slammed into place, like a video of shattering glass being played in reverse, the million shards of glass slicing back into position to form a whole mirror image, and in that mirror she saw herself and all the things she might have done or said that would have hurt him because she didn't truly know him, know who he was. She hadn't understood. She hadn't known.

It explained his moodiness as a child and a teen. It explained his need to sometimes go off into the woods on his own, and why he'd never wanted to take her to the ruins of that abandoned summer camp. Why he'd preferred to visit her ranch rather than have her come around to his home. Why he'd loved her father and mother so much, and Running Wind. Why he'd kept photos of her dad in his house. Why he'd rescued a dog just like her mom's. Ash Haugen had been a boy in search of a father figure and a family.

It gave a different context to why he'd tried to run away from home when Running Wind had found him in the woods.

She thought of Olav Haugen, a giant, gruff grizzly bear of a man. One swipe from that hand of his . . . She shuddered to think about it. She felt sick.

"He'd hit you?"

He nodded. "Sometimes he'd beat me. And worse. But he knew how to hurt me and not leave overt scars that could not be covered by clothing, and that would be questioned. Mostly the weapons of choice were psychological. Confinement. Withholding food, threatening to hurt an animal I loved, that sort of thing."

Ash's words from that day he almost shot her from the aspens curled back into her mind.

If you shoot my dog, I will kill you.

She looked up into his eyes and touched his scar gently with her fingertips. "This scar? Did he do this?"

He nodded.

She moistened her lips. Her brain raced. "Do you want to talk about it, Ash? The details—what he did?"

He shook his head, cleared his throat. "Not now. Not the details. Maybe never."

She nodded and squeezed his hand.

Part of Rebecca really did want to know the details, so she could fully understand what he'd been through. The other part of her wasn't sure she could bear to hear it, the acts of incest, rape. She could see now how her rejection of his sexual advances in the summer of 1998 might have shattered his terribly fragile sense of masculinity, of self.

She could see now why he'd fucked Whitney in the barn.

Tears filled her eyes as she remembered how harsh her words had been to him.

Only now could she begin to appreciate how desperate he must have felt upon believing Whitney was pregnant with his baby, and what it must have meant to lose his college fund—his means of escape from his father.

"I'm sorry, Ash," she whispered. "I'm sorry for not knowing. For not *seeing*. For not being there in a way that was helpful. I'm so terribly sorry you had to endure what you did. I . . . I wish you could have told me. I wish we could go back in time. God, I wish we could turn back time." She hesitated. "Your mother—did *she* know?"

He inhaled shakily. "I think so. She had to."

"But she never stood up for you?"

He snorted softly. "No. Not even when I was little and she had to have been aware my father was taking me out to those cabins under various farm-duty pretexts. She knew. God damn her, she *knew*."

"Running Wind?"

"He guessed. I think it was him who gave me the courage to fight back, to find a way to bury it all down deep and keep going forward. To not let it break me completely. He showed me how to track, hunt. He . . . I loved him."

"A surrogate father."

"A mentor. A way to be a man."

"It's why he asked you to fight for Ricky?"

He nodded. "It's why I couldn't refuse. It's why I'd die on that hill for him."

They sat in silence, just holding hands while snow swirled outside and built up in the corners of the windows. He was like a wild stallion broken and suddenly gone still inside his paddock. And Rebecca's heart swelled to near bursting with a deep and poignant affection. Compassion. And remorse. And pain for him. She felt the barriers she'd built around her emotions for Ash crumbling to soft dust. And what remained was love. Pure. Clear. Unadulterated.

"I've never told a single soul," he said quietly. "Not even breathed it. I couldn't. I . . . I locked it away in the basement of my being like something that never happened. Sometimes I even believed it never happened. But then . . . when they started searching that area with the K9 . . ." His words died.

"That day—the riding accident—"

"I'd dropped Whitney off, and was enraged by seeing Trevor there, them going off with my savings. I went home, and my dad was waiting for me, pacing outside. He'd been to the bank in town, and the teller, making small talk in her airheaded way, had mentioned to my father that she'd just seen me in there a day or two prior, taking out all my money in cash. He wanted to know why, and what I had done with the money."

He rubbed the knee of his jeans again. Rebecca watched his scarred knuckles, her mind going back in time as she listened to him.

"I told my father that the money was mine and it had been for school, and since he didn't want me to go anyway, he should be glad it was gone. He came at me with a backhand, struck me across the eye. And that was the moment." He wavered as memory appeared to crawl to life inside him.

He cleared his throat again. "That was the moment I reached my limit. The straw that broke the back of this thing. The moment, I think, Running Wind had been preparing me for in some way. I dropped low and barreled at him. We fought hard, down in the dirt, blood everywhere. I grabbed a shovel, and when he was down on the ground, I raised it high above my head, and I swear, I was going to kill him. Kill everything terrible he'd done. Kill the dark thing inside that I hid. But . . . I hesitated. He grabbed my leg, brought me down, wrestled the shovel away from me, and swung. The sharp end sliced my face open." He ran his tongue over his teeth.

"I groped for a log and struck him across the thigh, and again across his back as he went down. Hard. I felt the jolt of impact all the way up my arms and through my body and into my skull. And I left him bleeding there in the dirt. I don't really recall exactly what occurred next. I must have just started walking and walking. And walking. Away. And that's when you found me."

"What happened to your dad?"

"He took off. He dragged himself into the house, pulled some shit together, and hobbled off into the woods. He was away for three weeks. He didn't tell my mom he was going. She was in town, shopping. When she came home, he was gone. I thought he was dead. So did my mom."

"She didn't report him missing?"

He shook his head. "She'd seen my face. She knew we'd fought. I think she suspected I'd killed him. She also knew that if he was still alive somewhere, he'd be in trouble if she or I talked to police. Because the authorities would find out my father had been abusing me. Her life as she'd known it would be over." He inhaled deeply and blew out a shuddering breath. "So my mom just hunkered deeper into her preservation mode, and she kept quiet until my father finally limped back home three weeks later and said nothing, just went back to ranch business."

"He healed in the woods?"

"Sort of. There was a hunting cabin he sometimes went to. He always had a severe limp after that, and had a bad back and lung issues."

"I remember him limping in my last year of school," Rebecca said, almost as much to herself as to Ash. "You told us he'd had an accident with the tractor going over his leg."

"Yeah. That's what our little family said. That was the shameful front we presented to the town. And if others suspected anything over the years, they sure as hell never came forward to help me. My father never spoke to me again after that day. All communication was done via my mom. He died three years later. Maybe I did kill him."

Rebecca stared at him, the image of him walking down the road in that storm as fresh in her mind as if it had been yesterday. The look on his face when he'd turned to her in the rain. The bloody gash that had run from eye to mouth. The blood down his shirt. His raw knuckles. She saw it all in a different context now.

"The clinic—the ER?" she said softly.

"I . . . I couldn't, Becca. I couldn't have *anyone* know. I was unable to be coherent about it that day. I thought I might have killed my father, that they'd find him bled to death in the forest. I thought some doctor would call the cops if they saw me, that they'd know. There was already an ER doc there who was curious about injuries for which my mother had brought me in when I was younger. I think he suspected. He would've known for certain if I'd gone in that day." A long pause. "And I needed you. God, I needed you that day, Becca."

And now Rebecca understood why. Her heart collapsed under the weight of this new knowledge.

"It's why you ran away from home when you were eleven?"

He nodded. "Running Wind sometimes spoke to me about vision quests, and the need for a young warrior to prepare his mind so he could go out alone and kill a bear, and return home a hero." He gave a wry smile "I don't think he ever meant for me to literally kill my father, but that I should strive to kill this demon beast that lived inside me."

She regarded the scar down the side of his face, and she figured she knew why he'd never had it tidied up by a plastic surgeon. It was Ash's warrior wound from killing his bear. It was the wound she'd helped shape with her own hands in his blood.

Where did one go from here? Could Ash ever become truly whole again?

Was this why he'd been distant in his marriage with Shawna, causing its collapse? His words from that night in his house sifted back into Rebecca's mind.

I was absent in a sense, out in the bush a lot, doing my thing. I know I'm sometimes not easy to be with. And . . . she needed more.

"You can't tell anyone, Becca." His gaze locked with hers. "You can't tell Grace Parker, the other cops, no one. I *need* you to keep this close. For me."

She nodded, her eyes filling with tears. "It was a riding accident," she whispered. "That's all they need to know, but Ash . . . my burying it would be just like your mother. I—"

"No," he said firmly. "It wouldn't. I just want your trust. I need you to *believe* in me."

She swallowed and bit her lip as tears sheened down her cheeks.

"I do. I do." Rebecca laced her fingers tightly through his. "It's between us until a time you want to share. If ever." She held his gaze. "There are people you can talk to, you know? Groups. Therapy. Others have been through this. They could help."

"Not now. Not yet."

She swiped away tears on her cheek. "What do you need from me? What do you need from me now?"

"To be held. Can you just hold me?"

She nodded, unable to speak against the crush of emotion in her throat. Tears ran afresh down her face as she put her arms around him and drew him toward her. They lay back on the bed, and he rested his head on her chest. Rebecca stroked his hair, and the whole world felt changed.

She was holding the man she loved, always had, and there were no barriers left between them.

It was a raw and fragile and somewhat terrifying place to be. But it also shimmered bright and delicate with hope. In some way, Becca felt as though she'd finally come home. That everything had been dialed back to the beginning and they were finally getting a second chance.

"I love you, you know, Ash?" she whispered against the top of his head, breathing in the scent of his hair, of him. "I think I always have."

She just didn't know where they were going to go from here.

When they made love, it was slow and beautiful and poignant, a reclaiming of the years. A rediscovery of bodies, an exploration of what was new, and old.

Later, it was hot. Wild. Angry. A fierce mating. Then tender again before they fell asleep in each other's arms sometime near dawn.

CHAPTER 60

Ricky's headlights reflected off swirling flakes that hurtled at him like silver asteroids as he sped up the hills toward the dense forests.

Beyond the glow of his lights, the world closed dark around him. Under the low growl of Louie's snow machine, it was silent, everything muffled by the fresh snowfall and falling flakes.

It was almost forty minutes before he reached the snowed-in road that led to the little trout lake and the historic old mine. He slowed, peering into the blackness, wiping off the snow accumulating on his visor as he searched for a fence. The lights of a house. Or a gate lintel hung with antlers.

The adrenaline had long worn off, and now he felt scared. But as he rounded a bend, he caught sight of yellow squares of light shining through the curtain of swirling snow. As he neared, he saw that the lights emanated from the windows of a low, one-story ranch house. His beam hit the bleached whiteness of moose antlers hanging over the gate. The gate itself was closed.

He pulled into the cover of trees nearby and cut his engine. He lifted off his helmet. He could smell woodsmoke on the slight breeze. A deadened, cotton-wool quiet pressed down with the flakes, punctuated every now and then by a dull thud as snow that had grown too thick on a conifer branch was released and thumped to the ground, the branch springing back with a swish that made him think someone was there.

He listened and watched for a while, getting his bearings, thinking. Mostly he was now thinking this was a dumb-ass idea. He'd been too hotheaded, as usual. Too antsy for action, to *do* something for Ash rather than sit around and accept what came his way. It sure hadn't worked out for his dad the last time Ricky sat around and did nothing to stop the cops from taking away someone he cared about.

But his dad had done some bad shit. Ricky was convinced Ash was a good dude. He had to be.

If he could climb the fence, or find a hole through it, he could head around the back of the house on foot. He wouldn't do anything stupid. He'd just check out things at the rear of the property, see if there was a garage or a shed that housed the orange snowmobile. If he saw it, he could go home and tell the cops. And he could say, *This is where ketamine is trafficked. And other drugs. The guy who lives here sells it to kids and parents on the reserve. And this guy—Stu Henry—he's in bed with that big, bald biker from Devil's Butte.* And the police would come and bust them all, like on TV, come sneaking around the back with black gear and helmets and bulletproof vests. And the occupants would squeal and say they'd given ketamine to old man Noah North, then shot him dead.

Ricky had no idea why they would have done that—killed the old man. Maybe because Noah North was an old cop and it was payback or something.

Didn't matter—the why of it. It just mattered that it would give him Ash back.

He dug into his jacket pocket and pulled out his small LED flashlight. Also a gift from Running Wind. Ricky left the snowmobile and crept along the fence perimeter until he found a good spot to climb over, a place protected from the sight line of the windows by a big hemlock. He landed with a soft thump on the other side. He held still, listening for noise, for the possibility of dogs. All remained silent.

He crept in a low crouch toward the house, snow squeaking slightly beneath his boots. When he reached a leafless hedge, he crouched there and watched the house. The light from the windows painted yellow shapes on the snow. Parked out front were two trucks. One black with a row of hunting spotlights across the top, another smaller and a silver color. In the snowpack, leading around the side of the house, he saw sled tracks. Adrenaline dumped into him. The tracks were fresh. Someone had very recently arrived on a snowmobile. Ricky pushed up to his feet and moved quickly toward the tracks at the side of the house.

A dog growled.

He froze.

The animal barreled at him from nowhere, chains clattering against metal. It came up short, snarling and leaping and yapping. It was big and tied by a lead to a line that ran across the yard. It could only go so far.

Ricky dived back into the hedge. He huddled there, shaking, as the door of the house was flung open. A huge man silhouetted in yellow light peered into the night. The dog barked louder. It was a rottweiler cross with a huge head and a wide mouth full of teeth that glinted with saliva as it barked. Ricky's heart jackhammered. A voice came from behind the man. He turned to face the voice, and the light caught his profile.

It was the big, bald biker guy he'd seen in town before. Leather jacket.

Ricky's mouth went dust dry. He feared the man was going to let the dog off line to come after him.

But the man yelled at the dog instead. The animal hesitated, peering into the dark at where it could smell Ricky. It growled. The man yelled again, and the dog retreated back toward the house with a clatter along its chain.

When the dog reached the steps up to the door, the man unhooked the animal's lead from the yard line and took the dog inside. The door closed, and the wedge of yellow warmth that had sliced into the darkness vanished.

Ricky huddled there awhile until he regained his breath. Until he was sure they weren't coming out again. Then slowly he crept around the back.

More light from windows at the rear shone squares onto snow. Behind the house stood a large barn in a cleared area. The sled tracks led right to it. Behind the barn the forest looked dense. A small door in the side of the barn stood ajar, and Ricky crept up to it.

He edged it open wider. It made a loud cracking sound. He froze. Waiting. Snowflakes kissed his skin, melted down his neck. No one came from the house.

With relief he entered the barn and panned his thin beam around the interior. His light glinted off metal and plastic. His heart kicked. He moved closer. Two snowmobiles. Helmets on seats. A tarp covered a third—he could see the skis poking out beneath the cover. He went over and drew back the tarp. His heart stopped dead, then sputtered into a fast stammer.

The orange machine. And on the seat was the helmet with the black tarantula and web pattern. He'd found it. He'd found the fucking machine he'd seen fleeing from Noah North's cabin.

A creak sounded behind him.

He spun around.

A bright hunting spot flared into his face, blinding him.

"What the hell?" A man's voice. It was the bald man. Ricky tried to dart away, but the man lunged for him and flung him down to the floor. His flashlight went flying, and his face smacked against cold, hard concrete.

Ricky tried to scramble back up to his feet, but something struck the back of his head. It felt like a metal bar. He felt—heard—the crack. Pain exploded through his skull. His knees buckled as his legs crumpled beneath him. The man reached down and grabbed hold of his collar. Ricky could taste blood in his mouth and down the back of his nasal passages. His ears were ringing.

Another man with a flashlight appeared in the doorway.

"What's going on?" he said.

The bald man dragged Ricky along the floor toward the door. "Got us a little visitor. He was checking out our snowmobile under the tarp."

"Hey, that's Ricky Simon," said the other guy.

Ricky squirmed and was dealt another blow across the face. Pinpricks of light danced across blackness in front of his eyes as his vision began to fade. Sound grew tinny and distant in his ears. He felt his wrists being jerked behind him and tied there. He felt himself being dragged out the door and through the cool, wet softness of freshly fallen snow. He saw the lights from the house. He was dragged bump, bump, bump up the stairs. The bald man kicked the house door open. The dog inside barked.

"Hoi, guys . . . we got ourselves a bit of fun here."

CHAPTER 61

Cariboo Country. Saturday, January 26.

Ash's phone rang. He checked his watch. Five a.m. He took a second to orient himself. He was lying naked next to Becca. In her hotel room. Memories of sex washed through him. He groped for his pants on the floor, extracted his cell from his pocket. Answered.

"Ash here." He spoke quietly. Becca was still sleeping.

"You gave me your number." A woman's voice, slurred. Ricky's mother. "You shaid I could call any time of day or night."

Ash sat upright, abruptly wide awake. Becca's crime scene board peered at him in the dim light.

"Ricky hash not come home. I'm worried for his shafety. He took Louie's snowmobile, he went after thoshe guys."

"What guys?"

"Those ones on that ranch. Cousins."

She wasn't coherent.

"Listen. Slow down. Tell me what happened, in order, step by step."

"He wash mad—made Louie tell him."

"Tell him what?"

"I . . . worried about Ricky. Louie came over, said he could be in trouble. They'll kill him. Ricky . . . he wanted to know the name of the guy who shold ketamine."

Ash's pulse quickened. He shook Becca's shoulder. "Becca."

She blinked awake, switched on the bedside light. "What is it?"

"Ricky's gone after some guys who sell ketamine on the reserve," he said quickly. "He was speaking about 'Special K' in the truck, after we reported the accident to Buck. He told me some guys on the reserve deal in the stuff."

She hurriedly sat upright, clutching the bedsheet over her breasts, blinking as she pulled the world into focus. Her hair was a soft mess around her face, and Ash noticed her beauty despite the urgency of the call.

"Who is Louie?" Ash asked into the phone.

"My baby's father. My boyfriend."

"Are you okay, Mrs. Simon? Is Patty okay?"

She laughed.

He mouthed to Becca, *Ricky's mother. She's drunk.*

"Is Louie there, Mrs. Simon? Can you put him on the phone?"

"He'sh passed out."

"And the patrol officer outside your house? Still there?"

"Lemme go shee."

Noise sounded as Ricky's mother appeared to be crashing and bumping her way over to the window, or door.

"Cop car's shtill there."

"Listen to me. I'm coming over. Make yourself some coffee. Just . . . lay off the booze until I get there, okay? Make sure Patty is safe in bed, okay? Can you do that?"

She grunted and hung up.

He killed the call, swung his legs over the bed, and grabbed his clothes.

"Where is Ricky? What's going on?" Becca said.

"I don't know." He pulled on his shirt. "But what I do know is Ricky's mother doesn't usually worry about him. And because she's worried, so am I. I'm going out there to see if I can make sense of it all. He seems to have run off after these ketamine guys on her boyfriend's sled, and he hasn't come home."

"What about the officer stationed outside his house?"

"He seems to have ditched the cop. Snuck out the back, maybe."

She stared. Her eyes narrowed.

"I'm coming." She threw back the covers and swung her legs over the bed.

He stilled a moment, snared by her naked body. Her breasts. This woman he'd never stopped loving. Their eyes met.

Ash wanted to say so much to her suddenly. *Don't leave me, Becca. Don't leave me again.*

But he didn't. Because as he looked at her now, he knew she would. She had to. Her life, her relationships, her career, were hundreds of miles away from him and his ranch.

But the night had been theirs. In making love he'd felt whole, possibly for the first time in his life. For he'd shared with her the terrible dark weight of his secret. He'd laid himself absolutely bare for the first time ever—he'd trusted her with the weight of it. And she hadn't shunned him.

Instead, she'd taken him into her arms, into her very self. And Ash could not ask for more. In giving his secret to her, he'd allowed her to give him what he needed most. It was right. It was enough.

A veil had been lifted from his life. Perhaps now his vision forward would be clear. Step by little step. If only because he was not completely alone with his terrible secret.

"It could be nothing, Becca," he said quietly. "I want you to stay here. Stay warm."

She reached for her clothes. "I'm coming, Ash. You're supposed to stay away from Ricky Simon. At least if I'm with you, I'm a witness to whatever craziness this is."

"And you? You're supposed to stay away from me. Your career could—"

"Ash." She held his gaze. "I'm coming."

———

Ricky's eyes were swollen almost shut. He struggled to breathe through his split lips and smashed-up nose. There were three guys in the house, and they'd beaten him through the night as they argued and drank. After they'd kicked the stuffing out of him, trying to make him answer questions, they'd dumped him in a small room like a broken rag doll. The room was barely bigger than a broom closet, and the plywood walls were paper thin. He could hear almost everything they said through the wall.

"I told you to hide that sled, you fuckwit."

"It *is* goddamn hidden. Under the tarp in the barn. How did that kid come to be here anyway? One of you blabbed?"

"Jesus. No one squealed."

"Maybe it was Louie."

"We're screwed."

"No. We're not."

"Fuck, man, we *are* screwed."

"Listen to me—" It was the bald guy's voice. Through the course of the night, Ricky had learned his name was Jesse. Stu Henry had a low voice with slow cadence. The third guy was someone called Digby. Ricky reckoned Digby was Stu Henry's cousin.

"He's alone," the bald guy said. "We found his sled. No other tracks came with his. We get rid of the little shit, and nothing, nada, will link us to Noah North. Or that skeleton in the log."

"The kid was the fucking witness in North's shed. He saw me go off on the snowmobile." Stu's voice.

"But no one has found the machine yet, have they? Except for him. We get rid of it proper, and the kid. We're home clean."

"What about the skeleton?" said Digby. "Word is they found a bullet with the bones. What about CSI shit and linking it to a rifle?"

"That .30-30 slug? What can they link it to? Nothing. Got rid of that rifle years back."

"So how come the kid found us? Someone had to have told him something."

Silence. Clinking of bottles against glasses.

"Yeah." Jesse's voice. Calm suddenly. "We can get that information out of him."

"Yeah, before we beat his little brains out and smash him to bits and throw him down some old well like Trevor." It was Digby speaking.

Another few moments of silence. They were doing something— moving about. Ricky tried to sit up higher and lean against the thin wall in order to hear better. His head pounded. A dull buzz sounded in his brain.

"What about the mine?" Stu Henry's voice. "We can dump him down one of the old mine shafts."

"Too close to this property. You don't shit in your own backyard."

"The caves up Sleemack Creek?" Stu's voice.

Silence.

"That's an hour out on sleds from here," said Digby. "No one goes there in winter. We dump him down one of those narrow cave shafts, they go down for kilometers into the earth. Black as pitch down there, and water underground. They'll never find him. Like they never found Trevor."

"Yeah, and this snow is forecast to keep falling for another two days at least. Will cover our tracks good." It was Stu Henry speaking again.

A few more moments as this idea was considered.

"Get your gear." Jesse. "We head out before full light."

Ricky heard movement, banging. A closet opening. He heard them calling the dog and feeding it—the sound of kibble clattering into a tin dog bowl.

A faint light eked in through the window of the small room Ricky was being held in. Dawn was approaching. The hard plastic zip ties used to secure his hands behind his back were cutting into his wrists beneath the sleeves of his snow jacket. He still had all his waterproof gear on. He figured he might be dead from all the blows and kicks if he hadn't been wearing heavy winter gear.

He groaned as he tried to roll over. He retched from the blood and mucus going down the back of his nose and throat.

A short while later the door opened. It was Jesse.

He came over and hauled Ricky up by the collar. Ricky tried to stand but couldn't.

"Come, you little shit." He dragged him by the collar out of the room. Ricky saw the puddle of blood where he'd lain. It made a trail under the heels of his boots as he was pulled along the floor into the living room. The dog looked up from its bowl briefly, but was far more interested in his breakfast than in beaten-up little Ricky Simon.

"You stuck your nose where it's not wanted, buddy boy. No ways out now. You're going the way of Whitney Gagnon and Trevor Beauchamp."

"What . . . happened to them?" He coughed and spat a glob of mucus and blood onto the floor.

Surprise shot across Jesse's face, as if he couldn't believe Ricky had actually dared ask the question after being mashed half to a pulp. But then he grinned, as if he rather relished the idea of telling Ricky.

"Beat him to a pudding, slit his throat, and down the well he went. Sealed and done. The girl? Well, we had a bit of fun with the lass, now didn't we, boys?" He made a lewd pumping motion with his arms and hips. "All had a go, eh, boys? And got paid for the pleasure."

Laughter.

"Start of the Wolf Pack hunt club," jeered Stu with a fist pump. "Extreme hunting. Nothing like chasing a piece of naked white-girl ass bouncing through the forest. Beats whitetail deer any day, hands down, eh?"

Ricky thought about the wolf logo Tori had described on the black truck that had run them over the bank.

"We thought she'd clean disappeared that day," Stu added with a dark chuckle. "Freaked us out when we found we *were* chasing a deer in the end, and she'd just vanished near those ruins. Like a ghost. Turns out she was there all the time. Crawled into that log and never came out."

———

Ash banged on the door of Ricky's house while Becca stood in falling snow speaking to the officer in the cruiser stationed across the road. Ash had to bang several more times before the door opened.

Ricky's mom swayed in the doorway, bracing her hand against the jamb for support.

Ash pushed past her, brushing snow off his brow. "Tell me where he went."

She tried to hold her eyes open as she stumbled toward the kitchen table. She leaned on the table with both hands.

The cop and Becca entered behind him. The cop was calling Sergeant Parker on his phone. He looked ashen. He had reason to. He'd let his charge slip away.

"Look, you have a choice," Ash said to Ricky's mom. "Your children or the drink. Pull it together now, and I can get you help. I *will* help, but you need to help me find Ricky first. And if you choose the booze instead of your kids, I'm going to call social services and help them take your kids away. Understand?"

She sniffed, nodded, wiped her nose with the back of her hand.

"Now where's Louie?"

She jerked her head toward the living room. Ash looked around the dividing wall. A man lay passed out—dead to the world, mouth open and drooling—on the sofa.

"Okay, so Louie's out. Can you tell me where this place is where Ricky went?"

She rubbed her face. "I . . . I think Louie said it was a spread near an old mine. And a little trout lake or something like that."

Ash shot a glance at Becca. "I know it. I've been tracking past there several times. It's at least an hour or two out via the road. But if I can get back to my place, pick up a sled, I can go in through the forests from the back end. Will take a quarter of the time." He began to move toward the door.

"Ash, stop," Becca said.

He spun to face her.

"You need to stand down."

The cop raised his phone. "Orders from Parker—she says to leave it to her."

He stared at them, heart thumping. "I know who lives out there. Ricky's life is on borrowed time, if he's not dead already."

"Who lives there?" Becca said.

"Guy named Digby Henry. Rumored to be a dealer for a gang up north. Also rumored to work as an enforcer. His cousin Stu hangs out there, too. Had a run-in with them both when I was out there hunting a wounded cat."

"You cannot go out there," said the officer. Ash regarded him. A kid, really, all of maybe twenty years old with a pink, fresh face. "Parker is mobilizing a team as we speak."

"And how long will that team take to get out there? With the rate this snow is falling, if those guys leave that ranch with Ricky, we'll never be able to track them."

"You need to stand down, Ash," Becca said again.

Ash stared at her, conflict, urgency—desperation—crowding his chest, suffocating his breath, pounding through his blood.

The image of Running Wind on that mesa flashed through his mind.

I will. I vow it. I'll see Ricky through that rough patch. I'll die on that hill for you, okay?

He met Becca's eyes. "I gotta do this. I can't sit by. I'm going to pick up my sled, head through the forest. It'll be quicker."

She opened her mouth, but before she could speak, he busted out the door and jogged down the steps.

Becca came running after him.

He climbed into his GMC, and so did she, slamming the passenger door shut.

"Becca—"

"Drive." She checked her service weapon as she spoke. "Grace will send backup."

CHAPTER 62

Ash slowed his snowmobile as he and Becca and Kibu drew up to a gate with a log lintel upon which hung a rack of bleached moose antlers thick with snow. Stu and Digby Henry's house. Gray clouds smothered the forest, and the day had dawned dim and bleak. Snow continued to fall heavily.

Two trucks hulked like white beasts under heavy blankets of snow outside the front door. One of the vehicles was black, one silver, judging from the bits that stuck out. By the snow accumulation, Ash figured the trucks had been parked there all night.

He lifted his visor. "Hunting spotlights," he said with a tilt of his chin to the row of lumps in the snow atop the black truck. Becca raised her visor, studied the trucks, nodded.

Kibu began to growl low in his throat. Ash turned to watch him. It was the sound he made when another dog was near. He studied the lay of the property more carefully, saw the chain.

"A dog somewhere," he said. "I'll need to secure Kibu to the machine before we go in."

"We should wait," she said.

"For how long? They're going to take another hour—two, even— to get here via the road in these conditions. If they even can. It's not plowed, barely ever is."

"Grace will organize snowmobiles. Buck's detachment is equipped."

He frowned and studied the windows. No lights glowed inside. No smoke issued from the chimney. A sense of desolation blanketed the place. Torn plastic on one of the windows flapped in the breeze.

"I don't think they're here," he said. This worried him. It would mean they'd already taken Ricky someplace else. "I know there's a barn out back. I'm going to take a look at the rear. We can drive the sled around and come in under cover from the forest at the back."

Becca checked her watch, hesitated, then nodded.

They went around and dismounted among the pine trees. They removed their helmets. Ash secured Kibu by his leash to the sled carrier. He did not want him with them if there was a hostile dog on the property. They crept forward.

Becca carried her firearm in the tactical way she'd been trained to. Ash held his shotgun loaded, ready. They moved along the fringe of the trees. He stopped her, pointed.

"Tracks," he whispered, breath clouding around his mouth. "Looks like three sleds, one of them dragging a trailer."

The tracks led from an open barn door into the forest, heading in a southwesterly direction. The indentations were fast filling in with snow. Ash studied the barn. No movement.

He made a motion to Becca. She nodded, and they approached cautiously around the back of the barn, Becca going to the left, Ash coming around the right. As Ash rounded the side of the building, he kept his attention on the house. It remained dark inside. Quiet.

They entered the barn through the big, open doorway. It was dim inside. Becca clicked on a flashlight Ash had given her. The barn was empty inside, apart from a workbench, some tools on the walls, and one sled. Blue in color.

Rebecca shone her flashlight on the concrete. "Blood," she said quietly.

They followed the faint smears of blood to a smaller door in the side of the barn. Outside, a broad depression in the snow led from the barn door to the back entry of the house. It contained pink traces of blood.

"Whatever was dragged out or in here, it was a while ago," he said, worry fisting inside his chest. "Tracks have already filled in a fair amount." He glanced at the low ranch-house building. "I'm going up to the house. Can you cover me from here?"

"Ash—"

"There's no one around. If there are, they're sleeping. The windows are uncovered. I just want to look inside."

He crept forward. Rebecca held back, her sidearm ready, an extra rifle slung across her back, her eyes fixed on the windows, watching for movement.

Ash reached the house wall. Pressing against it, he peered cautiously up into the first window. A dog barked inside. Kibu barked in response from the forest. *Shit.* Ash ducked down.

He waited.

Nothing.

He glanced at Becca. Her posture was tense. But she made no sign that she'd seen anyone move.

He peered up again. In the dim interior a large rottweiler cross was tied to a short chain that appeared bolted to a beam on the living room wall. Ash could discern no other movement. He moved to the next window, edged up, and peeped in.

His pulse quickened. Blood smeared the floor, some spatters on the wall. A smeared trail of blood led from the middle of the floor to the door. Moving faster, he checked the other windows. Two bedrooms. Unmade beds. Some scattered clothes. No one in sight.

He tried the back door. It opened.

Ash motioned to Becca he was going in. Before she could protest, he slipped inside. The dog went ballistic, yanking against its short chain secured to the living room wall. Ash vowed internally he'd be back for that animal with the SPCA. The house was a mess of bottles, a bong on a coffee table. Cigarette rolling papers. Cans. Whiskey bottle. Overflowing ashtrays. He followed the blood smear to a small room. Anxiety torqued through him as he gazed upon the blood on the linoleum floor.

Becca appeared behind him. She stared at the blood.

"You think it's Ricky's?" she said.

"It's got to be. Those sled tracks lead out the back and into the forest heading southwest. Keep going that way and you end up heading into the mountains. I think they're taking him there. My guess is he's on the trailer one of the machines is towing."

Becca checked her phone. "No cell reception."

She moved into the living room. The dog barked and growled, baring teeth. A froth of saliva foamed on its jowls. In the kitchen Becca found a phone on the wall. She picked up the receiver. "Dial tone," she said. She dialed quickly.

Grace Parker must have answered, because Becca said loudly over the noise of the dog, "Looks like Ricky Simon was here at the Henry residence." She spoke fast, one hand over her ear. "There's a lot of blood. He might be seriously injured, or worse. Fresh tracks show three sleds and a trailer left the property and are heading in a southwesterly direction through wilderness. We're going to follow."

Ash watched Becca listening to the voice on the other end of the line. She appeared agitated. She glanced at the poor barking animal.

Ash interrupted. "Tell Parker with the rate this snow is falling, we'll lose any trace of them if we don't get on those tracks stat. We'll lose her key witness."

She relayed the message, then said, "Ash Haugen is an expert tracker. He wants to save that boy. Trust me, Grace, when I say Ricky Simon is like a son to Ash. He's *not* going to harm the kid."

Silence as she listened.

"Understood." She hung up. "Let's go." She made for the door.

"What did she say?"

"To stand down."

He stared at her. But she pushed past him, exited the house, and began running through the thick powder to where they'd left Kibu and the machine.

———

Rebecca snugged herself close in behind Ash as he wove a hair-raising slalom among the trees, following the indentations in the snow left by the three machines and the sled trailer.

Every now and then she caught sight of pink stains in the snow— blood—and feared the worst for Ricky. Behind her, Kibu hunkered down in his carrier, at ease and familiar with the experience of travel-ing in this manner with his master.

Ash pointed his gloved hand at another stain of blood as they rounded an old hemlock. Rebecca ducked out of the way of low branches, worrying that they might not find the kid alive. She hoped Ricky was holding on, but time was of the essence. That was why she'd made the decision to defy her superior's order. She understood why Grace had demanded they stand down and leave the pursuit to an Emergency Response Team when the ERT did eventually arrive.

Grace probably still viewed Ash as a key person of interest, too. Plus, her team needed Ricky's unfettered testimony when and if this all went to trial.

But if they delayed, Ricky could die, if he wasn't deceased already. A dead witness would be no help to Grace or a prosecution team. Rebecca also knew she could no more hold Ash back than stop the earth turning. His words about Running Wind and Ricky raced through her mind.

It's why I'd die on that hill . . .

Her hope was that Grace's ERT guys would get out here fast and be hot on their tail before things got out of hand.

They traveled for almost thirty more minutes at high speed before the terrain started to climb, twisting up through forest that grew sparser and trees that grew shorter as they gained elevation. Ash slowed as they found themselves in a narrowing valley. They came through the tree line into snowy fields that undulated into foothills, then mountains that rose steep and craggy.

He stopped the snowmobile, lifted his visor, and pointed to where the tracks crossed the snowy meadows, heading toward the mountains.

"Looks like they went up that way, up the Sleemack Creek drainage."

"That's where the Marble Caves are," Rebecca said.

"If they went up there, they're heading directly for the caves—can't figure any other reason for them to go up into that watershed." He fell silent, studying the terrain. "It's a choke point," he said. "Extremely narrow valley between steep flanks on either side. Only one way in and one way out. They'll hear our snowmobile coming for miles. Sound echoes among those rocks and through the caves. We'd be ambush meat."

Rebecca stared at the jagged black rocks that jutted like dragon claws through snow on either side of the tight valley through which Sleemack Creek churned glacial waters during the summers.

Rebecca had visited the caves once, during a school outing. They consisted of warrens of caverns and tunnels that burrowed down for miles into the earth. If those guys were dragging Ricky up there on that trailer, she was thinking dump site. The odds that the kid was dead already had just gotten higher in her mind. But she didn't say so to Ash. She allowed him his hope.

"Is there a way in from the opposite side?" she asked.

"It would take a full half day to go around that part of the mountain and come down from the top over there." He pointed. "Extreme avalanche danger in this powder, too."

He glanced at the pair of technical snowshoes strapped to the side of his machine. Only one pair.

"You're not thinking of going up there on foot?" she said.

"You'll have to stay here—I've only got one set. Wait for the team." He pulled off his helmet, dismounted, and rapidly started unstrapping his snowshoes from the side of the sled.

She yanked off her helmet. "No, Ash. You're not going alone. One guy against at least three armed and desperate men who could be killers? No freaking way."

He started to release Kibu from his box.

"No," Rebecca ordered. She clamped her gloved hand on his arm. "Not happening."

His gaze warred with hers. Mist clouded around his face. He was breathing hard. She could feel tension vibrating in his arm.

"I'm a cop, Ash. I've been on this case, and I have a duty here. I can't allow civilian life to be endangered."

"Ricky is—"

"Triage. Think triage. He could be dead. I can't have you dead, too."

"Becca." He spoke low, his arctic eyes cold, fierce. "I have *got* to do this. I can't sit here and wait to find out later that Ricky died in the space of time it took for the ERT guys to get in. If this costs me my life, so be it. At least I tried."

"Ash—"

"No." His face turned hard. "You listen to me. My life has been a fuckup. I've damaged everything I've touched. It's no great loss to the world if I flame out now." He shook off her hold on his arm and released Kibu.

The dog hopped out of his carrier and bounded through the powder snow, exhilarated.

"I'm going up that side, on the left flank." He pointed and waved his arm across to indicate the easterly span of the mountain beneath the caves.

She unholstered her weapon.

He hesitated. "What are you doing?"

"I swear, I'll use this. I'll detain you with force if I have to." She held her sidearm at the ready. Emotion burned fierce in her eyes. "You can't do this, Ash. Not now. You're wrong," she said. "You haven't damaged things you've touched. You've made things grow. Your ranch. Your dogs. Your work with predators is good work. You save livestock, save wildlife. You're one of the most caring people I know. You have worth, goddammit." She swallowed, her voice going hoarse. "*Worth*," she said again. "To me. Don't do this to me after you made me love you all over again."

He stilled.

He stared at her.

Wind gusted and swirled flakes.

"Becca, I can't leave him. I can't. You'll have to shoot me."

He bent down and began to strap on the shoes.

Her hands, holding the gun, shook under the power of the emotions that took hold of her. At her realization that she wanted this man. Alive. In her life. She would reengineer her career, everything to accommodate this, to make it happen.

"Fine," she snapped. She reholstered her weapon. "Get back on the machine."

He paused in buckling up his snowshoes.

"We'll take the sled up to that point there—that rock." She pointed to an outcrop several meters in elevation up the left flank. "Wind is blowing from the northeast. Sound is less likely to carry toward the ravine and the cave entrance if we go that way."

He glanced up to where she pointed.

"From there we go on foot. Across the flank toward the gulley and caves. It's shorter than you walking in from here. It'll be faster."

"There's only one pair of snowshoes. That powder is too deep across that flank without—"

"We do it like wolves. You're heavier. You wear the shoes and break trail. I follow behind in your tracks. This stuff is powder, Ash. Light as fluff. It won't be too bad."

He wavered and glanced once more at the outcrop Rebecca had indicated. "No." He faced her. "I'm not letting you go in—"

"You don't have a choice, bud. I'm the cop with legal authority here. Get on. You do this with me, or you don't do it at all."

CHAPTER 63

Ash picked his way carefully through ragged black rocks as he broke trail along the snowy flank toward the gulley where he believed they'd find the three snowmobiles parked with the trailer.

Becca was right. The snow was fluffy, light powder. Once he'd broken trail with his snowshoes, she was able to follow relatively easily in his wake, Kibu behind her. Their breath misted in clouds, and snow squeaked as they went. Huge flakes, the size of dollar coins, continued to waft to the ground around them. It provided good cover and deadened sound.

As they progressed, Becca's words rolled over and over in his mind.

You have worth, goddammit. Worth. *To me. Don't do this to me after you made me love you all over again.*

He swallowed at the thought. The idea was like gossamer in his chest. She instilled in him a sense of meaningfulness, of value, that began to chip away at the deep-seated shame he'd carried with him always, because of his father. Because of the abuse.

He glanced over his shoulder. She met his eyes through the falling snow. An energy crackled between them. Blood coursed hotter in his veins. The irony was not lost on him, though. Just as he'd been ready to risk death, Becca had given him everything to live for. And now he'd brought her into danger, too.

Fuck, buddy, you better not screw this one up now. Not this time.

He walked faster through the deep snow, breathing hard.

They'd left the snowmobile at the rock outcrop about two hundred meters back. They were almost above the cave entrance now. On his back he carried a rifle and the pack of supplies he customarily took with him when he hunted large predators. In his hand was a shotgun. Becca had a rifle strapped to her back, and she carried her sidearm.

He stilled for a moment and panned his binoculars across the snow-covered creek bed that nestled in the gulley ahead of them. He tensed as he saw the tracks where he'd anticipated he would, coming up the snow-covered and frozen creek.

He pointed and handed the scopes to Becca. She studied the tracks.

"Pretty fresh?" she said quietly.

He nodded, urgency biting him. They moved faster. Powder cascaded softly from under his snowshoes as the ground to their right fell away more steeply.

They reached a powder-covered rock ledge that jutted out over the gully. On the opposite side of the gully, a mountain flank rose sharply.

Ash stopped and checked his compass.

"We should be right over the main cave entrance," he whispered. "Those snowmobiles wouldn't get any higher up the creek than this anyway—it turns into a steep series of waterfalls from this point."

They moved carefully onto the ledge. Ash ordered Kibu to lie down at his boots. "Shh, stay, boy."

Kibu gave a little moan and acquiesced, settling with his thick fur into the snow.

"Wait here," Ash said to Becca.

He got onto his stomach and inched through powder toward the very lip of the ledge. He peered over the rock ledge to where the cave entrance was located below. His pulse spiked.

Beneath him three snowmobiles and the trailer were parked. One machine was blaze orange and decorated with a giant spider and web. The orange spider helmet rested on the seat. Snow was settling on the machines. By the amount, the men hadn't been here long. He took out his scopes again and studied the snowmobiles and trailer more carefully. Two of the machines had rifles strapped to the sides. Tracks and a pink trail of blood led from the trailer and disappeared directly below him, where the large cave entrance lay. His mind wheeled through his options.

Time was critical. Ricky was seriously wounded, or as Becca had said, maybe he was no longer alive and the guys had just come out here to dump his body. But if Ricky was still alive, they needed to move fast to keep him that way. Ash panned his scopes toward the snow-covered creek nestled in the V of the steep gully, then up the sheer incline on the opposite side of the creek bed, then back to the machines. Ash knew that beneath all that loosely packed powder lay ice from the recent extended freeze cycle. That powdery snow would be highly unstable atop that base layer of ice.

Ash inched backward to where Becca and Kibu waited. "They're down there," he whispered, shrugging off his pack. "I've got a plan."

He crouched down, opened his pack, and removed several bear banger cartridges and the gun designed to fire them. He loaded the gun. He then took out some pencil flares. All standard stuff he customarily carried with him.

"Here's what we do."

CHAPTER 64

Rebecca got into position, per Ash's plan, leaning against a rock near the lip of the ledge that jutted out over the cave entrance. She aimed one of the bear bangers that he'd given her, curling her finger into the trigger guard. She fired the projectile.

The cartridge rocketed across the river and exploded as it hit the snowpack on the sheer mountain flank on the opposite side of the gulley. Sound boomed—like a bombshell—down the narrow and deep valley, rebounding over and over. It happened almost at once. A line chased through the snow parallel to where she'd placed the banger. A creak. A groan. And the whole snowpack released below the line.

The avalanche gathered girth and speed as it churned like lethal white water down the flank and hit the riverbed with an explosive crash. It boiled and bounded through the gully and foamed up the other side and over the snowmobiles, rolling them over and covering them before settling.

Her pulse raced. She couldn't see Ash and Kibu from her vantage point. They'd climbed down from the ledge farther upstream of the cave entrance. The plan was for Ash to find a position from which he could train firepower on the entrance of the caves in the event that the men—alerted by the avalanche and fearing they might be trapped—exited them.

She fired a second banger. More to the right this time, setting off another massive slide that rumbled and crashed down the flank and filled the riverbed lower down the valley, blocking off an escape route.

She heard a yell, then another.

Below her a man appeared from the caves. He wore a toque and black jacket. He held a rifle. Relief washed through Rebecca. As they'd hoped, the cave entrances lay far enough back from the gully that the avalanche had not had enough momentum to boil all the way across and block the cave entrance off. Yet it had spooked at least one man into exiting.

He stumbled toward the mounds of chunked-up snow where the snowmobiles had been parked. He turned around and called the others. Two more men appeared. They joined the first.

She waited in anticipation of Ash's gunfire. It was to be a warning shot, a distraction.

The crack retorted sharply down the valley, making it seem as if the shot had come from all directions.

The men spun around, looking up and down, searching in panic for the origin of the gunshot. One pointed up in the direction in which Ash and Kibu had vanished. The man with the rifle whipped stock to shoulder as the other two stumbled back toward the cover of the cave. Either they had more weapons in the caves, or they were seeking cover because their rifles had been buried with their machines.

The man fired. Rebecca tensed.

She heard a bullet hit rock. Another crack of a rifle boomed down the gully. The man staggered backward. Ash's bullet had struck home.

"Self-defense," she whispered to herself. "The suspect fired at him first." That would be their story.

The man's knees buckled as his legs gave out under him. He fell with his rifle into the snow.

Rebecca waited. Tense. If the other two did have weapons inside the cave, they might hole up. Or they could have sneaked out below her, gone downstream, and started coming up the mountain to the south of her. There was also a good chance they were not armed. She'd seen those two long guns strapped to the now-buried snowmobiles.

She caught a blur of movement below. Her muscles snapped tight. One of the men ran from the caves toward his fallen colleague. He bent down and grabbed the fallen man's rifle out of the snow. As he did, Ash fired again. The bullet kicked up snow near the men. The unwounded man lurched for the cover of a rock. He returned fire quickly. So did Ash. His bullet hit. His target went down clutching his shoulder. His rifle fell into deep powder, vanishing from sight.

Rebecca waited. Silence descended. The man with the injured shoulder tried to drag himself through the snow, groping to find his gun. Ash fired next to him. He yelped and scrambled on his belly toward the cover of the cave, leaving a trail of red on white. He screamed something, and the third guy came into view. He tried to grab his fallen buddy by the arms and pull him under the safety of the ledge. Rebecca shot a third bear banger into the mountain in a southerly direction. The cartridge exploded like a bomb as it hit the flank. Sound boomed all around them. Snow started to slide.

She launched another banger into the air, aiming even farther up the creek. The cartridge exploded. The two men below froze. The uninjured one spun to face in the direction of the most recent explosion, apparently confused into thinking he might be surrounded and that shots were coming from the opposite side of the gulley now, from higher upstream. As the new avalanche rumbled down the slope and into the creek bed, Rebecca reached for the rifle Ash had left her. She aimed very carefully to place her shot.

Curling her gloved finger around the trigger, she pulled on a slow exhalation. The rifle crack ricocheted through the falling snow. The man standing above his fallen buddy went stiff. He staggered forward, stumbled, then went down into the snow.

Silence descended once more. She waited, blood booming against her eardrums. Nothing moved.

She saw Ash appear higher upstream of the caves. He was making his way down to the entrance, Kibu behind him. Hurriedly she slung the rifle over her shoulder and gathered up the pack Ash had left with her.

She began to make her way down to the caves, following the tracks Ash had left with his snowshoes.

But when she reached the rock slab where the men had fallen, there were only two. The third man—the one she'd shot—was gone.

So was Ash.

CHAPTER 65

When Ash reached the ledge outside the main cave entrance, one of the men had disappeared. Two still lay injured. He could not see the rifle with them.

The cave entrance loomed big and black to his right. It seemed to exhale cold and the dank smell of earth. He saw a trail of fresh blood leading into the maw.

"Stay here, Kibu," he whispered. "You wait for Becca."

His dog whimpered and sat in the snow.

Ash took his flashlight from his pocket, stepped toward the entrance, and panned his beam into the gaping darkness. The shot was almost instant, the sound deafening.

Ash flung himself sideways against the rock wall, dropping his flashlight. The bullet whizzed past him. His heart hammered. His mouth went dry. He edged backward, seeking cover.

Another crack of a rifle split the darkness. The bullet exploded rock above his shoulder.

Fuck.

He dropped to his stomach in the snow. He was trapped without sufficient cover. He tried to leopard-crawl backward and away from the entrance in a retreat, but his snowshoes hampered him. Another shot exploded from inside the caves.

He heard a yell, then a man's scream. Followed by growling.

Shit.

Kibu?

He spun to face the spot where he'd ordered Kibu to wait.

His dog was gone.

More screaming issued from inside the caves. Then came a terrible wet sort of growling—the sounds of a dog fighting a man echoing over and over as the labyrinth of tunnels amplified noise and overlapped it like a giant rock musical instrument in the bowels of the mountain. Ash fumbled to unbuckle his snowshoes. He kicked them off, panic whipping through his chest. He groped in the powder, searching for his flashlight, found it. He held still for a moment, listening.

The echoes faded slowly, swallowed by the caves, sucked deep into the mountain. Chills rippled over his skin. A moan came from one of the men he'd dropped earlier. Ash waited a moment longer. Still no sound.

He gave a whistle.

No dog came.

His chest cramped tight. He whistled again. No response.

Ash came carefully to his feet, ready to drop at any moment. He held his rifle forward. There was no reaction to his movement. He stepped into the cave entrance, listened. Silence now, just a sense of the mountain breathing slowly in, then out. He panned his flashlight across the darkness.

"Kibu?" he whispered. The caves whispered it back as they breathed out cold air. *Kiboooo.*

He went deeper in. Shadows leaped and quivered. The walls glistened with moisture and ice. He heard it, a whimper. Ash's stomach tightened.

He moved carefully over ice and rock toward the sound, stopped, listened again. Another whimper. The cry echoed softly, over and over, seeming to come from all directions. Ash slipped on a slick slab of ice and smashed down hard. His heart rate spiked. He came to his feet again, moving more carefully, holding his center of gravity lower, his rifle and flashlight aiming forward.

His beam bounced off something white. Then something white and black. Fur.

"Kibu?"

The dog gave a yip. He was lying with his paws on a small, unmoving shape. Ash's flashlight beam lit upon a hand resting on Kibu. A small hand.

Ricky!

Ash hurriedly panned his beam over the dog and the boy as he approached them. Ricky's face was swollen and bloody, his eyes shut. He lay dead still. Kibu whimpered.

"Kibu? Are you okay, boy?"

Kibu got up and wiggled in a low and sheepish fashion toward him. He'd never seen his dog act like this before. Then he saw what lay behind Kibu. A man. On his back, faceup, hands loose at his sides. A gun glinted near one hand. Tension roped through Ash's chest. He ran his flashlight over the man. Blood covered the man's face. His throat was a ragged, wet, and bloody mess of meat and cartilage. Ash shot his beam to Kibu, saw the blood around his dog's muzzle and on his paws.

His stomach doubled in on itself. He moved fast toward where Ricky lay, confident they wouldn't be shot at now.

He dropped to his knees beside Ricky and scanned the boy's face with his flashlight. Shock rammed through Ash. The kid had been beaten to a pulp, his face so swollen and his nose mashed in a way that rendered him virtually unrecognizable.

Hurriedly he removed his gloves, felt for a pulse. "Ricky?" he said. "Ricky, can you hear me?"

Ash felt the faint flutter of a pulse beneath his fingers. Ricky moved his head and moaned. Emotion surged into Ash's chest.

"Can you hear me, Ricky?"

The kid tried to open his eyes in their slits. "A . . . Ash?"

Tears pricked Ash's eyes.

"It's going to be okay. It'll be okay. We've got you now."

"I . . . I found it," Ricky whispered. "The . . . the sled."

"Shh. I know. We saw it outside the caves. Don't talk."

Noise came from behind him. He tensed.

"Ash?"

Emotion seared through his chest at the glorious sound of Becca's voice.

"Over here, Becca! We got him—I need help!"

CHAPTER 66

Relief torqued through Ash as he heard the distant whine of snow-mobiles approaching through the woods. He was seated on the snowmobile trailer that he and Becca had used to bring Ricky down the mountain, and he cradled the broken boy in his arms. They'd wrapped him in a survival blanket, and they'd managed to give him small sips of water.

"That's them!" Becca said, leaping off the snowmobile she'd been sitting on, hope firing into her honey eyes. "That has to be them."

Ash and Becca had carried Ricky out of the cave and secured him on the trailer, which Ash had managed to dig out of the snow.

While Becca administered some very basic first aid, stanching blood flow and making sure Ricky could breathe, Ash had dragged the two injured men into the caves to protect them from the elements. One was Jesse Scott. The other was either Stu or Digby Henry, and whichever one it wasn't lay dead in the cave with his throat ripped out.

He and Becca had then begun the arduous task of hauling Ricky on the trailer up the slope upstream of the cave entrance, then even higher uphill again to the ledge from which Becca had caused the avalanches. Once there, exhausted from the climb—the sled was heavy—Becca had fired two emergency flares into the air. They'd

mushroomed and hung in eerie pink clouds. It had stopped snow-
ing, and the cloud cover was thinning, but it was still unlikely the
flares would be spotted. Ash had then activated the SOS function of
the emergency GPS beacon he carried on him whenever he went into
the wilderness. The signal would broadcast to the GEOS International
Emergency Response Center, which in turn would locate the appro-
priate 911 agency in this country.

Pocketing his emergency GPS locator, he'd checked on Ricky
again. The kid had been fading in and out of consciousness. He
needed medical attention stat. Ash and Becca had then proceeded to
drag him all the way back to where they'd left the snowmobile. Kibu
with his bloody muzzle had followed behind. Once they'd reached
Ash's machine, they'd hooked up the trailer with Ricky on it and proceeded down the mountain to the wide valley, where they could be
easily spotted from the air.

As Ash peered into the forest toward the sound of machines that
grew louder and louder, a snowmobile popped out of the trees. The
rest came after it like a swarm of hornets from the dark forest. Relief
whammed through his chest, and emotion seared into his eyes.

Rebecca placed her gloved hand on his shoulder. "It's going to be
okay. He's going to make it."

Ash nodded. He willed it to be so.

Grace Parker had dispatched an ERT of eight officers on four
sleds, one of them a trained paramedic who got to work examining
and treating Ricky. The ERT officer in charge immediately called for
a medevac using satellite comms. A chopper was dispatched from
100 Mile House. Seventeen minutes later, Ash heard the faint thud
of the bird's approach.

He shielded his eyes and peered up into the clouds as the thudding grew loud. A lump swelled in his throat. There was nothing quite
like a rescue bird arriving from the sky in remote wilderness—a link
to help, to civilization. To warmth, safety.

He caught a glimpse of it in a cloud gap. Red and shining and metallic against the whiteness of the world around it.

As it lowered through the clouds, the sound became deafening. They all turned away and crouched low, closing their eyes as the downdraft hit and sent a blizzard of powder boiling through the air. The bird set down delicately in the clearing. Rotors slowed but did not stop. The doors opened. Two paramedics in flight suits hopped out carrying a litter basket and medical equipment. They ran through the powder in a crouch toward them.

Ash felt Ricky squeeze his hand.

"Hey, bud, they're here for you. The royal treatment."

Ricky's eyes opened in slits. The sound of the chopper quieted a little as the paramedics neared, but the pilot kept the rotors turning in anticipation of a fast takeoff.

Ricky groaned, tried to say something.

"Shh, don't talk, bud. Save your energy," Ash said.

"Trev . . . Trevor," he whispered.

Becca shot a look at Ash. She came closer as Ash bent his head forward, bringing his ear to Ricky's mouth.

"Trevor," he managed to say again. "They beat him. Pulp. Slit throat . . . Down well." He swallowed, trying to moisten his lips. "Sealed . . . the well."

Tension whipped through Ash. "They said that? They said they killed Trevor? Put him down a well?"

"Jesse said down . . . well."

Becca leaned closer. "Did they say where the well was, Ricky?"

Ricky tried to shake his head but groaned in pain. "Don't . . . shit in backyard."

"What?"

He faded out.

"Ricky," Ash said, "did they say anything about Whitney?"

"Raped . . . Whitney. All of them raped her."

"Jesse said this?"

He nodded slightly.

"Who is all of them?" Becca asked quickly. The paramedics were here, setting the litter down. Five of the ERT members were already heading off on the RCMP snowmobiles, making for the caves where Ash had told them they would find the injured men and snowmobiles. One of them, he'd explained, was deceased.

"Boys," Ricky whispered. "Called them boys. Wolf. Pack. Hunting. Got paid."

"Paid?"

The paramedic placed his hand on Ash's shoulder. "Sir, could you step back? Ma'am, step aside, please."

Ash and Becca stood back as the paramedics checked Ricky and eased him into the litter. Ash reached for Rebecca's hand, and they watched the men in orange flight suits hurry back to the chopper with their young patient.

The rotors sped up and the *thuck thuck thuck* of the blades shuddered back into the sky. Snow whirled in another blizzard around them as the chopper lifted into the clouds.

Ash shaded his eyes, watching as the metallic bird was swallowed by the sky. He felt Becca's hand slipping into his. They'd removed their gloves to help treat Ricky, and Becca's fingers were ice cold as they laced through his. She squeezed.

"You did it, Ash," she whispered. "You saved him."

He looked down into her eyes. Emotion choked his words. He struggled for a moment to find his voice. "*We* saved him, Becca." He swallowed, cleared his throat. "You and me. A team."

She smiled, wiped her nose, and nodded.

CHAPTER 67

Rebecca sat with Grace Parker and her detective colleague Corporal Ben Stammer in the interview room in the Clinton RCMP detachment. Night had fallen outside. The wind had died and the air was still. It felt as if a peace had settled over the town. Grace debriefed her as Ben observed. The interview was being recorded. Rebecca was aware several more officers watched from behind the two-way glass.

She told Grace, step-by-step, what had transpired since Ash had received the call from Ricky's mother.

Grace took notes and asked more questions. Her expression, as was to be expected, was unreadable. She offered no opinion, gave no verbal reaction at all.

Rebecca reached for her cup of water, sipped. Ash would come under Grace's microscope next, maybe tomorrow morning because he was still up at the Devil's Butte hospital with Ricky. Doctors had rushed Ricky into emergency surgery as soon as the paramedics had brought him in. So far the prognosis was good. He had a broken left arm, broken ribs, crushed fingers, some serious contusions, and a hematoma on his back, and they'd operated on his broken nose. But he was out of the woods and was expected to make a full recovery. Rebecca had to marvel at the suppleness and resilience of youth. Those and Ricky's sheer spunk and stubbornness and determination, his refusal to let go of anything he'd set his eyes on, including his life. And Ash.

Rebecca anticipated that several of Grace's officers would be at the hospital now, waiting to be able to speak to Ricky. And waiting, also, for Jesse Scott to come out of the operating room where he was being treated for a gunshot wound to his shoulder and expected to make a full recovery.

Stu and Digby Henry had not been so lucky. Kibu appeared to have flown at Digby Henry—whom Rebecca had wounded—and ripped out his throat in the dark cave when the man had fired at Ash. The dog had killed him. Ash would need to find a way to deal with the fallout from that.

Ash would also be grilled over wounding Jesse Scott and inflicting a fatal gunshot wound on Stu Henry, who had been pronounced dead by the ERT when they'd reached him in the cave. Rebecca had already been interrogated over wounding Digby Henry before he'd been killed by the dog. She'd surrendered her weapon pending the outcome of a police-involved-shooting investigation.

Ash had a solid argument for self-defense, though. Rebecca wanted to believe the cops would go easy on him, especially since he'd brought Ricky out, and the boy had managed to tell them what Jesse Scott had said. He'd cracked the case wide open.

"Did you hear Ricky Simon say anything about any other people involved in sexually assaulting and hunting Whitney Gagnon?"

"Negative," said Rebecca. "But he did say something odd after he mentioned the words 'wolf' and 'pack' and 'hunting.' He said the word 'paid.'"

Grace's eyes ticked up from her notes. "Paid?"

"Yes."

"As in they were *paid* to attack Whitney Gagnon and Trevor Beauchamp?"

"I don't know."

Grace exchanged a glance with Ben. "What about the location of the well into which Trevor's body might have been dumped?" she asked.

Rebecca relived the moment in her mind. "When I asked Ricky if the men had told him where the well was, all he said was, 'Don't shit in backyard.'"

"What does that mean?"

"I don't know. Maybe that the guys were unlikely to use a dump site close to their base?" She rubbed her brow, feeling exhausted. "The location where Frank Hatfield reported seeing blood and something fleeing through the woods—a few klicks east of that is an area that used to be an old homesteading site before the province acquired the land for the creation of a provincial park. I remember being told in childhood there was a covered well on the land. It's probably still there."

Grace noted this in her book. She raised her pen.

"Did anyone mention to Ricky who the father of Whitney Gagnon's baby was?"

"Not to my knowledge."

Grace moistened her lips. She closed her notebook, looked up. "We'll follow up with Ricky Simon when he's able to cooperate fully, but we can act on this information to date." She eyed Rebecca. "You defied an order to stand down."

"I made a decision to follow and remain with a key suspect in the investigation who was in a position to save the life of a key witness."

Her gaze remained locked on Rebecca's. Rebecca concentrated on not blinking.

Grace came to her feet abruptly. Ben followed suit. Grace reached her slender hand across the table. "Thank you, Sergeant North." She shook Rebecca's hand, then exited the room.

"Thank you, Sergeant," Corporal Ben Stammer said, then followed his boss out of the room.

Cariboo Country. Sunday, January 27.

Rebecca found Ash sitting beside Ricky Simon's hospital bed. She'd driven up at first light and arrived in the Devil's Butte hospital parking lot to find several RCMP vehicles already parked outside the building. The door to Ricky's room was open. Ricky lay propped up against pillows, his nose and face bruised and swollen and covered in bandages. His eyes were closed, and he appeared to be sleeping. His left arm was in a cast, and he had bandages around splinted fingers on his left hand.

"Hey," she said softly as she pushed open the door.

Ash came to his feet. She entered the room, took his hand, and drew him toward her. She leaned up and kissed his stubbled cheek. "You look beat."

He brushed a fall of hair back from her face. "I've been worse." He smiled, and it lit his eyes and cracked her heart. She felt the warmth of love in her veins.

"I brought breakfast." She held up a travel mug of hot coffee and a bag containing a warm breakfast sandwich.

"I always knew you were an angel," he said as he took the mug and bag from her.

"Ricky doing okay?"

Ash nodded and set the bag down on the windowsill. He took a sip of the coffee. "The cops were here earlier this morning, getting a statement from him. It exhausted him. He's sleeping again."

"How about you? Holding up?"

He nodded.

"They questioned you yet?" she asked.

"Not yet. They want to do that formally at the station." But the light that danced in his tired eyes told Rebecca that irrespective of what was still to come down the pike, he felt he'd won. Ash had gone

415

out there and triumphed in his battle for Ricky Simon. For Running Wind. For Trevor and Whitney and her dad. For her.

"I love you, you know?" she whispered.

He held her eyes for a moment, then looked away.

Rebecca swallowed. She knew he was thinking about the future, about the fact that she had to return to her job.

"Did Ricky say anything new to the detectives?" she asked.

He inhaled deeply, took another sip of coffee, then said, "It seems like the Henry cousins and Jesse Scott, and maybe some other guys—but we don't know that for sure yet—beat Trevor to death, dumped him down a well, and then raped Whitney before releasing her like game to be hunted in the woods near my land." He sipped again, seeming to need the warmth, the energy kick the coffee offered.

"That would be consistent with Hatfield's story of the blood, and seeing something—possibly a woman with golden-blonde hair—running through the woods," she said. "The bullet in Hatfield's truck was also a .30-30, like the one found with Whitney's remains. Ballistics will show if it came from the same weapon that day."

He nodded. "Ricky seemed to think from what the cousins said that this incident was the start of an extreme hunting club."

"Wolf Pack?"

"That would be my guess."

"And Buck is a member of this club? He has the sticker on his truck."

"Possibly. Who knows if they ever did anything like this again? Maybe not. Maybe it just bonded them all in some kind of bloodlust moment, but they stuck with hunting game thereafter. Or maybe it was just this core group of guys who were really dark. They're all connected with the drug trade in the Cariboo, though, and farther north. That's what one of the officers who was in here told me. And they found ketamine in the Henry ranch house when they searched it last night."

"Did they tell Ricky anything about my dad?"

He wavered, as if he'd been skirting the issue for fear of hurting her. "Yes. I'm sorry, Becs. From what Ricky heard, it appears the man fleeing your dad's cabin was Stu Henry. The cops said the machine is registered to him. The design was done by Wes up at Scott's MotorSports, but I don't think Wes is connected other than that he works for his uncle."

Ricky moaned. Rebecca's attention shot to him. He was waking up, his lids fluttering.

"Why?" she asked softly. "Why did Stu Henry do it? He had to have known my father had found something that would implicate them all. But what had my dad found, and how had they learned about it?"

"Maybe they just heard he had new information and was getting close. Maybe they thought Oona Ferris had told Noah something over the phone. It could have come out in any number of ways that Noah was on their case."

She ran her hand over her hair, feeling the weight of it all. "Grace's guys found latents on my dad's gun safe. If they can match those to the registered owner of the snowmobile, and in conjunction with Ricky's witness testimony, they could place the registered driver inside my dad's cabin." She paused, watching Ricky struggling to open his swollen eyelids. "And there's the ketamine possession," she said as she went up to the bed. Ricky's eyes opened in tiny slits, and his gaze settled on her.

"Hey, Ricky."

He tried to smile, but moaned as the facial movement caused him pain.

"Don't," she said, reaching for his good hand. She smiled at him. "Thank you," she said. "You're a true hero, do you know that?"

His eyes filled with tears.

"Your grandfather Running Wind would be proud, do you know that?"

He managed to give a small nod, and he closed his eyes again.

CHAPTER 68

Cariboo Country. Saturday, February 2.

The Moose and Horn was packed to capacity. The whole town, it seemed, and then some, had shown up to celebrate the life of Corporal Noah North. Music filled the place along with chatter and laughter and the clink of glasses and the smell of good food coming from the kitchen. Much of the gossip was about the murders and the takedown of Jesse Scott and the death of the Henry cousins. About how they'd all killed Whitney and Trevor. But the investigation continued. Jesse Scott was not talking. And who else might have been involved was not yet known. Still, Grace was closing a case around Scott, and he'd already been charged with the murders of Whitney and Trevor, her father, and Oona Ferris, although the evidence in Oona Ferris's case was still only circumstantial.

So far there'd been no paternal DNA match for the little fetus that had been found with Whitney's remains in the log. Whoever the father was, he might be totally unconnected to the murders. And his identity might never be learned.

Rebecca had suggested to Grace it could be Buck. But securing a warrant for Buck's DNA would be a stumbling block unless Grace's team found some evidence that a crime had been committed in connection with someone fathering the child.

Rebecca had also asked Grace whether her team had learned anything more about Ricky's statement that the Wolf Pack had been "paid" to hurt Whitney Gagnon and Trevor Beauchamp. But all Grace had told Rebecca was that the investigation was ongoing. And she'd pointedly reminded Rebecca that she was off the case.

So for now, Rebecca was going to focus on enjoying the celebration of her father's life with the rest of the town.

She sat at a large round table near a small stage where a trio of musicians played a fiddle and pipes and sang up-tempo, foot-stomping Irish tunes—something her dad had loved. Rebecca wanted this to be a joyous if poignant occasion, one that didn't feel like a wake.

Sitting with her at the big table were Ash and Ricky. Ricky's nose remained splinted and bandaged, but his facial swelling was receding, and he was in fine spirits. Also at their table was Thora Battersby with Don Barton and Jerry Phibbs—her father's drinking mates. Plus old Clive Dodd, who was still hanging on to a thread of life in spite of himself, and had been wheeled in with his oxygen for the occasion. And Dixie and Bob McCracken, who had so very generously offered to foot the bill for rounds of drinks.

Rebecca watched Thora for a moment, thinking about how she'd provided the trigger—the information about Whitney's pregnancy—that had launched her father's investigation. As Thora threw back her head and laughed at something Jerry Phibbs had said, Whitney's mother's words suddenly sifted back into her mind.

The Battersbys were good neighbors. I could always count on Jake to help when things like the dishwasher or washing machine broke, or if I had plumbing issues. That kind of thing. A real old-school handyman type. Always had a smile, too.

A dark, inky thought leaked into Rebecca's brain. Jake had been a regular inside the Gagnon household. Whitney was often left home alone by her absentee working mom. Whitney had been needy, craving attention, and promiscuous. Could Jake Battersby possibly have been the father of Whitney's baby? Could he and Thora have paid to make Whitney go away? Could Thora have misled both Rebecca and her father, maybe even be behind her dad's death? The words Ricky had whispered as he'd lain on the trailer surfaced in her mind.

Wolf. Pack. Hunting. Got paid.

Rebecca frowned as she began to turn this new suspicion over in her head. She'd also briefly toyed with the possibility that the charming and seductive, "hands-on" Lewis Meacham might have had an affair with his young housekeeper back in the day. Rebecca thought back to the conversation she'd had with Solly when she'd questioned the woman about her dad. At the time Whitney had worked for Lewis—and at the time she fell pregnant, given the age of the fetus— she still would have been sixteen. It was an age of consent, but if the man she'd engaged in sex with had been an adult, and in a powerful position, like her employer, it could be seen in courts as statutory rape. It could be motive.

"Hey." Rebecca felt Ash's hand reach under the table for hers. His fingers laced through hers. "Stop thinking about the case for a few minutes," he said.

"I just can't help wondering . . . what those guys meant about the Wolf Pack being paid."

"Leave it to Detective Parker for now," he said. "She's the real deal. She'll get there eventually."

Rebecca heaved in a deep breath. "Yeah. You're right."

"Lewis and Solly have outdone themselves," Ash said with a nod to the spread on their table, nudging her back to the event at hand.

She smiled. "They have."

The Meachams had indeed been generous. They were donating food from their kitchen, and Solly was clearly in her element working the bar with her barkeep, Hank, while Lewis helped ferry plates of pub fare to the tables. The old photos of Noah North had been moved into positions of prominence on the bar counter, and Rebecca had added her own—the framed photo of her father in red serge that Ash had given her.

Among the gathering Rebecca could see newspaper publisher Rennie Price. Buck. Gonz. Wes was also there. He'd come in spite of his uncle's being charged—he seemed determined to keep a brave face and divorce himself from his uncle's actions. He might have been tasked to work on his uncle's truck, and he might have suspected his uncle had done something untoward, but he apparently had no knowledge of the crimes, and so far Grace and her team had not found proof otherwise. Rebecca was also pleased to see that Janet Gagnon had accepted her invitation. Janet was in a corner talking to Marcy Fossum and Marcy's man.

"Noah would have liked this," Ash said, following her gaze.

"I think he would have." Emotion surged suddenly into her eyes, and tears threatened to leak down her cheeks. "I . . . I just wish I'd come home earlier. That I'd been here for him."

"You *are* here for him, Becca. *You* did this. You brought the town together tonight for him. Noah is here in spirit, and he knows you love him."

"Thank you," she said quietly. She wanted to believe that.

Ricky watched their exchange. There was something in the kid's eyes Rebecca couldn't read. But it looked like pride. She smiled at him, and he looked away as a flush of embarrassment colored his cheeks.

Olivia and Cole appeared in the saloon doorway with Tori. Ricky got up and hurriedly wended his way through the crowd to call them over.

"Did you hear I bought a new truck?" Rebecca said to Ash.

His brow crooked up. "Why? You going to stay awhile?"

"My superior called. I'm needed on a case. It's a desk job so I won't need a weapon, and it won't interfere with the investigation into my shooting. He wants me back day after tomorrow," she said. "But I thought I'd try commuting back and forth for a while. At least through the end of next summer. I hired a contractor to start demolishing and removing what's left of my dad's cabin when Grace releases it, and when the weather allows." She hesitated at the sudden raw intensity in Ash's eyes. She cleared her throat. "I . . . I thought I'd rebuild. Nothing huge."

"To sell?"

"Maybe. I'll see. Part of my dad is still there. Part of me, too. I'm not ready to let it all go yet." She paused. "And there's you."

His gaze held hers. His face changed and his eyes darkened. Music and noise seemed to fade.

"What about Lance?" he asked very quietly.

"It's over with him." The music stopped. Clapping began. "It was never properly on." His gaze locked with hers, and the memory of their making love surged between them. She leaned forward and whispered in his ear, "You ruined me for every man I was ever with, Ash Haugen."

He put his hand around the back of her neck, his grip firm, his mouth inches from hers. "I'm glad you came home."

She hesitated, then kissed him, not worried about who would see. The clapping died down.

"I need to give a speech," she murmured against his lips.

He pulled back. And he smiled. It was a smile such as she'd not seen since before that hot summer night of the rodeo fair. A smile that danced in his eyes.

Warmth surged through her chest as she came to her feet.

She took the stage as the musicians stepped back. She reached for the mike and cleared her throat.

"I want to thank you all for coming." She looked out over the sea of faces clustered into this warm venue and cleared her throat again.

"A few days ago, when I was having dinner with Mayor Bob McCracken and his wife, Dixie, Bob called this place 'the village living room.' And he's right. This was my father's home away from home. It's where he came for friendship, for connection. He came here to meet and spend time with all of you. This was Corporal Noah North's town, and this was my dad's—"

The saloon doors were slammed open. Everyone spun around.

Five officers in uniform entered. Rebecca's gaze shot to the windows. Red-and-blue police lights strobed as cruisers pulled up outside. No sirens.

Grace Parker appeared behind the men. She wore an RCMP cap and a bullet suppression vest over an RCMP jacket. "Everyone, please stay calm," she said as she scanned the crowd. The female officer standing beside her pointed toward the table where Ash sat. Grace gave a nod and an order.

The uniformed cops in bulletproof vests pushed through the gathering. "Stand back, please, stand back."

They came to a stop in front of the round table where Ash sat. His face paled. Rebecca's heart stalled.

The tallest cop placed his hand firmly on the shoulder of Bob McCracken. "Could you please stand up, sir?"

"What is this about?"

"Stand up, sir."

He came to his feet, shock on his face. "What are you doing?"

"Turn around, please. Hands behind your back." The officer cuffed Bob. "Robert McCracken, you're under arrest in connection with the murders of Whitney Gagnon, Trevor Beauchamp, Noah North, and Oona Ferris."

A collective gasp sounded across the venue. Murmurs started.

Bob looked confused.

"I don't understand. I had nothing to do with . . . This is insane!"

The officer took Bob's arm and forced him through the crowd toward the exit. Bob looked over his shoulder at his wife. "What in the hell?"

Dixie shot to her feet, face white. "This is not right, this cannot be right. What on earth is going on here?"

"Ma'am." It was Grace Parker. She took hold of the slight coroner's upper arm, turned her, reached for her other arm, and cuffed the coroner's hands behind her back. "Dixie Scott McCracken, you're under arrest in connection with the murders of Whitney Gagnon, Trevor Beauchamp, Noah North, and Oona Ferris. You have the right to retain and instruct counsel without delay. You also have the right to legal advice from duty counsel by making a free telephone call. Do you understand?"

"I . . . I haven't done anything."

Grace handed Dixie over to a uniformed female officer, who led Dixie from the room. Grace followed.

Rebecca climbed down from the stage, glanced at Ash, made a motion for him to remain with Ricky. She hurried out of the Moose and Horn after Grace.

"Sergeant Parker!" she called as Grace headed for the lobby exit doors.

Grace stopped. Rebecca hastened up to her.

"What is this about?"

Grace took her aside, lowered her voice. "Jesse Scott has confessed in exchange for a deal. He said he wasn't going to take the fall for this alone. He informed us Dixie McCracken offered him a cut, twenty years ago, of over fifty thousand dollars if he got rid of Whitney Gagnon."

"*She* paid them?" Rebecca blinked. "*Why?*"

Grace hesitated, as if deciding how much to tell Rebecca. She glanced toward the pub entrance. People were filing out, talking in excited tones.

"Bob McCracken, her husband, is allegedly the father of Whitney Gagnon's baby. She was his patient. He'd been engaging in improper touching and then sex with his patient when she was under the age of majority."

"That's statutory rape."

"And there might be more patients who come forward."

Rebecca swore and ran her hand over her hair. She'd always had a weird feeling about Dr. Bob when she was a kid, but had put it down to her dislike of visiting any kind of doctor or dentist. And Bob now seemed changed, a benevolent mayor, a champion of this small town and the people in it. Her world spun as a new lens settled over everything.

"Whitney and Trevor blackmailed Bob? Is that how they came into the cash?"

"Allegedly, according to Jesse Scott. If word got out that he'd fathered a patient's—a minor's—child, he was done."

"They blackmailed him in addition to lying to Ash and extorting money from him as well?"

"Allegedly."

Ash was a victim. So was she. And her father. They all were. The fallout from that crime had rippled down more than two decades and was still playing out now.

"And there'd have been no doubt Bob McCracken would have paid," Rebecca said softly. "A lot. Whitney's revelation would have destroyed him. His practice. His family. And Dixie."

"She was allegedly present when Bob McCracken handed the cash to the teens. Apparently, when Whitney was leaving after getting the cash, Whitney said something that made Dixie believe this wasn't over. That the kids would be back for more, again and again, and that they would continue to hang like a threat over her and her husband for the rest of their lives. She contacted Jesse Scott, a known henchman—a fixer—for a biker sled-neck group in Devil's Butte."

"The Sled-Nex."

Grace nodded. "Dixie told Jesse Scott he could take the money he would find on Whitney and Trevor if he got rid of them. And time was of the essence because he had to get them before the bus took them out of town and Dixie lost her opportunity to contain this."

"So Jesse Scott picked them up at the bus stop, allegedly offering a free drive south?"

"And killed them. After he and his mates took some bonus extras with Whitney—'had a bit of fun on the side.' Those were his words," Grace said, with no emotion. Flat delivery. "When your father reopened the inquiry into the teens' disappearance twenty years ago, Jesse Scott became fearful and coerced Oona Ferris into lying about the white van with Oregon plates. Then, when Dixie learned your father was getting close again now, twenty years later, she and Jesse Scott conspired once more to attempt to contain the damage and to keep their secret."

"Why Jesse Scott? I mean, how did Dixie McCracken know about him? What made her think she could just call this guy up and contract him for a killing?"

"Jesse Scott is Dixie Scott McCracken's half brother."

Rebecca blinked as it hit her—Dixie *Scott* McCracken. Not just a coincidence of a common surname.

"They share the same father?" she asked softly.

"And a history of impoverished backgrounds and divorced mothers. Although they never interacted or socialized in public, they had a bond. A tight one."

And maybe a dark, opportunistic, sociopathic gene. Dixie was the woman who'd looked on and feigned sympathy as Rebecca had been broken over the sight of her father's charred body.

Rebecca stared at Grace as she processed this news. "What about my dad?"

"Dixie orchestrated that. She knew what would fly in a self-inflicted-death investigation. She was in a unique position to control the outcome as coroner. She and Jesse Scott paid Stu Henry to do the work. They just got lucky with the kids causing the fire. The only mistake they made—partial prints on the gun safe. They're a match to Stu Henry."

"And two small witnesses."

"And two small witnesses," echoed Grace.

"Trevor's body?"

"Not yet. We have an additional cadaver team coming in for a larger search." Grace turned to go, but hesitated. "Rebecca," she said, "I'm sorry about your father's memorial celebration."

Rebecca blew out a chestful of air, then offered a wry smile. "I actually think he would have enjoyed this. He brought me back to town for this. To finish his case."

"And you have. You did him proud. Good job, Sergeant."

Emotion burned in Rebecca's eyes. She could not have asked for more from this cool-tempered homicide detective with a spine of steel. Respect.

"Thank you."

"I'm putting in a request to the commissioner's office for a full regimental funeral in Corporal Noah North's honor," Grace said. "A regimental funeral, as you know, may be accorded to a deceased former RCMP member who has served with distinction." She paused. A hint of a smile played over her mouth. "I have a feeling it will be granted." She turned and left.

Rebecca stared after the woman as the lobby doors swung shut behind her.

Ash appeared behind Rebecca. He put his arm around her. "What happened? Everything okay?"

She nodded, her chest bursting with emotion, barely able to keep it in. Her eyes filled with tears. "I did it, Ash," she whispered.

She looked up into the eyes of the man she loved, the man she knew on some level she was going to find a way to spend the rest of her life with.

"I did right by my dad. I got him his honor."

Ash hugged her closer. "I don't believe he ever doubted you would, Becs." He paused, and his gaze held hers. "It's why he phoned you that day. It's why you came home."

THE GROWING SEASON

Cariboo Country. Sunday, May 12, spring.

Rebecca thrust her shovel deep into the dark, loamy earth, her breath misting in the dawn air as she worked. She pushed it deeper with her boot. The day had dawned clear and cool, but by noon it would be baking. She wanted to dig her beds before the sun rose too high.

Up on the rise behind her, the ruins of her old family home had been cleared. Contractors had moved in as soon as the snow had receded. Construction on her new cabin had begun where the old one had stood.

But today was Sunday, and the hammers and saws and other equipment had fallen silent. Today she was working on reestablishing the once-flourishing vegetable garden her mother had cultivated in this spot. And beneath her shovel she'd found evidence that the soil was still rich.

She stopped to catch her breath and moved a strand of hair off her brow with the back of her work glove. She watched Ricky and Tori for a moment. They were stringing wire along the bottom of the garden for the deer fencing. She heard them laugh, and Rebecca was struck by a time warp as a memory suddenly folded over reality. She saw herself at Tori's age, her long, dark hair in a braid down her back, working the earth alongside her mother, their dog sniffing in the birch trees nearby, the same smell of rich soil, the same sensation of cool, clean air in her lungs. The same lightness of being. And suddenly Rebecca felt as if her mother were here, felt her presence in this garden that she was rebuilding over the old one. And for a strange, shimmering moment, Rebecca stood gripped by the idea that from somewhere down deep in this soil, lying dormant for all these years, had come seeds that had been brought to the surface, where they'd reached light and water, and it was all unfurling inside her, coming alive again.

Rebecca had given Ricky weekend work, and she'd promised him a job through the summer. She needed the extra hands, and he needed the cash. That, and he was quite simply fun to be around— he made her laugh. The kid possessed a wicked wit that belied his thirteen years. She supposed that was what happened when life was rough—you grew up fast.

Tori chuckled again at something Ricky said, and the sound of the happy teens made her heart smile. Tori usually came over to help whenever Ricky was around, and the extra company was welcome. Rebecca's place was beginning to feel like a home again, even though the cabin was still a work in progress and she'd been commuting back and forth from her case work in Ottawa.

She'd arrived again on a flight into Kamloops and driven up to Broken Bar country yesterday. She was camping in her dad's moonshine shed, which she'd converted into a tiny house with a cot, a makeshift kitchen complete with gas stove and small fridge, a propane heater, and warm bedding. She'd stay a week for this stretch. She needed to meet with her contractor and oversee the next stage of construction.

But one of the first things she'd done was task a craftsman in Clinton to brand the words NORTH FARM into a length of old cedar she planned to raise above her ranch gate for a lintel.

As she stood there, hand on her shovel, a dog nuzzled her leg. She started and glanced down. "Kibu?"

She spun around.

Ash stood there, up near the moonshine shed. Watching her.

She raised her gloved hand, and he came down to where she worked.

"I didn't hear you," she said as he neared.

"I didn't want you to." He kissed her, wiped a smudge of dirt off her nose, and held up a backpack. "Brought coffee and breakfast sandwiches."

She grinned. "I could get used to this."

He held her gaze for a moment, then said quietly, "I hope you do." He nodded toward Ricky. "He working out?"

"More than."

For a moment they stood side by side as they watched Kibu bound over toward the teens.

"Do you ever think of it? Kids?" Ash asked.

She stilled, glanced up at him. "Sometimes."

He nodded, but said nothing more.

"You make a good father figure for Ricky," she offered, trying to feel his mood, to sense where it was coming from.

He inhaled deeply and shoved his hands into his pockets. And she knew he was thinking about Whitney's baby. Of that old-growth cedar coffin on his land, in that place where his own father used to take him.

She'd told him there were support groups, therapists. But he said he didn't want to go there. Not yet. Maybe never. It was enough that she knew. But Rebecca also knew it would probably still affect him in tricky ways. Perhaps always. Such was the nature of trauma and abuse. Damaged kids were like seeds landed in the wrong ground. Parts of them grew crooked. But they could still grow strong with the right care.

"It's coming along," he said of her garden.

She laughed. "Hardly. But just you wait until the end of summer. There will be rich, red tomatoes over there. Ones that taste like summer sun. And zucchinis there." She waved her hand over her land. "And basil in a greenhouse on that side, and—"

"Becca, how long are you staying this time?"

She fell silent. A breeze rustled the new green leaves in the aspen grove. Quietly she said, "A week. But I return next month, and then I'm not going back."

His gaze fired to her. "What?"

An odd feeling of nerves shimmered through her now that she was voicing it to him. "I go back to pack, to finalize a few things . . . but . . . I got a transfer."

"Transfer?"

"I put in for Buck's job. I heard on Friday that I got it."

He stared at her. "Buck?"

"Yeah, Buck Johnstone. He's been cleared by internal after Grace initiated an investigation into his handling of my dad's murder, and the rest of the hunt club has been cleared, too, but it cast a professional cloud over him. RCMP brass tried to relocate him to a small community on the Yukon border."

"Demotion?"

"It was certainly seen that way. He handed in his resignation instead. I asked for his post."

Words eluded him. Emotions warred through his features, chased through his posture.

"Are you *serious*? You? A small-town cop, basically a one-man show?"

"One-woman show. Kinda like a US sheriff." She grinned. She'd been insanely nervous about putting in the request, worried it would be a serious and odd backward step in her career. But now that approvals had come through, she felt she was on the right track. "Hey, it was good enough for my dad."

"What if they transfer you again in five years?"

"If that happens, I'll face it then. Maybe I'll try something else." She looked out over her land. "Meanwhile, I need a horse. Or two. And some chickens."

Silence.

She met his gaze. His eyes gleamed with emotion.

"Hey?" She removed her glove and touched his scar. "This makes you sad?"

He laughed. Kissed her, hugged her. Laughed again. "And a dog, you definitely need a dog."

"I know. I'm on it."

He crooked up his brow.

"Olivia's driving me and Tori up to the pound at 100 Mile this afternoon. She says there are two puppies there. They were rescued at a reserve in the Northwest Territories with their mother. They're not ready to be homed yet, but Liv figures one would suit me, and the other she wants for Tori. She plans to teach Tori to track with the pup. She feels it'll help her with a lot of things, and soften the blow when Ace bows out."

He shook his head in amazement, a crooked smile curving his beautiful mouth. "You've been good for Tori and Liv," he said. "Liv told me. It's the cop link you share with Tori and her adoptive dad, I think."

Rebecca shrugged. "Are you going to grab a shovel and help me dig a row before that breakfast, or what?"

Ash regarded this woman, the smudge of dirt still on her nose, the sun coming over the mountains casting a yellow light around loose bits of her hair. And his heart nearly burst. He could see it again in his mind's eye. Becca in the kitchen with her mom.

She really had come home.

And so had he.

"The town cop?" he said again.

She angled her head. "You got a problem with that, cowboy?"

"Hell no. Where's that shovel?"

As he dug beside her, and the sun climbed higher, he said, "Your dad's got this great big grin in heaven right now, you know that, Becs? This"—he leaned on his shovel for a moment, surveying the progress of their work—"*this* is what would make him so very proud. To see that everything he did for you held worth enough for you to want it, too."

She laughed. And from the light in her eyes, Ash knew. He just knew his dream would come true one day. He'd make it so. He'd marry the cop's daughter, and she would come live on his ranch. And their kitchen would be filled with the yellow light of laughter and fresh vegetables from the rich, dark soil in their garden.

ACKNOWLEDGMENTS

As always, I owe a huge debt of gratitude to Charlotte Herscher for her sharp editorial eye and wonderful work manner. A novelist cannot but feel secure in her experienced hands. Thank you also to my acquisitions editor, Alison Dasho, and to Montlake managing editor Anh Schluep for their editorial midwifery and magic in bringing *The Dark Bones* to life, and in helping deliver it to readers everywhere. I remain deeply humbled by the continued and incredible response from readers for *A Dark Lure*, and it's because of this reader support and encouragement that *The Dark Bones* has now grown out of that same story world. A big thanks is also due my agent, Amy Tannenbaum Gottlieb, for her career guidance and support, and to the rest of the dynamic Montlake crew at Amazon Publishing. No book is an island, and I am grateful for my team.

ABOUT THE AUTHOR

Loreth Anne White is an internationally bestselling author of thrillers, mysteries, and romantic suspense. A three-time RITA finalist, she is also the 2017 Overall Daphne du Maurier Award winner, and she has won the *Romantic Times* Reviewers' Choice Award, the National Readers' Choice Award, and the Romantic Crown for Best Romantic Suspense and Best Book Overall, in addition to being a Booksellers' Best finalist and a multiple CataRomance Reviewers' Choice Award winner. A former journalist and newspaper editor who has worked in both South Africa and Canada, she now resides in the Pacific Northwest with her family. Visit her at www.lorethannewhite.com.